Thicker Than Water

Melissa Good

Yellow Rose Books

Nederland, Texas

ISBN 1-932300-24-4

First Printing 2004

9 8 7 6 5 4 3 2 1

Cover design by Donna Pawlowski

Published by:

Yellow Rose Books
PMB 210, 8691 9th Avenue
Port Arthur, Texas 77642-8025

Find us on the World Wide Web at
http://www.regalcrest.biz

Printed in the United States of America

Chapter
One

THE DAY WAS a perfect one for a festival: the sky a perfect deep blue, and the sun mitigated by a cool breeze coming off the aqua and green ocean waters. The infectious rhythm of salsa mixed with voices in a kaleidoscope of languages, moving through air filled with spicy scents and the pungent aroma of Cuban coffee.

One tall, one shorter, one dark, the other fair—but both had the same subtle confidence and the tanned skin of a native, and they rambled through the Latin festival with a sense of comfortable familiarity.

The shorter, blond one stopped at a stall and examined a long, striped skirt in a multitude of loud colors. "What do you think, Dar?" she asked, holding it up to her body. "Is it me?"

Her taller companion studied the effect. "Only if you're Carmen Miranda on mescaline." Dar plucked the skirt from the blonde's fingers and hung it back up. "C'mon, Kerry. I think I see something more your style."

They walked a little further and stopped in front of a booth selling embroidered vests. "There." Dar pointed with one hand, her other held close to her body by a sedate muslin sling. "I like the one with the parrots."

Kerry selected the indicated garment and slipped it on. It fit her neatly, and she buttoned it, then held her arms away from her body. "Yes?"

Dar dug a twenty dollar bill out of her pocket and handed it over to the woman behind the booth. "Yes." She bumped Kerry, indicating the area where all the food booths were. "There're a lot more people here this year than last year."

Kerry looked around. The beach area was packed with bodies, a stage on either end spilled music into the air while the center was filled with arts and crafts exhibits, vendors, and rows of Hispanic and Latin inspired foods. "Sure is."

It was colorful and loud and fun, and a sorely needed break

for both of them after a very long week at their mutual workplace.

Kerry took off her new vest and tucked it inside the canvas bag slung over her arm. She was dressed in a tank top and denim shorts, which nearly matched what Dar was wearing save that her partner's shirt was red and Kerry's was a light, placid blue. "How's your shoulder?"

Dar shifted her arm slightly. Injured several weeks earlier by a maliciously aimed baseball bat, the limb had been slow to heal, and she'd returned to using a sling that morning to try and ease the nagging ache. "Better. Want to go sit down and watch the dancing?"

"Sure."

They walked over to the right hand stage, sat down at one of the few empty tables, and leaned back to watch two experienced salsa dancers giving an exhibition. After a few minutes, Kerry moved closer to Dar. "Can we try that?"

Dar cocked her head. "What, salsa? Ker, you know dancing isn't one of my many skills."

"Hm." Kerry rested her chin on her hand. "It looks fun. Maybe we could take classes. I think the club on the island has them."

"I don't think my hips are structurally capable of doing that move." Dar pointed. "Without dislocating a major joint, I mean."

"Mmm...I don't know, you've got some pretty good moves." Kerry saw Dar's eyebrows lift and she relented, chuckling instead. "Ah, it's nice to have a weekend off, isn't it?"

"Yeah," Dar answered. "It really is." The past month had been a difficult one and not what Dar considered entirely success-ful. In the process of executing a government contract, she'd stumbled on a criminal scandal and the news had been less than welcome. She exhaled. "Glad the Navy's investigation is under the bridge and we can move on."

"To the next base?" Kerry asked, inwardly hoping that wasn't on the agenda. The investigation that Dar had triggered had thrown the naval base where she'd grown up into chaos, along with some old family friendships. It had been tough on her emo-tionally as well as physically, and by extension, tough on Kerry as well.

"Probably not," Dar answered. "That contract's on hold right now."

Kerry straightened in surprise. "On hold?"

Dar shrugged her good shoulder. "I expected it. Waves that big probably washed up on the White House steps. Alastair said there were some questions being raised."

"Questions? What kind of questions? We didn't make that

stuff up."

"I know." Dar comfortingly patted her on the back. "But it's a lot of stink, and they'll probably have to figure out who to blame now. Other than us, of course."

"Great." Kerry frowned. "Why didn't you tell me?"

Dar signaled the waitress. "Dos cervezas, por favor." She half turned to Kerry. "I wasn't ready to rush into the next one anyway. Things'll settle down." She hesitated. "And I didn't tell you because Alastair just told me last night. I didn't want to ruin our dinner with business."

A nice, romantic dinner out on the boat. Kerry scrunched her face into a wry expression, unable to disagree with the motive. "You have a point there."

"Glad you agree."

The music altered and two new dancers, dressed in flamenco outfits, came up on stage. They danced with a great deal of energy, stamping and kicking with gusto.

Kerry watched them, her mind turning over Dar's words. She gave the waitress a brief grin as she was handed a cold bottle, then she touched her beer to Dar's. "Well, here's to better luck in the next few weeks. I don't want another couple like the last few."

Dar clinked her bottle. "You're on."

IT WAS VERY late afternoon before they got home. Kerry put her bag of goodies on the couch and wandered into the kitchen, her mind sorting over the possibilities for dinner. "Hey, you in the mood for chicken?" she asked as she passed Dar standing in the open back door.

"C'mon, Chino." Dar closed the door and allowed their Labrador retriever to precede her into the living room. "Sure." She thumped down onto a seat at the living room table and sorted through their mail. "You feel like watching a movie tonight? They have some decent stuff on pay per view."

"You, me, a movie, and some popcorn?" Kerry grinned. "I think I could handle that. Pick something nice and gory." She removed a few things from the freezer and set them on the counter before she joined Dar in the living room.

Their mail was a collection of the usual junk she noted as she picked up a few pieces and turned them over. Free software, applications for mortgages, pre-approved credit cards... "Spam." She noticed a purple envelope, extracted it from the pile, and turned it over to look at the address.

"Hm." The envelope was addressed to her and she acknowlededged the logo on the top with a grimace. "Ah."

"What's that?" Dar looked up from a catalog of geek toys.

"My high school." Kerry opened the envelope and pulled out the contents. After a moment's perusal, she shrugged. "Just asking for money." She turned and wandered off. "I'm going to grab a shower and change. Be right back."

"Join you in a minute." Dar continued to flip through the catalog and stopped when she spotted a glow in the dark trackball. "Oo. Now that has possibilities." She rested her chin on her fist and considered the thought of the cleaning staff entering her darkened office and seeing it floating on her desk. "Heh."

KERRY SAT DOWN behind the desk in her upstairs office and regarded the note she'd taken with her. Part of what she'd told Dar was true—her high school was always looking for donations, and this was no exception. However, the second part of the card was an invitation to her high school reunion.

"Ugh." She exhaled. High school had been a tough time for her and going back there wasn't something she really wanted to put on the table for both of them, though she'd talked Dar into attending her own reunion. It was different for Dar, or so she'd convinced herself.

Dar had gone to public school. Dar had already been a rebel when she'd attended, and Dar strutting back into the circle of her old classmates, as successful as she was, had been a good thing for her. The black sheep had lifted its hind leg and pissed on them all, so to speak.

Kerry hadn't gone to public school. Her high school was a very conservative, Christian establishment, and while she was there, she'd been under a tremendous amount of pressure to uphold her father's image of her. It hadn't been fun, and save for a very scattered few, she had no truly fond memories of the place.

Having had little choice in the matter, she had done well there. She had kept her nose clean and gotten good grades, and joined the appropriate team sports, avoiding the scandalous behaviors of her classmates. Debating had been her one real outlet for expression, and even then she'd been careful when she'd presented her opinions.

The perfect little senator's daughter. Kerry's lips curled in reaction and she felt a touch of disgust at her younger self.

She turned the invitation over and studied it. Going back there as the vice president of global operations of ILS wouldn't be terrible, though she knew she wouldn't be considered nearly as successful as her classmates who'd married into big money and raised large families. Her professional success would, however, be noted and congratulated.

But going back there with Dar—dear God. Exposing their life-style to those people would be like rolling in a fire ant hill, and Kerry felt sick to her stomach just thinking about it. When they realized she was gay, the look in her classmate's eyes would not be anywhere near the bemused, somewhat wary acceptance they had found at Dar's reunion. Oh no.

Even though she knew many of them would have seen the televised senate hearings where she had been outed, that would have been in the abstract. Seeing her and Dar as a couple up close and in person would be something else entirely.

Kerry wasn't embarrassed about their relationship, but she had no intention of subjecting herself, much less Dar, to a night of half pitying, half disgusted stares and the cutting remarks of her family's social circle.

No way.

"Ker?" Dar called from downstairs. "What do you think about a cellular pen?"

Kerry had to smile. "Nerd!" she yelled back, getting up from her desk and heading for the shower. Dar really did get way too into techno toys sometimes. Then she stopped and considered. *A cellular pen?* "Wait. Does it come in pink?"

THE STUDY WAS mostly wood panel, leather, and the scent of old money. The walls were lined with bookshelves stocked with frequently dusted and never read books, and one end was filled with a huge mahogany desk.

Behind the desk sat a man in his fifties, stocky and gray haired, in a crisp white shirt with the sleeves rolled back two turns. He held a stack of papers, and studied each page carefully before he turned it over and set it on a growing pile on the desk.

The door opened and a gray haired woman entered and closed the door behind her. "Roger, the Millisons are having a dinner party next week, and the Vice President is attending. Will you be available for it?"

Roger Stuart leaned back and pondered. "Do I want to be seen with him this month? What has he done lately that I hate? Oh, hell, why not? Millison at least serves a decent meal, especially when he's trying to suck up."

"I'll confirm for us, then," Cynthia Stuart replied. She turned, left the room, and closed the door behind her.

The phone rang. Stuart picked it up and listened, then grunted. "What's the news this time?"

The voice on the other end sounded perkier than was perhaps

normal. "Sir, we finally got that hearing you've been asking for, the one about ILS. They're going to schedule it. I'm sure it'll bring things right out into the open, just like you've hoped."

Stuart hesitated, his eyes going to the stack of papers. "They put it on the listing yet?"

"No, sir, but Jayson promised me it's just a matter of an hour or so."

He drummed his thick, knotted fingers on the papers, making a pattering sound. "All right, listen." He sighed. "Tell him to hold off."

"Sir?"

"Something's come up. Just tell him to hold off until he hears from me," Stuart barked. "Is that understood?"

"Uh...yes, sir." The voice sounded puzzled, but chastened. "I'll tell him."

Stuart hung up and went back to the report. "God damn it! Would you just leave it to that..." He paused and made a face. "To find something like this." He thumped the desk. "Damn it, damn it, damn it!"

He crinkled the papers under his hands, their damning words in stark black against the creamy white of the quality surface on which they were printed. Idly, he flipped a page over and frowned at the typing on the back.

He leaned closer, examined it, and found nothing more interesting than a weather report, then shook his head as he turned it back over. He snorted. "Recycling. Must be a Democrat."

He had to give the woman credit, though. The analysis was crisp, to the point, and did not beat around the bush in regards to its findings, which was something he appreciated regardless of the source. Most of the reports he had to read were full of verbose puffwords saying nothing. Reading Dar Roberts' report was like a breath of fresh air. He could appreciate the content while despising the author, couldn't he?

Stuart sighed. But damn if it had to be her. Having had little choice, he had grudgingly come to accept Kerrison's decision, regardless of how stupid and mindless, not to mention embarrassing, he'd considered it. Finding out his daughter thought she was gay had been a shock, but even worse—she'd shamed him by not even having the grace to keep the fact hidden and discreet.

Disgusting. Just the thought of the two of them... His lip curled. *Disgusting.*

At least he knew that when it inevitably ended, the woman would make no financial gains from his daughter, and in the meantime the two of them lived in what even he considered acceptable style.

There would be no Enquirer stories about Kerrison living in a shack somewhere. The reporters had learned to keep clear of her, especially since her office fended them off and she lived on that private island. At least she'd had the sense to do that much for him.

Now he had this to contend with. Stuart glared at the papers. Roberts had picked him for a reason; he knew it. She hadn't just dropped the documents into his lap out of patriotic fervor, that was for sure.

Had she gotten wind of the incipient investigation into the ILS contracts? Was this her way of trying to buy him off to forget about it? If it was, she was definitely, sadly mistaken. Stuart snorted softly and went on to the next page. As soon as he read through everything, he'd get that hearing right back on...

Stuart bent closer, staring at the next page. "Jesus Christ."

THE SMALL GROUP sat in a circle, in chairs so mismatched that it looked like it was done on purpose by a designer with a decidedly twisted streak. All of the occupants were young, most in their late teens, except for the woman seated cross legged in the large overstuffed chair nearest the door.

"Okay, Barbara, what makes you think he's got it out for you?" Kerry asked quietly, focusing her mind on the problems of these troubled youngsters, halfway between children and adults and dealing with an emerging sexuality they weren't sure they understood. Weren't really sure they wanted, for that matter, being different at an age where different meant outcast in so many poignant ways.

She shared her counseling duties with two other older women and found she enjoyed her time with the group. It meant having to listen to and dealing with problems vastly different from the ones she normally handled, and reminded her all over again that her own acceptance of her lifestyle had been smooth in comparison. Right now, the youngest member of the discussion group, Barbara Gonzales, had confessed that she thought her boss at Burger King had figured out she was gay and was trying to get rid of her because of it.

"I don't know." The slim, brown haired girl wrapped an arm around one knee. "He changed my shift, and now he makes me do all the hard stuff–like figuring out how much bread and meat to order for the next week, and making me check out the bathrooms, and stuff like that."

"Hm." Kerry sat back, aware of Barbara's eyes on her. "Did you ask him why he did that?"

Barbara shrugged. "No. I just figured it was because he saw me and Sally in the freezer that one time. We were so stupid about that."

"Hm." Kerry imagined Alastair McLean walking into a wiring closet and finding her and Dar kissing. She suppressed a giggle. "Is he very conservative?"

"Yeah, kinda." Barbara nodded. "He's all into that community stuff, you know, like Hibiscus."

Hibiscus? Kerry blinked. "You mean Kiwanis?"

"Yeah, whatever."

"Do you do a good job?" Kerry asked.

"I guess. The customers like me. I get stuff done, and I'm always on time and all that stuff."

"Well, he could be coming down on you, but there's another possibility," Kerry said. "He might be trying to nudge you into a more responsible position in the restaurant."

Barbara blinked at her, obviously never having even considered that prospect. "Huh?"

"If I were a fast food manager," Kerry speculated, "and I had a position I needed to fill—say, an assistant manager or a shift leader—I'd find someone who was trustworthy, who was prompt and neat and got the job done, and give them a little more responsibility every day to see how they handled it."

"You would?" Casey cocked her head, which was covered in an explosion of dark curls.

"Sure." Kerry smiled. "Asking Barbara to do the ordering projections and supervising the cleaning of the bathrooms seems to me to be an indication that the man trusts her, and maybe wants to see if she's ready to be promoted." Her eyes twinkled at Barbara, who was staring open mouthed at her. "Tell you what. Think of it that way for a week, and try to look at everything he does positively instead of negatively. See what happens."

Barbara pushed a lock of hair behind an ear. "Wow...okay, yeah, I guess I could do that. Maybe I could, like, iron my shirts and stuff. See if he notices." She smiled and her face lit up. "Thanks, Kerry. You're so cool."

Kerry stood up and circled her chair. She leaned on the back and gazed at them. "Sometimes, it's easy to get into the mode where you think everyone's against you, or that your sexual preference automatically makes you a victim. It's not true." She paused and considered. "Not that it doesn't happen. Of course it does. We all watch the news, or have had stuff happen, so you know it does." A brief smile touched her lips. "But not always."

"You're pretty out at work, aren't you?" Casey asked curiously.

Kerry nodded.

"Do you get shit for that?"

The girls watched her closely, intensely interested in her answer. Kerry tended to turn talk away from her life to theirs, and they were always digging for little nuggets about her personal side. They knew she worked for a big company and that she was gay, and not a whole lot more. Most of them hadn't even met Dar, since the current group had formed after the last picnic her lover had attended.

"Sometimes, there are people who find out and they don't like it," Kerry said. "But mostly, I just do my job and they don't really care."

"Your boss doesn't care?"

She couldn't suppress a smile. "No. Definitely not."

"Cool." Casey nodded. "Maybe I'll get me a job there, then. They sound all right."

Kerry reviewed the stocky young woman, whose dark hair was dyed in three shades of purple to match the six different kinds of earring stones and to contrast with the tattoos dancing across her neck. "Give me your resume and I'll give it to Personnel."

"All right." Casey grinned. "You're pretty cool, for an old lady."

Kerry's eyebrows lifted. "Just how ancient do you think I am?" She put her hands on her hips in mild outrage. "I only have three gray hairs, you know."

Casey grinned, then bashfully dropped her eyes. "I know, I was just ragging you. It must be so cool–to have it all so together like you do."

Hm. Yeah, as a matter of fact, it is pretty darn cool. "I've been really lucky. I've had good opportunities given to me and I've managed to find someone I want to spend the rest of my life with. I thank God for that every day, believe me, Casey." She circled the chair and sat down.

"Okay, so next subject." Kerry pulled her legs into a cross legged position and leaned on the arm of her chair as she regarded her small group of teens. "Did you have a good Thanksgiving?"

Five sets of eyes rolled. "I hate holidays." Lena groaned. "We had the whole family–my grandparents, the cousins, everyone, at our house. I had to dress up. It sucked." The tiny, blond girl made a face.

Kerry chuckled. "Oh yeah, I remember those days. Thanksgiving was always big at my parents' house. We had thirty or forty people there sometimes."

"Did you like it?" Lena asked, sounding doubtful.

Kerry thought about that. "Sometimes. When I was really young, I did, because all my cousins would come over. We were too little for anything really formal, so they'd let us loose in the solarium with a couple of the nannies and we'd have a ball."

"Oo, nannies." Erisa pushed a lock of dark hair back off her forehead. "You were, like, super rich, huh?"

"My parents are well off, yes," Kerry replied.

"So, what did you do this Thanksgiving?" Lena asked. "Did you cook that turkey you got?"

How did we end up talking about me again? Kerry wondered. "Yes and no. I did get to cook it, but it was a few days late. I was out of town for the holiday."

Casey sat up. "You took off? What'd your SO think of that?" Everyone's ears perked up, and they watched Kerry with visible interest.

"Mm. Well, Dar knows my job entails a lot of traveling, so she understood." *Sort of.* "But as it turned out, she was traveling too, and we both ended up in Chicago together. So, it worked out." *Time to change the subject.*

"I dunno." Lena sighed. "For two days I had to listen to my folks tell me how I should get a boyfriend. They're so clueless, I mean, like, hello. Those are not pictures of Leonardo Dumbasa-Fishio on my wall, okay?" She twisted her limbs into a position that made Kerry wonder if she had bones or plastic rods in her body. "You think they'd know, you know? Do I have to paint, like, my whole room in friggin' rainbow stripes?"

"They'd probably think you were just doing that retro seventies thing." Casey snorted. "My freaking father finally caught a clue when I dumped a box of friggin' condoms he'd left in my room into his cereal bowl and told him I wasn't in'erested in letting anything that fit in them fit in me."

Kerry bit back a snort of laughter. "What did he say?"

Casey shrugged, then laughed without humor. "He said, thank fucking God, at least I wouldn't go out and get stupid and pregnant, and make him pay for it."

"Yo, he'd rather you be gay than a slut, right?" Lena remarked. "My folks would rather I be dead than gay."

Kerry sobered. "You don't know that."

"Sure I do." Lena looked directly at her. "My mom told me that right to my face, after she watched some fucking Oprah shit about gay kids." She snorted. "She said if she ever found out I was gay, she'd shut me up in my room and gas me."

Holy crap. Kerry took a breath to steady herself. "I don't think she meant that. Parents say things like that to scare their kids, sometimes."

Lena shrugged. "Yeah, maybe, but I know why so many gay kids pretend they ain't. You get so sick of people thinking you're just so fucked up."

"Yeah." Elina nodded. "I was thinking the other day, is it even worth it?"

Kerry sat up and put both feet on the ground. She clasped her hands between her knees as she leaned forward. "Listen." She spoke slowly and quietly. "My parents don't like me being gay either, and that hurts, because I love my family very much." She sorted through her feelings. "I hated having to make a choice between them and the truth about myself."

"They just don't get it," Elina remarked softly. "It's like they don't understand it, so they have to hate it."

Kerry nodded. "That's true, and believe me, I was scared when I realized I was going to have to face that. I didn't want them to hate me." She paused and collected her thoughts. "You know, I never knew what it would be like to fall in love. So when I fell in love with Dar, it was all so much of a surprise to me—how good it felt and what an amazingly powerful emotion love is."

They all looked at each other, then back at her.

"It's worth it," Kerry said simply. "I wouldn't give Dar up for all the money, or the approval of my parents, or anything else in the world."

There was utter silence, and Kerry glanced from face to face as they stared. "C'mon, it wasn't that profound." She chuckled, then realized they weren't staring *at* her, they were staring *past* her. She turned her head to find Dar leaning in the doorway, her arms folded and a quiet, pleased smile on her face. "Ah, it's you."

"Yes, it is," Dar said.

Kerry was aware she was blushing. "C'mon in. Guys, this is Dar."

Dar entered, rounded Kerry's chair, and perched on an arm of it as she regarded the circle of young faces. "Hi," she said, then turned her attention to Kerry. "You're late."

Kerry gave Dar a bewildered look. "I am? For what?"

"You have an appointment with me, some of my stone crab friends, and a tall bottle." Dar watched the startled delight creep into Kerry's features. "With lots of bubbles in it." She turned her head and peered at the girls. "You'll excuse her, right?"

Five heads nodded.

"Good." Dar turned her attention back to Kerry. "Well?" She lifted an eyebrow and held out a hand, palm up. Kerry clasped Dar's hand, their fingers curling warmly around each other's. Dar stood and tugged, and waited for Kerry to stand up.

"Um." Kerry faced her group, who were now smiling and giggling at her. "I guess I'll see you guys next week, huh?" She flashed them a rueful grin. "See? She's definitely a keeper."

Still clasping hands, they walked out of the meeting room and through the church, respecting the peaceful silence until they pushed through the large outer door and went from the slightly close air into a cool fall night and a gusty breeze tinged heavily with salt. "Wow." Kerry regarded Dar's profile outlined in stars. "That was a surprise."

Dar nodded. "I know. I had a tough day and ended up getting through it by planning the night with you. C'mon. Let's go count stars."

Kerry smiled and turned her face to the wind as they walked to a nearby small, seaside restaurant, its table candles fluttering in the breeze. Her hand felt warm in Dar's and the concrete sidewalk seemed to turn into a cloud.

Chapter
Two

"ANGIE?" CYNTHIA STUART looked up as she heard footsteps in the hall. "We're ready to sit down for dinner. Is Richard back?"

"Not yet." Angela entered the solarium, took a seat, and straightened her skirt as she tucked her feet under the chair. "He said his meeting might run late. I just put Andrew to bed." She fiddled with her hair—a dark brown, very unlike her older sister Kerry's. She was also taller than her sibling, with a thin build that made her seem almost gaunt.

"Well, all right. It can wait a few minutes," Cynthia replied. "Your father's still in conference, at any rate. But I think they are wrapping up shortly. He rang the bell about five minutes ago."

Angie nodded and they were silent for a few moments.

"Have you spoken to your sister recently?" Cynthia asked.

Angie shook her head. "No. I tried calling there a few times, but I didn't get an answer. I guess they're busy." She looked at her mother. "You know."

"Mm." Cynthia nodded once. "They do seem active." She sighed. "I do wish—"

"Mother, don't start," Angie said. "Kerry's happy, isn't that enough? Just leave her alone."

The study door opened and Roger Stuart emerged. Spotting them on his way to the dining room, he changed direction and entered the solarium. "What's going on here? Are we not sitting down to dinner tonight? I expected to have soup on the table already."

"We were waiting for you, Roger," Cynthia responded mildly. "And Richard isn't back yet. But we can go sit down now. I'm sure he'll join us shortly." She got up and motioned for Angie to join her. "Was your meeting successful?"

"Tsh." Roger shook his head. "Jackasses, all of them." He stood back to let Cynthia and Angie precede him into the dining room. As they walked across the corridor the youngest Stuart sibling, brother Michael, joined them. "Ah. Come to mooch dinner again? They out of Happy Meals down the street?"

Michael colored, but didn't answer. They all filed into the dining room and took seats. The dining room staff came in silently and placed platters of an orange, creamy looking soup on the table.

"What's this?" Roger asked, poking the soup with a spoon. "Is it that damn tomato I told you never to give me again?"

"No, sir," the head server replied respectfully. "It's cream of carrot."

"Mmph." Roger tasted it, then made a face. "Barely edible. Does anyone in this house like carrots?"

"Kerry does," Michael remarked, and sipped a spoonful of the soup. "I bet she'd like this." He jerked slightly as Angie kicked him under the table.

Angie sighed. "She probably would, if it were being served anywhere but here."

Her mother frowned. "Angela."

Roger looked up and gave his children a dour stare. "I'm sure she would. But it'll be a cold day in Hell before you ever find out, hmm? So keep your mouths shut until you have something intelligent to say." He gave each of them a pointed look. "Should be a quiet meal."

There was a long moment of tense silence, then Cynthia sighed again. "Well, so, how was your day, Michael? Did you meet any new clients?"

"Um...no."

Roger laughed again, this time with a disgusted edge to the sound. Then he looked up abruptly. "Damned ironic that the one person in this family who could handle an intelligent discussion won't ever be here for it."

Silence settled in against the soft clanking of spoons.

DAR ENTERED HER office, tossed the report folder down on her desk, and watched it slide across the polished surface as she walked around behind it. She neatly caught the packet as it slid off the desk, and threw it into her outbox with a little noise of disgust.

Mondays. I hate them. Dar took a seat, nudged her trackball, and watched the screen come up. It was full of dark messages, some with red exclamation points. She rubbed her eyes and started to read them, cursing under her breath. "No." She clicked delete. "No." She clicked delete again. "Kiss my ass." She selected three and deleted them. "Son of a bitch, what is wrong with these people today?" Her phone rang and she hit the button. "Yes?"

"Dar, I have Mr. Alastair on *numero uno*," Maria replied.

Jesus. "Okay, thanks." Dar punched the line open. "Hi."

"Morning, Dar." Alastair sounded relatively relaxed. "Anything new going on there?"

Dar stared at the phone. "Were you expecting there to be?"

"Nah," Alastair answered. "Just felt like touching base with you. How's the shoulder?"

"Fine, Uncle Al. How's your bursitis?" Dar replied, half amused and half aggravated. "You hear from Gerry?"

"Nope, not a word," Alastair answered. "But I figure that as far as that goes, no news is one less thing I have to have chewing my shorts up, if you know what I mean."

"I know what you mean," Dar said. "To answer your original question, it's quiet here for a change. Just a lot of annoying crap in my mailbox I'm trying to catch up on."

"Good to hear," Alastair said. "Kerry doing okay? I got the feeling she was a little shook up with all that activity, eh? She settle down?"

Dar frowned at the phone. "Alastair?"

"Eh?"

"What the hell's going on?"

Alastair sighed. "I'm trying to work on my subtlety, Dar. You're not helping."

Blue eyes blinked a few times. "And it's supposed to work on *me*?"

"Not really, no," he said. "Fact is, I got wind that a relative of hers could be behind all this mish-mosh of questioning our contracts with the military." His tone was serious. "So, I was wondering if she'd been in conflict with him again, maybe stirred him up."

Dar snorted. "If that's all it takes to stir him up, he's not worth the six dollars per square yard of linen my tax dollars pay to clothe him."

"Mm."

"No," she went on. "Kerry hasn't spoken to her folks for a while. Nothing's going on. He's probably just being an asshole because he is one...and because of me."

"Ah."

Dar drummed her fingers on the desk. "This just start?"

"Nah," Alastair answered. "Apparently he instigated it right after we first signed the deal. It's just now bubbling to the top."

Not because of what I gave him, then. "Well, I can't help it. I can't change what's pissing him off. You think it's real trouble?"

Alastair sighed again. "I think it might be. I know you can't fix it, Dar; I was just curious. I'll take care of it on my end. Don't fret over it."

Dar suspected they both knew that bit of advice wasn't going anywhere. "You think he's coming after us? God damn it, Alastair, I saved the bastard's life. What more does he want from me?"

"I know." Alastair's voice modified to a gentler tone. "Dar, it's not you, it's him. Let me handle it. I just wanted to know if there was anything going on with him and Kerry before I start hitting below the belt. Understand—I don't give a damn if he's her father. If he scotches this contract, we're in big trouble, lady. I can't make those dollars up at this late date in the fiscal year."

No kidding. Dar chewed on the inside of her lip. The contract had been a huge plus for them when they'd announced it. "Do you know what it would mean if we had to go back on that now?"

"Lady, do I ever," Alastair remarked dryly. "Talk at you later, huh? Have a good day, Dar."

"Yeah." Dar hung up the phone and grimaced. "*Now* you say that."

HER PHONE WAS ringing as she entered and she contemplated letting it go to voice mail, then sighed and answered it. "Operations, Kerry Stuart."

"Hey, Kerry, this is Ilene, from the church?" The voice hesitantly added, "I do the youth group counseling with you?"

"Oh, sure." Kerry's mental train jerked onto a new set of tracks. "Sorry. What's up?"

"Have you heard from Lena, the kid in the group? You know the one I mean?" Ilene asked. "She was supposed to meet me for lunch yesterday, and she never showed."

Kerry started shutting down her computer. "Well, maybe something came up; you know how it is. She didn't call or anything?"

"No. And yeah, I know stuff happens, but two of her friends were here just now looking for her. They said she hasn't been around for a couple of days, and they're a little worried. I thought maybe she might have contacted you."

"Me?" Kerry's brow creased. "No. I don't think I gave my number out to the group and I'm not listed in the phone book. If she does contact me somehow, though, I'll definitely get in touch with you. Do they think something happened to her or—"

"No one's sure. It's just weird for her not to be around for that long. She didn't say she was going anywhere." Ilene sighed. "Well, it was a long shot, but Casey said Lena really likes you, so I thought maybe you'd given her your number or something. Thanks anyway, Kerry."

"No problem," Kerry replied. "I'll keep an eye out for her, okay?"

"Much appreciated. Talk to you later."

The unexpected call left Kerry a bit unsettled. She finished closing down her system, then checked her caller ID and copied Ilene's number into her Palm Pilot. She'd met the other counselor a few times at church functions and rather liked her, but they hadn't spent much time talking to each other since then.

Pity, really, since Ilene shared her general background and upbringing. She'd been born in Detroit into a family of old car money whose reaction to her coming out had been, if not as spectacular as that of Kerry's parents, at least as vicious. They'd taken just about everything she owned and had thrown her out of the house, forcing her to move somewhere, anywhere, and support herself.

Just like Kerry, Ilene had made the transition, but for Ilene it had been much harder since the only job she'd had prior to moving was as a movie usher. She'd mixed in with a tough crowd there in Miami and gotten into a little trouble, but had ended up taking vocational courses and scraping together a career as a mechanic.

It puts things into perspective, sometimes, when you look at other people and realize how lucky you are. Kerry leaned back and wished her Advil faster sailing as it headed towards her pounding headache. It was making her slightly sick to her stomach, and she hoped that the nausea faded before she had to make a dash for the restroom.

Meetings didn't usually bring one of those suckers on, but she'd been a little tense when she'd woken up late, and rushing to get to work never helped. Dar had shrugged off the timing problem, but Kerry was very aware of the eyes and ears monitoring her, and the last thing she wanted was people commenting that she took advantage of her relationship with Dar to wander in whenever she felt like it.

Dar told her not to give a crap if they gossiped, but that didn't really help her insides any. Of course, she also didn't have the cojones to handle the comments like Dar did. When her lover was confronted with a caustic comment on her late entry, she merely replied with a smirk and the words, "Don't you wish you had the reason I do?"

It was flattering, in a way, but Kerry knew she turned brick red every time she heard it. "Ah well." She flexed her shoulders, her fingers working a knot at the base of her skull. Maybe the rest of the day would be peaceful, and she could get her mailbox cleaned out after she'd ignored it all weekend.

A soft knock sounded on her inner door, and she swiveled to see it open and reveal Dar's dark head poking through. "Hey."

Dar entered, walked over to her, and leaned on the back of her chair. "Can I kill Eleanor?"

Ah. "What now, honey?" Kerry folded her hands over her stomach and gave Dar a loving benign look. "Did she promise a prospective client you'd take them to dinner again? You know it's just because of your reputation."

"She promised a prospective client I'd give him free bandwidth if he signed a multiyear contract," Dar replied with a dour look.

"Oh. What a bitch." Kerry sat up and reached for her keyboard. "Let me go tell her what she can do with her promise of free—"

Dar covered Kerry's hands with her own. "I told her. But I know she's going to come to you with a sob story to get you to try to change my mind."

"Hah!"

Dar gave her a kiss on the top of the head. "She'll learn, one of these days." She stepped away as Kerry sat back and swiveled around to face her. "Meeting go all right?"

"Eh." Kerry exhaled. "It gave me a headache. I'm waiting on the Advil."

Dar sat down on the desk, and brushed Kerry's hair back and then stroked her cheek.

It brought a smile to Kerry's face and banished some of the tension. "Quiet by you? Maybe we can get out of here a couple minutes early. If they're going to talk anyway, I might as well just take advantage of it."

"Sure." Dar saw Kerry's line light up. "I'll let you get back to work."

Kerry circled Dar's leg with one arm as she answered the phone. "Operations, Stuart."

"Ms. Stuart, this is Ramon in the ops center," a tense voice responded. "I think something's going on."

Kerry felt Dar lean forward to listen. "Something? Like what?"

"There's a huge file transfer going on from the banking T1's, nothing like I've ever seen before. Can you take a look? I was trying to get hold of Ms. Roberts, but she's not in her office."

"We're on our way." Dar hit the button and popped up off the desk, with Kerry right behind her. "Well, one thing—at least—"

"We don't have to answer our mail?"

"You got it."

The door slammed after them, leaving the room in somber silence.

"DID YOU HAVE to do that?" Angie asked, as she walked her brother out to his car. "I mean, good grief, Mike."

"Yes, I did," Michael replied stubbornly. "God damn it, Angie, she's our sister. I don't care if our parents wish she wasn't, she is."

Angie walked a few steps, glancing up at the clear, star filled sky. "I know."

"You don't know. You don't give a piss, Angie. You went right along with them when they wanted to give her the cold shoulder at the trial, and you could give a rat's—"

"That's not true!" Angie grabbed his arm and swung him around. "I love Kerry. Don't you take that high and mighty attitude with me. You went right along with it, too."

"I didn't. I went over there where she was sitting." Mike jerked his arm free. "You didn't."

"For crying out loud, Mike! I was nine months pregnant," Angie shouted. "What in the hell did you expect me to do, make a scene?"

"Yeah," Michael replied. "You could have stood up for her."

"Oh, you're just impossible." Angie turned and started back for the house. "All you want to do is start trouble about her to keep him from taking pot shots at *you*." She slammed the front door, leaving Michael out in the chill of the fall night.

"Yeah." Michael exhaled. "Maybe." He gave his head a half shake and went to his car. Several men walked towards the house and he stepped aside to let them pass. They spared him a glance, then continued on without acknowledging him.

"Does he know what he has? Is he sure?" one asked in a doubtful tone.

"He's sure," a second answered. "What I want to know is, where'd he get the dirt from? I thought the guy he had inside turned on him?"

"Dunno. Guess we'll find out shortly."

They passed out of earshot, leaving Michael standing there. He shook his head and sighed. "What now, I wonder? Did he get those pictures of old what's-his-name and the hooker? Anything to make a scandal and take the heat off, I guess." He paused as he turned towards the car. "Maybe we are related."

KERRY LEANED OVER Dar's shoulder, watching her key in rapid commands on a console. Dar's legs were locked around the base of the chair, and she rocked slightly—the energy coming off her was almost palpable.

"What is it?" Kerry asked in a soft voice.

"Dunno...dunno, yet," Dar muttered, trying to wrestle an analyzer into place on the line. "Jesus, it's big." She gave up on her work, then keyed another screen. "I'm going to mirror and dump it."

"Ma'am?" The console operator sounded nervous. "We're not supposed to do that."

"*You're* not supposed to do that." Dar finished her task. "Until I can see what this is, I'm not taking any chances." She went back to work on the sniffer. "Damn port's pushing so much data, I wonder if I can...Damn."

"Can you just put a...Ah." Kerry closed her mouth and watched as Dar managed to get a handle on the traffic by throwing it to their packet analyzer. "Okay, let's see what we...Oh, hell."

"Yeah."

"Encrypted," Kerry said. "Well, that's a good thing, right? I mean, you want your data to be encrypted."

"Mm." Dar traced something with a long fingertip. "I don't like that header."

Kerry leaned forward again and studied the packet Dar pointed at. "Why?"

"Unusual port," Dar murmured. "Do me a favor. Get Charles Ettig on the phone and feel him out. See if he's got a big transfer going on. Just say we saw a usage spike on the pipe."

Kerry sat down and lifted the phone on the console. She pulled out her PDA and checked the number to dial, then punched it in and waited for a connection. "Charles Ettig, please. Kerry Stuart, from ILS."

Bad Musak happened for a few minutes, then it cut off. "Hello? This is Charles Ettig speaking."

Kerry kept her voice casual. "Charles, this is Kerry Stuart."

"Oh, hello, Kerry," Charles responded. "How are you?"

"I'm fine, thanks. Listen, one of our measuring systems caught a spike on the usage of your primary line. Are you guys moving some files?"

There was a moment of silence. "Moving files?" Ettig asked. "No, not that I know of. I mean, it's Monday, y'know, and we do have all the reconciliation transfers coming from the banks in here, is that what you mean?"

Dar shook her head and pointed to herself.

"No, this is something coming out of your building," Kerry said. "Like if you were putting out a software upgrade, that kind of thing. We thought maybe you were distributing patches to your database."

"Oh." Ettig pondered a moment. "Well, I guess we could be. Let me call around and find out." He hesitated. "We aren't being charged for it, are we?"

Kerry chuckled. "No, it just seemed a little out of the ordinary, so we thought we'd ask."

"Okay." Ettig now sounded more confident. "Thanks for keeping an eye on things. You know we really do appreciate that, huh? I'll call you back."

Kerry hung up and gave Dar a quizzical look.

"Beautiful," Dar said. "I'm going to see if I can track down where it's going." She typed in a command and observed the result.

"Be careful, Dar, you're walking a very fine line here." Kerry laid her hands on Dar's shoulders and flexed her fingers against the powerful bone and muscle under them.

"Got it." Dar went to another screen and typed in a query. "Let's see who you are, hm?"

"It could very well be legitimate."

"Could be."

Dar waited, drumming her fingertips on the keyboard. "California. Okay." A few more moments passed as the trace continued. "Well, it's heading for a DSL node in San Francisco. They got anything in San Francisco?"

"Three branches," Kerry said. "But they're on Frame Relay lines, Dar. Not DSL."

"Uh huh."

"Where are they tapping in? Is it on our network?" Kerry inhaled. "Did we have a breach?"

"Shit." Dar started typing again. "Switch in Detroit." She picked up the phone and dialed. "Mark? It's Dar. Pull up all the changes and adds in Detroit over the last three weeks. Get them to Ops." Without waiting for the answer, she hung up and started tracing ports. "It's in the cloud."

"The Frame cloud? In the Tier 1?"

"Yes."

"They were breached."

Dar's fingers hesitated over the keys. "I'm going to cut it off."

The phone rang and Kerry picked it up. "Operations, Stuart."

"Kerry? This is Charles Ettig. Listen, I just talked to my people and they say there's nothing going on."

Dar's hands were a blur.

"Okay, Charles," Kerry replied. "Tell you what. We're going to drop the traffic, and we'll analyze it—see if we can figure out what it was and let you know. How's that?"

"Sounds just great, Kerry. Thanks again for taking such good care of us, okay?" His tone was grateful. "I know we can trust you guys."

"Thanks, Charles. Call you back." Kerry hung up and exhaled. "Dar, if there was a breach, is it our fault?"

"Depends where it is. Let's trace it, then we can figure out what the hell we're going to do. Damn. The last thing we need is a security crack right now." Dar stared at the screen. "Even if it's the Tier 1's breach, it's still our managed circuit. Damn it, damn it, damn it." She thumped a fist against her forehead.

Kerry put her hands back on Dar's shoulders and gave them a squeeze. The tension was evident, and without really thinking, she gently massaged the muscles. "Let's find out what the deal is, first. At the very least, Dar, we saw it happening." She turned and looked at the console operator, who was studiously looking elsewhere. "Ramon, you did a great job finding this."

He glanced furtively at them. "Thanks, ma'am."

Kerry's brow knit, then she realized he was uncomfortable with her interaction with Dar. For a second, she almost stopped and backed off. Then Dar's skin shifted under her touch, and she stepped closer instead, adding her body's warmth to the massage and thinking, *To hell with it.*

To hell with it. This woman in front of her was what mattered, not a bug eyed nerdy boy standing by watching. "Dar?"

Dar leaned back until she rested her head against Kerry's stomach. "Yes?" She tipped her eyes up and looked at Kerry. "This could be a ranking fubar, Ker."

Kerry managed a smile. "You'll handle it. We'll figure it all out. Mark's provisioning process is a solid one. I'm sure we can find an angle."

Dar's shoulders relaxed, and she nodded. "I'm sure we can." She typed a note into the console. "I'll have him put that data dump somewhere so I can check it out tomorrow. Maybe I'll get some clues from that."

Despite their stated optimism, Kerry knew they were both crossing everything they could.

HANDS CLASPED BEHIND his back, the tall, dark haired man paced back and forth across Senator Stuart's home office. "Roger, I appreciate what you're saying, but how can you be sure it's real data? You said someone just gave it to you? I don't understand."

"You don't have to understand." Roger glared dourly at him. "Just look at it. Look at the names and the numbers, and you tell me, Bradley, you tell me if it's real or not." He threw a stack of papers on the desk towards Bradley.

Bradley picked them up and studied them, impatiently at first, then slowly turning the pages. He paused, then sat down in a chair across from Stuart and stared at the writing. "Dear God."

Roger leaned back in his chair. "So you tell me, Bradley," he repeated with deep sarcasm, "do we have a problem?"

Bradley looked up. "We have a problem. Roger, we need to pay off whoever got this to you and fast." To his surprise, Roger laughed. "I'm not joking."

Stuart got up and started pacing. "Oh, but you are; you just don't know you are. The source I got this from not only can't be bought off, I wouldn't even try it." He turned and pointed. "What I want to know is, how is it that someone," he stared pointedly at Bradley, "was so god damned stupid as to put incriminating information in something so accessible? Tell me that, Bradley?"

"Sir—"

"Tell me why details about deals neither of us officially knows anything about are sitting in a military database in the sticks!"

"Sir." Bradley held up a hand. "Let me get Stevens and Perlamen in here; maybe they can make sense of it." He went to the door and called out, "Gentlemen, we need you."

The two men entered, faced with the angry senator on the other side of the room. "Sir?"

"They can't explain it. You can't explain it." Roger's voice rose. "No one can explain it, because I'm surrounded by idiots! The irony of it all is that the goddamned bitch who gave me this crap makes you all look like mental *midgets*."

"Sir, take it easy, please," Bradley begged. "I'm sure there's an explanation. Someone must have—"

"Idiots!" Stuart bellowed. "'It's a simple deal, Senator.' Isn't that what you told me? Just some surplus military garbage being traded, nothing important. You stupid son of a bitch, did you see what's in that data? Idiot! Idiots! All of you!"

"Sir!" Perlamen said. "We can incriminate—"

"We're all incriminated, you jackass!" Stuart yelled at the top of his lungs. "This is not in the hands of any friends of ours. For God's sake...For God's sake..." He clutched his head. "Ah!"

"Sir?" The men rushed forward. "*Sir!*"

Chapter
Three

"UGH." KERRY SLID down into the hot tub and cradled her neck on its edge. "Thank God that's over."

Dar had her eyes closed. "Yeah." She squirmed around, taking advantage of the heavy jets of water. "Thank God it turned out to be a firmware glitch, not a stolen file. Even if it took us most of the night to figure it out."

"Mm." Kerry turned her head, captured her straw, and sucked in a mouthful of peach iced tea. "It's not quite ten. We've stayed later."

Dar tangled her legs with Kerry's and exhaled. "Uh huh. Glad we didn't have to. I'm tanked."

"Fish tanked?" Kerry snickered, splashing her a little.

"Wench. Get your snorkel ready." The cordless phone rang, and, after giving it an evil look, Dar picked it up and answered it. "Hello?"

There was silence, then a gasp. "Um...um...can I talk to Kerry?"

Dar's brow creased. "Sure." With widening eyes and a shrug, she handed the phone to Kerry. The voice had sounded very young.

Kerry took it and put it to her damp ear. "Hello?" Dar sidled over and pressed her head against Kerry's to listen.

"Oh, Kerry, hi." There was a sharp intake of breath. "I'm really sorry to like, bother you this late and all that, but—"

"Lena?" Kerry's mental recognition kicked in. "Is that you?"

There was silence for a breath. "Yeah."

"Hey, folks have been looking for you," Kerry said. "Where are you?"

Lena hesitated. "Um...not in a good place."

Dar nestled closer and listened.

"What's 'not a good place'? Are you in the hospital?"

"No," Lena muttered. "I'm in jail."

Dar's eyes widened in surprise. She and Kerry exchanged

startled looks.

"In jail? What are you doing there?" Kerry sputtered. "What did you...?" She half turned and pushed the wet hair out of her eyes. "Are you okay?"

"Yeah." Lena sounded tired. "It's just really stupid, you know? My folks clued into like, me being gay, and they grounded me."

"Grounded you?" Kerry's voice dropped in pitch. "Did they think that would fix it?"

"Fuck if I know," Lena replied glumly. "A window got busted in my old man's car, and they called the cops on me."

"Ah." Kerry's eyes narrowed slightly. "You need help getting out?"

Lena was very quiet for a few seconds. "You're the only person I know that doesn't make minimum wage. My folks told me to rot in here."

Blue and green eyes met. "We'll be right down there. You at the main jail? The one off Flagler?"

"Yeah," Lena whispered. "Thanks, Kerry."

"No problem. Take it easy until we get there." Kerry hung up and put the phone down. "Stupid son of a b—" She was stopped with a kiss. "Damn it, Dar. What the hell is wrong with people?"

"I don't know." Dar wiped a bit of water off Kerry's cheek. "But we'd better get dressed and go bail your little buddy out. Then we can worry about her dimwitted genetic contributors."

"Pah." Kerry sloshed out of the tub, grabbed a towel, and handed Dar hers. "Poor kid. How could they let her be taken down there? She's probably scared half to death."

"She the one with the tattoos?" Dar asked.

"Yeah."

"Mm. And the nose ring?"

"Yeah."

"She'll be fine."

They walked into the condo and were halfway across the living room before Kerry stopped and turned with her hands on her hips. "Do you know this from personal experience?"

Dar rubbed her face and just kept walking, a faint chuckle escaping her.

"Oh, I can't wait to hear *this* story." Kerry followed, with a chuckle of her own.

THE DADE COUNTY primary jail was, as most jails are, a supremely depressing place. The walls were institutional beige, and the floors were repeatedly shined heavy tile. Kerry was sharply aware of the glances thrown her way as she entered and was glad of Dar's light touch on her back as they walked across the starkly lit lobby to the processing desk.

Thick, bulletproof glass protected the woman seated behind it and it took a moment before she realized someone was there and looked up. "Yes?"

Ew. Kerry exhaled. "A friend of ours is in here. I'd like to see about getting her out."

The woman looked at her, then pushed a pad across the desk and through the small opening in the glass. "Name?"

Kerry glanced at the pad, then fished in her purse for a pen. She realized she didn't know Lena's last name at the same time Dar handed over her favorite heavy, silver-cased ballpoint. "Thanks." Kerry scribed the first name, then hesitated. "I'm sorry. I only know her first name."

"Real good friend of yours, huh?" The officer took the pad back and studied it. "Could be worse; could be Maria. Lemme go look." She ripped the top sheet off the pad, got up, and disappeared into a cluttered area full of files and tall cabinets behind her.

"Hm." Kerry rocked on her heels. "I feel pretty stupid about that."

Dar shrugged, laced her fingers together behind her back, and glanced around the lobby. "Hasn't changed much." She accepted Kerry's curious look. "After I..." Dar paused and inclined her head. "That little incident at the club I think you mentioned once."

"Ah." Kerry did, indeed, remember. "They brought you here?"

"I was pretty young," Dar said. "They wanted to make sure one of the jackass's friends didn't come after me. They called Dad and he came down to pick me up."

Two officers with an obviously inebriated young woman slung between them pushed by. Kerry moved out of the way and ducked as the woman wildly swung an arm. "Whoa." Dar pulled her to one side and hovered protectively over her. Kerry decided a distraction was appropriate. "So, Dad picked you up, huh?"

Dar's nose wrinkled at the sudden stench of vomit. "Yeah." She took another step backwards, tugging Kerry with her. "He was, um..."

"Proud." Kerry tried to breathe through her mouth.

"Well..."

"Paladar Katherine Roberts, I can just stand here and picture your father coming in here to get you. I bet he made every cop who was there tell him what you did."

Two men, arguing in loud, strident Spanish, brushed by. They had badges on chains around their necks. Another yelling man, pointing a finger at one of the detectives, approached. The detective slapped his hand and yelled back.

"Hey!" The clerk had returned to her desk, and now she used the microphone. "Take it inside!"

The three men gave her a look, then shoved through a worn, wood paneled door off to one side, which opened into a large room filled with desks and papers. The clerk watched them, then looked up, made eye contact with Kerry, and curled her finger inward.

"Officious little—"

"Dar." Kerry patted her lover's leg. "C'mon, let's get this over with." She led Dar over to the counter and rested her elbows on its chipped Formica surface. "Find her?"

"Yeah." The woman shuffled some papers. "You a relative?"

"No. Just a friend." Kerry moved a little closer and tilted her head to see the officer's nametag. *Funk. Hm.* "She had a little trouble with her folks."

"No kidding," Officer Funk said. "All right. The bail's a thousand dollars."

Kerry saw the officer's eyes lift to her and she suspected she was waiting for a reaction. Kerry smiled pleasantly. "Okay. Do you take checks? Credit cards?" She waited a moment and there was still no reaction from the officer. "Animal pelts?"

"Cash," Officer Funk replied. "Ten percent."

Dar removed her wallet from her hip pocket and sorted through its contents. She removed a hundred dollar bill and tossed it onto the counter. "There."

Kerry opened her mouth to object, then realized she didn't have that much cash on her. She pushed the bill closer to the officer. "There."

They stood there while the paperwork was completed, what looked like an eight or nine part form along with a sheaf of other documents. "I didn't have to sign that many things for my new car," Kerry commented idly.

"You weren't buying it from Dade County," the officer muttered. "All right. Jack, c'mere. Get me this one from the holding area." She thrust a piece of paper behind her, and it was taken by a shorter man in uniform, sporting a thick, dark mustache. "This is your receipt." She pushed a form to Kerry. "She comes up for a hearing in ten days. Make sure she's there, or you're in the hole for the other nine hundred."

Dar leaned forward. "What is she charged with?"

The deeper tones caught the officer's attention and she looked up to find Dar's piercing eyes pinning her. "Destruction of property."

"What did she break?" Kerry asked.

"Car window."

Dar's brow creased. "Wouldn't it be cheaper to just pay for the damn window?"

Officer Funk shrugged. "Her parents pressed charges. Guess they figured the kid couldn't pay."

"Bastards."

The policewoman stopped from standing up to put away her papers and peered through the glass at Dar. "I don't know. If my kid told me she was queer, I might do the same thing." She shrugged and walked away.

Kerry turned and met Dar's eyes, and they looked at each other in silence. After a moment, an inner door opened and the short, male officer appeared, one hand grasping Lena's arm. The girl was very quiet, her face showing signs of rough handling and her clothes ripped and stained. She looked up and saw the two of them and a look of utter gratitude lit her face.

"Hey, Lena." Kerry smiled at her. "C'mon, I bet you want out of here."

"Oh." Lena closed her eyes, then opened them. "You bet your ass I do." She paused awkwardly. "Um...I mean..."

"I think you said exactly what you mean," Dar drawled. "Let's get out of this place." Her eyes drifted and met Officer Funk's. "It stinks."

They went out through the large double doors and into the cool night air. Lena stopped on the stone steps and took a breath, tilting her head back to look up at the night sky. "Thank you." She hugged herself. "I'll pay you guys back. I've got some money in my savings account." She looked around with a lost expression. "I'll have to take it all out anyway. I'll need clothes before I can go back to work tomorrow." She paused. "If they haven't fired me."

Kerry and Dar exchanged glances. "C'mon." Kerry put a hand on her arm and steered her towards the Lexus. "The first thing you need is a shower and some clean stuff to wear. We've got both back at our place."

"I can't ask you to do that." But Lena looked pathetically grateful.

"You're not. Let's go." Dar keyed the doors open and motioned her inside. The poor kid looked so ragged, and so at a loss, Dar felt like...*Like what, Dar?* her conscience pricked her. *Like you want to go punch her mother?* She closed the door after Lena climbed up inside, then walked around and started to get in. She paused and rested her arm on the edge of the windowsill as she gazed down the sidewalk.

She remembered walking down it, dressed in her scary, punky best, with parts of her aching from the fight but happy, because her daddy was there next to her. They'd stopped on the corner and leaned back against the coral wall, across from the parking lot where she'd spotted her dad's truck. Andrew had looked her over and shook his head. "Lord. You are mah kid, ain't you."

Dar had stuck her hands into her ripped pockets and just nodded.

"Y'know, they don't much give medals to folks who do what I do," Andrew had said, looking off into the distance. "And I sure ain't got none to give up, but here." He'd taken off his dog tags and put them around Dar's neck.

Dar remembered looking up at him, and she knew her face must have shown how she felt, because he'd smiled and cupped her cheek with one callused hand.

They'd just gone on home after that, after a stop at a gas station mart to pick up a couple of ice cream bars and two bottles of pop. Even her mother had listened to the story and, with a sigh, given her a pat on the knee and told her she'd done a good thing.

It had felt like winning the lottery, that winning of her parents' praise, and listening to Lena, Dar realized all over again how different it could have been for her.

"Dar?" Kerry leaned over and tugged on Dar's shirt. "You okay?"

"Yeah." Dar slid behind the wheel and closed the door. "I was just thinking of something."

Kerry studied the angular profile for a moment, then patted Dar's thigh and half turned in her seat to address Lena. "You're doing data entry, aren't you?"

Lena was running her fingers over the soft leather of the seat. She glanced up guiltily. "Um...oh, yeah, yeah, I do. It's a telemarketing thingie. I put in the orders." Her eyes dropped. "Or, I did. My boss hates when people are late. I can just imagine what his reaction was when I didn't show for work for two days."

"Don't worry about it." Kerry smiled at her. "So, what exactly happened?"

Lena pushed some very dirty hair back off her forehead. "Oh, my God, it was like...It was so incredibly stupid." She exhaled, but her spirit was rebounding a little. "I can't believe it. It's like some dumb weird ass dream thing, you know?"

"No. But if you'd tell me, I would," Kerry replied patiently.

Lena emitted a sigh. "Okay. Like, I told you I was really into this Internet thing, right?"

Dar and Kerry exchanged looks. "We can relate to that," Kerry said.

Lena was momentarily distracted. "Are you guys on the Internet?"

"We run the Internet," Dar said as she pulled carefully onto the highway. "So, yeah, you could say we're on it, under it, inside it, crawling all over it."

"Wow. For real?" Lena watched Dar's profile with interest. "That's so cool. Are you, like, hackers?"

"No."

"Sometimes."

Kerry gave Dar a look. "We are not."

"You've never seen what I can do with a data analyzer, have you?"

Lena started laughing. "You guys are funny." She relaxed into the leather seat. "So, anyway, I'm like really into this Internet stuff and I found some really cool places, with people...um..." She hesitated.

"Like us?" Kerry hazarded a guess.

"Yeah," Lena said. "Anyway, we all get together and we chat, and do stuff, and a lot of them write these story things." She rubbed her fingers together. "Some of them are okay, and some are pretty good, and some...ew." Lena made a face. "So, I figured I could try doing it, too, and just see how it went."

"Stories?" Kerry leaned against the seat and considered that. "What? Stories about...school and things like that?"

"Uh, no." Lena blushed. "Not about school. Well, one of them was. This girl wrote this one about her and two other girls and some gym equipment, but—"

Kerry cocked her head. "Gym equipment?" She looked at a laughing Dar. "What?" Her brow knit, then relaxed as she realized what sort of stories Lena was talking about. "Oh. Kind of...romantic stories, huh?"

Lena chewed her lip. "Well, I guess some of them might be called that."

"So, did your parents catch you reading this lesbian erotica?" Dar asked in a low, amused tone.

"No way." Lena shook her head. "I'm way too careful for that, and my parents wouldn't know what they were looking at in my computer anyway." She folded her arms. "I wrote my first one, and I posted it, and you know, everyone liked it. It was so cool."

"Hey, that's great," Kerry said.

"Yeah, except I printed out a copy to take to school, to show Casey and them, and it was on my printer, and my mother came in and took it." Lena looked out the window. "Wow, we're driving onto a boat? Where do you guys live, Cuba?"

"That'd be a commute," Dar muttered. "I'd say your mother got what she deserved if she walked in and just took what wasn't hers."

Kerry sighed. "Some parents are of the opinion that they own whatever's in the house because they pay the mortgage. Boy, have I been there."

Dar looked at her sideways, one eyebrow lifting.

"Yeah, you're absolutely right," Lena blurted. "That's exactly what my parents think. My mom took it while I was in the shower and by the time I got out and got dressed, she was..." She fell silent for a second. "She started throwing things at me."

Kerry took her hand.

"I tried to stay out of the way, you know? Because she does that sometimes, just goes off and shit. But she just kept coming at me." Lena took a shaky breath. "She chased me into the garage, and...oh my God, everything was falling, and she threw a baseball bat at me. Then I don't know what happened, something, and a sled we had up in the overhead fell down right on my dad's car."

"So that's what broke the window," Kerry murmured.

"It broke everything. And that sports car is his, like, best child," Lena said. "She locked me in there, and the next thing I knew, the cops were there and they took me off."

The ferry docked and the conversation ended as Dar piloted the Lexus onto the island and turned down the road leading to the condo. Lena slid over to one side and peered out of the window, looking around curiously until they pulled up next to the condo and parked. "Wow. Holy shit, Toto, we're not in Hialeah anymore."

They got out of the car and headed up the stairs.

KERRY LED THE way upstairs, leaving Dar to putter around and put on some coffee. Lena crept along behind Kerry, trying not to touch anything as she walked in the very center of the stairs. "Let me get you something to change into; you can use the shower in there." She gestured to the guest bathroom, tucked in neatly next to its attendant bedroom.

"Wow." Lena peeked inside, then hurriedly followed Kerry into her own bedroom. "This is a way amazing place."

Kerry pulled open a drawer and rooted around inside it. "It's pretty big, yeah." She removed a shirt and a pair of shorts. "Here. These'll be big on you, but not too bad. They're old ones of mine from when I was a lot smaller."

Lena took them gingerly and eyed Kerry. "You're not fat."

Kerry smiled. "No, but I used to be a lot lighter before I started all this wall climbing and weight lifting." She turned Lena around and pointed her towards the guest bathroom. "There's lots of soap, and everything you need in there. Help yourself."

"Okay." Lena carefully folded the clothes over her arm. "Um...thanks, Kerry. I thought I'd be all tough and that, and just stay in there. You know, like—wow, so this is jail."

One of Kerry's pale eyebrows cocked. "Why? You're not stupid."

Lena fingered the clothes. "There were some really fucked up people in there. I figured I'd better find a way to get out before something stupid happened." Her eyes lifted. "So, thanks."

"No problem, but one thing is puzzling me," Kerry said as they walked down the hall. "I don't remember giving out our phone number here."

"Oh." Lena managed a wan, but cheeky grin. "Casey got that out of the church Rolodex. We were all, like, curious to see if we could figure out where you lived and stuff."

"Ah," Kerry replied. "I thought that was locked up in the office."

Lena grinned again. "And?"

Kerry sighed. "That's supposed to be private information. You could have just asked." She folded her arms.

Lena looked nonplused for a moment. "I didn't...I mean, we didn't think of that. It's just that, like, no one tells you anything when you're our age, you know? It's like everything's such a big secret, and if you want to know stuff, you have to go find it out yourself."

"Mm." Kerry understood that, having grown up in a very political household.

"What is up with adults?" Lena asked. "It's like, even in school, they say they don't teach things so we don't get 'ideas.' I thought the whole thing school was for was to, like, encourage us to get ideas. So they don't tell us about important shit, like what sex is all about. How brainless is that?"

"Very brainless," Kerry acknowledged wryly.

"Um...listen." Lena cleared her throat. "My cousin's got a place right down from the ferry base in Miami Beach. I can stay with her, if you can give me a ride back over there. I feel kinda bad about getting you guys all out at night and stuff."

Kerry pondered. "If you're sure that's okay, yeah, we can do that."

Lena shrugged. "I've been, like, talking to her anyway. After you said all that stuff about being out and all that, I figured maybe I'd give it a try." She scowled a little. "Didn't work out as good as it did for you, though, huh?"

Kerry exhaled. "Go take a shower. It didn't work out well for me in the beginning either."

"People suck," Lena commented. "I guess."

"Yeah. Sometimes they really do," Kerry said quietly, remembering waking up in a cold, sterile hospital room. "But that's why getting away from those people is sometimes the best thing you can do."

Lena nodded, started to turn, then stopped. "But hey, you know? Sometimes it's okay. Look at what happened to Barbara, yeah?"

Kerry blinked. "What happened to Barbara?"

"Oh, yeah. I guess you didn't hear. That guy at work likes her. He made her, like, an assistant manager. How do you like that shit?" Lena seemed amazed. "So I guess you were right."

Guess I was. "Mm." Kerry smiled. "So, see, you never know."

"Yeah."

Lena disappeared into the bathroom, leaving Kerry to a moment of silent reflection. Shaking her head, she headed back downstairs to the sounds of brewing coffee and Dar.

"SO." DAR FLEXED her bare toes against the floor tile. "Now what?"

Kerry trudged across the kitchen and ended up next to her partner. "She's got a friend she can stay with. I'll ride her over after she gets cleaned up."

Dar poured her a cup of coffee and mixed some sugar and cream into it before she handed it to Kerry. "I can go with you. It's late."

Kerry kissed her on one shoulder. "You should rest your arm. I can handle this." She took a swallow of the coffee. "Dar, I feel so bad for her."

"I know." Dar took a sip of her own coffee. "So do I."

"As bad as my father is, it's not like that."

"No." Dar leaned against her. "Your father's a bastard and he's just thinking of himself, but sick as it is, I really do think he thought he was helping you."

Kerry sighed. "I keep wondering if I should try giving him a call. Maybe for Christmas. What do you think?"

Dar's nose wrinkled a bit. "Well, it's worth a try. Look at me and my mother."

"Mm." Kerry took another sip of coffee. "C'mon, let's go sit inside. Isn't the croc man on now?" She gently guided Dar towards the living room and its soft leather couches. "You know what I think I'm going to do, Dar?"

"Get her a job with us?" Dar suggested wryly.

"Did you read my mind?"

"No, your heart."

Despite how tired she was, Kerry had to smile at that. "You're such a sweetie."

"No, I'm not!"

"Munchkin."

HOURS LATER, THE phone pulled Kerry out of a deep sleep, which caused her to stare at the ringing object for several long seconds before she got her brain in gear and grabbed it. It was still dark, and a glance at the clock showed barely six a.m. Dar stirred against her as she got the receiver to her ear. "Hello?"

"Kerry?" The voice was familiar, if strained. "It's Angie."

A surge of adrenaline cleared Kerry's mind as she put together her sister's voice and the time. "Ang? What's wrong?" She hadn't spoken to her family in over a month and a pang of guilt made her grimace.

A sigh filtered through the receiver. "It's dad. He's had a stroke."

Kerry drew in a shocked breath. "Oh my God." She felt the pressure of Dar's arm around her and she turned to see the dim outside light reflecting off her lover's pale eyes. "My father's had a stroke," she told Dar. "How is he?" She directed that to her sister.

"Not good," Angie replied quietly. "If you..." She hesitated. "Maybe you should think about coming up."

Very bad, then. Kerry's thoughts were whirling and scattered. "How's mom?"

Angie was silent for a moment, then she sighed. "She's not dealing with things really well. No one is. It's kind of a real mess right now." A pause followed as Angie collected herself. "It happened last night. He was at a meeting with some other people, over some bill or something, and he got mad, like he does, and the next thing we knew, they were all yelling, and calling out and..." She stopped. "Anyway, it's been a really long night."

The speech gave Kerry time to sort out her thoughts. "Yeah, for us, too. I just got to bed two hours ago. All right. Let me get my wits together and I'll book a flight up." She paused. "Did you say you were calling me?"

"I told mom, yeah," Angie said. "I'm not sure she understood what I meant, but I think it's okay."

Great. Kerry scrubbed her face with her free hand. "Okay, thanks for calling me, Ang. I'll see you soon." She listened to Angie's quiet goodbye, then set the receiver in the cradle. Then she turned around and faced Dar.

"Bad?" Dar's voice was burred and husky from sleep.

"Sounds like it," Kerry replied. "Not good timing, I know."

"No way to help it." Dar shrugged. "I'd offer to go with you, but I'm thinking my presence wouldn't do a thing for his condition, or make it any easier with your family."

"No," Kerry had to regretfully agree. "But I wish that wasn't true, Dar."

Dar's smile was barely visible in the gloom. "I know." She drew in a breath and rubbed her neck to ease the headache brought on by her sudden awakening. "All right, let's get this show on the road."

"Hey, sweetie." Kerry gently pushed her back down onto the pillows. "There's absolutely no sense in you getting up just because I have to. Let me go book my flight and you go back to sleep, okay?"

Dar gazed at her. "Too late." She smiled wryly. "Phone calls at six a.m. tend to wake me up pretty thoroughly." She tugged on Kerry's Tweety Bird T-shirt. "How about you go start coffee and I'll book your flight?"

Kerry sighed. "Sorry about that. All right. Feel like anything for breakfast?"

Dar considered. "Steak," she replied as Kerry rolled out of bed, paused in mid motion, and looked back over a shoulder at her. She shrugged sheepishly. "You asked."

"Really?" Kerry asked, getting a nod in response. Dar generally was a very light eater for breakfast, usually contenting herself with her coffee, and either a bowl of cereal or a banana. Kerry herself preferred a simple muffin, but had learned recently to supplement that with a protein shake to fuel her early morning exercise. "Guess I'll call the beach club. I don't think we have any sirloins lying around."

DAR POKED HER head into Kerry's upstairs bedroom, where her lover was busy packing a small overnight bag. "You're set." She entered the room and went to the bed. "You've got a plane change in Detroit."

"Always. I think we even change planes in Detroit going from Saugatuck to Grand Rapids," Kerry murmured, neatly tucking a sweatshirt into the bag. "Thanks for taking care of that for me. What time is the flight?"

"Nine thirty." Dar slipped the folded piece of paper with the details into the side pocket of the carry on. She was dressed in a pair of worn cutoffs and a sweatshirt, with her hair pulled back into a neat tail. "I'll drop you off at the airport, then just go in to work."

Kerry looked at Dar. "Like that? Damn. No fair. I don't want to miss José's expression."

Dar chuckled softly. "I'll bring a change of clothes. I don't want to scandalize the entire building by walking in looking like a beach bum."

"A very cute beach bum, but I see your point. Nothing would get done all day." Kerry sighed and pulled the zipper closed on her bag. "That's that." She had packed enough clothing for a couple days and her traveling kit. And her black suit. Just in case.

Dar sensed her change in mood. "Got everything you need?"

Kerry nodded somberly. "I guess I'd better—"

"I booked you into the Marriott."

A faint smile appeared. "Thanks. This is going to be tough enough without sharing space." Kerry took a deep breath. "Hopefully it won't be for long."

Dar put her hands on Kerry's shoulders, turned her around, and faced her with a serious expression. "Take as long as you need. Don't worry about what's going on here."

Kerry kept her eyes locked on Dar's shirt. "Thanks. But to be honest, I'd rather that you tell me you desperately need me here and not to take a minute more than necessary." She felt shaky and knew her voice showed it. She wished she knew why.

Dar tipped her chin up and gazed into her eyes. "I need you desperately. Every minute you're gone is going to seem like a lifetime to me." The look on Kerry's face brought a smile to Dar's. "And we'll miss you at work, too."

It didn't untwist her guts, but it did make her feel a lot better. Kerry put her arms around Dar and hugged her. "Please take care of yourself while I'm gone."

"You mean I can't start that skydiving class I'd planned?" Dar teased gently. "Or the I-95 rugby league?" She kissed the top of Kerry's head. "You be careful, too, okay? I want you back in one piece, safe and sound."

"I will be," Kerry promised.

"I hope your father's okay," Dar said, in a very quiet voice. "For what it's worth."

Kerry didn't answer, not sure of how she felt about that herself.

Chapter
Four

DAR GOT TO work before eight and figured she was safe enough to enter the building dressed as she was, with her change of clothes tucked into the gym bag she was carrying. "Morning." She met the door guard's eyes, daring him to look down as she strode past.

"M...ah, morning, Ms. Roberts," the guard stammered.

Dar stopped and looked back over one shoulder at him. "Problem?"

He shook his head vigorously.

"Good." Dar resumed her progress to the elevator. She entered the car and let the doors close, then turned and regarded her reflection in the mirrored surface. *Hm.* She crossed her legs at the ankles, and watched the powerful muscles in them tense and move under her tanned skin. *Maybe wearing shorts this short isn't the smartest thing I've ever done, even this early in the morning.*

The elevator perversely slowed to a halt on the 10th floor and the doors opened.

Crap. Dar exhaled silently. *She would pick today to come in early.* "Morning, Eleanor." She was glad she was wearing sunglasses, which hid what she was sure was a mildly sheepish expression.

Eleanor entered the elevator and chose a spot on the side wall to lean against. "Good morning, Dar." She smiled. "You're a little casual today, aren't you?"

Dar shrugged. "Had some things to do before work." She kept her voice neutral. "What brings you here this early?" The elevator floors seemed to crawl by, taunting her as she resisted the urge to fidget under Eleanor's appraising eyes.

"Marketing meeting, what else?" the Marketing VP responded drolly. "You want to come? Those shorts'll wake everyone the hell up, at least."

Dar rolled her eyes and shrugged.

"Hey, I'm not the one wearing them," Eleanor said.

Dar straightened as the doors opened on fourteen. *Finally.* "Well, good luck on it." She escaped from the elevator, only to pull up as she almost crashed into Mark and three other MIS techs. "Morning."

And Maria. "*Buenos Dias*, Dar." Her secretary managed to mask a smile. "I was going to get *café*. May I get you some, as well?"

"Love some," Dar replied. "You blocking my hallway for some reason, Mark?"

Eyes up, face front. "Uh, no, actually, boss, I was just taking the guys down to pick up that new box for you. We'll just get going now." Mark gave the nearest tech a shove towards the elevator. "Be right back."

Dar eyed them as they marched purposefully away. She couldn't quite avoid hearing their hissed conversation, though.

"Holy shit, did you see those legs?"

"Shhh!"

Dar sighed. "Okay, so I've made my bad management decision for the morning. What's next?" She exchanged a wry look with Maria.

"I think you look very cute, *jefe*." Maria laughed. "What is the occasion?"

A sober look appeared on Dar's face and she removed her sunglasses. "Kerry got some bad news this morning." She opened the outer door and allowed Maria to precede her. "Her father's had a stroke."

"*Dios Mio.*" Maria's eyes widened and she stopped in shock. "I am so sorry to hear that, Dar."

"Me, too." Dar nodded. "I dropped her at the airport before I headed here."

Her secretary frowned. "Should you not have gone with her? That is terrible, to have someone so sick."

Dar glanced at her. "Her family's not fond of me." She felt herself blushing a little at discussing something so personal. "They're already stressed—I don't think my being there would help matters."

"Ah." Maria folded her hands. "*Si*, that is right. I remember now." She seemed at a loss for words. "I feel for Kerrisita, though. She has always felt such trouble with her family. Is there something we can do? Send something to them?"

Dar paused in the doorway to her office, considering the question. "For them? No." She gave Maria a direct look. "But call the Marriott in Saugatuck and make sure Kerry gets treated to the best service they have there. I booked her a suite, but upgrade her to the best they have, and have them stock it with the works."

"*Si.*" Maria smiled. "I will do that, Dar." She glanced at the door, where voices were growing louder. "Now, I think you maybe will change, yes?"

"Yeah." Dar grimaced and swung the door closed after her. "Before they start snapping pictures."

KERRY TOOK A deep breath as she walked down the airline ramp from the plane. It had been two uneventful flights, and now that she was finally there, she wished they'd been longer. The white of the ramp gave way to dull brown brick and the familiar sights of the airport near her home.

A quick glance around told her she wasn't being met, not that she'd expected to be since she hadn't informed Angie of her flight plans, but part of her felt a tiny bit disappointed, all the same. On second thought, maybe that was for the best, Kerry decided, as she shouldered her bag and headed off towards the rental car counter.

Best for me to do this on my terms, right? Isn't that what I told Dar?

She thought about that as she walked. Keeping a little distance from everyone seemed like a good plan, especially since tensions would be high, the press would probably be present, and the last thing anyone needed was a family spat right in the middle of a crisis.

In fact, on the way up, not going at all had crossed her mind several times. It was only Angie's quiet finality that had pushed her forward, knowing in her heart that staying away and letting her father die without at least saying goodbye to him was something she just wasn't capable of.

Or am I?

Kerry sighed unhappily and stepped up to the counter. "I'd like a car, please." She'd picked the chain ILS usually used from habit.

"For how many days, ma'am?" the young man behind the counter asked politely.

Good question. "A week." Kerry supplied her credit card and Florida driver's license.

"Thanks." The man took them and keyed in something, then paused, evidently surprised at something. "Oh, Ms. *Stuart.* We already have a reservation here for you." He handed back her card. "ILS is taking care of it."

One of Kerry's eyebrows lifted. "They are, huh?" She found herself unable to be upset with Dar. "Okay." She took the proffered keys and went outside, wincing as the cold wind bit her face. "Ugh. Forgot about that."

She tugged her jacket closed and zipped it, then searched out her assigned car and opened the trunk to toss in her bag. *Hospital first*, she decided. *Let's find out the bad news.* She got in the car, then drove carefully out of the parking lot and onto the icy streets.

It wasn't that big a town and the drive to the hospital was fairly short. At midday, the place didn't seem that busy, and she parked in the half empty visitor's lot. She spotted a news truck parked near the back entrance, though, and several cars haphazardly pulled up near it, and her suspicions were confirmed when she entered the main doors and saw the cluster of men and women, complete with cameras, standing nearby.

Will they recognize me? she wondered. The national news people had pegged her in DC, but it had taken a while, and these locals hadn't seen her in a few years, if at all, given the turnover rate.

Certainly, if they were old timers, they wouldn't expect the girl they'd known in lace blouses and knee length skirts, with carefully styled hair and a model slim build, to have morphed into the muscular figure in jeans and a leather jacket she knew she presented today.

Her attitude had changed as well. Kerry had studied Dar's use of her considerable charisma and personal energy when she interacted with others, and she'd tried to inject a little of that dynamic into her own personality. Part of it was self confidence, which success at her job had given her, and part of it was an awareness of herself and her effect on other people. "Excuse me." She moved past the reporters with a polite nod.

They didn't even give her a second glance. Kerry repressed a smile as she went to the reception desk. She waited for the woman behind the desk to look up, then leaned forward a little. "Could you tell me where in CCU Roger Stuart is?"

The woman gave her an immediate, guarded look, and glanced behind her at the reporters. "Are you family, ma'am?"

Kerry removed her driver's license and showed it to the woman. "Yes."

A quick look at the license, then at Kerry's face, and the receptionist replied, "Hold on a moment," as she got up and motioned for a guard. "George will take you up. George, CCU 4, okay?"

"Yes'm." The tall, red haired guard nodded. "Come this way, please."

Kerry followed the man through a restricted access door and down a long hallway to where a small elevator was located. Very few people were in the hall, just two orderlies pushing beds and one man with an X-ray machine. She followed the guard into the elevator and waited while he inserted a key and pressed a floor.

"You part of the senator's family?" the guard asked.

Kerry nodded. "Yes. He's my father."

"Hm." The elevator reached its destination and he held the door for her. "Second alcove on your right, ma'am."

Kerry stepped out and walked quietly across the tile floor. Her heart pounded and shivers went up and down her spine. She could hear, faintly, the sounds of machinery around her—beeps and the gurgling of oxygen and it reminded her unpleasantly of Dar's stay in the hospital down south.

Outside the room she paused, hearing voices. One was her mother's. It didn't sound good.

Oh boy. Kerry steeled herself, then took a deep breath and forced her legs to move forward into the room where a circle of strange, familiar faces ringed a bed full of lines and machines, and the almost hidden form she realized was her father.

Eyes shifted and looked at her, some in surprise, some in distress, as the doctor who'd been speaking broke off his speech and turned. "Are you part of the family here?"

It was a very awkward moment. Kerry had no idea what the real answer to that question was.

"That's my daughter," Cynthia Stuart murmured. "Please, go on, Doctor. Kerrison, come here."

There wasn't much else she could do. Kerry walked across the silent room to her mother's side, shocked when her hand was grabbed and held in desperation. She felt Angie move closer to her as they turned and faced the somber looking man in the white coat.

"Ms. Stuart," the doctor said gently, "we were just going over what we mean when we talk about a coma."

DAR ALMOST HAD to laugh when she looked up to see Mark peeking cautiously around the door to her office. "Yes?" she growled.

"You...um...ready to review that firmware?" Mark asked. "I've got my whole bunch of guys reviewing how something got upgraded and we missed it."

She picked up her cup of steaming coffee and sipped it. "Sure." Now soberly dressed in her iron gray suit and silk shirt, she leaned back and watched as he entered with a clipboard. "So, how'd we do?"

Mark took a seat across from her. "I have no clue." He

grinned briefly. "Here's the network paths to the dump; I figured you'd know what to do with them." He handed the clipboard to Dar. "There you go."

"Thanks." Dar accepted it and reviewed the page, then glanced up to catch Mark intently studying her. One of her eyebrows lifted. "Something wrong?"

He hesitated, then gave her a slight shrug. "Didn't expect to see you here so early."

"Earlier I start, earlier Alastair has his answer," Dar replied. "Why don't you take off?"

"I got some sleep in the center," Mark said. "What about you?"

Dar sighed. "Kerry had to fly up to see her family. Wasn't much time to sleep."

Mark nodded. "I saw on the newscast he was sick. Stroke, they said, right?"

"Yeah."

"That sucks," Mark said. "I know stuff is all screwed up between her and her family, but it still sucks." He glanced around. "Listen, Dar, if you want to head up there, I can try and..."

It was almost funny. Dar rubbed her temples with the tips of her fingers and wondered how she had managed to get her entire staff to morph overnight into solicitous nannies. "Mark, get your ass out of here and go figure out how the hell we slipped up by not testing that new release before it got put into production. Something got missed." She pinned him with a look. "Now!"

He jumped. "Okay." One hand lifted. "Okay, I get the message, boss. No problem." He slid out of the chair and ducked around the door, leaving Dar in peace.

Silence settled for a moment before she pulled her keyboard in front of her and called up the files, glad of the large, flat screen with its crisp display. However, tired as she was, she couldn't avoid acknowledging the fuzziness of the characters unless she squinted at them, and she admitted to herself that her long deferred trip to the optometrist's had to be well and truly scheduled.

Damn. Her lips quirked in annoyance. *The hell if I want to wear glasses.* A scowl appeared as she started up her analysis program. *Or contact lenses.*

Hey. She studied the screen for a moment, then tapped it with one long finger. *If I only need the blasted things when I look at the monitor...*A sly grin crossed her face. *Why not just have whatever adjustment I need built into a screen shield?*

"Yeah." Dar felt a little more cheerful. She settled back and reviewed the files. As the screen filled with data, she searched for patterns, trying to ignore the growing unease inside her guts.

THE WAITING ROOM for the critical care unit was small and discreet, tucked away behind the medical area and reserved for the families of the patients who were sequestered there. Kerry cradled her cup in her hands, using the coffee's mottled surface as a concentration point while she thought.

My father is dying.

Kerry felt the styrofoam surface under her fingers dent slightly as she flexed her hands. The interruption of blood supply due to the stroke had hit in the worst place imaginable—the parts of his brain that kept him alive and breathing without assistance from the noisy machines that dominated the space he was in. The machines that were the only thing keeping him alive.

Around her, the family was seated in grim silence. Her mother, breathing in short, sobbing gasps, sat between Kerry and Angie. Michael was on the other side of her, nervously twisting a tri-fold napkin into a thin, tight line. Richard paced back and forth on the far side of the room, where one of her aunts also sat with an uncle. Nobody wanted to talk.

Kerry knew she was the focus of uneasy attention. She'd heard the ugly whispers as they'd left the CCU unit and walked down the hall: how she didn't belong there, how her father had hated her. How it was her fault—causing the strain he'd been under that finally got to him.

Kerry couldn't even lie to herself and say it wasn't true, because she knew at some level it was. She'd come to terms with that in her heart, during that week they'd spent in Key West after the hearings. Come to terms with the fact that she'd done what she'd done for the reasons she'd done it, and reluctantly accepted that if she'd had to make the decision all over again, she probably wouldn't have done it.

But she had, and good or bad, she had to live with that decision for the rest of her life. She'd always held out a faint hope that someday, somehow, after enough time had passed, she'd have a chance to go home and maybe she could sit down with her father and just...talk.

Kerry drew in a breath, feeling the finality of the moment. *There will be no chance of talking now.* The doctor had been gentle and kind, but he'd held out no false hope to them. He'd just given them some time to sit down and absorb the truth, and told them of their limited options. The machines could not give him a life again, but they could keep him alive; did they want them to?

Kerry was surprised to feel tears gathering behind her eyes.

Surprised that losing him hurt as much as it did—after all that had happened and everything that had come between them, he was still her father.

"Mama." Angie's voice was shaky. "Can I get you a drink?"

Kerry looked up to see her mother jerk her head up and down, one hand pressed to her mouth in evident agony. Their eyes met and Kerry slowly extended her cup. "Here, mom, take mine. I haven't touched it."

For a moment, she thought her mother would refuse, but then her hand lowered and accepted the cup, spilling it a little as Kerry released it.

"Thank you," her mother whispered, as she brought it to her lips and took a sip.

Kerry exhaled, slowly looking around the room. The tension was almost a visible fog, and suddenly she wanted nothing more than to be out of there. She stood up. "I'm going to," she could almost feel the stares on her, "stretch my legs. I'll be right back."

Before anyone could think of joining her, she made it to the door and slipped out into the hallway, a puff of cooler air from the vent overhead feeling very welcome in the warm indoors. She'd forgotten what needing heat was like and had shed her jacket when she'd found herself sweating after a few moments inside the building. At least she thought that was because of the heat.

Kerry stuck her hands in her pockets and paced across the tiled floor, threading through a maze of conflicting emotions. When she looked up, she found herself outside the CCU unit, looking through the multiple glass windows to the alcove in which her father lay. For a moment she simply stared. Then, with a quiet breath, she went to the quiet corner full of hissing noise and soft beeps...and lost chances.

DAR SAT WITH Duks and Mariana in the lunchroom; the busy crowds lessened in the late afternoon, leaving the big room mostly empty and pleasantly quiet.

"Sure you don't want a bite of this, DR?" Duks nudged his plate of chocolate cake towards her. "You're getting me worried about you today."

Dar waved a hand at him, settled back in her chair, and nursed her glass of milk. "No thanks, Duks. Damn painkillers I'm taking for my shoulder are making me queasy." She indicated her mostly uneaten lunch. "I'll take a rain check."

Mariana chewed a bite of her salad and swallowed. "Dar, why not go home?" She studied her friend's face. "We can cancel the staff meeting."

Home. Dar felt the strain of the long day and longer night, and the thought of lying down and letting her wound up body relax was very, very tempting. Then she remembered how quiet the condo was without its other occupant, and scowled a little. "Maybe later."

"Heard from Kerry yet?" Duks asked casually. "News is very circumspect from there."

"Not yet." Dar shook her head, somberly studying her milk. "Hey, anything come of the internal audit this quarter?"

Duks gracefully accepted the change of subject. "One or two very small things, but they are inconsequential. We are very good at chasing our own tails, is it not true?"

"True," Dar said. Duks' alert and aggressive internal auditors watched the computer systems like hawks. One digit out of place brought them sniffing around, even in her area, where the problems usually tended to be misplaced receipts and forgotten cellular bill overages rather than anything more criminal. Their one line woven in the carpet was the one leading to inside her office— if any of them had any questions, they fed them directly to Duks, who could be depended on to pay Dar a visit and present them.

Or not. Dar had been surprised to find out that Duks would sometimes merely sign off on things that were slightly out of line from Operations, and she'd cornered him on it once. The big VP of Finance had laughed, then seriously told her that just as her judgment was trusted without question in her realm, she should extend the same courtesy to him.

Good point, Dar had admitted, after a moment.

Duks had shaken a finger at her. "Just don't try to get away with anything more than a stick of chewing gum."

"Worst thing I think you found this time was José taking home cases of Bustelo," Mari commented with a dry chuckle.

"Mm." Dar shrugged. "Sounds about right." She decided she'd had enough chitchat, and got up. "I've got problems in the Northeast. Later." She picked up her tray and deposited it in the collection bin, then left the café.

DAR'S PHONE WAS ringing as she entered her office, and she hurried over to it as she realized it was her private line. "Yeah"

"Hello, Dar?"

Ah. "Afternoon, Gerry." Dar circled around her desk and sat down. "What can I do for you?"

The general cleared his throat. "Just came from a meeting,

Dar. Me and a few top brass going over your report."

"Ah." Dar felt a touch of unease. "Guess it's going to stir up a lot of crap, huh?"

General Easton paused, then sighed audibly. "Dar, I wanted to talk to you myself about this. Wasn't the thing we were looking for when we brought you in here, y'know."

"I know," Dar replied. "I wasn't glad to find it."

"Of course, of course," Gerry acknowledged hastily. "You wouldn't, after all, would you? You grew up there, mostly."

"Mostly."

There was another awkward pause. "Damnable thing, Dar. If half of what's in here pans out, it's a disaster. A big disaster: for the Navy, for the country...Damnable thing."

Dar drew in a breath, then released it. "Guess they should have thought of that before they did it. You sound like you're regretting the project."

Easton cleared his throat a bit. "I have to shut it down, Dar. We can't use this." His voice took on a cooler tint. "The government doesn't accept the results of your investigation." He paused and then had the grace to add, "I'm sorry."

For a moment, Dar wondered if she'd heard right. "What?"

"Look, we'll pay off the contract, no worry about that," Easton said. "You won't be the loser for it, Dar. But it has to stop. I'll discard this package, and you have to destroy any copies you have."

Dar blinked. A sense of shock made her skin prickle and she stood up in pure reflex, animal energy surging. "Am I hearing you right?" She paced around the desk. "Are you saying you're not going to do anything?"

"Now, Dar." Easton tried to sound offhand. "I'm sure a lot of this can be explained in any number of ways. Not everything's a plot, y'know."

Dar slammed both hands on her desk and leaned over the speakerphone. "Plot? Goddamn it, Gerry, it's not some kind of damn plot; it's a criminal act of major proportions! Are you telling me you're just going to sit back up there and let those son of a bitches get off scot free?"

"Dar."

"Don't you 'Dar' me." Dar's temper built. "I risked my damn life going back in that hell hole because you asked me to, and now you tell me never mind?"

"You don't understand," Easton responded forcefully. "There's more at stake here than one measly base, Dar. This could rock the entire Navy. Do you want that? Do you want everything your father fought for dragged through every inch of muck between Key Largo and DC?"

Dar stared at the phone. "The people in that report," she took a breath, "deserve that."

"I don't give a damn about them," Easton shot back. "It's the Navy I care about. I'm not going to let something like this make us the laughingstock of the damn country. Of every other country. I'm just *not* going to do it, Dar!"

Dar settled into her chair, folded her hands carefully on the desk, and leaned forward. "If you don't," she enunciated the words very, very carefully, "I will."

For a moment, dead silence reigned. Dar waited, anger pulsing through her veins and making her nostrils flare as her breathing deepened and her heartbeat slowed. Her hands twitched, as though sensing an impending battle.

"You wouldn't do that," Easton said quietly. "I know you, Paladar."

The very faintest hint of a wry smile appeared on Dar's face. "You only think you do," she growled softly, reveling in the tension. "I will do it, Gerald." She paused. "I have to."

A final parry was inevitable. "Think of your father, Dar. Don't you care what he thinks, how he'll feel if you do this? You know how he loves the Navy."

A sense of peace settled over Dar. "I am thinking of him. He'd whup the tar out of me if I did any less, Gerry, and we both know that."

Another silence stretched between them. "Well, damn it." Easton sounded more than frustrated. "I'm calling that boss of yours in here tomorrow and I'll see if I can talk sense to him then, if I can't get through your thick skull!" He slammed the phone down, leaving a ringing in Dar's ears.

Damn it.

She took a deep breath, surprised to find herself shaking a little. "Damn." She lowered her head into her hands and closed her eyes, thinking about what she'd said. Did Easton have a point? Would the report do irreparable damage to the service? "Guess I better warn Alastair."

"DAR."

Dar jumped almost a foot in her chair and whirled, shocked to see her father standing just inside the door that led down the back hall to Kerry's office. She stared at him, then relaxed back into her seat. "Dad."

Andrew Roberts removed his hands from the pockets of his pullover, walked around the desk to her, and looked down, his face quiet and very serious.

Dar knew a moment of self-doubt. Gerald Easton had been right in one thing, she knew her father's love and loyalty to the service ran very deep and very strong. She looked up into those pale blue eyes so like her own and wondered, *Is the general right? Is this too big a sacrifice?* "Guess you heard all that."

"Yeap." Andy cupped Dar's cheek in rare, gentle touch. "I ain't never whupped you, Paladar."

She gave a faint, mildly embarrassed shrug. "Sounded good." Dar looked down, then back up. "Was I wrong?"

A grin remarkably like her own appeared. "Hell no, you weren't wrong." Andy eyed the phone. "But that there's gonna be a hell of a problem."

Dar nodded.

"Heard about Kerry's pop." Andy's expression sobered. "Don't rain but it pours, don't it?"

Dar nodded again, tiredly. "Yeap." She thought about what Alastair would say and winced.

Trouble. Oh yeah.

"I was about to head home," Dar said. "Been a long day."

"C'mon." Andy offered her a hand up. "Got me some dog hairs I need to give back over by your place." He put an arm around Dar's shoulders as they walked to the door.

IT WAS ALMOST like looking at a stranger. Kerry curled her fingers around the cold metal bars and gazed at her father's face, half-hidden by the tubes and machinery keeping him alive. His eyes were taped closed and there was no expression on his face, as though he were no longer a person but rather a mannequin used for training.

He would hate this so much, Kerry thought. *Hate their pity, and the helplessness, and the indignity of it all.* She lifted her eyes and studied the machines, then returned her gaze to that still, closed face. It was hard to know what to feel.

Kerry tried to remember the last time she'd felt joy in her father's presence. When he'd been "daddy," and she'd smiled just to see him. Her eyes moistened as she acknowledged just how long ago that was and how very young she'd been.

Too young to understand.

Maybe, five, six? Kerry's lips tightened as a dimly remembered scene flickered before her—a birthday party. She'd gotten a pair of roller skates she'd desperately wanted, blue ones with silver tassels, and she'd thrown her arms around her father in sheer delight because she knew he'd gotten them for her.

Five, then, before she'd gone to school, when life had been as simple as peanut butter and jelly sandwiches and the long days of fall she could skate in. She had a picture, somewhere, of herself in those skates, with kneepads and a grubby T-shirt. Grinning.

He'd hugged her back. Patted her. Called her his little girl.

Kerry flexed her hands on the bars, and released a shaky breath. That had been a very long time ago, indeed. She reached through the bars and laid her hand on her father's arm, the skin feeling dry and papery beneath her touch. Then she slid her hand down until she curled her fingers around his, a simple touch she hadn't felt since she'd been a child.

What she chiefly felt right now, Kerry acknowledged, was a deep sense of regret. "I'm sorry, daddy. I wish it hadn't been like this." She watched the unresponsive face. "I never meant for us to hate each other."

She blinked, feeling a few tears spill down her face. "I hope you find peace with God."

For a few moments, she simply stood there, holding his hand. Then a sound made her look up, to see one of the nurses coming in. They exchanged awkward glances. "Sorry." Kerry released her hold and backed away. "I know I'm not supposed to be in here."

"It's all right," the nurse replied with quiet compassion. "Is that your father, honey?"

Kerry nodded.

"I'm sorry." The woman, who was probably twice Kerry's age, had a sweet face and a warm expression. "I know it must be tough for you." She walked around to Kerry's side and fixed a tube next to the bed. "Take your time. Everything we can do for him, we're doing."

"I know you are." Kerry wiped the back of her hand across her eyes. "How...um..." She cleared her throat. "How long could he stay like this?"

The nurse faced her and met her eyes honestly. "As long as you let him." At Kerry's look of pain, she put out a hand. "I'm sorry, honey. I know that sounds harsh. But you know something? I've worked in this unit for a long time, and sometimes death isn't our enemy."

Kerry found a place on the tile floor to focus on.

The nurse took a step back. "I'm sorry." She fell silent. "I didn't meant to upset you. I thought the doctor had already spoken to the family about this."

"He did," Kerry murmured softly. "But I don't think we're ready for that decision yet."

They were both silent for a few moments, then Kerry shifted and put her hands on the bars. She felt sick to her stomach, the tension creeping up her back and making her head pound. The nurse watched her, then adjusted a wire and left quietly, her steps muffled by the overhead speakers making soft, urgent announcements.

DAR AND ANDREW sat side by side on the couch, sharing a bowl of ice cream and a good deal of conversation. "If that's what you found there," Andrew portioned off a scoop of vanilla, "what else they got to look forward to? Can't blame 'em for sticking their heads back down underneath the manure, Dardar."

"Dad, it's not like this is Tailhook," Dar said. "Or some half assed misuse of government funds crap. This is documented evidence of big money smuggling and money laundering."

Andrew grunted.

Dar removed a cherry and bit down on the stem as she considered all that had happened. "Hell if I'm going to let that jackass get away with this. Alastair's just gonna have to take a stand on his morals on this one."

Andrew glanced at her. "Ah don't think Jeff Ainsbright's the mover and shaker, Dardar. Just the nitwit they done got to front it all. Figgured he done just used his kid to roadblock you."

"A pair of stooges." Dar sighed. "Yeah, you're probably right. But damn it, someone has to be behind it, Dad."

"Yeap." Andrew nodded. "Problem is, that feller pro'bly ain't gonna get hisself nailed for it. Big shots always find some little feller to squash."

"Maybe. But I'm not going to help them hide it." Dar glanced at the sliding glass doors, which showed a peaceful darkness outside. She was a little surprised she hadn't heard from Kerry, but maybe no news was good news. The television had reported several times that the senator's condition was "guarded," and Dar figured that at least sounded all right. "Thanks for keeping me company for dinner, by the way."

"Heh." Andrew chuckled. "Your momma's done gone to one of them art things tonight. I figured pot luck with you was gonna beat out that crackers and cheese mess they always have."

"Ah. Yeah, I'm not much into the rubber chicken circuit myself." Dar smiled. "I used to leave business cocktail parties and stop at Burger King on the way home." She jumped a little as her cell phone rang. "Whoops." She dug it out, checked the caller id, and opened it. "Hey."

There was silence for a moment, then a sigh. "Hey."

Dar sat up, reading the tension and grief in her lover's voice. "What's wrong?"

"What isn't?" Kerry whispered. "Oh, Dar."

Panic set in. Dar's pulse jumped, and her mind raced. "Are you okay?" Her voice took on a sharp edge and Andy put the bowl on the table and watched her in evident concern. "Where are you?"

Kerry leaned against the car door and closed her eyes. "Outside the hotel. In the car. I just wanted to talk to you before I went in." She wished her head didn't feel like it was exploding. "They want us to pull the plug."

Dar sucked in her breath. "God, I'm sorry, Ker."

"Me, too," Kerry replied softly. "Everyone's a wreck. I don't know what the hell I'm going to do." She'd gone back from the CCU unit and faced her mother, who was in hysterics and everyone else in pieces, and just dealing with the barrage had been difficult enough.

Getting out of the hospital had been worse. The press had rubbed them raw and she'd finally torn herself free, outran two of the most persistent and jumped over a low wall that had led her to where her car was parked.

Her relatives had all gone to her family's house. They expected her to follow. Kerry had huddled inside the car, knowing she couldn't. It was just too much. Now she was outside the hotel and reaching for her lifeline. "Shit."

"Want me on a plane?" Dar asked. "Screw everything."

Kerry's defenses broke down. Her throat closed and her eyes fill with tears and she suddenly wanted to be in Dar's arms so badly it hurt. She gasped and held the phone close, trying not to start sobbing.

"That's it. I'm on the way." Dar's voice went from concerned to decisive in quick order. "Just hang on, okay?"

Kerry took several deep breaths. "No...wait," she managed to get out. "Dear God, I'd love for you to be here." She sucked in another ragged breath. "But they can't take it, Dar. It's too much."

"Fuck them," Dar replied. "I don't give a damn about them. I give a damn about you and what you want, and that's all there is to it."

Kerry watched several couples walk by.

"So what do you want?" Dar asked very quietly.

"I want you," Kerry whispered.

"You've got me."

"Give me a day with them, Dar." Kerry felt very, very tired. "I think we're going to make the decision tomorrow night. I could use a friend around when that happens."

"I'll be there," Dar said. "Are you all right?"

She could feel the tunneling starting. "No." The light outside was suddenly garish. "Let me go inside before this migraine hits."

"Call me later," Dar said. "Please?"

"I will," Kerry replied. "I love you."

"Love you, too."

Kerry closed the phone and gathered her strength, then opened the door and let in the cold night air.

DAR SET THE phone down and stared at it. "Damn it."

Andrew put his plate down. "Not doing too good up there?"

"He's on life support and they want to end it."

"Ah." Her father drew in a sobering breath. "Wall, I got to say I never had much use for that feller, but I feel bad for Kerry having to go through all that."

"Yeah." Dar went over and over Kerry's words, and more importantly, the tone behind them.

"You going up over there?"

"Tomorrow. Probably," Dar replied. "Kerry said her family's pretty shook up."

Andrew's eyes twinkled. "Think she'd want you up there just to take their minds off her."

"Huh." Dar stood up and walked across the living room. She stopped at the back sliding doors and gazed out over the porch to the sea. The sunset poured across the sand and water, a lone seagull drifted over the waves as though searching for something in its depths.

Kerry had specifically asked her not to come up until she was ready. Dar respected her partner's desire and almost understood the ambivalence between Kerry wanting the comfort of her presence, and not wanting the antagonism it would cause.

She understood it. Really, she did. Her ears twitched, hearing the echo of that stifled sob as Kerry told her to stay, and she balanced it against the knowledge that between the network problem and the military, things were going to come down at work the next day. "Dad?"

"Surely I'll give you a ride to that thar airport, Dardar," Andrew said placidly. "'Member to pack them long johns. It ain't tropical up there."

Dar met her own eyes' reflection in the sliding glass door. "Well, worst she could do is throw me out of her hotel room. She doesn't have to tell anyone I'm there, right?"

"Yeap."

Dar turned. "Thanks for the ride offer, but I don't know how long we'll be out there. I'll just leave mine at the airport."

A grizzled brow moved upward. "Dangerous, them parking

lots, Dardar."

"Um." Dar's eyes twinkled sheepishly. "I use the valet." She escaped to the bedroom, taking her yuppy confessions with her.

Andrew merely chuckled and got up to put the dishes in the sink.

AT LEAST THE lobby was quiet. Kerry brushed past the tastefully decorated Christmas tree, causing the ornaments to tinkle softly, and sidestepped a heavyset man intent on gaining the bar. The Marriott tended to attract business travelers, and the lounge seemed to be full of them, bending forward in intent conversation as a ball game played mutely in the background.

The front desk was devoid of guests, and Kerry gratefully set her bag down and fished for her wallet as the clerk looked up and gave her a friendly smile. "I have a reservation. Under Stuart."

The young clerk, a well scrubbed boy with short blond hair obligingly tapped a few keys on his computer, then smiled. "Yes, ma'am, Ms. Stuart; we certainly do have it."

God bless you, Dar. Kerry leaned wearily on the counter, hoping she'd taken her painkillers in time. She handed over her credit card.

"Do you need help with your luggage, ma'am?" the clerk asked, ignoring the card and presenting her with an envelope. "Your key's in there. It's the twelfth floor, turn right, first door."

Kerry took the envelope. "Thanks." She put her credit card back into her wallet, too tired and sick to argue about it. Dar's planning, she was sure, but there would be time enough to change it when she checked out. She shouldered her bag and trudged to the elevator, wishing the perkily playing holiday Musak tape would break and leave her in peace.

But no. The music continued in the elevator, which climbed leisurely to the twelfth floor and finally released her into a cooler hallway. "Turn right, first door," Kerry muttered, following the instructions and finding herself unsurprisingly in front of a hotel room door set in an alcove by itself. She fished in the envelope and pulled out the electronic key, slid it in and listened for the click, then pushed the handle down and shoved the door open.

It took her three steps before she noticed something unusual—the door slammed shut behind her as she stood and simply stared.

"What on earth?" Kerry whispered. The room was huge, roughly three times the size of a regular room, and laid out as though it was a... She stuck her head into the bathroom and saw the heart shaped tub. "I'm in the honeymoon suite. What in the hell am I doing in here?"

She walked to a plush, leather chair and sat down and took in the fully stocked bar, plates of pretty good-looking fruit, and the half-sized refrigerator.

Exhaustion overtook her. She slumped forward and leaned her elbows on her knees, too tired even to care. Feeling the pain building, she cradled her head in her hands and decided that if she was going to be sick and miserable, it might as well be in such luxurious surroundings. She hadn't eaten anything all day, but the thought of food almost made her gag. With a groan, she pushed herself to her feet, dragged her bag over to the bed, lifted it up, and unzipped it.

The soft smell of home wafted out. Kerry's fingers stilled, then she pulled out her sleep shirt and buried her face in it, detecting Dar's scent faintly around its edges. As the tears rose in her eyes, she dropped onto the bed and just let them out, the moisture soaking into the cotton fabric.

It only lasted a few moments. She sniffled and dried her face, debating whether to just stay where she was, fully dressed, instead of expending the effort it would take to get up and get undressed. Finally, she rolled over and got up. She shrugged off her jacket and tossed it onto the chair, and then pulled off her shirt and unfastened her jeans.

A chill made her shiver, and she pulled her sleep shirt on and sat down on the bed, unlaced her sneakers, and pulled them off. She flexed her toes against the carpeted floor and sighed, then tossed the scuffed Reeboks over near the chair, as well. "Brr," she muttered, rubbing her arms as she got up, wandered into the bathroom, and paused when she was confronted with her reflection in the mirror.

Disordered blond hair framed a pale, haggard face with bloodshot eyes and lines of tension across the forehead. Kerry grimaced, then ran water in the sink and splashed some onto her cheeks, causing another chill to almost make her teeth chatter. She straightened, dried herself off, then walked back into the main room and headed for the bed. Just as she reached it, her stomach rebelled, and she sat down quickly, and reached for the garbage can as she half convulsed.

It was mostly dry heaves, save for the bitter taste of the aspirin she'd taken. But it made her head pound all the more fiercely and she uttered a soft oath as she leaned against the nightstand, breathing hard. The nausea increased, and she dropped the basket and stumbled into the bathroom, just making it to the toilet before her stomach heaved again.

She truly saw stars. Her vision blacked out from the pressure, and as her body was gripped in a convulsive spasm, all she could see was sparkles. Her legs buckled and she dropped painfully to her knees onto the tile, holding on to the basin for dear life. At last it eased, and she slumped, shivering and gasping, against the tub.

It was the absolute worst she'd ever felt in her life. Even her dislocated shoulder hadn't been that bad. Kerry felt like her head was going to split right open, and she whimpered softly, holding her temples with both hands. Her whole body was shivering, and she grabbed the bath towels, and pulled their scant warmth around her as she crouched there in agony.

She didn't know what else to do. She moaned softly as her stomach twisted again, and her body convulsed, forcing nothing but bile up out of her guts. *Oh, God.* Her teeth chattered uncontrollably and made her headache even worse.

IT WAS ALMOST midnight as Dar got off the elevator and emerged into the hallway. She paused as she collected her thoughts and tried to figure out what she could say to Kerry that would excuse the disregarding of her wishes.

Then she simply shrugged and faced the door, hesitating before she knocked. There was no sound coming from the room, and Dar realized that on top of everything else, she'd be waking her partner up. *Well,* she glanced at the key she'd been given, *might as well get this over with.*

Gingerly, she slid the key into the lock and opened the door. She slipped inside and closed the door behind her. At once, she realized something was wrong. The lights were on and the room was empty, Kerry's clothing strewn about with uncharacteristic sloppiness.

Dar heart started to pound. She glanced around, then pushed the door to the bathroom open and froze for a shocked instant before she jumped across the tile and dropped to her knees beside the pathetic figure curled up in the corner.

"K..." Dar could barely speak as she carefully lifted the disordered towels off her lover and turned her over. Kerry had been throwing up, she could tell, and crying, and Dar was a split second from calling 911 when Kerry's eyes fluttered open and tracked to her in dire confusion. "Hey...easy."

"D...Dar?" Kerry whispered hoarsely. "Oh...dear God...I was...praying you'd come." She reached out a shaking hand. "I hurt so much."

"Easy." Dar fought down the panic with difficulty. She sat on the cold tile floor and gathered Kerry clumsily into her arms, unsure of what to do to help her. "Where does it hurt, sweetheart?"

"M...my head." Kerry moaned. "How long...have I been here? It's tomorrow already?"

"No. Shhh." Dar cradled her gently, rubbing her neck with one hand. "They told me I'd get a fifty percent discount if I flew up tonight. I couldn't resist."

"Uhngh." Kerry curled an arm around Dar's leg and pressed her lips against the denim covering her thigh. "Tried...to take something...Kept coming back up."

Dar reached over her head, turned the water on, and dampened a washcloth under the warming water. She pulled her arm back down and gently cleaned Kerry's face. "So I see."

The green eyes flickered open to peer at her, so bloodshot they seemed almost ochre in the bland light. "I've nev...never felt like this before. I th...it got really b...bad there, I wasn't...I think I blacked out."

Dar finished her task. "How's your head now?" She pushed the damp hair out of Kerry's eyes.

"Hurts." Kerry closed her eyes. "Everything hurts." She plucked at Dar's sleeve with shaking fingers and tried to get closer. "It's so cold."

"C'mon, let's get you into bed." Dar took a deep breath and braced herself. She got an arm under Kerry's knees and one around her shoulders, and prayed as she stood up, biting the inside of her lip as a bolt of pure agony ripped through her shoulder.

"Dar...put m'down...you're gonna hurt yourself," Kerry protested faintly.

"Shhh, I'm fine," Dar said. "Hold on to my neck."

Kerry obediently clutched at her, shivers moving through her body. "But your shoulder—"

Later for that. "It's fine." With a grunt of sheer will, Dar turned, walked stolidly to the bed, and let Kerry down onto it. She pulled the blankets down and tucked them around her lover's chilled body, hearing and feeling the sigh of relief as Kerry relaxed onto the soft surface. "That's my girl."

Kerry peeked at her from half closed eyes. "Am I?" she murmured, licking her dry lips.

"Oh, yeah." Dar managed a smile. "Still cold?"

"Yes."

Dar stood up and took her jacket off, then removed her sweatshirt. "Hang on, and I'll do something about that." She glanced around the room, then retrieved a bottle of water from the small bar and brought it back with her. "Sweetie, you need to drink some of this."

Kerry grimaced. "Only if you want it back in your lap."

"Just a little." Dar knelt and removed the bottle top, then spotted a neatly wrapped stack of straws and grabbed one. "Here." She guided the straw to Kerry's lips. "Just sip it."

"Don't say I didn't warn ya," Kerry mumbled, but sucked weakly at the liquid. She swallowed the mouthful then waited, apparently very surprised when it stayed put. She drank some more, then stopped. "'Nough."

Dar watched her quietly for a moment, then put the bottle down. She kicked her shoes off, slipped out of her jeans, and laid them neatly across the chair before getting under the covers. "Easy."

Kerry kept her eyes closed, but turned over and burrowed into Dar's body, letting out a piteous little sound as Dar folded long arms and legs around her. "Ohh. Thank God you're here."

Thank God I listened to my heart instead of my conscience. Dar hugged her. "I'm here, Kerry. It's going to be okay, I promise." She could feel the shivers slowly abate, and she gently stroked Kerry's hair until the rigid muscles relaxed under her touch. "Easy. I've got you."

"Mm," Kerry murmured. "Thank you, Lord, for hearing me begging for my Dar." She exhaled, her teeth discontinuing their clenched chattering at last.

Dar smiled. "And here I thought you were going to be mad at me for showing up early. Should have listened to Dad. He said not to worry."

Finally, and even though it hurt, Kerry also smiled. She tangled her hands in Dar's shirt and made a low, contented sound. "He was right. I needed you."

Dar rubbed Kerry's back very gently. "You've got me." Everything happening elsewhere faded out, becoming unimportant as she focused on this one thing that did matter. "So, I'm forgiven?"

Kerry nodded weakly. "Even for putting me in the honeymoon suite." The agony faded enough for sleep to make inroads. "I love you."

Dar kissed her head. "I love you, too."

Chapter
Five

IT WAS VERY quiet in the hotel, even after dawn had burnished the window with a pale light and thrown a slender stripe of it across the large bed. Dar's eyes drifted open to take in her surroundings, and she was a trifle confused until her memory kicked in and she remembered where she was. And why.

She was lying on her back with Kerry sprawled half over her. Kerry pinned her firmly in place and used her shoulder for a pillow.

Dar watched Kerry sleep, noting the shadows under her eyes and the drawn look that characterized her face, even now. *Yesterday was such a trial for her*, she mused, *and today will be worse. But at least I'm here now and can give moral support, if not much else.*

She couldn't take charge of the situation, couldn't shield her lover from the events or their consequences. Dar grimaced a little, unused to being in such a passive role and not liking it much. All she could do, really, was just be there for Kerry.

Like I was last night. Dar shuddered, imagining how many hours Kerry might have been crouched on the tile in misery if she hadn't decided to just chuck everything and jump on the next plane heading north.

To hell with everything else. Dar closed her eyes and reveled in the warmth of her human blanket. She could feel Kerry's breath through her cotton shirt, and she floated for a few minutes while she decided what to do next.

First things first. Dar reached out a hand, lifted the phone receiver off its cradle, and brought it to her ear. She stabbed at the keypad and was rewarded by a pleasant Midwestern voice that sounded a little like Kerry. "Room service, please."

A click, some canned "Sleigh Ride," and then the phone was picked up. "Good morning! Will this be breakfast or a late night snack?" The operator chuckled.

Dar's brow creased and she glanced at the window. "Breakfast," she muttered.

"Okay, well," the woman said, "our special for you this morning is lovebird muffins with sweetheart jelly."

Dar turned her head and stared at the phone. "What?"

"We also have splits of champagne and berries with whipped cream."

"How about oatmeal," Dar replied. "And a large pot of coffee, and," she considered, "a stack of pancakes."

There was a momentary pause. "All righty then. Anything else?" the voice chirped. "That's for two, right?"

"Um...right." Dar's brow creased. "How did you know?"

"Just a lucky guess. It'll be right up, okay?" Now the voice sounded vaguely patronizing.

"Okay, thanks." Dar hung up, puzzled by the odd responses. Then she remembered what suite they were in and chuckled quietly.

"What's so funny?" Kerry asked softly, not stirring an inch.

"If I spread sweetheart jelly all over you, would you be my lovebird muffin?" Dar asked.

Very slowly, Kerry lifted her head and peered at Dar with a look of mild disbelief. "Excuse me?" Her voice cracked a little, and she cleared her throat. "Bah. Dry air."

Dar handed her the bottle of water she'd left by the bedside. "Here." She guided the straw to Kerry's lips and watched as she sucked down half its contents. "Does that mean you won't be?"

Kerry finished, and put her head down, seemingly exhausted. "Right now I feel more like a meadow muffin," she muttered into Dar's chest. "A really flat one that was out in the sun a long, long time."

Dar stroked her back and scratched it lightly with her fingertips. "I ordered breakfast."

"Ugh." Kerry shook her head. "Not for me."

Dar hesitated. "Did you eat anything yesterday?"

Did I? Kerry's brow creased. "Just breakfast with you. I was way too stressed to eat after I got here."

Dar drummed her fingers on Kerry's back. "I'm no expert, but that might be why you feel so lousy. You know how you get."

"What's that supposed to mean?" Kerry asked crossly.

Dar gently cleared her throat.

Kerry sighed and burrowed back into Dar's body. "I don't think I can handle eggs and bacon."

"Damn good thing, because that's not what I ordered." Dar smoothed down Kerry's hair and peered at her dimly seen profile tucked against her chest. "So just trust me, okay?"

It was so nice and warm where she was. Kerry closed her eyes, wishing with all her heart they were both home with nothing more to look forward to than a Saturday's cartoons and a diving trip. "Can I just stay right here?" she asked softly, as Dar's arm closed around her in a hug. "I don't want to go over there, Dar. Call it cowardice if you want, but I don't want to face those people...or that place." She paused. "Or him dying." Her chest tightened, and she blinked sudden tears from her eyes.

Dar felt very much at a loss. "I know it's tough." She kissed the top of Kerry's head. "I'm sorry."

Kerry sniffled. "Me, too," she whispered. "Thank you for being here." She ran a finger along Dar's ribcage. "I feel incredibly selfish, but thank you."

Dar kept up her gentle stroking, not sure of what else to do. "It's not selfish. I'm glad you want me here. I know how easy it is to shut everyone out when you're hurting."

Kerry shifted and looked up at her. "Thinking of your mom?"

Dar's shrug spoke volumes. "And myself. I had friends who tried to talk to me after Dad...died." It seemed so strange to say that now. "I pushed them all away. Had to put up that tough front, like I thought he'd want me to."

Kerry's lips tensed in wry compassion. "That big mushball? Nah."

Dar smiled a little.

"You don't have to worry. I won't ever lock you out, Dar; I need you too much." Kerry gave Dar a painfully open look, then sighed and rolled over, reluctantly releasing Dar's body. "I guess we'd better start day, huh?"

Dar ran her fingers through Kerry's hair, making her lay still as she savored the contact. "How's the head feel?"

Kerry ran her thumb along the inside of Dar's forearm. "It's okay." She shrugged one shoulder. "I just feel really washed out." She didn't feel like moving an inch, as a matter of fact. "Tired."

C'mon, Kerrison, her conscience sternly prodded. _You're a big girl. Life sucks sometimes, so get your ass up and deal with it._ She girded her philosophical loins and lifted her head–then was pulled back into Dar's arms and back into her safe, warm nest.

Well, I tried. She greedily absorbed the hug. _Sort of._ "You know something?"

"Mm?"

Dar rubbed her all over, easing tiny tensions she'd hardly been aware of. "Love rocks." Kerry sighed. She felt Dar chuckle, and the knot in her gut abruptly unraveled, making her almost dizzy with relief. She knew the day wasn't promising to be any better than she had thought it would be the night before, but from Dar she could borrow the strength she'd need to live through it.

DAR WATCHED HER mail download as she stood near the small table, preparing two bowls of gray, glutinous matter. She kept glancing at the bed where Kerry was tucked, the covers pulled around her and a quiet, almost remote look on her face.

She's too pale, Dar realized, as she continued her work. "Kerry?"

"Mm?" Green eyes turned her way, abandoning CNN.

"I know how your family feels," Dar kept her gaze on her oatmeal, "but do you want me to come with you today?"

Kerry had to literally bite her tongue to keep the instant yelp of "yes" from emerging. She took a breath and watched Dar's face for a moment, seeing the careful unconcern plastered on it. Her family would hate it, yes, but at that moment, she just didn't care. "Yes, I would," she heard herself say.

After a moment's silence, Dar looked up. "But?"

Kerry simply shrugged. "But nothing. If they have that much of a problem with it, we can both leave."

Dar's pale blue eyes widened a trifle, and then she smiled. "Okay." She picked up a bowl, carried it to the bed, and set it down on the covers. She handed Kerry a spoon. "Go on. You should be able to keep that down."

Ah. Kerry took the spoon and examined her bowl. "You know, Dar, I don't think I ever mentioned this, but...um...I really don't like oatmeal."

"Just try it." Dar said. "Trust me."

Kerry, she flew a thousand miles in the middle of the night to be here for you. She managed to get a spoonful of the sticky stuff balanced and lifted it. *She loves you. Remember that. She loves you.* "Mmph." For a moment she mouthed the oatmeal, a substance she hated with a passion.

"Yeess?" Dar's low drawl answered.

"How'd you get oatmeal to taste like tapioca pudding?"

Dar sat down with her own bowl, and smirked, just a little. "I have many skills."

"Mmm." Kerry swallowed another spoonful. "So I see."

THE CLOCK FLIPPED over to eight-o clock. Kerry glanced at it, then sighed. "Hospital opens at nine. Guess we'd better get started." She pulled the covers back and sat up, stifling a yawn. "Can't believe I'm still tired."

Dar gave her a sympathetic look. "Stress. On top of a killer migraine."

"Mm." Kerry scrubbed her fingers through her hair. The room phone rang and she glanced at it, then at Dar. "Probably for me, huh?"

Dar held up her cell phone and shrugged. Kerry picked up the receiver. "Hello?"

"Ker?" Angela's voice was low. "I know it's early."

The pressure of the situation came down on her again. "It's okay, I was up."

"We missed you last night," Angie said. "Thought you were right behind us, then you disappeared."

Kerry's brow creased in displeasure. "I didn't disappear; I was being chased by those damn news people. I just barely got out ahead of them and got across the parking lot." She waited for Angie to comment, but there was only silence. "Then I got a migraine, and it was all I could do to get back to the hotel."

A sigh echoed through the receiver. "You okay?"

"Now," Kerry said, "yes. But it was a very miserable night. I wouldn't have been much use."

Angie cleared her throat. "It was pretty rough here, too. Mom's in pieces."

"I know," Kerry replied softly. "And given what Uncle Harold was saying, maybe it's better I wasn't there."

The ensuing silence was definitely awkward. "He didn't mean that," Angie said. "Everyone's just so stressed; you say stuff."

A lie. "Sure."

"You'll come back with us tonight, right?"

Kerry gazed across the room at the compassionate blue eyes watching her. "I don't know. That's probably not a good idea."

"C'mon, Kerry. We're your family, and this... Of course it's a good idea. Why not?" Angie sounded distressed.

Kerry took a breath. "Dar's here. She flew in last night."

"Oh." Angie let out a heartfelt sigh. "Well, it can't make things any worse, I guess. I'm glad she's there for you, at any rate."

That brought a faint smile to Kerry's face. "Me, too. Listen, I'll meet you guys at the hospital, then we'll see from there, okay?" She knew Angie wasn't happy with that. "Angie, you know how the rest of the family feels about me. Let's not make things harder than they already are."

"All right," Angie replied very quietly. "See you soon."

Angie disconnected and Kerry replaced the receiver in the cradle, then stood up. "I won't be long. Don't go anywhere."

"I won't." Dar waited for Kerry to duck into the bathroom before she rummaged in her bag and pulled out her bottle of pain-killers. *No sense in advertising stupidity,* she reasoned as she removed the cap and shook out a large pill, then recapped the bottle and tucked it back inside her bag. She washed the tablet down with a swallow of orange juice, then sat down and began to review her mail.

Today isn't going to be fun, she mused, *but we'll get through it.* With quiet determination, she put the thought out of her mind and concentrated on her work.

Jesus. Dar's brow creased. *What the hell's going on back there?* She scrolled down the long list, then remembered she had not only her own mail, but Kerry's being forwarded to her as well. She scanned the headers, then sorted them by priority and started clicking.

"Everyone's getting short answers today," she muttered, pecking out a reply as she kept her injured arm still by resting its elbow on her thigh. "Don't like it? Too bad." She typed, "No." Click. Type. "No." Click. Type. "Ok." Click. Type. "Bite me."

Backspacing to that note, Dar sighed. Given her current position, Alastair had asked her to at least try to be a little more dignified in her responses. She studied the request, a whine from José about getting the sales staff new laptops. "Why? Did they run out of sand on their Etch A Sketches?"

"What's that, hon?" Kerry poked her head out of the bathroom. "Were you talking to me?"

Dar peeked over her screen. "No, I was making fun of José. He wants new toys for the sales department."

Kerry scrubbed her teeth while she thought. "Figureth ouf there'r Fither Prith, eh?"

Dar snickered. "Yeah." She did the mental math. "He's got them in his budget...Should I be nice?"

"Eh."

Dar forwarded the mail to Mark. "Ok," she typed in, and clicked send. "You got lucky, José. Those pancakes mellowed me out."

Kerry disappeared into the bathroom, then emerged, wiping her mouth with a small towel. "Dar?"

"Mm?" Dar looked up.

"You're typing one handed." Kerry walked over to Dar. "Does your arm hurt?"

Uh oh. "Yeah." Dar shrugged. "Slept wrong, I guess."

Kerry cocked her head, then leaned on the desk and caught Dar's eye. "No, you didn't. You picked my ass up last night."

Dar grinned rakishly. "And the rest of you, too." She chuckled, leaning back in her chair. "Yeah, I had to brush the dust off my butch card; what can I tell you?" She made light of the charge, not wanting Kerry to feel guilty about it. "Relax, I'm fine."

Kerry stepped closer and circled Dar's neck with her arms,

pulled her close and kissed the top of her head. "I'll make it up to you, Dar," she murmured. "When we get home, I'm going to pamper you, and make sure you don't do anything until that shoulder heals."

Dar found herself in a very advantageous position. She gently nibbled Kerry's skin through her shirt. "Anything?"

Kerry cleared her throat. "Well..." She kissed Dar's head again, then released her and turned back towards the shower. A thought halted her. "You know, if that shoulder's really stiff, it might be a lot easier if I scrubbed you."

"Oh, reaallly." Dar was glad to see a touch of spirit coming back into Kerry's demeanor. "Are you propositioning me?"

Kerry smiled and held out a hand. Dar rose and went to her. She took the hand and wrapped an arm around Kerry as they entered the steamy bathroom. Kerry helped Dar pull her shirt off over her head, then stood as Dar peeled her out of hers.

She still felt shaky. The breakfast and the night's sleep had helped, and Dar's presence had helped even more, but she wanted a good dose of the comfort only her lover could provide to buffer her against the day. This was as good a way as any to get it, and still be doing something productive at the same time.

They stepped into the shower, and Kerry took the tube of soap she'd packed and squeezed out a handful. The steam put little wisps between her and her target, so she moved closer and studied the body before her. Dar's chest moved as she took a breath, then moved again as Kerry spread her fingers and slipped them over the tanned skin, leaving lather in their wake.

She loved how Dar felt. She had such smooth, soft skin, and it was stretched over an incredible supple and strong form that moved under her touch in a flow of muscle. There were a few tiny scars across her ribcage, and Kerry carefully cleaned all of them, aware of Dar's feather light touch on her side.

She cleaned Dar's breasts, her lips twitching a little as the touches tickling her own ribs became more insistent, then her hands moved down Dar's muscular belly and past the indentation of her navel.

The pressure of the water was starting to feel good against her sensitized skin. Kerry deliberately let the memories of the previous day dissolve as she rubbed her skin against Dar's as they slid together. She lifted her head and Dar's lips found hers, then started a slow, teasing journey down her neck.

"Oo," she whispered into Dar's ear, just before she started suckling the lobe. "I like that."

"That?" Dar rumbled, and gently closed her teeth on a very sensitive part of Kerry's anatomy.

The answer was a low groan.

Dar shifted her attentions slightly. "Or that?" She chuckled softly as the groan became a squeak.

KERRY FLUFFED OUT her hair and stared pensively at her reflection. She tugged a little on the snug teal turtleneck she hadn't had occasion to wear in over a year. "I'm going to sweat in this, aren't I?"

Dar came up behind her and put a hand on her shoulder. "Probably." She brushed a speck of dust off Kerry's sleeve. The sweater nicely outlined her lover's athletic build and contrasted against her pale hair. "You look nice, though."

Kerry turned and regarded her. Dar was wearing a beautifully knitted red pullover with an embroidered pattern on it and a pair of black corduroys. The pullover had a rolled collar, and it looked casually elegant. "So do you. I like that on you."

"You should; you bought it." Dar smiled, having found the surprise laid out on her dresser after the first cool morning they'd had that fall. She didn't like sweaters, as a rule, never having had occasion to wear them much, but she did like this one. It was incredibly soft, for one thing, a very fine, silky weave that felt nice against her skin. For another thing, she looked good in it, and she was self aware enough to know that. "Where did you get it? I should get you a blue one, and we can wear them on the same day at work." She straightened Kerry's shoulder seams. "You ready?"

Kerry's eyes dropped. "As I'll ever be. Dar, I want to apologize to you in advance for all the crap you're going to have to witness and be subjected to today."

Dar tipped Kerry's chin up so their eyes met. "I'll live. Don't worry about me, okay?"

A thin lipped smile flitted on Kerry's face, then disappeared. "Okay. Let's go." She slipped into her leather jacket and zipped it, then headed for the door with Dar following behind her. "Good God." She stopped in mid stride, almost making Dar crash into her. "Dar, what happened with the Navy investigation?"

Dar put a hand on her back and pushed her gently forward. "C'mon." She pushed the elevator button, debating whether or not to go into the subject.

Kerry didn't budge. "Dar?"

Pale blue eyes regarded her seriously. "Gerry called me."

Kerry waited. "And?"

Dar sighed. "He...wants to dump the whole thing."

Kerry's jaw dropped. "What?"

Dar fiddled with the catches on her heavy jacket. "I can see where he's coming from, Kerry." She glanced up and down the empty corridor. "The scandal could destroy a lot of people."

Kerry just stared at her. "And you accepted that?" Her voice was flat with disbelief.

Dar studied the carpet, then looked up. "No. I told him I'd go public with it if he didn't." The doors opened and she put out a hand to keep them that way. "Alastair's frothing at me for that."

Kerry walked into the elevator, her mind churning. She knew Dar would keep her word, but at what cost? "Is it worth it? Maybe Easton's right." Dar's silence made her look up, and she found her lover studying her seriously. "Maybe the damage outweighs the benefits."

Dar seemed to understand where she was coming from. "I thought about that. After I did the analysis, I sat at my desk for hours, debating with myself over whether or not to give it to your father." She half shook her head. "Maybe I knew this was going to happen."

The doors opened at the bottom floor and they exited. Kerry thought about what Dar had said as they crossed the warm, gaily decorated lobby and passed through the revolving door into the bitterly cold wind. "Did you think you might be doing it just because you were mad at Ainsbright?"

Dar stuck her hands in her pockets. "No. I thought I might be doing it to stroke my own ego."

Kerry looked at her in surprise. "What?"

Dar gave an embarrassed nod. "I figured there's a part of me that hates losing and hates letting someone get one over on me, and that's what was driving me to force the issue."

Kerry stopped at her rental car and opened the doors. She waited for Dar to slip inside, then joined her and closed the door on the icy air. "And you decided you weren't?"

Dar smiled at the bleak scene outside the car. "No. That was very much a part of why I did it." She gave Kerry an honest, open look. "But the other part of it was that people are getting hurt by this, and it has to stop." Her jaw tensed. "And it will stop, one way or the other, no matter what that takes."

Sometimes, Kerry mused, as she started the car and let the engine warm up, *sometimes life's lessons come at you from the strangest directions, and at the weirdest times.* "Does your father know about this?"

Dar nodded silently.

Kerry didn't have to ask how Andrew felt about it. She knew, simply by the set of Dar's shoulders and the almost unconsciously proud lift of her chin. It definitely gave her something to think about. "Well. I don't think my father had time to do anything with it."

"Mm." Dar leaned back in her seat.

Kerry exhaled and put the car into gear. She backed out of the parking spot and headed towards the main road. The landscape was bleak and gray, trees dressed in winter brown with their coating of snow and ice.

It made Kerry feel cold, despite the heater in the car. This had once been home. She'd grown up here, played in some of the fields they were passing, skated on those frozen lakes. They drove past a group of young people walking along the sidewalk, laughing and joking with each other, obviously headed for the church youth center not far away.

Kerry remembered being one of them, pampered and privileged, wanting for absolutely nothing. Sure of her place in the world and secure in her family's solid circle. Lacking only the one thing that Dar, raised without any of her advantages, had been given freely.

Life is so strange, sometimes.

Kerry felt almost lightheaded. She pulled over to the side of the road, stopped, and leaned on the steering wheel as she stared out at the trees.

"Ker?" Dar asked, hesitantly.

"It...um..." Kerry started, then paused. "I think part of the reason why I leaked that dirt on my father was because I was so angry at him." Her voice was shaking a little, and she appreciated the sudden warmth as Dar laid a hand on her thigh. "I don't think it had anything to do with wanting to do the right thing. Knowing that, and seeing him in that bed...it's killing me."

"Hey." Dar leaned over the shift console and put an arm across Kerry's shoulders. "It's not your fault, Kerry."

She gazed at Dar. "Isn't it?"

"Don't be an idiot." Dar's voice was warm, taking the sting out of the words. "Yeah, that was stressful, but your father spent his whole life in politics, Kerry. You think that was the only stress in his life? C'mon, you know better."

Kerry remained silent.

"Don't do that to yourself," Dar said. "He made the choice to do what he did, knowing it might get out. You think keeping that secret wasn't tough?" One dark brow lifted. "In the long run, lying is harder than truth." She stroked Kerry's cheek. "We found that out, didn't we?"

A memory of the tense months early in their relationship surfaced, when even bringing Dar lunch was looked at with suspicion. "Yeah," Kerry had to admit. "It was a lot easier once we came out. But this isn't the same thing, Dar."

"Isn't it?" Dar echoed her earlier statement. "Think about it."

Kerry exhaled. "Maybe. Guess we'd better get moving."

Dar rubbed her neck a little. "Want me to drive? That should keep you distracted until we get there."

Kerry unexpectedly smiled as she put the car back into gear. "I'm okay." She put the turn indicator on and watched for passing cars. "But I'll keep the offer in mind."

THEY MET ANGIE and her husband on the way into the hospital. Some of the press interest had waned, it seemed, or maybe the weather had deterred them. Snow was falling, and Kerry shivered a little as she joined her sister on the walk to the back entrance. "Hi."

"Hi." Angie rubbed her arm. "Hi, Dar. Thanks for coming up."

Kerry didn't have to look behind her to see the raised eyebrow. She gave Angie a heartfelt smile and a hug. "Sorry about last night."

"Richard, this is Dar Roberts, Kerry's partner," Angie went on in a determined Midwestern twang. "Dar, this is my husband, Richard."

Dar mentally gave Angie several more points as she extended her hand. "Nice to meet you." She met Richard's wary eyes, on a level with her own, as they shook hands. "Sorry it has to be on this kind of occasion."

"Ms. Roberts," Richard said quietly as he released her hand. "Good to finally meet someone I've heard so much about."

Oo. Talk about your loaded statements. Dar returned his brief smile. "Likewise." She turned to Angie. "How's Andrew?"

Everyone relaxed just a little as Richard turned to open the door to the hospital.

"Growing like a weed," Angie said. "He's made up for having such an exciting birthday by being just the sweetest, calmest child." She waited for her husband and Kerry to enter the hospital, then she turned and lowered her voice. "Dar, I'm really glad you're here."

Dar managed a brief smile. "I know I'm not wanted here, but I couldn't let her go through this alone." She held the door open for Angie to pass. "Besides, unfriendly family isn't exactly foreign to me."

Angie sighed as she walked inside and Dar followed. "I know. I just wish it wasn't so damned hard. The whole situation's so lousy, and then on top of it...Oh, crap."

Dar glanced ahead of them to where Kerry was standing,

bracketed by two older men. Her body posture was so defensive it brought an immediate response from Dar, who brushed past two vaguely familiar looking women and bore down on Kerry with determined strides.

"Uncle Albert, you don't have a right to ask me to leave," Kerry said firmly. "This is my father—"

"You sure didn't think of that when you turned against him, did you?" her uncle snapped, his face flushed. "Look, I'm not going to stand here and argue. I'm not going to put up with my brother being mocked by the likes of you, you little traitor. Get your ass out of this hospital before I throw you out."

Kerry felt a wild rush of anger that was so unexpected, it almost made her lightheaded. "You just try it." She balled her fists. "You stupid, useless windbag. I haven't even seen you since I was twelve. Now you show up here like you own the place, like you matter?"

"Might have figured it was you giving someone bullshit," Dar said.

Kerry's uncle turned and stared in utter shock.

A cold smile graced Dar's face. "Aren't you going to say hello, Al? Or did you forget what I looked like after I fired your ass for the rankest incompetence in the history of business?"

"You son of a—"

"Oh no." Dar slipped between him and Kerry, very aware of the watching crowd. "I didn't have a dick then and I don't now, but let me tell you, Al, you say one more nasty word to Kerrison and you won't have one either, because I'll pull it off and beat you to death with it."

The elevator doors opened into a frozen silence. Dar put out a long arm and blocked them from closing. "Ladies first." She motioned Kerry and Angie to go on, then joined them in the car, and let the doors close before anyone else could get on.

The sound of Angie pushing the elevator button was loud as they all took a breath at the same time. "Wow." Angie wiped her brow. "This isn't a good way to start the day, is it?"

Kerry turned and looked at Dar. "Uh..."

Dar had been staring at the doors, now she turned and exhaled. "Sorry. Temper got the better of me."

"It's okay." Kerry lifted a slightly shaking hand. "Better yours than mine, Dar. I was about to start swinging at him." Dar slipped an arm around her shoulders, and she leaned gratefully against Dar's tall form. "Sorry we left Richard down there with them, Ang."

"He'll live." Angie shrugged. "I'm sorry. After the past few days and listening to all the righteous bullshit I've had to listen to, with daddy in here helpless, I'm just...damn it to hell...over it."

Kerry peeked at her. "Angela, that's the most curse words I've ever heard you use."

"Yeah, well." Angie drew in a long breath and let it out. "I've been spending time on the Internet, what can I tell you?" The doors opened and she exited, followed by Dar and Kerry. They turned to the right and went to the waiting room of the critical care unit.

Cynthia Stuart was already there, alone. She was sitting in one of the chairs, her hands folded in her lap, her body in an attitude of pained patience. She looked up as they entered. "Oh, Angela...Kerrison...I'm..." Her eyes slipped past them and rested on Dar. "Oh."

Kerry heard the elevator doors opening behind them, and she figured the entire situation was either going to resolve itself or turn into an undignified free for all more suited to the soccer field than a hospital. "Mother—"

Cynthia stood, brushed past her, and stopped in front of Dar with a serious expression. She held out both hands. "I'm so glad you came."

It was one of the last things Dar had expected to hear. She clasped Cynthia's hands in sheer reflex, her battle ready mind scrambling to reassess the startling attitude. "I'm sorry," she managed to get out. "I really am," she added in a softer tone.

"As am I," Cynthia replied. "For many things."

Loud voices at the doorway made them both turn. Kerry's uncles entered with Richard and one or two others. They all stopped and stared at Dar, who stared impassively back, her hands still clasped in Cynthia's.

The tension in the room was shattered when the inner door opened and a tall, good looking man entered, wearing a white lab coat over a set of green surgical scrubs. Everyone's attention went to him, and he paused, collecting his thoughts before he continued.

Dar released Cynthia's hands and stepped quietly back to join Kerry, who slipped a hand around her arm as they waited for the doctor to speak.

"Hello, Doctor Bridges," Cynthia said quietly. "How are things this morning?"

The doctor's lips tensed a bit in compassion before he put a hand on her shoulder and walked her to a seat. He sat next to her and rested his elbows on his knees as everyone else sat across from them.

"There's been no change, Mrs. Stuart," Dr. Bridges told her

gently. "You know we didn't expect there to be any; we talked about that yesterday."

Cynthia Stuart looked very small and very alone. "Yes, I know. But you live your whole life thinking prayer can change things, so you do what you can." Her eyes searched the doctor's face. "It seems so odd, with everything we can do these days, that nothing can be done for my husband."

Dr. Bridges nodded, seeming to accept the gentle rebuke. "Sometimes we can achieve what appear to be miracles, that's true. But some things are still beyond us, and restoring energy in a brain where there's none left is one of those things."

Not caring who was watching, Dar put an arm around Kerry. She could feel her lover's whole body shivering, and she wished there were some way, any way to change the words the doctor was forcing them to hear about her father. Even if she hated the man's guts.

"There really is no hope, is there?" Kerry asked softly. "Not even one in a million?"

Dr. Bridges hesitated, studying his hands before he looked up and met her eyes. "Ms. Stuart, in my business, I've learned never to quote odds. Because human beings have the damnedest way of finding a way around them."

Kerry blinked. "But?"

The doctor sighed. "But, Ms. Stuart, I know our limitations. Your father is beyond them." He patted Cynthia's hand. "I'm sorry."

Kerry's mother nodded numbly.

"I'll be in my office if you want to see me," the doctor said to Kerry. He stood up and headed out the way he'd come in.

For a few moments, they were all silent. Then all hell broke loose. Both of Kerry's uncles stood up and faced her, their voices rising in mindless outrage in counterpoint with too few voices protesting in her defense.

Finally, Cynthia Stuart simply stood up and screamed at the top of her voice, "Silence!" It shocked everyone so much, it achieved its purpose, and silence did, indeed, fall over the waiting room.

Kerry's uncles were squared off on one side, facing Kerry, Angie, and Dar, with Richard sort of hovering off to one side.

"Cynthia, I won't have it," Edgar Stuart said flatly. "My brother is lying in there dying, and I won't have that little bitch here." He pointed at Kerry. "She put him here."

Kerry opened her mouth to respond.

"*No.*" Cynthia almost spat the word out. "Now that's enough." She was shaking, but clearly in control. "Is it not bad enough we're here for this, without this nonsense? Kerry did not put Roger anywhere."

"What are you talking about?" Edgar yelled. "You know—"

"Enough!" Cynthia out-yelled him. "Hatred put him in that bed. I won't have it; I won't. Now you stop this at once, or I will have you thrown out."

"Mother." Kerry put a hesitant hand on her shoulder. "It's not worth what this is costing. I'll leave."

"Please," her mother turned and whispered, "hasn't there been enough anger?"

Kerry dropped her eyes and her hand fell from Cynthia's shoulder.

Dar stepped up behind Kerry and laid a hand on her back in silent support, gazing with quiet impassivity over Kerry's shoulder at her mother and her uncles.

"Now, let's all sit down," Cynthia said shakily, "and have a moment's peace."

Someone had to sit first, and Kerry decided it would be her. She took a seat against the wall as Dar settled next to her, and, reluctantly, everyone else did as well. *God.* Kerry was shaking inside and her head ached again. She was very conscious of Dar's presence, almost feeling the tension radiating from her silent lover.

"What I want," Cynthia Stuart had seated herself and was now speaking firmly, staring at the opposite wall, "what I want is for all of us to come together and support each other during this horrible trial."

"Cyndi," Edgar broke in.

"Edgar," she said, "that's enough."

Kerry just kept quiet, leaning forward with her elbows on her knees and her head in her hands. She felt chilled and welcomed the warmth as Dar put an arm across her shoulders, despite the fact that she knew if she looked up, she'd see disgust and loathing in her family's eyes. It was so hard. She let out a breath and felt like crying.

"Mom's right." Angela's voice broke the silence. "This is hard enough for all of us. Let's not make it worse." She reached past Dar and rubbed Kerry's back. "Fighting gains us nothing."

The two older men stared at her. "It gains me the satisfaction of knowing I didn't sit by and let my brother's memory be sullied by the likes of her," Edgar spat. "He'd hate her being here, with that...that..."

Dar stood up. "Let's cut to the facts. Kerry's father's in there dying. Kerry wants to be here." She let the words sink in. "I'm not leaving her here to face that alone, so unless you think you can physically remove either one of us, why don't you just shut up and use your energy for something other than moving the hot air around."

"You—"

"Heathen? Dyke? Sinner?" Dar refused to lose her temper or her acidic humor. "Save it. I've heard it all, and I'm not the one here making everyone sick to their stomachs." She stared Edgar down.

"Aren't you?" He got up and left, and Albert followed him.

Kerry lifted her head and gazed at Dar, then she slowly straightened and slumped back into the chair with a sigh as Dar resumed her seat. "I'm sorry," she said quietly to her mother.

"Kerrison, this was God's will, not yours," Cynthia said. "We've spent too much time railing against that. It's time we stop and bow our heads to it and listen to His word." She folded her hands and gazed at them.

Kerry propped her head against one hand and rubbed her temples. Her stomach was aching again, and a flash of the torment she'd gone through the night before made her shiver in pure reaction.

"Ker?" Dar leaned close, a concerned tone in her voice. "You all right?"

Kerry met Dar's eyes. "Not really," she murmured. "Got any ibuprofen?"

"Yeah." Dar nodded. "Let me go grab you a drink." She got up and squeezed Kerry's shoulder before she walked to the door and disappeared.

Kerry exhaled heavily and closed her eyes, leaving them that way when Angie slid from her seat into the one Dar had vacated and pressed her shoulder against Kerry's.

"Hey, sis."

One green eye appeared. "Hey."

"I'm glad you're here," Angie said. "Even though I know you're not."

Kerry managed a faint smile. "Thanks." She glanced at her mother, who was now whispering to her Aunt Helen. "I'm glad Dar's here, even though I know she's not."

Angie smiled. "Yeah, I bet you are." She sighed. "I've missed talking to you." She patted Kerry's shoulder. "I've just been so busy with Andrew." She lowered her voice. "Brian's coming over later with Mike. That'll tip the scales."

"Mmm." Kerry closed her eyes against the throbbing. "I'll be glad to see them." She peeked cautiously past Angie's shoulder. "Bet you will too, huh?"

Angie sighed. "I was seriously considering spilling my little secret the other day before this happened. I figured, what the hell, right?"

Kerry leaned her head against Angie's. "What a family of rebels we turned out to be." Her humor faded. "What are we going to do, Angie? How can we ask mom to make that choice?"

Angie's eyes went to their mother's face, then flicked back. "I don't know," she whispered. "I just don't know."

Chapter
Six

DAR FOUND THE cafeteria and lost Kerry's relatives with equal success. She'd spotted Al and Edgar near a bank of pay phones, busily speaking in low, angry tones. Avoiding them meant dodging into the stairwell, but that was okay too, since it was much, much cooler in there, and she appreciated the chill as she went downstairs.

She was worried about Kerry, though, and as she exited the stairs and spotted the cafeteria, she set her mind to figuring out a way to get her lover through what was turning into Hell's own sideshow.

Dar studied the contents of the cooler case, then smiled and retrieved two cartons of chocolate milk. She knew the sweet beverage would serve two purposes—give Kerry something to wash the Advil down with and provide an almost food-like substance to keep her metabolism on an even keel. With the emotional overload Kerry was currently experiencing, Dar didn't want to take any chances.

She paid for the milk, a banana, and two cookies, then opted for the stairs to regain access to the CCU floor. Halfway up, her cell phone rang.

"Shit." Dar stopped on the stairs. She tucked the banana under an arm, dug out her phone, and opened it. "Hello?"

"Dar." Alastair's voice was very serious. "I have a real problem."

Dar glanced up at the stairwell ceiling, dully lit with bland incandescence. "Yeah?"

"They've called me to the Pentagon," Alastair said. "It's no joke, Dar. Easton wants that data and he wants it today, or we're looking at sanctions and God only knows what else. Every contract we have with them is at stake."

Dar leaned against the railing. "Is he nuts?"

"He's a very angry man. You need to come here and talk to

him," Alastair said. "I had Bea book you a flight."

"Alastair—"

"No excuses, Dar," Alastair said. "I need you here; I need you now. This is critical."

Dar blinked at the wall opposite her, tracing the bricks with her eyes as her mind worked. "I can't. I'm not in Miami."

"What do you mean yo...Not in Miami? Where are you?" Alastair demanded. "You didn't say you were going out of town."

"I'm in Michigan," Dar said.

"What? What problem do we have there?"

Dar felt the press of the cold metal against her back. "We don't." She exhaled slowly. "It's personal."

There was a momentary silence. "Dar, what in the hell's going on? Have you lost your mind? I told you I need you here or there'll be hell to pay!"

"I can't," Dar repeated.

"The hell you can't!" Alastair spluttered. "What the hell's going on that you can't get on a damn plane?"

A pause kept Alastair waiting for his answer for just a few seconds. "Kerry's father's dying. I'm not leaving her here to face that alone." The funny thing was, she realized much, much later, it had actually been one of the easier decisions she'd ever had to make. "General Easton is going to have to wait."

Alastair seemed to be at a loss. "I can't tell him that. Jesus, Dar—"

"The answer's no, Alastair," Dar said.

Alastair sighed. "Dar." The phone crackled, as he apparently shifted position. "Now you listen to me, all right? You've scared the crap out of this man, and he's ready to do something stupid. He's going to do that stupid thing if you aren't here to talk about it, and a lot of people could get hurt."

Dar felt unusually calm. "I know, but I'm not leaving here."

"Dar." Now Alastair sounded a touch desperate. "He's not going to let me postpone this. He needs an answer, and he needs it this afternoon. Either you deal with him, or..." He left the thought unfinished.

Dar could hear her own heartbeat, and she closed her eyes. "All right." She paused, then surrendered. "What does he want?"

"What does he want?" Alastair's voice rose. "Nothing much. He wants that data, and your guarantee every part of it's going to be destroyed, Dar. You need to talk to him, work something out."

"All right," Dar said. "He can have the data. I'll sign a release."

"You will?" The shock was evident in Alastair's voice.

She drew in a long, long breath. "I'll give him what he

wants."

KERRY LOOKED UP as she felt a light touch on her wrist.

Her mother leaned closer and said softly, "We'll wait for your brother to get here." She paused, as though debating whether or not to continue. "I want you all together."

Kerry nodded in understanding. "Okay."

"In a way," Cynthia went on softly, "it's easier to come back today and think of these things. The shock, you know, it's over." She drew in a breath and released it. "But it was very difficult last night."

"I'm sorry I wasn't there," Kerry murmured.

"Angela said you were sick?"

Kerry glanced up at her. "I got a migraine." She watched her mother wince slightly, knowing she was prone to the debilitating headaches herself. "It was..." She faltered. "Anyway, I'm sorry I didn't come to the house to be with all of you."

"Kerrison," her mother put a hand on her arm, "this anger between us must cease. It has done far too much damage to us all, and I will not have it any longer."

What answer can I have to that? Kerry wondered. *That it wasn't my anger to begin with? Or that it was, but they'd caused it? This is no time to start that up,* she reminded herself. "All right."

Cynthia was about to continue when a stir at the door made them both look up. Dar entered, her tall body filling the doorway with its vibrant presence. Her pale eyes flicked around the room then settled on Kerry's face, a faint smile twitching at her lips as their gazes met.

Kerry smiled back and heard her mother sigh. Angie moved over, and Dar dropped into the seat next to Kerry, and offered up a brown and white carton and a banana.

"Thanks." Kerry stuck the banana between her knees, opened her milk, and took a sip. It was thick and sweet, and she took a few mouthfuls before she swallowed the tablets Dar handed her.

Dar leaned back and draped an arm over Kerry's shoulders, letting her other arm rest against her stomach. She could tell she'd walked in on some kind of discussion; the furtive glances and general air of discomfort were boringly familiar to her, usually duplicated whenever she entered the restroom at the office when it was already occupied.

Though, that hasn't happened that much lately, Dar admitted. Apparently, settling down and gaining a steady partner had eliminated her from most of the racier personal gossip, and everyone still seemed a little embarrassed over the last false rumor about

Kerry and Andrew. She didn't think she'd be getting any invita-
tions to Tupperware parties any time soon, though.

That is, if Alastair forgives me for this one, Dar reflected quietly.
*For putting my personal life before the company's well being for the first
time.* He'd been very angry; even through the slightly raspy connection and the distance between them, Dar recognized that.
Angry and disappointed and more than a little frustrated.

But what choice did she have, really, between her honor and
Kerry's well being?

Well, I'm here. Dar firmly put work and the conversation with
Alastair out of her mind as something she could no longer do anything about and concentrated on the situation at hand. She shifted
her hand a little and gently rubbed the back of Kerry's neck,
which had a knot in it the size of a plum.

"Mmm," Kerry murmured appreciatively, rocking her head
forward to loosen the muscles Dar was working on. The warmth
of her touch was almost as effective as the strong massage, and
the tension eased out of her body after a few minutes. It was an
odd sensation, because part of her knew that doing what she was
doing, where she was doing it, was making everyone else uncomfortable.

Is it selfish? Kerry lifted her head and stretched, then eased
back as Dar's long arm curled around her shoulders. Her mother
was staring off into the distance, and her aunts were pointedly
looking elsewhere. Only Angie seemed unaffected, and as she met
her sister's eyes, Angie gave her a tiny, rueful shake of her head
and the barest of winks.

Yes, Kerry decided. *It is selfish of me.* Everyone was hurting.
She was making it worse. She'd always been taught to deny herself for the comfort of others, and this was a prime example of the
opportunity to do just that. Right. Now she just had to clue in her
other half.

Kerry glanced at Dar, who was gazing down at the chocolate
milk in her other hand. Dar's profile was tense, and she could see
the shift of the muscles along Dar's jawline as she clenched and
relaxed it. Dar was as uncomfortable as her family was, being
there in a place where almost everyone hated her, and involved in
a highly emotional situation she had little experience and less
skill in dealing with.

Hm. My lifelong flowchart, Kerry realized, *has gained a branch.
Sacrificing my comfort for others is fine—unless it hurts Dar.* The
solicitous attention was Dar's way of dealing with the situation,
focusing her concentration on something she could do something
about and gaining some measure of balance from that.

Push Dar away, and it would please her family. Kerry swallowed as Dar looked up and their eyes met. She saw the tiny furrow form over the bridge of Dar's nose, and in pure reflex she reached out and smoothed it away.

Dar relaxed and sat back, holding up her milk with a wry grin. "Open this for me?"

"Sure." Kerry glanced casually around as she pulled the carton's top open, then handed it back. Then she peeled her banana, took a bite, and chewed it thoughtfully.

MICHAEL AND BRIAN arrived just after noon. Kerry stood near the window in the waiting room, and she turned as she heard the footsteps. She met her brother's eyes as he entered, followed by her old friend.

Mike went to her, and she pulled him into a hug. She gave Brian a pensive smile over her brother's shoulder. "Hey, Mikey."

"Hey." Michael sighed, releasing her. "Sucky day."

"Yeah. Big time." She gave him a final squeeze, then ducked past him and found herself being hugged by Brian. Michael joined Angie and her mother on the other side of the room. "Hey, Bri," she greeted her onetime boyfriend.

"Hi, Kerry," Brian replied shyly. "Sorry about all this."

"Me, too."

They parted. Kerry tipped her head back and they regarded each other for a moment. If things had been different, she realized, they'd have been married by now. She tried to imagine that, and found she really just couldn't—it was too remote from who she was now. Though she felt an echo of warm affection when she looked at Brian, she knew she'd never loved him enough to spend her life with him. She wondered if he felt the same way.

"How are you?" She took his hands. "Angie said you got promoted?"

A brief smile flickered over his face. "They made me a junior partner, yeah. Not too bad for less than a year, but nothing like your career's been."

"Mm." Kerry smiled back. "Thanks for coming down here. I know it's a zoo downstairs." She exhaled, glancing behind him to see her uncles reenter the room. "Not that it's been much better here."

"Yeah, Mike was telling me." Brian gently rubbed her hands. "It's good to see you, though. You look great." His eyes twinkled slightly. "I'll have to come down to Miami sometime to see where you get that tan from."

"Anytime," Kerry said. "Plenty of sun to go around, I promise you."

"Kerrison."

Kerry glanced at where her mother was now standing, with Angie and Mike next to her. Kerry gave Brian's hands one last squeeze, then released them and straightened her shoulders before she started towards her family. Her eyes flicked to the far corner of the room where Dar was leaning against the window and gazing out at the snow. After a brief instant, Dar turned and met her gaze, her lips tensing in sympathy. Kerry returned the look, then walked to her mother. "I'm here."

"Let us go into that area there." Cynthia indicated a small office tucked inconspicuously in a corner. The doctor was standing there, obviously waiting for them. "It's time."

They filed into the room and closed the door behind them, leaving the rest of the assembled family and friends in a somber, chilly silence.

IT WAS GRAY outside. Dar could feel the chill through the thick glass of the window, and she watched in idle bemusement as the snow fell harder onto the parking lot below.

The weather seemed appropriate to the situation, though. Dar glanced down at the television news trucks gathered near the back entrance to the hospital, their lights glowing dimly in the winter gloom. It also matched the atmosphere inside the room, she acknowledged wryly as she glanced up to catch the reflection in the window of what was behind her.

Center of attention, Dar resisted the urge to straighten. She could see Kerry's aunts and uncles glaring at her back, and the half furtive, half curious looks she was getting from the tall, blond Brian. Her...rival? Dar almost smiled. Kerry had called Brian a good friend, but she hadn't gotten a chance to talk to him at their first meeting, a brief few minutes at Angie's bedside after the birth of her infant son.

Brian's son as well, in fact. Dar wondered if Angela had ever told anyone else about that. Even having only exchanged a nod with Brian, Dar thought he'd be a better match for Angie than her husband Richard. She looked at her own reflection, seeing the pale light glint off her eyes. Would that change now?

For Kerry's sake, Dar felt badly about the whole reason they were there. She was honest enough with herself, however, to admit she wasn't sorry to see the end of Senator Stuart. The man was a bastard who'd made his kids miserable most of their lives, in Dar's view. And while she wasn't glad, exactly, that he'd been stricken the way he had been, she also didn't feel any reason to pity him.

Dar sighed and watched the snow covering the cars. She was surprised at just how depressing it appeared.

"Excuse me."

Dar's eyes jerked up at the sound and she turned to find Brian standing right behind her. He met her surprised gaze warily, then pursed his lips and stuck his hands in his pockets. "Yeah?"

"I...um." Brian peered at her from under sandy eyebrows. "We really didn't get a chance to meet last time." He stuck a hand out. "I'm Brian Evans."

"I know." Dar allowed a half smile as she took his hand and gripped it firmly. "Dar Roberts."

"Yeah, I know," Brian replied, returning his hand to his pocket. "Well, I just wanted to say hello." He seemed at a loss for further conversation.

Dar leaned back against the glass and crossed one ankle over the other. He was fairly good looking, she decided, with an angular face and a gentle demeanor that reminded her just a little of Kerry's. "I'm glad you came."

He peered at her. "You are?"

Dar nodded. "Kerry needs all the friends she can get." She glanced pointedly around him at the rest of her lover's family, who were glaring at her with venomous intent.

"Ah." Brian followed her eyes, then exhaled. "Yeah, it's been tough, or so Angie told me. I guess it's more important for some people to nurture their hatred."

"Yeah." Dar exhaled. "More I see of it, the more I appreciate my parents." She shook her head a tiny bit. "What a waste of energy."

Brian gave her a wry smile, then a motion at the door caught his eye and he turned. "Ah."

Dar looked over his shoulder. In the doorway, stood a tall, very distinguished man with steel gray hair and a clean-shaven face. She glanced at Brian. "Someone you know?"

Brian exhaled. "Charles Durham." He kept his voice low as the rest of the occupants of the room went to greet the newcomer. "He's been a friend of the family for many years."

"Lawyer?" Dar asked.

"Worse." Brian hesitated, then apparently made his decision, moved closer to Dar, and folded his arms. "Their very, very conservative pastor."

"Oh." Dar sighed, wishing she and Kerry and the unexpectedly nice Brian were three hundred miles away. "Great."

THE INNER DOOR opened and the family filed out, followed

by the doctor, who clasped Cynthia's shoulders before he walked towards the ICU.

As Dar watched in concern, Kerry straightened her shoulders with an obvious effort, then turned to meet her eyes. The look in them was quiet but resigned as Kerry held out a hand in obvious invitation.

"Excuse me," Dar murmured as she left her spot by the window and crossed the tile floor to Kerry's side. She took her hand and clasped it. "You all right?" she whispered.

Kerry nodded, swallowing audibly. "I didn't think it would be that hard to let him go," she murmured. "Damn it hurts. Even after everything he did."

Dar briefly rested her cheek against Kerry's hair, trading trite words for the comfort of touch. They waited for the rest of the family to join them, everyone blessedly silent for a change, before they proceeded to the ICU.

The pastor joined Cynthia and they spoke quietly, heads bent together. His eyes flicked to Kerry, but Cynthia quickly raised a hand, in an almost impatient gesture. The pastor nodded and patted her shoulder, but couldn't resist a slight shake of his head.

Kerry didn't miss any of it, but she remained silent, firmly squeezing Dar's hand as they stood waiting. Memories of stern lectures from their pastor rang within her, but she hoped with all her heart the old man would focus his energies on her father and leave her alone.

Dar squeezed her hand in return and took a step closer, bringing a welcome sense of security totally at odds with the chill, disapproving atmosphere in the room, and managing to carry off an air of somber, yet potent intimidation.

Just when the tension was almost unbearable, Cynthia sighed and turned towards the door. "Please, let's all go now."

The hallway was quiet, save for the scuffs and squeaks of their shoes as they walked towards the critical care unit. As they entered, a nurse looked up and pressed her lips together in sympathy before she intercepted them.

"We've just taken him off the machines. You can stay as long as you want to," she told them with professional gentleness, and waited for them to move past her before she pulled the privacy curtain around them and left.

Kerry was surprised at how quiet it was. They'd turned off all the alarms and all the pumps—machines stood mutely dark in the corner, save for one single monitor that showed an already irregular heartbeat.

She focused on the still figure in the bed, watching the hesitant breaths with a surreal sense of distance. It was almost like this was happening to a stranger. In a way, her mother had been right, she realized. Yesterday she'd said her goodbye, an inner part of her knowing there would be no recovery from this. Now it was just a matter of waiting for the end.

Kerry felt a warm touch on her back and she looked up at Dar, then glanced around the room. Everyone was solemn, leaving their differences outside for a brief time while they gave death its due dignity. Even Dar's presence was accepted, however grudgingly.

Pastor Charles held Cynthia's hand, his head bowed in prayer. Kerry pensively studied his profile, remembering long hours spent in Bible study and his uncompromising view of the world and all their places in it.

"Go with God, Roger," the pastor said softly as he finished his prayer. "Knowing the Lord will watch over your family and keep them safe until you meet again."

A shiver passed over Kerry, and she grasped the railings of the bed. The reality of the situation came clear as she watched her father's chest move more slowly, more erratically.

She glanced at the slack face, its half open, glazed eyes staring off into a strange realm none of them could yet see. There was no expression there, no familiarity.

The green line on the monitor rippled, its bumps jerking and hesitating.

Kerry found it hard to breathe herself, and she focused on the railing between her hands, its faintly reflective surface showing a flash of blue green from her sweater. Dar's hand settled on her shoulder, feeling warm and incredibly real in all that cold silence, and she only just resisted turning and hiding her face against her lover's chest.

No. She forced her eyes up, forced herself to watch that damn green line as it pulsed, the ridges and valleys becoming more and more indistinct.

If she turned her head, she wondered if she would sense Death's presence, yet another silent, patient watcher in the room. It was a creepy feeling, and suddenly Kerry felt afraid. As if sensing that, Dar moved closer, her body a wall of solid warmth behind Kerry, so close she could almost hear Dar's heartbeat.

Kerry drew in a breath and released it, steadying her nerves. Then she fixed her eyes on her father, only blinking a few times when the chest jerked, moved, then finally, gently, fell for the last time. It was accompanied by a soft, almost inaudible gasp.

The green line rippled, and went still. There was no alarm, no rush of nurses, just an eerie silence as everyone in the room seemed to hold their breaths.

And then it was over. Cynthia drew in a shuddering breath and started to cry.

"MS. STUART?"

Kerry looked up at the voice, surprised to find the doctor standing next to her. She was outside the CCU waiting room, taking a moment to settle herself before she went back inside. "Yes?"

"I'm very sorry." Dr. Bridges put a hand on her shoulder. "If it's any comfort to you at all, he had no awareness of what was going on."

Kerry studied his face. "I know. Thank you. I'm glad. He'd have hated being like that."

The doctor nodded. "So your mother said." He paused. "Do you have...ah...plans yet, as to..."

Dar returned from her walk down to the water fountain at that moment and joined them. She glanced questioningly at the doctor, then at Kerry, who reached a hand out for her in reflex.

"There's something being planned, yes," Kerry said. "The family counsel is arranging things and taking care of the press."

"Good." Dr. Bridges exhaled. "Well, you take care, Ms. Stuart. I'm sorry I couldn't have done more."

"Thank you," Kerry replied and watched him walk away. She turned and looked at Dar, feeling suddenly exhausted. "Ugh."

Dar put an arm around her and pulled her into hug. "C'mere."

Kerry went willingly and abandoned herself into a dark, warm haven that smelled of wool and Dar and blocked out the reality of the coldly lit hospital corridor. She suspected she was still in shock, because it hadn't even occurred to her to cry or feel sad, a mixture of regret and relief filled her instead. "You know something?"

"Mm?" Dar murmured very close to her ear.

"Now the hard part starts."

Dar sighed. "Yeah." She glanced into the waiting room, where she could see the pastor with his arm around a distraught Mrs. Stuart, next to Angie and Michael. Dealing with all the family now that the immediate crisis was over was shaping up to be a tough ride. "Sorry."

Kerry exhaled, warming Dar's skin right through her pullover. "Thank God you're here," she whispered. "But I'm sorry I'm putting you through this."

Dar rested her cheek against Kerry's hair. "I'm not sorry at all. So don't you be either, Kerrison."

Kerry tipped her head back and gazed up at Dar. "Do you

know, you're the only person who has ever said that name in a way that makes me want to hear it more often?"

A tiny smirk appeared as Dar gracefully inclined her head. "You do the same to me with mine. But don't tell anyone, all right? It'll wreck a lifetime of conditioning people not to use it."

"No problem, Paladar." Kerry found reason to smile, which felt strange after the past two days. "We're going to have to go back to my parents' house, you realize."

Dar nodded. "I know."

Kerry sighed and put her head back down on Dar's shoulder. "I don't even know what to feel, Dar. Should I be crying?"

Dar was silent for a moment. "When they came and told us that Dad had died," her voice was soft and reflective, "I didn't cry at all."

Kerry's brows contracted. "Really?"

"Yes. Not for days. Then, I was at work and I was at my desk and..." A flash of that memory surfaced, twisting Dar's guts. "It just hit me." She paused. "That I was never going to see him again. And I lost it."

"Mm."

Even now, Dar felt the tears all over again. "I went into the Xerox room and locked the door and went to pieces for hours."

Kerry thought about that. "Knowing how you feel about him, I'm not surprised. I don't think that's going to happen to me, though."

Dar hugged her. "Maybe not. But give yourself a little time, okay?"

"Okay." Kerry closed her eyes and wished it was over. "Dar?"

"Let me guess." Dar gently scratched the back of Kerry's neck and got a contented murmur. "You love me, right?"

"No," Kerry said. "I love that you love me." She gave Dar a big hug, then slipped an arm around her waist. "Let's go get this started."

"WAIT, MS. STUART! Can we get a statement!"

"Hold, on—look, that's the brother, there. Go on!"

"Ms. Stuart, look this way!"

Kerry just kept her head down and kept walking, almost slipping as her boots stepped off the swept sidewalk and onto the snow covered parking lot. "Jesus." She kept her hands in her pockets, aware of her uncles herding everyone along and her mother huddled between her and Michael. "Fucking ghouls."

Cynthia Stuart's head jerked up. "Kerrison!" she whispered, shocked.

"Well, they are," Kerry replied, as they dodged between two parked television news trucks and escaped the glare of spotlights. Behind them, she could hear a spokesman yelling in vain for attention, and she was glad when the noise faded back, leaving them to the labored sounds of their own breathing and the crunch of snow underfoot.

The family limo and its driver were waiting for them, and doors opened quickly, allowing a gust of leather and wax-tinged warm air out. Kerry helped her mother inside, then stepped back. "We'll follow you."

"Kerry, there's room," Angie protested. "Come on."

"You go." Kerry gave her a gentle shove and took a backwards stride almost into Dar's arms. "We'll be right behind you, I promise." She closed the door behind Angie, then turned and let out a huge sigh, until she saw two reporters running their way, one with a camera balanced on his shoulder. "Oh, pud."

Dar turned, saw them coming, and made one of the instantaneous decisions that marked her long career. She stooped and grabbed a double handful of snow, then wadded it, let it go sidearm, and nailed the man with the camera right in the face. He stumbled, fell sideways on the ice, and knocked his companion right over.

"Let's go." Dar grabbed Kerry's arm and plowed towards the rental car. "I'll drive."

"Oh no." Kerry wrestled for the keys as they half walked, half slid together. "Now c'mon. Dar."

"Let me," Dar said. "For crying out loud, Kerry, I have an engineering degree. I can figure out how to drive on snow." With a stern glare, she keyed the door lock and pulled the passenger side door open. "In."

Kerry was about to argue, but spotted more reporters heading their way and decided she could always wrest control of the car from Dar after they got clear of the parking lot. She slid inside, closed the door, and leaned over to open the opposite one. Dar dropped in next to her and slammed the door, sending a tiny puff of snow cascading down the front windshield.

Dar cranked the ignition and turned the lights on to combat the fast gathering twilight. Then she paused, looking at the frosted windows. She pointed. "What the hell are you supposed to do with that?"

An exhausted Kerry stared at the window. "With what?"

"That." Dar pointed at the ice. "Wipers won't take that off."

Kerry stared at her. "You use the defroster, Dar." She leaned over and turned the device on. "What on earth did you think it was there for?"

Dar frowned. "Clearing out the humidity when it rains." She peered through the clearing glass, glad to see the reporters were now chasing the limo as it made its stately way out of the drive. It was cold out and she was shivering, unused to the damp chill which ate through her sweater and made her already aching shoulder throb. Add the fact that she'd left her medication at the hotel room and they'd missed lunch, and it made for a truckload of misery.

And now they were headed for more of it. Dar cautiously put the car in drive and pulled out of the parking space, following the tail lights of the limo. She tested the brakes and felt the lack of control in the car, her muscles automatically compensating for that. *All right,* Dar decided. *I can do this.*

She didn't see Kerry half turned sideways in her seat, watching her with gentle, tired eyes, the faintest of smiles on her face.

"They going to want you to stay overnight?" Dar asked.

"Probably," Kerry said.

"We don't have a change of clothes."

"We can sleep naked," came the reasonable answer. "We usually do."

Dar fought the desire to turn her head and stare at Kerry. "Not in your family's house, we don't."

"Mm." Kerry exhaled. "That's true." She blinked slowly. "I have clothes left there, but I bet none of them fit." The thought seemed to please her. "Maybe some old sweatshirts, if they didn't get tossed, but definitely nothing that'd fit you." She watched their progress along the street and grudgingly admitted that Dar was doing pretty well with the ice. "Maybe we should detour past the hotel."

"Just what I was thinking," Dar said. She pulled carefully to a halt at a red light, as the limo ahead of them went on. "You doing okay?" She glanced at Kerry, whose drawn face was painfully evident even in the low light. Before Kerry could answer, Dar's cell phone rang, startling both of them.

"That's been quiet," Kerry murmured.

Dar took it out and opened it. "Yeah?"

"Dar."

Alastair's voice sounded much, much calmer than it had earlier. That served to make Dar's stomach tie up in knots, and she wondered if she was on the verge of being fired. She decided she really didn't care. "Evening, Alastair," she said, putting the car into motion as the light turned green. "Right, up ahead?" Kerry nodded. "What's up?" she asked Alastair.

"Just saw the news," Alastair said. "Tell Kerry I'm sorry; that's a tough thing."

Dar exhaled. "I will."

There was a slight pause. "Easton took the deal. Didn't think he would, but he did."

"Good." Dar felt a sense of relief. "Thanks for telling me."

"Anytime, Dar." Now, at last, Alastair's voice gentled. "Take care, y'hear? Both of you."

"We will," Dar replied. "Talk to you tomorrow." She hung up, folded the phone, and tucked it back into its cradle. "Alastair sends his condolences, and wants you to take it easy."

Kerry watched her closely. She'd lived with Dar for over a year, and she'd learned through trial and error to be able to read almost every twitch of that very, very expressive face. "And?"

There was a glint of streetlamp off blue eyes as Dar glanced at her. "And?"

Kerry saw Dar's hands flex and resettle on the steering wheel. "And, what else is going on?" She waited through the obvious hesitation. "C'mon, Dar, you can bluff an entire roomful of stock analysts, but not me. What's up?"

Dar inhaled, then squared her shoulders. "Things went south with the Navy." She pulled into the hotel's parking lot. "Easton called Alastair on the carpet and demanded he produce the information we found and turn it over, or face some pretty strong consequences."

"What happened?" Kerry sat up straighter, perversely glad to have something else to focus on. "How'd he get out of it?"

Dar stopped the car in a parking spot and rested her hands on the wheel as she gazed thoughtfully out the window. "I agreed to a deal." She turned to Kerry. "To turn over the data and not press forward with it."

Kerry blinked at her with a look of utter shock.

"He had a deadline. I had to be there. I wasn't going to be." Dar shrugged. "So, that's what's going on." She shut off the car and opened the door. "Come on, I need to change into something warmer." She got out into the still falling snow and closed the door, then trudged around the back of the car and peered in the passenger side window. Kerry was still sitting there with a stunned look on her face. It almost made Dar smile. She opened Kerry's door and gave her an inquiring look. "Coming?"

Kerry finally turned and reached for the doorframe to pull herself up. "Dar—"

"No." Dar touched two fingers to Kerry's lips. "There was no option, I don't regret it, there was no choice to be made. Got it?" She stared seriously at Kerry. "Being here for you was that important for me."

The snow drifted and flakes settled on Kerry's upturned face.

"Was Alastair mad?"

"Livid." Dar pulled Kerry the rest of the way out of the car and closed the door. "But he understands." She wrapped an arm around Kerry as they started towards the hotel. "He knows me."

Kerry thought about that as they walked. "Does he?" The shock of Dar's revelation was still ringing inside her, evoking an alternating mixture of dismay and awe.

A smile crossed Dar's face. "Yes, he does."

THEY HAD A surprise waiting in the hotel room. Dar entered first and switched the light on, then stopped in mid stride causing Kerry to crash into her back. "Whoa."

"Wh...Dar, why did...Oh." Kerry peered out from behind Dar's back and saw the table covered in baskets. "Good grief."

"Yeah." Dar walked to the table and examined the items. There were four in all—two sedate ones that contained subdued flower arrangements, one stocked with a variety of chocolates, and one with other snacks such as crackers and cheese. "Someone worried there weren't any restaurants all the way up here?" She picked up the cards and read them. "Ah."

Kerry peeked. The flowers were from Maria and Mariana, the snacks were from Colleen, and the chocolate... "Your folks certainly know you."

"Me?" Dar glanced at her wryly. "Oh, does that mean you don't want any?"

Kerry's nostrils twitched as Dar removed the cellophane wrap from the chocolate basket, releasing a sweet, delicious scent. "I didn't say that." She plucked at the snack basket. "But I'm going to have some crackers and cheese, too, or I'll be bouncing all over the place."

"Good." Dar selected a truffle and popped it into her mouth. "While you do that, I'm going to put on my damn thermal underwear."

Kerry picked up the bottle of pills and handed it to Dar. "And take this, right?"

"Mm." Dar accepted the bottle, but put it down for a moment as she pulled her sweater off over her head. Or tried to, at any rate, when she unthinkingly used her bad arm. "Shit." She hissed and paused in mid motion.

"Hey!" Kerry dropped her crackers and jumped to her side. She eased the fabric off over Dar's head and carefully lowered her arm. "Oh, damn, Dar!" She was shocked at the new mottled bruising that covered Dar's shoulder joint and spread across the front of her chest. "Sit down."

"Why? Is that supposed to take strain off my arm?" Dar did as she was told and sat quietly on the bed as Kerry examined her. "Just a bruise, Ker."

"It wasn't like that when I left Florida yesterday," Kerry said. "You did this last night."

"Yeah, so?" Dar shrugged.

Kerry seriously studied her, then she unclipped her cell phone, opened it, and dialed a number. "Hey, Ang."

"Kerry, where did you disappear to?" Angie asked. "You were behind us, then you vanished. I thought you got lost."

"In my own hometown? Not likely," Kerry replied. "We stopped by the hotel for Dar's medication."

The phone juggled. "Hang on." There was a moment of silence, then Angie's voice came back, clearer and with less noise in the background. "Maybe it's for the best. This place is a circus, Ker. The press is here, and all of dad's staff, and it's a madhouse."

"Ugh," Kerry murmured.

"And," Angie hesitated, "with everything that's going on, I think the general feeling is it might be better if you didn't come over here." She seemed almost embarrassed. "With all the press here, they don't want any controversy."

Kerry felt a burn of anger. "You mean, it'd be okay if I came, but not if I brought Dar with me."

"Something like that, yeah." Angie sighed. "That's not from mom, but there're so many—"

"Fuck them." Kerry enunciated the words carefully.

Angie was prudently silent.

"But you know what? I'm glad," Kerry went on. "Because I was just calling to tell you we weren't coming over anyway. Dar hurt her arm again last night picking my butt up, and I'm going to spend the evening relaxing, eating very good chocolate, and taking care of her."

Angie still remained silent. Dar's eyebrows crawled up into her hairline and lodged there.

Kerry smiled mirthlessly. "So, if the press asks, you can tell them that."

"Lucky stiff," Angie finally muttered. "Mom wants you to come by in the morning, is that okay?"

"I'll think about it," Kerry answered. "Bye." She closed the phone with a snap. "Sons of bitches."

Dar circled the back of Kerry's thigh with one hand and squeezed gently. "Easy." She could see the anger flaring along the lines of Kerry's body. "Everyone's under a lot of pressure."

"Bullshit," Kerry snapped back. "Most of those people couldn't give a damn about my father. They're just polishing up the old image, so their memoirs will..." She paused, visibly upset. "Can't have the family disgrace messing that up, can we?"

Dar pulled her a little closer and nuzzled her side in wordless comfort. Kerry leaned forward and laced her fingers through Dar's hair, then touched her head to Dar's and exhaled. "Bastards," she whispered.

Dar nodded. "Uh huh."

They stayed like that for a few minutes, rocking gently back and forth, then Kerry released a held breath and straightened a little. "On the other hand," she pushed Dar's hair out of her eyes, "I'm tired, I'm hungry, and spending the night alone with you is sounding more superfantastic by the second."

Dar issued her a rakish smile. "I was hoping you'd arrive at that conclusion. I kinda liked the idea of being pampered and fed chocolate all night." She took Kerry's hand and relaxed back onto the pillow, giving her an inviting little tug. "C'mere."

Kerry crawled over her and laid down at her side, never taking her eyes from Dar's. She released Dar's hand and stroked Dar's soft bare skin with light, curious fingers. "This is that silver lining thing, isn't it?"

"Mmhm," Dar agreed, brushing Kerry's cheek and watching her fair lashes flutter closed at the touch. "Don't let them get to you, Kerry. When people are hurting or confused, it's easy for them to lash out at things they don't understand."

Kerry lowered her head to Dar's shoulder and snuggled close, wrapping an arm around her stomach. "I know that. It just makes me so angry that all they think about is themselves." A sigh warmed Dar's skin. "It's so unfair."

"Life is, sometimes," Dar replied. "You just do the best you can with it." She thoughtfully regarded the ceiling. "Like now, for instance. We could be at your family's house."

"Mm," Kerry murmured.

"With one third of the crowd glaring at us, another third of them making veiled but snarky comments, and the remaining third being sweet and sympathetic."

"Uh."

"Having," Dar thought a moment, "pate canapés and white wine?"

Kerry nodded. "Probably."

"So, instead, we're here in this nice hotel room, with a lot of chocolate, a big room service menu, and a heart shaped hot tub."

Kerry had to smile at that. "You've got a good point there." She relaxed a little, her fingers absently tracing patterns over Dar's belly. "You gave up a lot today, Dar. Standing by me."

"Nah," Dar replied. "Besides, that's what friends do, isn't it?

Stand by each other?"

Kerry hitched up on an elbow and gazed seriously at her lover. "I mean it, Dar." Her brow creased. "That meant a lot to me; don't minimize it."

Dar met her eyes and a smile tugged on the edges of her lips. "It felt good." She twirled a lock of Kerry's hair between her fingers. "Now, what was that about feeding me chocolate?"

"Did anyone ever tell you that you have a one track mind?" Kerry gave in with a smile. "All right, you beautiful hedonist. Lie still, and I'll get the chocolate and a menu." She leaned over, kissed Dar on the lips, and licked them lightly. "Mm...speaking of chocolate." She felt Dar's hands ease her sweater up and slide beneath it. Part of her knew Dar was trying to keep her mind off the terrors of the day, but the larger part of her decided it didn't care, and that maybe it wasn't such a bad idea.

She didn't really want to think about the hospital. She didn't really want to think about her family and the raw hatred that had battered her all morning. She didn't really want to see the slack, blank look on her father's face, or the lines on the monitor flattening to even.

For right now, she decided, she'd focus hard on the beautiful body poised just under hers, and the touch that was making her guts burn, and the soft, enticing growls chasing the shadows far away.

"HOW'S THAT?" KERRY adjusted the heating pad so that it covered more of Dar's shoulder, and gave it a solicitous pat.

Dar eyed her arm. "Kerry, you know it's—"

"Ah ah ah!" Kerry put a fingertip on Dar's lips. "Do you have that other medicine with you?" She could see Dar debating whether to answer. "Don't make me go through your bag, Paladar K. Roberts."

"Heh." Dar chuckled sheepishly. "Yes, in the right pocket. Two bottles...but..."

Kerry got up, rummaged in the specified pouch, and came up with the plastic bottles. "Listen, tiger, I know you hate taking this stuff, but you'd make me feel better if you did."

Dar sighed. "It makes me space out. Just the pain medication's bad enough, Kerry. I don't need that other stuff."

Kerry perched on the bed and pushed a lock of pale hair back behind one ear. She was dressed in her Tweety T-shirt and nothing else. "You sound like such a kid when you talk like that."

Dar pouted.

"Aw." Kerry grinned, biting her lower lip a little. "That's just so adorable, I wish I had a digital camera."

The pout disappeared and an eyebrow lifted. "For what? Where would you be putting that picture, Ms. Kerrison?"

"On my desktop." Kerry relaxed onto her side, crossed her ankles, and wiggled her feet. "Right next to the little shot I have of you in your swimsuit."

Dar blinked. "In my...swim...Oh, you don't really."

"Mmhm. I sure do." Green eyes peered innocently back at her. "The really nice one, that black, semi see-through number." She grinned. "The picture I took on vacation."

Dar just stared at her. "That's on your desktop?" Her voice cracked on the last word and she blushed. "Kerry, that's almost—"

"Oh yes, absolutely." Kerry very much enjoyed Dar's discomfiture. "And let me tell you, looking at that when I come back from some of those afternoon marketing meetings...ahhh." She waggled her eyebrows at her lover, who looked mildly alarmed. "Dar, c'mon. You're an incredibly sexy looking woman and you know it, so stop looking at me like I'm nuts."

"W...it's not that. I'm just...it's..." Dar spluttered to a halt.

Kerry held back a smirk. "Do you have any pictures of me on your PC?"

It was amazing how quickly a grown woman could manufacture the impression of a small child caught with its fist in a nice, big cookie jar. "Um..." Dar scratched her ear and tugged on the lobe a bit. "Yeah."

"Oh yeah? Which ones?" Kerry squirmed a little closer. "The one on the boat?"

"No," Dar drawled. "Not that one."

Kerry considered for a moment. "Oh...not that one you took when we were parasailing."

"Nope." Dar studied the ceiling, aware of the ridiculous blush that was coloring her skin. "I don't think you've seen these."

Both of Kerry's eyebrows lifted. "I haven't?" She crawled even closer, until she was almost nose to breast with Dar. "Which pictures are they, then?"

Dar evaluated her tactical situation; it wasn't pretty. At least she'd gotten Kerry's mind off those damn drugs. "A couple I took out at the island the last time we were out there. After we went diving."

"Oh." Kerry frowned, trying to remember the outing. It hadn't been that long ago, after all, and they'd been diving for hours, then...Her mist green eyes opened wide, and she lifted her head to peer at her lover. "Dar, wait a minute." Baby blues blinked at her with devastating innocence.

"Hm?" She watched as Kerry blushed, the color making her fair brows stand out vividly. "I got some gorgeous shots."

Kerry covered her eyes. "You're not telling me you took pictures when I was sunbathing in the buff, are you?"

Dar ran a finger across Kerry's scarlet cheek. "All that beautiful orange sunset and you. Incredible."

"Oh, my God," Kerry murmured weakly. "Please don't tell me you have that on your desktop where Maria can see it."

"Why not? She appreciates fine art when she sees it." Dar almost burst into laughter when Kerry removed her hand and gazed at her in total shock. "Relax. They're not on my desktop." She gently patted Kerry's cheek. "I would never do that to you, honey."

Kerry exhaled, rubbing her face with one hand. "Guess that teaches me to start a teasing war with you, huh?" She gave Dar a rueful look. "Here I thought I was doing so well." She rolled over and got up, then trudged over to the table and poured herself a glass from the pitcher of iced tea. "Whoo."

Dar watched her fondly. The thin, almost threadbare cotton of Kerry's T-shirt clung to her body, outlining it and emphasizing her athletic build. "Wanna see the pictures?"

Kerry almost spat a mouthful of iced tea across the room. "Pft." She managed to swallow. "You have them here?"

"Sure." Dar chuckled softly. "I said I didn't have them on my desktop." She pointed. "They're on the laptop."

Kerry looked at her, then at the computer, then back at her. She firmly turned her back on the machine, returned to the bed, then leapt lightly over Dar and curled up at her side. "No thanks, sweetie." She rolled onto her back, exhaled, and let her body go limp. "The room service we ordered should be here soon. What do you want to do afterwards?"

Dar cupped a hand around one of Kerry's neatly outlined breasts. "Have dessert."

Kerry turned her head and met Dar's eyes. "Dar?"

"Mm?" A lazy smile appeared.

"If you're trying to distract me," Kerry took in an unsteady breath, her body already reacting to the sensual touch, "it's working."

"Good." Dar rolled stiffly onto her side and continued her exploration. "My vote is for dinner, dessert, and a nice soak in that tub." She leaned closer. "'Cause that's gonna make me feel a *lot* better than those damn drugs."

One green eye opened and regarded her suspiciously. "Is this a plot?"

Dar eased the thin cotton fabric up. "Oh yeah."

Kerry half sat up and captured Dar's jaw, then she kissed her with quiet passion. "If that room service guy knocks in the next few minutes, you're in so much trouble."

Dar chuckled deep in her throat.

Chapter
Seven

WELL, KERRY EYED the snow-covered landscape going by, *at least I feel a hell of a lot more relaxed than I did yesterday*. She flexed her hands inside her lined gloves and tightened her grip on the steering wheel, sparing a glance at the passenger side. "Depressing, isn't it?"

Dar was examining the view out the front and side windows. "Um…" It was mostly flat land with dead trees, though the occasional evergreen, dripping with heavy white snow, threw a splotch of color into the mix. "It's definitely sort of," she paused, "bland."

"Yeah. One of the things I noticed first when I moved down to Florida was how damn colorful it is." Kerry pulled off the highway and turned onto the road that would eventually lead to her parents' house. "Sometimes I forget how much it's not like that in the north in winter."

Dar settled back, folding her arms across her chest. "Must be nice in summer, though. And it's kinda pretty, with all that snow and all. Looks like something off a Currier and Ives print."

"I guess," Kerry said. "It can be fun around here. I used to have a good time in winter, sledding down hills and ice skating. And in summer, on the lake." She noted the new buildings on the low horizon. "They're finally getting Starbucks out here. Good grief."

Dar chuckled. "I don't know, Ker. Doesn't seem like a bad place to grow up." She reviewed the passing countryside. "No worse than where I did, at any rate."

"Hm." Kerry watched the once familiar landscape go by. She turned right onto a sloping street, bordered on one side by stately walls, the houses behind them hidden from view. On the other side the road pitched down to a snow covered hillside, giving a view across a small valley of more isolated homes on the far side.

How many times had she turned up this road? Walked up it—from the church, from school…and now it just looked cold and strange to her. Someplace she no longer belonged.

"You definitely fit better in the tropics," Dar commented out of the blue. "You have to wear too much clothing up here."

Kerry gave her a quick glance, then she turned into the opening in the long, brick wall they'd been driving alongside. "It's definitely a whole different world." She pulled up next to a gate and opened her window, allowing a cold, wet draft in. The gate guard bent down to look at her, then almost jerked back in surprise.

"Ms. Kerry!" The older man, dressed in a thick winter parka, smiled. "Been a long time."

A year. Kerry nodded. "Yes, it has, John. How are you?"

"I'm doing great." He leaned closer. "I'm sorry about your father." His eyes flicked briefly to Dar, then back to Kerry. "Terrible thing."

"Thanks." Kerry gave him a small smile. He straightened and opened the gate, and she drove carefully through and continued up the driveway. At the end of it was a circular drive and the imposing, classic outline of her family's home.

A tiny shiver passed over her as she remembered the last time she'd driven down that road, the night she'd revealed her relationship with Dar, the night her father had thrown her into a mental institution.

The night Dar had claimed her, powering her way into the hospital with a ruse so incredible, she still didn't believe they'd had gotten away with it.

That night, when they'd driven back to pick up Kerry's things and she'd had her one, last, furious confrontation with her father and left the house, crossing the line in no uncertain terms to go back home to her new life, her new job, and her new lover.

Kerry pulled up on one side of the circle and put the car into park. Fortunately, there were only two other cars there. She suspected they were Angie and Michael's, and the press seemed to be completely absent. "Well," she looked at Dar, "here we are."

"Let's go then." Dar smiled at her. "Nice to see this place in the daylight this time."

Ah. Kerry got out of the car and shut the door, taking a deep breath of the cold air before she trudged around and joined Dar on the short walk up to the front door. Halfway there, Dar wrapped long fingers around hers. It felt wonderful.

Kerry lifted her shoulders and almost smiled as she used the huge, brass doorknocker. She heard footsteps behind the door, then the lock turned and the portal opened. Her brows lifted. "Hey."

Angie looked profoundly relieved. "Good grief, get in here before you freeze." She pulled Kerry and, by default since their hands were still linked, Dar, into the house and shut the door behind them. "I'm really glad you decided to come over, sis." Her eyes shifted. "Good morning, Dar."

"Morning," Dar replied.

"Seems quiet here today," Kerry ventured. "Where is everyone?"

"It's just us," Angie answered. "Mom, Mike, and me. Everyone else is someplace else, and I for one am damn glad of it." She took Kerry's arm. "C'mon, we've just started breakfast."

Kerry resisted the tug, giving Angie a direct look. "Was that on purpose?"

Angie hesitated. "Ker."

"It's all right. I wasn't looking forward to a screaming match with uncle Al over coffee," Kerry said. "And God knows we don't want the press to know Dar and I are normal people who eat with forks and shave our legs."

Dar's eyebrows lifted. She patted Kerry on the back, but was at a loss for words.

"Kerry, c'mon now, that's not fair," Angela said. "Maybe we wanted a little peace too, you know? It's been really tough around here the last few days."

"Yeah." Kerry pointed towards the dining room. "Whatever. Let's go."

Angie sighed, but she turned and led the way inside, straightening her blouse as she entered the foyer and crossed its marble emptiness.

Dar followed behind the sisters, taking a moment to look around at the interior of the house. She remembered it somewhat differently than it was now, probably due to the circumstances and the late hour. In the daylight, the house was a large, airy, well designed place with vaulted ceilings and a beautiful curved stairway going up to the second story.

They walked through the foyer and under an archway she vaguely remembered, then turned and entered a small dining room with a vaulted skylight that let in the wan winter sun. Seated at the table were Cynthia and Michael, and both looked up as the trio entered.

Dar watched them carefully for a reaction, pleased when she saw welcome and relief. She'd figured that might be the case, but with Kerry's family you never knew, and she had no intention of standing quietly by if it were otherwise. She was rested, her arm was much better, they'd had a great night together, and she was feeling pretty feisty.

"Ah. Kerrison." Cynthia stood and came over to them. "I'm so sorry about yesterday." Michael got up also and went to hug his sister.

"It's okay." Kerry decided to be gracious about it for the moment. "I needed a break last night anyway." She returned Michael's hug and gave her mother a smile. "How are you?"

"As well as you might imagine," Cynthia replied. "Come sit and have something for breakfast." Her eyes drifted up and met Dar's. "And you as well, Dar."

It was a peculiar experience, Dar mused. She followed them back to the table and sat down on a chair she recognized as antique, at a table covered in fine linen, china, and silver service. *For breakfast.* Dar shook her head a little, turning when she sensed a presence at her elbow.

A young woman stood there with a tray. "May I put this down, ma'am?"

Dar nodded, and was presented with a plate of fresh fruit and gently steaming eggs, then the woman put an identical plate in front of Kerry. Dar noticed that Kerry, though giving the woman a quiet thanks, otherwise treated this as a completely natural thing, and it struck her how different this was from their normal lives.

Breakfast at home, such as it was, generally consisted of a glass of something—milk for her, juice for Kerry—and something that would give them energy for running. Usually eaten standing in their kitchen, while the sky outside the window turned from inky black to the pearly pink of dawn.

Hm. Dar had known Kerry's family was well off. She'd known, at an intellectual level, that her lover had been brought up with the proverbial silver spoon in her mouth, and little things like her impeccable manners sometimes reminded her of that. But it was strange to actually see her fitting in here. She listened to the talk, slightly strained and very general, everyone staying away from any controversy, and wondered if that was normal, or just put in place because of the uncomfortable things between them all.

"Excuse me, Dar?"

Shaken out of her musings, Dar looked up and met Cynthia Stuarts' eyes. "Yes?"

"Kerrison told Angela you weren't well last night?"

Huh? I was g... "Oh." Dar cleared her throat slightly. "It's not really anything. I managed to do a little damage to my shoulder recently, and it was giving me some trouble. Maybe the weather." She inhaled in surprise as Kerry poked her under the table, and she shot her partner a look. One of Kerry's eyebrows was raised and a half smile tugged at her lips. "What?"

Cynthia gazed at both of them with a mildly puzzled look. "Well, I certainly hope you feel better today, after resting."

"Resting?" Dar asked with a slight drawl, seeing Kerry's eyes widen out of the corner of her own. "Oh, right. I feel much better today, thanks." There was an awkward little silence, which Dar used to ingest a forkful of eggs in peace.

"So, what project are you working on now, Ker?" Michael asked, neatly changing the subject.

"Well," Kerry took a sip of juice, "I just finished reorganizing one of our operational divisions, and we added two brand new support groups in the western US. My life's been a lot nicer since Dar put our new network online."

"Everyone's has," Dar said wryly. "Even mine."

"How does it help?" Angie asked. "I remember reading in the paper about your company doing something that revolutionized something or other, and it was very fast."

Kerry took a biscuit, sliced it open, and neatly added a pat of butter to it. It gave her a moment to try and come up with a way to explain to her family what she did. *How do you describe high speed, high bandwidth WAN networking to someone who never even turned on a computer?* "Well..."

"A network is like a highway," Dar said. "If you have a few cars on it, everyone goes fast. Add more cars, everyone starts to go slower. Find a spot in the road where it narrows, and everyone bottlenecks and comes to a standstill."

"All right." Cynthia nodded. "That seems clear."

"We had mostly two and three lane highways. I made them forty lanes across," Dar said. "And took out the speed limit."

"And made everyone buy Ferraris," Kerry murmured.

"Ah!" Cynthia looked pleased. "Yes, that's very clear. I understand."

"Yeah, so do I," Michael added. "Outrageous. Can you explain what a chip is next?"

Dar looked him right in the eye. "You sure you can handle it? It involves a lot of silicon."

Michael gazed uncertainly at her, not sure if she were joking or not. "Does that hurt?"

"Only if you get some up your wazoo," Kerry replied dryly. "So, what have you been up to, Mike?" She neatly cut off a square of biscuit and collected some eggs with it on her fork. It was stressful and uncomfortable, and Kerry realized they were all putting a conspicuous gloss over a lot of things. *But haven't we always? Why should this be any different from any other time?*

"We've made some plans," Cynthia murmured into the small silence that had fallen. "The service is scheduled for three tomorrow." She paused and took a breath. "I realize it's quite short notice, but the staff seems to feel—"

"Mother," Kerry put her fork down, "who cares what the staff thinks? Is that what you want to do?"

Cynthia shifted uncomfortably. "Well, dear, it's really not..." She stopped. "There are quite good reasons for it, you see—"

"Bullshit." Kerry found herself getting really angry. She stood up. "First they have the balls to tell me to stay away, then they tell you when you should bury daddy? Where are these assholes? I want to talk to them, right now."

Dar blinked in mild alarm, put out a hand, and laid it carefully on Kerry's back. She could feel the tension vibrating through her lover. "Hey," she murmured. "Easy."

"Kerrison!" Cynthia protested. "Come now, your language. They're doing what they think is best for all of us; surely you understand?"

"No." All of a sudden it became too much for Kerry. "I don't understand. It's never what's best for us, only what's best for them. Always." She ducked out from behind her chair and just started walking, needing space and air, an overwhelming fury buzzing around her head like a swarm of bees. She got through the dining room door and kept moving, one hand grabbing the door edge and slamming it shut behind her. The solid crash of wood against wood gave her primal satisfaction.

THERE WAS A definite silence after she left. Dar felt all eyes turn to her and she took a breath before she looked back from the now closed door to her lover's family. "Um..." She set her silverware aside.

"Well," Cynthia Stuart put her napkin down, "I must go speak with her."

"No." Dar stood. "I'll take care of this," she said with quiet firmness, then put her own napkin down and followed Kerry without waiting for them to respond.

The door closed again behind her. "This is outrageous," Cynthia said.

"What did you think was going to happen?" Angela asked. "I told you she's still really ticked off, mother. Did you really think she'd just waltz back in here and everything would be peaches and cream again?"

"She could make an effort. We are her family," Cynthia replied.

"Maybe it would help if she hadn't been tossed in the looney bin last time she was here," Mike replied bluntly. "Or if you hadn't told her she wasn't welcome here last night because she's gay. That would put me in a bad mood, too."

"She wasn't coming anyway," Angie muttered.

"We've discussed that." Cynthia looked annoyed. "You know your father was just doing what he considered best for Kerry."

"Bull." Angie slapped her cup down. "I'm so tired of hearing that. He had no interest in what was best for Kerry, and you know it. All he cared about was not letting the press find out he had a gay daughter."

"Angie." Cynthia gave her an exasperated look. "Please."

"It's true." Now Angela was upset. "I've had to listen to two days of everyone saying what a freaking saint he was, and I'm sick of it." She took a breath. "No one here's grieving, mother; we all know that. He never cared about any of us, just himself."

Cynthia sighed. "He was a very forceful man."

"And Kerry was the only one of us who had the guts to stand up to him," Mike said. "Now she's paying for that big time, when all these freaking people should be patting her on the back and saying 'good job.' If they treat her like that again this afternoon, I'm going to kick their asses out of the house."

"Michael!" Cynthia stared at him.

"I don't care!" Mike stood up. "I don't give a shit about any of them. Kerry's the person I care about. She's my sister, and I'll be God damned if those two-faced, lying bastard uncles are going to give her grief. And if I can't do it by myself, I'll get Dar to help me. I bet she could kick their asses sound asleep." He pushed his plate back and stepped away from the table. "I'm outta here."

"Me, too," Angie said. "And if any of those weasel aides say a word, I'm going to slap them." She followed Michael out the door, leaving her mother in pristine silence.

Cynthia released a breath and sat back. The door opened and a tall, slim man, carrying an appointment book and a pen, entered. He took a seat next to her.

"We've got everything scheduled, Mrs. Stuart. Here are the details." He offered her a sheet. "Now, the press will be by later, as the more important guests arrive. We need to discuss how you want to present the family." He gave her a little, sympathetic smile. "I know we've got some work to do on that."

Cynthia looked the paper, then looked at him. She placed a fingertip on the page and moved it back to him. "I'm afraid you've got it a bit wrong. My family's perfectly capable of presenting itself, and you would do well to remain uninvolved."

He looked a little surprised, but regrouped quickly. "There are certain things—"

"No, there are not," Cynthia said with calm finality. "If the press wishes to come and make a spectacle of itself, it may do so. My children are free to speak to them or not, as they please. I will not tolerate any interference with any of them."

"But—"

"Henderson, have I not made myself clear?"

"Mrs. Stuart, you know we're only working to present a united front and a positive image of your late husband in these trying times—"

"Nonsense," Cynthia said. "Please let's stop using euphemisms. You are anxious about the press asking after Kerrison, is that right?"

He hesitated briefly. "The more sensational papers, yes. It really doesn't conform to the image we're trying to build, you see, and—"

"Mr. Henderson," Cynthia sharply tapped him on the arm, "my husband is dead. He no longer cares about his image. It's difficult for Kerrison to be here, and I simply will not allow you to make it more trying for her. Is that clear?"

"Mrs. Stuart—"

"If you were even slightly intelligent," Cynthia finally lost her patience, "you would realize that antagonizing my eldest daughter is an extremely stupid idea." She paused. "Her father learned that lesson far too late." She stood up. "If we're finished, I must go and change. Goodbye."

Henderson was left alone in the large dining room, its walls still ringing with Cynthia's last words.

DAR PROWLED THROUGH the uneasily still house, following a logical guess as to where Kerry had run off to. Kerry's unusual explosion of temper had surprised Dar, but she could tell the tension was ratcheting Kerry up to a point where almost anything could happen.

Ahead of her, she spotted daylight, and she turned into a small corridor and found herself inside a solarium. Its thick, insulated glass panes hazed the scene outside, but it provided natural light and she had a feeling if she poked around inside, she'd find what she was looking for.

A soft creak signaled her, and Dar walked quietly between two rows of precisely trimmed flowers. Near the back of the solarium was a two person, padded swing, only half occupied. *Ah.* Kerry's back was to her, but as Dar approached, the blond head turned in her direction.

They regarded each other for a moment, then Dar slipped into the seat next to Kerry and simply took her hand, and laced their fingers together in silent sympathy. They sat quietly, rocking a little on the bench as they watched the snow come down outside.

Finally, Kerry took a deep breath, pulled Dar's hand up, and tucked it against her heart before she spoke. "If I ask you something, will you promise not to think I'm a coward?"

"Sure," Dar answered. "When do you want to leave?"

Kerry leaned against Dar's shoulder. "I don't want to, but I think I have to, Dar. If I stay through this, it's only going to get worse." Dar's fingers tightened around hers. "I can't deal with it, and I don't want you to have to."

Dar understood, possibly far more than Kerry imagined. "I remember being at Daddy's funeral service. A service, not a burial, because they told us there wasn't anything left to bury."

Kerry remained very quiet.

"And I hated everyone." Dar had to stop for a minute, as a vivid memory of that cold day sharpened in her mind's eye. "All these people getting up and talking about him...they had no clue who he was, or how he'd lived his life." She slowly shook her head. "They wouldn't let me talk."

Kerry just closed her eyes.

"So, I ran," Dar said. "I ran out of there and kept running, all the way home."

"From Connecticut?" Kerry asked, very softly.

"Yeah," Dar replied, just as quietly. "I hitched back...walked...took a bus once in a while. Gave me time to get it out of my system."

"The anger?"

Dar shook her head. "The grief."

Kerry regarded the frosted glass in front of her. "You know something, Dar?"

"Mm?" Dar slipped her arm around Kerry's back.

"I wish I'd had a father worth that kind of feeling." Kerry's eyes closed as Dar encircled her arms around her and pulled her close.

Dar rested her cheek against Kerry's hair. "You do."

That's true, Kerry acknowledged. After knowing them less than a year, she was closer to Andrew and Ceci than she had ever been to her own parents after most of her lifetime. She loved Dar's parents deeply, just as she did their daughter, and she was grateful beyond words that she had them in her life.

Is it even worth staying for the service tonight? "Let's go home," she whispered. "I can't change how they feel about me, Dar. I'm going to leave them to their hatred and stupidity."

"All right." Dar hugged her. "Home sounds good to me, too."

DAR FOLLOWED KERRY out of the solarium and across the

quiet, spacious parlor. "It's a nice place." she glanced around. "Plenty of room."

Kerry slowed her steps and turned around. "I guess it is. I never really thought of it that way, though, because so much of the house was pretty much off limits to us as kids." She paused, then walked to a painting on the wall and looked at it, and touched the canvas with a curious finger. "We used to get punished for grabbing anything."

Dar had wandered next to Kerry. "Punished?"

"Yelled at," Kerry clarified. 'Sent to our rooms, mostly." She eyed the painting. "I only got hit once that I remember, and all because of this damn stupid thing."

"Really?" Dar examined the painting. "What's there to this that's worth being hit for?"

"It's a Renoir." Kerry indicated the signature. "And I always thought it was way too dull and ugly, so one day I took my box of one hundred and twenty-eight Crayola crayons and changed that."

Dar bit the inside of her lip, but a tiny snort of laughter escaped anyway. "Oh boy."

"Mm. Yeah, it wasn't pretty." Kerry smiled faintly. "I had to drag one of those antique chairs over here and climb all over it to get all the squares filled in. Did I mention it had been raining outside, and I was covered in mud?"

"Oh, Kerry." Dar covered her face with one hand. "You want to know something really funny?"

"What? Did you do the same thing when you were a kid?" Kerry turned and grinned at her. "Don't tell me that."

"No." Dar shook her head. "If I'd shown the least bit of interest in drawing, my mother would have thrown a party. But on the way up here, I was thinking of how much I wish we'd met sooner." She rested a hand on Kerry's shoulder. "I would have liked a friend like you."

Kerry spared a moment to remember the increasingly lonely years after her childhood, a life full of acquaintances and parties, activity and publicity, but very few real friends. She would have loved to have known Dar then, but she also knew the sad reality of the fact that her parents would have prevented their friendship. "I'm glad we didn't." She covered Dar's hand with her own to soften the words. "I wasn't ready to know you back then." Dar cocked her head in mild consternation. "I still believed in my parents, and they..." Kerry glanced away, then back up at Dar's face. "I'm glad I met you when I did."

Dar's lips twitched into a smile. "Do you really think I'd have let your parents stand between me and a friend, even at that age?

We would have been tabloid city: 'Wild child corrupts senator's daughter—film at eleven.'"

Kerry had to smile, both at the sentiment and the mental picture.

"Besides," Dar pointed at the picture, "anyone with the will to color by number a Renoir would have been right up my alley." She surprised Kerry with a gentle kiss. "My mother would have adopted you in the vain hope you'd rub off on me."

Kerry drew in a breath, then released it as a certain tension eased out of her. She put her arms around Dar and simply hugged her as hard as she could. Then she released her. "C'mon. Let me give you the ten cent tour then. I don't know if I'll have another chance." She held out a hand, which Dar took, then led the way through the labyrinth of rooms.

The first place they went was the library. Kerry pushed the door open and was hit with the inimitable smell of a critical mass of books. The room had traditionally dark paneling and a thick wool rug, with heavy leather and brass bound furniture and floor to ceiling shelves of books on all four walls.

"This was a favorite spot," Kerry said, as Dar roamed around the room and studied the books. "Not so much for the subject matters—I brought my own books in here—but it was always a nice, quiet place to hide in." She walked to a chair near the corner and settled into it. "Seems a lot smaller now."

Dar walked to the chair and leaned on it. "I also had a spot I used to disappear with a book into. Wasn't as cushy as this, but I know what you mean."

Kerry nodded. "Your dad's a big reader. Was that really *Wuthering Heights* on his workbench the other day?"

"Mmhm," Dar murmured.

"Incredible." Kerry got up and tugged Dar after her. "One of the good things about all these doors is that you could always escape out one way if anyone official or anything was coming in the other way." They walked down one hallway and turned into another. "Here's another favorite spot." She pushed open a swinging door and peeked into the kitchen.

Dar poked her head in also, to see a large, well laid out room with commercial quality cooking equipment. A tall, black woman entered from the other side, then stopped in surprise at seeing two faces looking back at her.

"Ms. Kerry? Is that you?" the woman asked, setting down a bundle of clothes she'd been carrying. "C'mon in here!"

Kerry eased the door open and entered. "Hello, Betsy. Yes, it is." She walked over and gave the woman a hug. "Been a while, huh?" *A year, to be exact.* "You look great."

Betsy smiled. "Honey, so do you." She looked curiously at Dar. "This your friend?"

It didn't even feel strange, which, in and of itself, was very odd. "This is my partner, Dar." Kerry smiled. "Dar Roberts. Dar, this is Betsy Stonewright. She's been a part of the staff here since before I was born."

"Now, don't you be revealing how old I am, Ms. Kerry." Betsy shook a finger at her, then extended a hand to Dar. "You take your horns off before you come in here, Ms. Dar?" She had a mischievous twinkle in her eyes. "'Cause I heard you had a nice pair of them."

Dar chuckled, took her hand, and returned the strong grip. "Yeah. I left them with the tail and the pitchfork back at the hotel." She ruffled Kerry's hair. "She's got a little baby pair, too."

Betsy snorted. "Honey, I've seen hers, and they ain't little. I could tell you some stories about how this little angel used to turn this place upside down."

Kerry blinked innocently. "Who, me?" She pointed at her own chest, then smiled. "I was just telling Dar about my artistic assault on Renoir."

"Lordy, that was some day." Betsy shook her head, then sobered as she took Kerry's hand. "Kerry, I'm sorry about your daddy. I know you and him didn't get on, but still and all..."

"Thanks." Kerry accepted the words with quiet grace. "Well, listen, we don't want to disrupt anything; I was just showing Dar around. Is Mary here?"

"She'll be back shortly. Hold on now." Betsy ducked into the large walk-in refrigerator on one side of the kitchen, then reappeared with two small cups. "Here you go." She handed one to Kerry and offered the other to Dar. "Unless you done decided you don't like chocolate any more."

"Not hardly." Kerry accepted the treat with a smile. "I still have dreams about your mousse cups, Betsy. Thank you." She slipped her other arm around Dar and leaned against her. "Dar likes chocolate, too."

"A little. Thanks." Dar draped an arm over Kerry's shoulders. "Where to next?"

"Wanna see my nursery?" Kerry asked. "I think there might still be chuck-up stains somewhere."

"Lead on." Dar winked at Betsy. They left the kitchen, leaving the cook behind, shaking her head and chuckling.

"Lord." Betsy heard the sound of the back door opening. "That you, Mary?" She turned to see a short, well muffled woman with ginger white hair and gray eyes enter.

"Yes, ma'am, and who else would it be?" Mary took her coat

off. "Did I miss something?"

Betsy gave her a smug grin. "You most certainly did, woman." She crossed her arms. "You just missed meeting that infamous Dar Roberts."

"No!" Mary looked devastated. "You're having me on."

"I am not. She was just standing right here in this kitchen," Betsy said. "And, child, let me tell you, there was a lot to see. I always did say that Ms. Kerry had a good eye, and sister, oh, did she pick a nice one."

Mary chuckled. "Only one in this whole damn family with a lick of sense and a passel of taste."

THEY ENDED THEIR tour in the large foyer, standing at the foot of the large, curved stairway that led up to the bedrooms on the second floor. Dar had gotten the impression that the place was a beautiful, certainly impressive home with absolutely no sense of its occupants' personalities.

Now, Dar was honest with herself, *one could really say the same about the condo, right?* Her brows creased as she considered that, letting Kerry ramble on about the architecture. Her thoughts ran over the changes in her own home over the last year, and she had to sheepishly admit that her supposition was no longer valid.

How had she let Kerry convince her to have those damn doodlings framed? *Anyway,* Dar dismissed the thought, *this place has even less personality. Kerry's old apartment held far more.*

"Excuse me." A male voice caught their attention, and they turned to see a tall, slim man standing nearby, his hands folded primly in front of him.

"Yes?" Kerry replied warily. "Can I do something for you?"

The man approached. "I'm Tak Henderson. I'm part of the senatorial staff."

Dar bit her tongue to prevent ill thought out words from emerging. The man's smug attitude made her nape hairs bristle, and she moved instinctively closer to Kerry.

"Yes?" Kerry repeated.

"Ms. Stuart, I can appreciate this is a difficult time. It's hard for all of us," Henderson said. "I'm sure you don't want to make it harder than it has to be."

Kerry's green eyes narrowed. "Excuse me?"

"Listen." He lowered his voice. "I know this hasn't been very pleasant. I'm sorry you've had such a rough time of it, but is there any real reason to keep it going?"

Kerry's features settled into a cool mask. "You're suggesting I leave?"

"Wouldn't it be better?" Henderson asked evenly. "C'mon, Ms. Stuart, no one needs the trouble you've had to go through."

It was exactly what Kerry had been thinking. She was aware of Dar's silent presence at her side, lending a solid, tangible support just an extended hand away. Dar would be glad to go home. She would be glad. She wanted so badly to smell the salt tang in the air on their porch and feel Chino's warm welcome. If she closed her eyes, she could imagine herself there—snuggled up with Dar on the couch, a bowl of Thai chicken between them and glasses of chilled plum wine just within reach.

Kerry sighed. There was so much good about her life. She had a nice place to live, a good job, loving friends, a pretty dog, and a drop dead gorgeous partner who was inexplicably crazy about her. Maybe this dweeb was right, and her choice had been the right one. "That's true." She exhaled. "It's been a bitch."

Henderson seemed to sense his advantage, and he smiled. "I think you'd feel a lot better being out of it."

Kerry studied him. "You're right, I would." She made a decision and hoped her beloved partner wasn't going to wring her neck for it. "But, unfortunately for both of us, I'm not going anywhere, so you might as well take your clipboard out of your ass and find something useful to do."

Henderson got caught completely flat footed. He stared at Kerry with a slightly hanging jaw for a few seconds, then collected himself. "Now just wait a—"

Dar slipped in front of Kerry and closed in on Henderson, who backed up a step in reflex. "Henderson, you said your name was?" she asked in her silky, dangerous, boardroom voice.

"Yes."

"All right, Mr. Henderson," Dar said. "Let me tell you something. I've had it about up to here," Dar lifted a hand to her forehead, "with bullshit attitudes. If you don't leave right now, and keep clear of Kerry until she decides to go elsewhere, I'm going to call up every major news agency and spend a half hour telling them just what a bunch of skunks live up here in the woods of Saugatuck." She paused. "Got me?"

His whole face twitched. "I don't know that they—"

"Oh yes, they would," Dar said. "And if that's not enough, I'll call the tabloids and give 'em good shots of me and Kerry kissing on the doorstep out there. How 'bout that?"

That shut him up.

"I thought so." Dar pointed to the door. "Move it."

Surprisingly, Henderson did just that. He walked right past them into what was formerly the senator's study and closed the door. Dar considered the door, then released a satisfied little grunt. "So, we're sticking around, huh?"

Kerry sighed. "Are you going to kill me?"

Dar affectionately ruffled her hair. "Nah. You can make it up to me by finding me more two bit, half witted, stuffed socks I can practice my intimidation skills on." She chuckled softly. "I almost forgot how much I enjoy doing that."

"All right." Kerry took her hand and pulled. "C'mon. Let me show you one last place."

"Your bedroom? I've seen it," Dar teased.

Kerry smiled privately. "No, the attic."

"YOU THINK THE governor's really going to do it?" Mike asked, as they reached the room Angie had been staying in and sat down on the bed. "Name mom to take dad's spot?"

Angie shook her head. "It seems ridiculous. Why should our mother be a senator, just because she was married to our father? She doesn't know the first thing about politics. You know she always made a point of steering clear of all that."

"Yeah, I know," Mike said. "But you have all those scum-buckets who worked for him desperate to keep their jobs. And how else will they do it? Not like they can just dig up an election this time of year."

"Mm." Angie nodded. "That's true. Hope she tells them to go stuff it."

Mike's lips quirked into a smile. "You're in a feisty mood today."

Angie sighed. "I'm just sick of it. That stuff with Kerry pissed me off."

"Me, too." Mike nodded. "I mean, it's not like it's this deep dark secret anymore, so what's the big deal? If the lawyers hadn't been stupid enough to make Kerry just blurt it out on national television, that'd have been one thing, but, Jesus, like, who cares anymore?"

Angie shrugged. "That's what I was thinking, too. It's old news, and besides, it's not like she's done anything really radical, like buying a motorcycle or getting a tattoo."

Mike self-consciously cleared his throat.

Angie looked at him. "Oh, you didn't."

He batted long, dark lashes back at her with devastating inno-cence. "Don't worry. No one'll see it unless they get me really mad, and I show them where they can kiss my ass. Tony and Brad and I went out last week and got pretty plastered. They bet me I didn't have the guts to go through with it, so..."

Angie sighed. "Michael."

"I know, I know." Michael grinned. "I'm a jerk."

"You're hopeless. When are you going to grow up?"

Michael shrugged.

They were quiet for a moment. "You going to keep working for the publicity firm?" Angie asked.

Michael stared at the floor past his clasped hands. "I dunno. I haven't really thought about it. I don't have to now, do I?"

"No." Angie shook her head. "But he's not around to get your butt out of trouble anymore, either."

"I could run away and join the circus."

"Mike."

"You going to tell mamma about Brian?"

Angie fell back onto the bed and gazed up at the ceiling. "Maybe. I might have to. I slipped the other day and left Andy's medical papers out where Richard could see them."

Michael looked at her. "So? He doesn't have Brian's name branded on his ass, does he?"

"No, but my blood type is O and Richard's is A. Andrew's is B, just like Brian's," Angie said with a grimace. "I told Richard they must have made a mistake on the papers."

"Ah," Michael murmured. "Well, if things get real bad, you can reveal that little tidbit, I'll pull down my pants, and Kerry'll come out looking like the Republican in the family."

Angie paused a moment, then burst out laughing. Mike joined in, relieving some of the stress of the situation.

"What's so funny?" Kerry asked, as she paused in the doorway.

"Don't ask." Angie propped up on her elbows. "We were just comparing scandals. What are you two up to?"

Kerry and Dar entered the room. Kerry took a seat on the wooden side chair, and Dar merely lowered herself to the carpet, extended her long legs out, and crossed her ankles. "I was giving Dar the tour. She didn't get to see much last time. What scandal did you get into now, Michael?"

"I got a tattoo," Michael admitted.

Dar snorted and folded her arms over her chest. Kerry just rolled her eyes. "Oh, God, it figures. How drunk were you?"

"Maybe I wasn't," Mike retorted in an injured tone. "Maybe I just decided it was something I wanted to do for personal growth."

Kerry studied him, her fair head cocked, then she smiled. "No way, Mikey. You're the biggest chickenshit I know when it comes to pain. You were either drunk off your butt or unconscious."

Mike scowled, then stuck his tongue out at her. "You're just jealous because you don't have one."

Kerry's green eyes twinkled. "How do you know I don't? You haven't seen all of me in a very long time."

Mike looked at Angie, who looked back at him, then they both looked uncertainly at their older sister.

"I have." Dar came to their rescue. "Every square inch, and she doesn't." Kerry blushed a deep crimson, making her fair eyebrows stand out vividly. Everyone laughed, and even Dar chuckled at her lover's loss of composure.

"Stop that." Kerry covered her face with one hand and rubbed her skin. "Dar, you're so bad."

"Well, you don't," Dar said matter-of-factly.

"Wanna see mine?" Mike asked, to distract everyone.

"No," Dar replied. "Based on what I know about you, I can make a guess where it is, and that window's got a clear shot to the street."

Angie burst out laughing, holding her stomach as she rolled over. Kerry joined in, pointing at Michael's injured expression. "She's right, isn't she?"

Michael stuck his tongue out again. "You guys are such girls."

Dar pulled her collar away from her body and glanced inside her shirt, then nodded. "Guilty."

Now the laughter turned a little giddy, mixing amusement with relief and not a small touch of bittersweet-ness. It finally petered out, and Kerry wiped her eyes with her sleeve and regarded her siblings.

"Sorry I lost it before," she said. "I know you guys were trying to keep things under control."

"That's okay." Angie rolled over onto her side and exhaled. "After you left, we both did too. I'm just so over it. Mike's just so over it. We've had enough of all the political garbage, and we just want our sister back."

It caught Kerry by surprise, and she gave them a stunned look, her face going very still for a long moment. Finally she released a breath and rested her elbows on her knees. "I'd like that too. I never meant to hurt either of you."

Angie got up and went to Kerry's side. Dar remained very still, just watching. "Kerry, you never did. If you did anything, you helped us both realize there was another way to live." She put a hand on Kerry's arm. "You always were our ringleader."

"Yeah." Mike scrambled to them and stepped carefully over Dar's legs. "We love you."

Dar smiled from her spot on the carpet. Kerry's siblings were surpassing her expectations of them, and she was silently delighted at the look of surprised pleasure on her lover's face. She was glad, now, that Kerry had changed her mind, though Dar would have supported her either way. This was better. Kerry needed this.

Now, if she could just figure out a way to prevent the rest of the Stuart family from ruining it.

THEY TROOPED UP to the attic together. Mike opened an unobtrusive door set in a small alcove, and they walked up the heavy wooden stairs.

Dar listened to the door close behind her, and she exhaled, shifting her shoulders nervously before she followed Kerry. The stairwell was very narrow, and her shoulders only just fit in the space. The closeness made her uncomfortable, and she suspected Kerry realized that, because halfway up, a hand reached back and she took it and felt the comfort of Kerry's fingers curling around her own.

That was good, because the ceiling came down rather close to her head, and by the time they climbed up and out into the vaulted attic space, Dar was twitching. It was far more open, though, and she relaxed a little. It was warm—the heat from the house clustered up there despite the chill outdoors, and the eclectic nature of the place quickly drew her interest.

There were steamer trunks pushed against three of the four walls, and stacks of neatly bagged bedding and clothing. Two old rocking chairs sat peacefully in the corner, and there were containers of unknown items scattered around here and there. Dar had no idea why Kerry had wanted to go up there, especially after their footsteps stirred up a mild cloud of dust and they all sneezed, but she was willing to go along with it for a while.

"We stuck them here." Mike dragged one of the larger trunks out into the middle of the floor and knelt in front of it. He dialed the combination lock and threw the top open. "All of Kerry's stuff that Angie and I could find around the house before the thought police came through."

Ah. Dar's ears perked up and she slipped around Kerry to investigate the trunk. "What have we here?"

"Hm. Good question." Kerry scuttled to the trunk and knelt beside it. "Think I can just have this whole trunk shipped?"

Dar pulled out a pair of very old, yellow, obviously well worn footy pajamas that featured a threadbare cotton tail on the back. She grinned at Kerry, who was making a face at them, and pulled out her cell phone, flipped it open, and keyed in the memory. "FedEx? I'd like to schedule a pick-up."

"Oh, my God." Kerry covered her eyes. "Of all the things for you to save."

Angie snickered. "You know something? It was worth it, just to see your face right now."

"Dar, give me that." Kerry reached for the rags, but Dar lifted them up beyond her reach. "Dar!"

"Shh." Dar finished giving the address to the operator, then folded her phone shut. "These are...um," she lowered the pajamas to eye level, "cute." She examined the fluffy tail in the back. "Wanna model them?"

"Augh." Kerry lunged across the trunk and snatched the old things out of Dar's hands. "I haven't worn those since I was six, thanks." She tucked the fabric under her arm for safekeeping, then warily explored the top layer of the trunk. "Oh, God, Angie..." She lifted out a photo album. "I was wondering if you snagged this."

Dar settled at Kerry's side and peered at the book with interest. It was leather bound and age creased. Kerry opened the cover. Angie and Mike also inched closer, and sat cross legged on the floor at her side.

"Oo." Dar laid a long finger on the page. "I like that one."

"Dar." Kerry had to smother a chuckle. "That hoary, old baby-on-the-bearskin picture?" She eyed her naked infant self, sprawled over some fuzzy fabric and staring up at the camera with a look best described as astonished. "Can you believe that's me?"

Dar examined the picture. "Sure. Parts of you haven't change a bfwh." Kerry covered Dar's mouth with her hand as Angie and Michael started cackling.

"You are so dead," Kerry said. "You just wait, Paladar. I'm going to...to...to...yow!" Kerry pulled her hand away from the nibbling teeth and exploring tongue. "Stop that!" She grabbed Dar's tongue and pulled.

Angie almost hurt herself as she rolled onto the floor, narrowly missing the edge of the trunk. "Oh, my God," she gasped. "You guys are too much."

Dar retrieved her appendage and returned it to its normal location. Then she grinned, looking into Kerry's eyes, getting the hoped for tiny crinkle above the bridge of her nose and the faint smirk that meant her lover really wasn't as annoyed as she sounded.

What's gotten into her today? Kerry wondered silently. Being so demonstrative in the company of others was definitely not normal for her usually far more reserved partner. Dar would, on occasion, put a hand on her back or ruffle her hair, but never did she indulge in the kind of extremely personal horseplay she was displaying that morning.

So, since she was, there was a reason. Kerry knew Dar well enough to know that. Very, very seldom did Dar ever change well ingrained patterns without a solid, logical thought path behind it. Kerry glanced at her siblings, who were much more relaxed, and joking with Dar about the rest of the pictures on the page, daring her to guess which of them each one represented.

The realization clicked for Kerry. *Acceptance.* That's why Dar was acting the way she was, because she knew it would make Kerry feel better if her family liked Dar. So Angie and Mike were getting the cute, mischievous side of her lover that very few people ever saw.

Kerry was touched. She lightly scratched the back of Dar's neck and smiled into the inquiring pale blue eyes that turned her way. "Thanks," she mouthed.

Dar winked at her, then went back to studying the photographs. "Hey, there you are on a pony."

"Oh, yes." Kerry nodded, leaning over the book. "Tympani." She put a fingertip on the picture. "What a little bastard he was."

"Remember the time he bit Mike?" Angie said. "Nastiest temper I ever did see on a horse."

"Pony. Maybe he had a short horse complex," Dar added with a straight face. The others snickered and Kerry poked her in outrage. "Friends of ours down south had some horses when I was younger. It was always the little ones that were hell on four hooves."

Angie relaxed onto her side. "Did you ride, Dar?"

"Sure." Dar nodded. "We used to take three or four of them and just go on campouts in the Glades in the winter. Catch our own food, make our own shelter, that kind of thing."

Mike goggled at her. "Really?"

"Really."

"Like, hunting, and all that?" Angie asked.

"Yep," Dar said. "Of course, now that I've learned where the supermarket is, you won't catch me doing that again."

They all laughed. "Yeah." Kerry combed her fingers through Dar's hair. "Dar and I both agree the only camping we'll do is from the inside of an air-conditioned RV."

"With a satellite hookup," Dar amended. "Which reminds me, the sat company called before we left. The system for the cabin's in stock."

"Cabin?" Angie asked.

Kerry told them about the cabin. "It's a little place down in the Keys. Pretty run down, but Dar and I have been doing it all over on the odd weekend. It's cute. And very peaceful. We can pull the boat right up to a dock nearby, and it's getting to be pretty cozy."

"Wow." Angie sighed. "That sounds nice. Richard was talking about us getting a place up by the lake to take the kids, but..." She shook her head. "I don't know."

"The tough part was getting a dedicated pipe in there," Dar said. "The phone company was scratching their heads for weeks over that one. But we got it done." She paused. "You guys'll have to come down and help us christen it."

The stairs creaked and they looked at the door as it opened, revealing Cynthia Stuart framed in the doorway. "My goodness, it's dusty up here. I must have a word with the staff." She continued on into the attic, walking carefully on the wooden floor. "What's going on up here?"

Kerry indicated the album. "I was just showing Dar some of my baby pictures."

"Gracious, how did they end up here?" Cynthia asked in astonishment.

"I put them up here," Angie answered. "When father was looking to burn them."

There was an awkward silence. "I see." Cynthia sighed. "I had thought he'd gotten to them before I had and they were gone. We had a horrible fight about that." She gave her head a slight shake. "At any rate, I came up to find you, Kerrison, because I asked John to bring your and Dar's things upstairs." Cynthia paused, then took a breath. "I thought you might like the corner green room, perhaps."

Kerry opened her mouth to decline the offer, then stopped, as her memory of the house kicked in. She peered up at her mother in honest surprise. "Um...that would be fine; sure. Hang on." Kerry slid a hand down Dar's side and into her front pocket, and pulled out the car keys. "Here. Our bags are in the trunk."

"Excellent." Cynthia had regained her composure, and she took the keys. "Well, perhaps you'll all come down for lunch. The reverend will be here, and several others of the family who asked to come over early."

"Sure." Angie nodded. "Sounds great."

"Okay," Mike agreed.

Cynthia gave them all a slight nod and left, closing the door behind her.

All three siblings stared at one another. "Son of a bitch." Kerry snorted. "Can you believe that?"

"No." Angie shook her head. "No way, nu uh, not on this earth. What drugs are they giving our mother?"

"Wowza," Mike breathed. "Did you score, or what?"

Dar gently cleared her throat. "I think I'm missing something here. Someone want to fill me in?"

Mike crawled closer. "She put you guys in the green room."

"I have uncles and aunts who never got in there," Angie added. "For years."

Dar looked at Kerry. "And?" Her eyebrows rose.

Kerry actually smirked. "It has only one bed. It's where they put the honored, very married members of our family when they visit." She still felt a sense of shock and amazement. "You have no idea what a big deal that is here."

Dar absorbed this unexpected but gratifying news. "Does that mean we have to go out and get her a toaster?"

Kerry laughed, then got lost in wonder for a moment, her world suddenly becoming a topsy-turvey place where anything could, and apparently might, happen. "Yeah. I think it does." She pondered the idea again, then shook her head. "Hey, want to go for a quick walk outside before lunch? I could show you the tree I took a header into once."

"Sure." Dar was glad of a reason to get out of the dry heat, even if it was to get into damp chill instead. "I'll kick it for being so rude."

Kerry closed the album and held out her hand. "You're on." She gave her siblings a look. "You guys, too?"

"We're in." Angie and Michael got up.

"Lead on, sis," Angie added. "We're right behind you."

Chapter
Eight

THE WEATHER, HOWEVER, intervened. The snow came down harder, almost a blizzard, and Dar found herself in the infamous "green room" staring out the window at a white fog so strange looking she found it hard to comprehend. Rain she was used to—Miami's thundershowers were legendary for both their volume of water and speed of descent—but this white facsimile that made no sound was almost...spooky.

Dar turned as Kerry entered and closed the door behind her, then smiled as Kerry joined her at the window. "Hi."

Kerry didn't answer. She just wound her arms around Dar's body and snuggled close, putting her head on Dar's shoulder with a contented little grunt. "Can we sit down for a minute, because I'd really like to talk to you. I've got something I want to say, and I don't want to wait."

Dar blinked in mild alarm. "Sure." She glanced around and pointed at a padded bench. "How about over there?" Kerry led her to it and they sat down. "What's up?"

Kerry, staring very seriously into Dar's eyes, cupped Dar's cheek with her hand. The blue orbs widened slightly in reaction. "I expected the worst today," Kerry said very softly.

"I kind of thought so." Dar stayed still, only the flexing of one hand against the bench betrayed her unease. "I'm glad it turned out better. I know how much your family means to you, Kerry." Her eyes dropped a little. "And I know how it feels not to have one."

Kerry tilted Dar's chin up with her other hand, so their eyes met again. "Do you know what the most wonderful part of today was?"

"Me singing the praises of your butt?"

"No." Kerry did smile, though. "It was watching you lay yourself open to my family because you knew it would make me happy."

Dar blushed a little. "Ah. You caught on. I thought I was

being subtle."

"Mm hm." Kerry kissed her. "Like your usual freight-train-at-full-speed, bad self." She exhaled. "God, I love you."

Dar relaxed, the tension running out of her shoulders and torso, and she tilted her head to return the kiss. Kerry's hand slipped off her cheek and curled around her neck, pulling her closer for a long, sensual moment. Then they separated slightly and gazed into each other's eyes.

"I thought maybe you'd be a little upset with me, teasing you like that," Dar said. "I kind of crossed the line a few times." She touched noses with Kerry, and watched her struggle to focus on her and not cross her eyes. "Though those pictures *were* adorable."

"Thanks." Kerry gave up and closed one eye, then just closed the other one and decided to kiss Dar instead. That didn't require vision. "I personally think I was a goofy, chubby little kid, but if you want to think that's cute," she explored further with her lips, "who am I to argue?"

"You were gorgeous then," Dar brushed a bit of loose hair off Kerry's forehead and traced an eyebrow, "and you certainly are now."

Kerry smiled, obviously charmed, then chuckled softly. "I'm sorry, I'm finding this so ironic."

"What?" Dar traced Kerry's other eyebrow and outlined her eye.

"Where I am, why I'm here, who I'm with." Kerry captured Dar's finger in her teeth and explored the faintly ridged surface with a sensitive tongue. "Hey." She released the digit and gazed at Dar. "How's your arm?"

Dar flexed her shoulder very carefully. "Stiff. Aches a little." It was actually killing her. Even the drugs weren't helping much, and Dar was beginning to worry that she'd actually done some serious additional damage to herself.

"From the weather, probably." Kerry stood and held out a hand. "We're snowed in right now. C'mon and lie down, and I'll put some of that analgesic cream the doctor gave you on it." A faint warning bell went off when Dar acquiesced without argument, and she led her lover to the bed and gently pushed her down onto it.

It was a nice bed, all things considered—a four poster with a stately canopy, fitting the room's vaulted ceiling and wide expanse of mint green carpet to good proportion. The drapes on the window were also green, a slightly darker shade, and the furniture was whitewashed oak, providing a feeling of pleasant lightness to the room.

Kerry went to the divan where their bags were and rooted

around in Dar's until she found the cream. "That's pretty heavy
snow out there, huh?" she commented, more to break the silence
than anything.

"Yeah," Dar said. "I don't think I've ever seen anything like
this before." She paused. "How long does it go on?"

Ah. Good question. Kerry sat down next to Dar's reclining
form. "Well, I heard the staff saying it should stop before dinner,
so that's good." She unbuttoned Dar's shirt, continued down, and
tugged its ends out of her corduroys.

"Didn't think the bruises went down that far," Dar commented.

"They don't," Kerry replied seriously as she peeled back the
fabric. "I just like looking at you with your clothes off." She
watched the muscles just under Dar's skin contract as she laughed
in silence. "Hey, I'm not lying." She jumped a little when Dar's
cell phone went off, but then unclipped it from her waistband and
handed it to her. "Here."

Dar answered it. "Yeah?"

"Ms. Roberts? It's central ops," the voice answered.

Uh oh. "Yeah?" Dar repeated, mouthing the word "ops" to
Kerry, who winced in reflex, then looked around for her own cell
phone.

"I'm sorry to bother you, ma'am, but we have a big problem
and we can't reach Ms. Stuart."

Dar glanced at Kerry, who had found her cell and opened it, a
puzzled look on her face. Then she rolled her eyes, slapped her
forehead in eloquent mime, and keyed the switch that turned it
on. The device immediately beeped as stored messages sounded
alerts.

Dar suppressed a smile, then put a crisp note into her voice.
"She's taking care of some emergency family business. I told her
to turn off her pager. What's the problem?"

"Oh, sorry," the operator said. "There's a huge storm system
going over the Midwest."

Dar peered at the window. "Really?"

"Yes, ma'am. They're having massive power outages in Chicago."

"Again?" Dar murmured. "Hm. So how does that affect us?"
A thought occurred to her. "Oh, Jesus, don't tell me the processing
center's down again."

A sigh preceded the admission, "Yes, ma'am."

"Shit," Dar said. "Get me a contact list."

Kerry had eased down next to Dar and was gently spreading
some of the cream across her shoulder, while listening to the conversation. The Midway Center had been a bone of contention for

them for some months because, as Dar pointed out, it had no back up facilities and the giant UPS systems in the building had previously failed twice.

This close to Christmas, having a major center that cleared credit card purchases down was a bad, bad thing. "Power's down again?" she asked softly, smoothing the thick ointment over the point of Dar's shoulder and massaging the muscles just under the skin.

"Yeah," Dar said. "Stupid bastards. I'm going to have that damn Dick Stark's nuts for lunch."

"Ew." Kerry made a face, then held it for a different reason. "Dar, this is really bruised." She very gently touched the soft skin just above Dar's left breast.

"I know. It hurts like hell," Dar said. "Yeah, okay, you got a pen?" She spoke into the phone, focusing her attention away from the very concerned green eyes studying her. "All right. Have you started getting screaming phone calls from the banks yet?"

Kerry pulled Dar's shirt back over her and covered her injured arm, then she stood and walked to the small desk, picking up her laptop case along the way. She could, she knew, legitimately take the phone from Dar and do what Dar was doing—it was her job, after all, and if she hadn't been so dumb as to turn off her phone, she'd have gotten the call, not her boss. But she also knew that this one was going to come down to a screamfest, because if the weather in Chicago was half as bad as it was here, getting a repair crew out to fix the UPS wasn't going to take her kind of finesse. It was going to take raw, brute, sheer bitch, and when it came to that, Kerry would be the first to admit she was a rank amateur compared to her lover. She'd let Dar get things rolling, and spend her time getting hooked up to the system to see what she could do about shifting processing remotely.

"Don't give me that." Dar's voice rose into a familiar bark. "Get his ass on the phone right now or he'll be paying penalties on this for the next twenty years!"

Hm. Kerry regarded the figure in the bed. Then she went around the other side of the four poster with her laptop, squirmed into place next to Dar, and let her machine rest on her knees. A soft knock on the door made her look up. "Yes?"

The door opened and Angie poked her head in. "Hey."

Kerry motioned with her head. "C'mon in."

Angie walked quietly across the floor and took a seat next to the bed. "What are you guys doing?" she whispered as Dar's voice lifted again.

"Tell that son of a bitch I'm going to send FedEx to pick up his testicles if he doesn't get on this phone!"

Angie's eyes widened.

"Easy, DR," Kerry said in a soothing voice. She achieved her cellular connection and logged into the network. Alerts popped up on her screen like rabid weasels. "All right, all right, I get the picture; shut up already." She slapped a few keys and looked up at Angie. "We're running the world."

Angie's brow creased. "Right here, from the green bedroom?" She watched Kerry type, her eyes flicking over the screen with a startling intensity. This was new. She'd never really seen Kerry do whatever it was that she did, and she listened in shocked consternation as Dar said things to people in terms Angie hadn't even heard in gangster movies. It was sort of interesting, even though she hadn't any idea what either of them was talking about.

"Look..." Dar shifted in aggravation, sat up, and reached over to move the phone from one ear to the other. It was a bad mistake, and she froze in mid-motion, stifling a yelp and biting her tongue as something that felt like a hot coal pressed against the nerves in her shoulder.

"Dar!" Kerry shoved the laptop off her legs, swiveled, and grabbed Dar and eased her back down onto the pillows. Dar's face had gone pale, and she watched the blue eyes blink rapidly, faint twitches of pain making their way across her face. "Easy."

Kerry grabbed the cell phone out of her hand and put it to her ear. "Hello? Who is this?" She waited for an answer. "That's nice. Listen to me. My name is Kerrison Stuart. I know more people in Congress than you have brain cells. If you don't want six government agencies coming down on your doorstep on Monday morning, you'll do whatever it is Ms. Roberts was asking you to do and not say one word." She paused. "Do you understand me?" The sound of panic came through clearly. "Good. If you need me to get the snow removal people to clear your path, just say so." She paused for his reply. "No? Good. We'll be waiting for that repairman. Good bye." She slammed the phone shut and threw it across the room, where it bounced off the wall. "Jesus!"

She turned to see Angie staring at her, both hands covering her mouth. "What?" Then she shifted her eyes to where Dar was lying peacefully, her hands folded over her stomach, regarding her with a look of mixed amusement and pride. "What?" Her frustration surfaced. "You need a doctor!"

"Kerry," Dar laid a hand on her thigh, "would you take it easy?"

"No." Kerry scowled. "Dar, I'm really worried about your arm, and I..." She winced and rubbed her temples. "Shit." The pounding at her temples increased and made her stomach churn. She sucked in her breath at a wave of lightheadedness and was aware of Dar's sudden grip on her. "Damn it."

Angie leaned forward. "Ker, are you okay?"

Kerry exhaled, trying to release the anger that had boiled up unexpectedly. She took a few deep breaths and the dizziness faded, along with the tension along her brow line. "Yeah." She cleared her throat a little. "I'm fine...just aggravated."

Dar rubbed the inside of her wrist. "You sure?"

Kerry looked at her, seeing the honest concern in her eyes. "Yeah. I'm just worried about you, and frustrated." She considered for a moment. "And overreacting, I think." She gave Dar a wry look. "Sorry."

"S'kay." Dar gently squeezed her leg. "You've got a point, I do need to get this looked at. But we're not going anywhere in this weather, and unless an orthopedic surgeon is on your guest list, it's going to have to wait until we get home."

Kerry frowned.

Angie cleared her throat. "If you don't mind me asking, what exactly happened?"

Dar and Kerry exchanged glances. "It's complicated," Kerry finally replied, as the tension that had gripped her slowly ebbed. She pulled her laptop back onto her lap and stared at it. "What was I doing?"

"Finding alernative routes for the western and southern datastreams," Dar replied. "Try Atlanta and Kansas City. They should be able to handle the additional traffic. I think I put in big enough pipes there."

"Yeah," Kerry murmured, taking a deep breath and releasing it.

"Er...I meant to Dar's arm," Angie said delicately. "Not that what you're doing isn't interesting, but I'm seriously clueless when it comes to computers."

Dar watched Kerry work for a moment. "I...um..." Explaining the entire Naval base issue was just too much for her at the moment. "I got hit in the shoulder with a baseball bat."

"Oh," Angie murmured. "Wow, that must have hurt."

"Yeah, it did."

"And then she made it worse by picking me up the other night," Kerry muttered, her eyes focused on her laptop screen. "So there's a certain amount of personal guilt going on here." She smacked a few more keys. "God damn it."

Angie exchanged glances with Dar. "Know what I think?"

"What?" Kerry asked testily.

"I think you need a nap." Angie got up and tossed a pillow at her sister. "And you need to chill out." She left the room and closed the green hued door behind her.

DAR'S EYES CLOSED as she lay quietly waiting for a call back on her cell phone. It was dim and silent in the room, the snow was still falling outside, and Kerry was curled up on her side with her head pillowed on Dar's stomach, fast asleep.

Dar curled her fingers around a lock of Kerry's hair, and wondered if Kerry was half as worried about her as she was about Kerry. She could almost sense the fractures in Kerry's usually sturdy psyche and she only hoped the growing and renewed warmth with her nuclear family helped to heal them. Or else she'd take Kerry home and surround her with as much love and support as it took to do the job.

They'd gotten some of the problem resolved, as much as they could without fixing the broken equipment, and Dar had finally coaxed Kerry into taking one of the pills she carried around for stress headaches. Unfortunately, or perhaps fortunately, the dosage that merely relaxed Dar had knocked her shorter, lighter partner out like a light.

Dar's cell vibrated softly, and she lifted it up. "Yeah? " she murmured into the receiver.

"Dar, it's Mark." The MIS manager sounded upset. "Listen, we've got a real problem."

One of Dar's eyebrows lifted wryly. "Another one?"

"Some guy from the government's here. He's got a court order or something that says I have to give him the core dump you took from the Navy base."

Dar's other eyebrow lifted. "Really? Let me talk to him."

She could almost see the smug look on the man's face, and the carefully not smug look on Mark's when he handed the phone over. "Who is this?" she drawled softly.

"My name is John Bradley," a voice answered. "I represent the Military Appropriations Committee, Ms. Roberts. I assure you, this is all in order. Please have your staff here give me the information I require."

"They don't have it," Dar told him, enjoying the moment of stunned silence.

"Ms. Roberts, this is not a joke. I have a court order."

"It's not even remotely funny. But the fact is, it's not there, Mr. Bradley," Dar replied. "Mind telling me who you work for?"

There was a brief silence before he blustered, "We can search."

"Go ahead." Dar laughed softly. "But be ready for the lawsuit. You can drop a copy of that court order off at our legal department while you're at it."

"This request comes from some very important people, Ms. Roberts," Bradley warned. "You don't really want it getting out that this information is floating around out there, now do you? If you force me to take this public, I will."

Ouch. "You're barking up the wrong tree," Dar said.

"Am I? We'll see." There was a click.

Dar sighed. "This so sucks," she murmured in the direction of the canopy. For a few minutes, she just lay there, listening to Kerry's slow, even breathing, then she picked up her phone and scrolled through her address book, selected a number, and pressed it.

The phone rang three times before it was picked up. "Joint Chiefs," the young, female voice answered.

"I need to speak with General Easton, please," Dar said very quietly. "This is Dar Roberts."

She waited patiently, one hand tangling itself in Kerry's hair while canned Christmas music played in her ear. Finally, after a few minutes, the line clicked and she heard the faint sound of someone clearing their throat before speaking. "Gerry?"

The voice stilled, and she could hear the exhale. "Well, hello there, Dar." Easton's tone sounded wary, but also slightly surprised and hopeful.

Dar had used his first name for a reason. "Alastair told me we had a deal."

Easton cleared his throat again. "Why, yes, we do... Listen, Dar," he sighed, "I know what a bloody bastard this is, and I know it put your shorts in square knots."

A faint smile crossed Dar's face. "And I know how you feel about the service."

Another sigh was audible. "It's so damn hard, Dar. You know how fond I am of you."

"We've known each other a long time," Dar said. "I didn't want to find what I did."

"Don't you think I know that?" Easton said. "Damn it all, Dar."

Dar was silent for a moment. "If we have a deal, then why did I get a visit from the goon squad today? I didn't think you mistrusted me that badly."

For a long instant, there was dead silence on the other end of the line. "What?" Easton finally spluttered. "Visit from who?"

"Some guy named Bradley from the Military Appropriations Committee was in my office with a court order, getting that data dump you asked them to retrieve," Dar replied calmly. "Why, Gerry?"

"Errr..." Easton almost sneezed. "I didn't send a damn blessed soul anywhere near Miami today!" A chair scraped against wood. "What the devil are you talking about?"

Dar stared blankly at the phone, a dozen thoughts running through her head. "You didn't?"

"Certainly not," Easton replied.

"I talked to him myself," Dar murmured. "He said he had a court order." Her mind flicked over the conversation. "He wanted the core...Wait a minute. How in the hell did he know I had that?"

Easton paused. "Gave it to him, did you?"

"No," Dar replied. "It's not there. Gerry, are you sure you didn't ask them to do this? Don't..." Dar felt her heart rate pick up. "Forget the company; I need to know."

"Paladar, I swear to you I didn't," Easton said seriously. "No point to it, you see? Not with that bargain you drove. Sticky thing that was to push through, I will say."

"Then where did he..." Dar paused. "Huh." Could someone have found what her father had hidden? Anything was possible, though she knew her father well enough to know how careful he was. Oh well. A simple phone call could verify that.

"I say, Dar...do you mean to say someone knows about this whole thing outside us?" Easton suddenly asked, sharply. "John Bradley, was it?"

"I'll call you later." Dar hung up and immediately dialed her parents' cell phone number. It rang four times, then went to the voice mail. "Damn." She waited for the message to end, then left her name and cell number. As she closed the phone, she considered her next course of action.

"Dar?" Kerry's voice burred sleepily. "What's wrong?"

Dar gazed down at the half open green eyes peering up at her. "Hm?" She made a questioning noise, to buy herself some time. "How's your head?"

"Woozy." Kerry remained where she was, one hand stroking idly across Dar's belly. "That stuff's strong. You shoulda warned me." Her eyes closed for a moment, then reopened. "You didn't answer my question."

Should I? Dar didn't want to add to the stress already piled on her lover's shoulders, but she was reluctant to lie to her. "Someone from the government, or so they claim, came looking for that information at the office. I thought he was from Gerry's office, but..."

Kerry absorbed that. "Damn. I thought you took the core dump out of the building."

"I did," Dar said. "Dad has it."

Kerry shrugged. "Then it's okay, right?"

Dar met her eyes with a troubled look. "Except that now Gerry knows someone else is looking for it, because I was stupid enough to tell him."

"Oh." Kerry looked apprehensive now. "What does that mean?'

"I don't know."

"Could someone else have found out about it?" Kerry asked. "Or...did this come from my father?" She hesitated. "What does Dad say? Anyone been asking him?"

"I don't know," Dar said. "The folks are not answering the phone. Maybe they took the boat out." She opened the phone and dialed. "Hello? Yes, this is Dar Roberts; can I talk to the dock master please?" She waited. "Slip 1452, is it berthed?" There was a short wait before the man came back on the line. "Yes? Thanks." She hung up. "Boat's in the dock."

Kerry was now more or less awake. "Want me to call Colleen and have her run down there? I think she's the closest."

Dar nodded silently and handed her the phone. She listened to Kerry dial and watched as she pushed the disheveled hair back off her forehead and leaned on one elbow.

"Hey, Col," Kerry said softly. "Yeah. No, thanks. Thanks. I loved the basket." She listened. "No, what I...What? Where are you? Our place?" She looked at Dar. "Mom and Dad asked Col to puppy sit. Said they were going out of town for a few days."

Dar blinked. "When was this?"

Kerry asked. "About two hours ago," she relayed to Dar. "Did they say where they were going? No? I don't get it."

Out of town? "They didn't mention anything about going out of town," Dar said, in a puzzled tone. "Did they?"

"No, I don't think so." Kerry just sat there thinking for a minute. "I don't get it." She yawned and leaned against Dar. "Why would anyone be trying to get that information from you? The general already has it, and my father already had it."

"Beats me. Guy said he was from the military appropriations committee." Dar shrugged.

Kerry took hold of her wrist. "My father was on that," she said. "Could he have told them?"

Oh boy. "I don't know," Dar murmured. "But if he did, we've got a problem."

They heard the distinct slamming of a door somewhere nearby. They looked at each other, then at the door, as footsteps—heavy and determined—headed in their direction. "I think that problem's going to have to wait." Kerry rolled off the bed.

Dar got out after her and followed her across the carpet, but stopped when Kerry paused and put her hand out, touching Dar's chest. "What?"

"They're my family." Kerry intently searched Dar's face. "Please. Let me take a stab at handling them. Stay back for now."

Dar frowned.

"Please?" Kerry brushed Dar's lips with her own. "I have to face them sometime, Dar. You can't beat them all up for me."

"Why not?"

"Dar."

Dar sighed. "Okay." She opened the door for Kerry. "Go get 'em." She gave her a pat on the butt, and watched until she disappeared around the edge of the corridor leading to the stairs. She waited an additional moment, then slipped out, padded to the landing, and cocked her head to listen.

CYNTHIA STUART SAW the broad back go past her, and she hurried after it. "Edgar?"

Edgar stopped, then turned and looked at her. "Cyndi, I heard you had that whore under this roof." He stared accusingly at her. "We had a bargain."

"Edgar," Cynthia frowned, "this really is none of your business. If I choose to—"

"Cynthia, it is my business," Edgar said flatly. "Roger was my brother, and you know how he felt about that woman and the godforsaken way she chooses to live."

"Yes." Cynthia sighed. "I am well aware of how he felt."

"Then how could you?" Edgar asked. "How could you invite her in here, push her in all our faces, when we all know how he felt, how that ate at him. Good Lord, Cynthia, what the hell's wrong with you?"

"Edgar, listen to me." Cynthia was upset. "I know you have strong feelings, but—"

"Strong?" Edgar's voice rose. "No, you don't understand. I hate her. I hate her and everything she stands for, and I hate what she did to this family and to my brother."

"Don't be ridiculous," Cynthia snapped back. "You don't nearly know the truth of that." She stepped closer. "Do you think Kerrison simply decided to turn against Roger for no reason?"

"There is *no* reason that can explain what she did."

"Yes, there is." A quiet voice interrupted them. Both turned to see Kerry standing there, watching them with wary green eyes. "But you know what? I don't owe you any explanations."

"Kerrison," Cynthia put up a pacifying hand, "please, let me handle this. I'm sure—"

"Mother, this has to stop somewhere." Kerry looked her uncle in the eye. "What is it you want from me, Uncle Edgar?"

Edgar stared at her, his nostrils flaring. "I want you to go to Hell," he said softly and bitterly.

"Edgar!"

"It's all right, mother," Kerry replied softly. "Uncle, tell me something. Do you want me to burn in Hell for exposing my father's illegal activities to the press, or because I'm gay?" She held his eyes, her body shaking inside and her guts churning. Part of her regretted asking Dar to stay behind, but she knew she had to face this, one way or the other.

A flicker of indecision crossed his face, then his jaw firmed. "You're a disgrace to this family and an abomination in the eyes of God!" he yelled, then turned, walked down the stairs, crossed the foyer, and exited into the study.

Kerry released the breath she'd been holding, and relaxed her shoulders.

"Kerrison..." Cynthia lifted a hand, then let it fall.

"There's nothing you can say," Kerry said. "I'm sure there'll be a lot more people here tonight that feel that way." She looked at her mother. "But you know what? I don't care." She drew in a breath. "I can't change what I did, and I can't change who I am."

Cynthia hesitated, then twitched Kerry's sleeve straight. "This is so difficult. I wish I had a simple answer to this quite horrible situation, Kerrison. But I will tell you that despite how hard it has been, I'm very glad you decided to come here." Her eyes intently searched Kerry's face.

Kerry blinked, then gazed at the railing on which her hand was resting. "It...wasn't an easy choice." Her voice was a little husky. "I didn't really want to face this." Now she looked up. "But you're my family. I can't change that, either."

Cynthia pursed her lips and shook her head a little. "We should sit down and talk. I think that's been sadly lacking in this entire situation."

The doorbell rang. "Guess that's the start of it."

Cynthia sighed. "I suppose it is. I was hoping..." She let the thought die away. "Perhaps after the reception we can speak further."

"Sure," Kerry said quietly, knowing it would never happen. "I'll go change." She turned and went back up the stairs, deeply immersed in sober thoughts. She rounded the last bend before the landing and crashed into Dar. "Oh!"

Mild blue eyes regarded her as Dar steadied her with a quick grip.

"Thought I told you to stay behind," Kerry murmured.

"I did. You just didn't specify *how* far behind I had to stay." Giving Kerry an unrepentant look, Dar indicated the staircase. "That jackass was lucky he decided to give up and leave."

"Dar, don't you think I can handle my own family?" Kerry

asked with a touch of annoyance.

"No," Dar replied calmly. "I couldn't handle mine and needed your help." She laid a finger on the tip of Kerry's nose. "Don't think I didn't hear you at my grandmother's funeral, making sure they all knew how their poor ragamuffin relative from down South had made good."

Kerry smiled faintly at the memory. "That's true." She relaxed a bit. "C'mon, we'd better get dressed for this thing. People are starting to show up."

Dar circled Kerry's shoulders with one long arm as they went back to the green room. "You were the main reason my father decided to ask me to help him recontact Mom; you know that, right? And if I recall, a certain drawing exhibition..."

"Okay." Kerry held up a hand. "I get the point, Dar." She gave her a quiet look. "I guess I'm quite the little meddler, aren't I?"

"Yep." Dar pushed the door open and stood aside for Kerry to enter. "So don't you dare give me a hard time for doing the same thing." She followed Kerry inside and closed the door. "Speaking of which, let's talk strategy."

Kerry paused with her hand on her bag and turned. "Strategy?" She unzipped the bag and removed her dark suit. "For what?"

The room was darkened by the weather outside; only two lamps shed butter colored light across the room, and it splashed over Dar as she walked to Kerry. "What's your goal here, Kerry? What outcome do you want this evening to have, when it's all over? Is this where you tell your family to kiss your ass, or do you want to try to mend fences?"

Kerry blinked at her in total bewilderment. "Dar, what are you talking about?"

"Think," Dar replied, as she laid a hand on Kerry's cheek. "Everyone has their opinion of who you are. Do you want to change that?" There was only silence as Dar watched thoughts chase themselves across Kerry's expressive face. "Are you proud of who you are?"

Blonde lashes flickered. "I don't know." Kerry inhaled. "I should be, shouldn't I?"

Dar gazed intently into her eyes, allowing her own powerful personality to surge to the surface. "You have to believe in yourself before you can get anyone else to buy into that. And yes, you should be very proud of who you are." A faint smile curved her lips. "I know I am."

Kerry's eyes filled with tears and they spilled down her cheeks as she blinked. For a moment, she felt very alone, as though she were standing on a bridge high out over chill waters. There was no safe place around her, only harsh, buffeting winds, and if she closed her eyes, she could almost feel the swaying. It was frightening. She knew Dar was waiting for her on the other side of the bridge, but this was something she could only do by herself, a decision she had to make alone.

But there really isn't a choice, is there? Kerry realized. She considered her accomplishments, both personal and professional over the previous year, and felt a sense of wondering satisfaction settle over her. With steady confidence, she traversed the bridge and crossed over it, leaving her childhood behind her to enter a newly burnished realization of her own reality.

Dar watched intently as Kerry's eyes opened, a misty green still watery with tears that nevertheless met hers with startling clarity.

"What I want is for my family to understand that my life is exactly how I want it to be." Kerry took Dar's hand and ran her fingers over the strong bones and tensing muscles within it. "And I am very proud of who *we* are."

Dar kissed her, but remained silent, savoring the sweetness of the moment.

Chapter
Nine

SHE COULD HEAR the murmur of voices, a low wash of sound that mixed soft clinks and footsteps. It sent a wave of familiarity over her, bringing up memories of growing up in this house and hearing those sounds so very often. Kerry soberly regarded her reflection in the mirror. Her charcoal gray, wool suit jacket fitted precisely across her shoulders and draped over the slightly lighter silk dress. She wore her hair clipped back into a knot, and had on only a sober dusting of makeup. "You doing okay?" Her eyes lifted to the mirror, and watched Dar's reflection in it as she walked to her.

"I'm fine." Dar eased her collarless black silk jacket over a simple yet elegant dark bronze sheath. The jacket covered the ugly bruising and provided a somber draping to Dar's tall form. "Got plenty of drugs in me." She glanced at Kerry's profile. "You doing all right?"

Kerry nodded. "I'm fine." She removed two jade studs from her small kit and inserted one into her right earlobe. "Sounds like a crowd's finally arrived downstairs."

"So I hear." Dar put her own jewelry case on the dresser. "When you have a chance, it's tough for me to reach up—could you...?"

Kerry smiled a little. "Sure." She finished putting in her earrings, opened Dar's case, and took out the beautiful blue diamonds that were her favorites. "Sit." She indicated the low, padded bench. "Make my life easier."

Dar did as she was asked, stifling a small yawn with her good hand as Kerry moved her hair aside and tilted her head a little. She felt the warm touch of fingers against her earlobe, then the faint pressure as the posts went through her skin. "I like that dress on you." She touched the soft fabric that covered Kerry's hip.

"Thanks," Kerry murmured, attending to the other ear. "I got it to wear to that executive convention next month in New York."

She straightened and observed her work. "Those are so pretty."

"Should be, for what they cost," Dar said, jokingly. "Mind getting that necklace, too?"

Kerry fished in the bag and drew out the glittering crystal on its golden chain, then opened the catch and fastened it around Dar's neck. It matched the one already around her own neck and, with a tiny grin, she settled it into its spot above the hollow in Dar's throat. "Are we ready?"

Dar tilted her head and peered up. Kerry's face was grave but composed, and there was a peace about her that had been sorely missing for several days. "I think we are." She stood up and twitched her jacket straight. "Let's go."

They met Angie and Richard on the stairs, and walked down together. Richard had on a dark suit, and Angie had chosen a simple, dark gray dress. Dar was the last on the stairs and had the best view of what waited below. There was a small crowd in the foyer, men mostly, with a few women, and a local television reporter. As they descended they were spotted, and Dar watched the reactions.

Interesting. Eyes fastened on her, and she coolly returned the stares. The television reporter broke off his speech with an older man and turned and hurried in their direction. "Here we go," Dar murmured, giving Kerry's back a tiny scratch.

Kerry's shoulder blades shifted and she stiffened as they reached the foot of the stairs and were met by both the reporter and the stares of the gathered crowd. As she expected, the reporter made a beeline for her, and she met his eyes steadily as he advanced.

"Ms. Stuart?" The man seemed a little more excited than the situation warranted. "Can I get a word with you?"

Kerry sighed inwardly. "Sure." She stepped to one side and allowed the others to move on. Dar, naturally, didn't. Angie gave her a sympathetic look as she edged past. "What can I help you with?"

The man glanced at a piece of paper, then obviously organized his thoughts. He lifted his eyes and started to speak, then paused, his gaze drifting up and a little to the left. He blinked, then cleared his throat. "Ah...I know this is a very sad occasion, Ms. Stuart, but there are many people who are surprised to see you here."

"Really?" Kerry asked. "Why? My father died yesterday. Did you really think politics could interfere with my being here for my mother and my family?"

The camerawoman edged around, getting a better shot. It gave the reporter a moment to regroup. "Ms. Stuart, we're aware that there have been some strained relations with your family, and—"

"And?" Kerry cut him off again with genteel politeness.

Another shift of his gaze up and to the left. "And...ah...I'm...I mean, it's good to see the family giving each other support during this horrible tragedy."

"Thank you." Kerry rewarded him with a warm smile. "It's been a very difficult few days. Now, if you'll excuse us?"

"Uh...sure." The reporter backed off, with a nervous glance behind Kerry. "Thanks for speaking with us."

Kerry smiled and ducked around the camera. She waited until they were halfway across the foyer and almost to the large reception room before she paused and lowered her voice as Dar drew even with her. "What were you doing to him?"

"Me?" Dar's low, musical voice asked. "Nothing. Why?"

Kerry just gave her a look. "I can't wait to see this on the eleven o clock news." She glanced ahead and saw several of her extended family near the door to the reception room, and the coldness of their stares was almost a physical blow. She squared her shoulders. "C'mon."

Angie spotted them as they cleared the door and she hurried to them. "Hey, that didn't take long." She latched on to Kerry's arm and steered her away from the hostile crowd. "Mom's over there." She pointed to their mother, flanked by two aides, with a short, stocky older man opposite her. "Chatting with the governor. I think she could use some support."

"Sure," Kerry replied. "Aunt Mary looks like she wants to spit nails at me anyway." She gave her aunt, a chubby woman dressed in unflattering black crepe, a smile, which wasn't returned. "You'd think she hadn't spent the last twenty years telling everyone what a bastard our father was."

"Mm." Angie snorted softly. "Or that she'd been a flower child who burned her bra and voted Democratic just to spite the family."

"Hm," Kerry said. "I wonder if that look's for my lifestyle or the company I work for, then. Maybe I've got her staring daggers all wrong. She's been fighting big business since the Stone Age."

Dar chuckled softly.

"Don't laugh," Kerry murmured. "She thinks the high techs are the worst things that ever happened to the Earth." They arrived at Cynthia's side before Dar could answer, and they met the glares of the aides.

"Ah, Kerrison." Cynthia welcomed her warmly, ignoring the frosty expressions of the two men on either side of her. "Splendid. I was just discussing you with the governor." She turned. "James, this is Kerrison, my eldest daughter." Then she paused, almost infinitesimally. "And her...partner, Dar Roberts."

"Kerrison." The governor extended a hand to her with surprising good nature. They shook, then he turned and met Dar's eyes, a tiny smile crinkling the corners of his own. "Ms. Roberts."

There was, Dar realized, something faintly familiar about the man. She returned his strong grip and tried to figure out where she'd met him before. "Governor."

"And you know Angela," Cynthia continued. "The governor and I were just discussing—"

"Mrs. Stuart, a word with you." One of the aides tugged at her sleeve. "There's a phone call."

Cynthia looked very annoyed, but she gave the governor a graceful nod. "Excuse me a moment." She allowed herself to be drawn off to one side, where two other aides were standing, one holding a wireless phone.

"Kerrison," a male voice chimed in from behind them. "Hadn't expected to see you here."

Kerry turned to see one of her younger uncles on her mother's side standing there. "Hello, Brad." She exchanged wry looks with him. "I didn't expect to see you, either. Guess I took your place as the black sheep, hm?" Brad still had his earrings, though he'd taken out the one he usually sported in his nose for the occasion. Kerry was glad to see him, though they'd never been close.

"Made my life a little easier, yeah." Brad laughed. "'Specially after my band got busted for possession last year."

Dar watched the interchange, satisfied that Kerry wasn't going to get bushwhacked, then turned her attention to the governor, who was standing quietly, watching everything. Their eyes met. "Political minefield, eh?"

He shrugged lightly. "Aren't they all?" He cocked his head. "Roger was a bastard, but he knew his job and he was damn good at it. Lots worse could have been in that seat, though I'm betting you'd disagree."

Dar glanced around, surprised at the governor's candor with a relative stranger. "He wasn't my favorite human being, no. People who wish me, and those I love, dead and in Hell rarely are." She met his eyes evenly. "It's a fairly common attitude, though."

The faint smile returned. "That's damn true, Ms. Roberts. Damn true. Some of my closest friends feel that very way, matter of fact, and I'm not known as a liberal in many circles. Makes an already dicey decision even tougher now that Cyndi's publicly stated her support for young Kerrison, there."

"I bet." Dar smiled humorlessly. "Does she even want the job?"

"Not particularly." The governor shrugged. "S'why she's probably going to get it." He rocked back and forth on his heels a bit. "Hasn't got much time left on this term anyway, and anyone else I choose would just cause me other problems."

Dar's eyebrows rose. "Despite the," she paused deliberately and put a sting in the word, "complications?"

The governor chuckled for no apparent reason and looked at his laced leather shoes. "Y'know, Ms. Roberts, I gotta tell you something." He looked up at her. "I made the mistake of assuming things about gay people once, and I got my ass dragged into a torpedo locker and the bs kicked right out of me for it." He grinned at her visibly startled reaction. "I surely don't intend to make the same mistake twice, and have Andy Roberts coming after my ass again. I'm too old for that now."

Dar blinked, then chuckled a little in pure surprise. "You know, I thought I knew you from somewhere. You captained that hunter sub he went out on for two tours."

"That I did," the governor said. "Besides, I'd be a half-brained old sea salt to piss off someone who might prospectively bring more private sector jobs into my state, now wouldn't I?" He gave her a rakish grin. "Got any plans for expanding in Troy?"

Cynthia Stuart returned at that moment, having shed the two aides. "My apologies, Governor, but I see you were well accompanied." She gave Dar a nod. "Is Kerrison...? Ah, there she is. Kerrison, perhaps we can speak with your uncles now. Are you free?"

Kerry and Dar exchanged glances. "Sure. I don't honestly know what good it'll do, but I'm willing to try." *Maybe,* she considered, *in this very public venue, they'll at least be civil.* She put a hand on Dar's arm. "You'd better—"

"Stay here?" Dar completed the statement with a faint smile. "All right, but if voices start to get louder, I won't be responsible for my reactions." She watched Kerry walk to a knot of her family, relaxing a little when Michael slid in and put an arm around Kerry's shoulders.

The governor gently cleared his throat. "Chip off the old block, aren't you?"

Dar kept her eyes on her lover, but smiled with pride. "That's what they tell me."

"THAT THERE MAN is not worth this here suit." Andrew folded his arms over his broad chest and reviewed the passing countryside. "Ah will tell you that."

Ceci glanced at him, then returned her attention to the icy road ahead of her. "No, he's not worth a potato sack. But Kerry's worth that suit, and besides, I like you in it." She caught a pair of pale blue eyes reflected against the windshield and smiled. "Not as much as the white one, but still..."

Andrew merely grunted, shifting his shoulders inside his dark blue uniform jacket. "Spent enough time decorating it, now didn't you?" he rasped, giving her a wry look.

Ceci chuckled smugly. "Wasn't it a coincidence that box of medals from the Navy showed up yesterday? Amazing, I tell you, just amazing." She turned carefully onto a smaller road, grimacing as she felt the wheels slide under her touch. "Lovely."

"You want me to drive?" Andy asked.

"Honey," Ceci struggled with the wheel a moment more, then got the car straight, "I'm sure Kerry and Dar would like to see us in one piece sometime this evening." She accelerated cautiously. "Ah. That's better." It really was hard to believe they were actually there. Certainly it was only marginally their business, and their presence would not, she suspected strongly, be a welcome one.

That one shot of Dar and Kerry coming out of the hospital the night before, both faces strained to an almost scary extent, made their decision for them, for better or worse. Ceci exhaled and nodded to herself. They had the means, they had the method, and by the goddess, here they were about to turn into the driveway of the Stuart family manse.

"Think we should have warned them?" she asked, waiting in line behind a maroon Jaguar.

An unexpected smile crossed Andy's scarred face. "Nope. Better to just do it and fill in the paperwork later."

"Mm." Cecilia pulled up to the guard and opened the window. The man leaned over and peered inside as she marshaled several well thought out arguments to gain admittance, prepared to bombard the man with inescapable logic and plain intimidation if she had to.

"Go right ahead, sir," he murmured courteously. "Ma'am."

The gate opened. Ceci glanced at her husband who looked back at her, equally puzzled. "Well." She pulled the car through the opening gates. "I'm not looking that gift donkey in the ass."

"Musta been taken by your pretty face," Andy said.

"More likely by the glare off your chest, sailor boy." Ceci patted the front of his uniform, which was liberally bedecked with medals and ribbons. "He probably figured you run the Navy. C'mon."

They got out and Ceci pulled the lapels of her coat closer as the cold wind chilled her skin. After a second, Andy was next to her, and he put a hand on her back to steady her steps as they headed up the icy walk towards the house. "Stuffy looking, isn't it?" she commented as they rang the bell.

"'Bout what I expected," Andrew grumbled as the door opened. The staff member immediately retreated and allowed them to enter, offering to take their coats with a quiet word. They accepted the offer, and continued towards a large, crowded room off to the left.

Ceci checked out the house with a knowledgeable, patrician eye. The Stuarts occupied roughly the same social class as her own family, but there were differences. This was conservative, stolid, Midwestern money, concerned with presence and stability and tradition.

Ick. Ceci had a sudden, almost irresistible urge to throw a bucket of paint over the stately white walls. With an effort, she controlled herself and concentrated on studying the room full of dignitaries, searching for familiar faces. It was tough, being the height she was, but she managed to find Dar's tall, elegant form almost immediately. She had her back to the door and was speaking to a tall, silver haired man. "There's one."

"Yeap. Easy to spot. Prettiest girl in the room," Andrew noted with complete seriousness.

Ceci chuckled softly. Then she stopped laughing when she saw Kerry off to one side, ringed by a number of older men and women.

"That don't look so good," Andrew said. "Think I'll go scout."

"I'll go clue in our daughter," Ceci replied, and they moved off in opposite directions.

"WELL."

Dar turned her head and found a most unwelcome sight. Kyle Evans was standing there with a slightly mocking expression on his face. "Ah. What rock did you crawl out from under?"

One silver eyebrow lifted. "Not even a pretense of civility?"

"Not for you." Dar met his gaze evenly. Of all the members of the late senator's staff, this was the one she had the most reason to hate. And she did, with a completeness that allowed for no mitigation. Kyle had been Kerry's persecutor, the man who had carried out her father's rigid policies, and a nightmarish tormentor who had scarred her gentle lover's psyche in ways it horrified Dar to think about.

"Well." Kyle examined the room with cool eyes. "Finally got what you wanted, didn't you?"

"No. I've always had what I wanted." Dar met his sudden

look with an icy smile. "But he finally got what he deserved."

Kyle didn't answer. Instead, he continued to study the room. "Pity I was out of the country," he purred. "I'd have made sure you didn't join this little family reunion." He turned and smiled at her with no humor at all. "But look, there's the little prodigal. Let me go pay my," his lip twitched, "respects."

"I don't think she wants them," Dar said.

"I'm sure she doesn't." Kyle smiled again. "Maybe we can talk over...old times."

He turned and glided away, leaving Dar with an icy facade over wild inner turmoil. She felt her blood pressure rise, sending a surge of warmth to her skin and muscles as her body interpreted the emotion she felt with uncanny accuracy. Her hands twitched, and it was only by the barest of margins that she held herself back from going after him.

"Dar?"

Her head snapped to one side, and it took a few seconds for her rational mind to recognize the voice and register the sudden, completely unexpected appearance of her mother at her side. Her glare melted as she took a breath and blinked. "Mom? What are you doing here?"

"Well..." Cecilia eased closer, now that the impending eruption seemed to be under control. "Up 'til now I'd have said we were here just to piss everyone off and give you two some friendly faces." She studied her child with concern. "But after that little scene, I'm not so sure that *moral* support is the only kind you need. Who the hell was that?"

Dar's eyes darted over the crowd. "Dad's here?"

"Yes," Ceci said. "He was heading over to thump Kerry's relatives a moment ago. Why?" She put a hand on Dar's arm. "Dar, are you all right?"

Dar closed her eyes and took firm control of herself. "Yes. Thanks." Now that she knew they were safe, one worry was done away with. And she had another to take its place. She finally turned and regarded her mother. "I'm glad you're here." She drew a deep breath before addressing the question. "And that was Kyle Evans. He's...he *was* Stuart's chief bastard and whitewasher." Her lips twitched. "His personal assistant."

"Uh huh." Ceci relaxed a little. "Tight-assed looking creature. Sorry about the surprise. We saw you two on television last night and you looked like you could use a little support."

"I tried to call you earlier." Dar felt her pulse slow. "Colleen said you'd gone out of town, but she didn't know where." She scanned the crowd again and immediately found her father's tall form as he slid into place beside the unsuspecting Kerry, just as

Kyle approached from the other side of her.

An unexpected smile crossed Dar's face, which vanished just as quickly. "It's been a rough couple of days. Most of her relatives are giving her hell."

"So I gathered," Ceci murmured. "Shall we go rescue her?"

Dar glanced around the room. It was full of dignitaries, most of whom were watching the cluster of people around Kerry with thinly disguised interest. She watched a camera flash and saw the reporter angle for a better shot of Kerry's face as she stood holding her ground against her various aunts and uncles. She was tense; Dar could see that in the way she held her body and in the careful, controlled hand motions as she fought to remain civil.

"Yeah," Dar said. "Let's go do that."

KERRY RETURNED THE thin smile from her youngest aunt. *Viciously polite.* That was the term she was looking for. So far, though, she'd done all right. Even her uncles, aware of the cameras and the outsiders' stares, were behaving themselves. "Sorry, what was the question?"

"What's the social life down there like for you?" Marcia repeated. "I'm sure you participate, don't you?"

"Not really," Kerry replied quietly. "I do on a corporate level, naturally, but we have other interests besides parties."

"Oh, really?" Her aunt was a slim, hawk faced woman with silvered dark hair. "Like what, cooking?" she asked with a touch of sweet sarcasm.

Keep cool, Kerry, she reminded herself. "I dabble in it, sure. But mostly outdoor sports, really. Diving, underwater photography, that kind of thing." She smiled. "And a little distance running and martial arts."

"Funny," Aunt Marcia sniped. "You were never interested in those things before."

"Well, you know, there's a limited amount of scuba diving available in Lake Michigan," Kerry replied. "Miami's a little more climactically friendly to outdoor sports. It's been great for me. I'm having the time of my life."

"Well you certainly look different," her aunt said. "You definitely...filled out."

Kerry refused to view that as the insult her aunt undoubtedly intended it to be. "Thanks. You look good yourself."

"Yes, she certainly has changed." A voice came from Kerry's left, sending a chill down her back. She turned to find her worst nightmare looking back at her through cold, gray eyes.

"Hello, Kyle." Her stomach lurched as she remembered the

last time they'd met. She felt someone brush lightly against her on the right side, but she remained in place, warily watching her old adversary. She honestly hadn't expected this confrontation. Her mother had told her Kyle had been sent overseas months ago, and she'd figured... *Damn.*

"Yes, didn't expect me, did you?" Kyle laughed. "I've just arrived. I'm so glad to see you."

Kerry felt like throwing up. "Feeling's not mutual." She resisted the urge to look around for the comfort of Dar's presence. A thousand childhood fears reared their heads, a hundred memories of that smiling face echoed in places she'd thought well cleared. "Excuse me."

"Oh, but we've only started to talk." Kyle moved closer, very aware of the watching eyes. "Do tell me what you've been up to, Kerrison. I want to hear every detail."

Feeling trapped, Kerry studied him to give herself a moment to think. "Nothing you'd be interested in, Kyle. I don't think there's much for us to discuss."

Kyle put a proprietary hand on her shoulder. "Come now, is that any way to talk? Let's—"

A hand covered his and removed it from Kerry's arm with a power evident even in that brief contact. "Ah do believe this here young lady has other things she'd be liking to do."

Kerry whirled in startled, disbelieving shock. She tipped her head back to take in the tall, grizzle haired man in a Naval uniform right behind her, his scarred face set in watchful stillness.

"Ya'll might want to just let her get on with them," Andrew drawled.

Kyle's eyes narrowed. "Excuse me, but I don't think this is quite your affair...ah," he glanced at Andrew's chest, "Commander, is it?" Then he looked again. "Roberts. Ah."

Andy put a long arm around Kerry's shoulders. "Ah'd say you were wrong. This here young lady is very much mah business."

Kerry exhaled her tension, and threw her arms around him in a hug. Kyle had truly rattled her, and to have Andrew show up at just the right moment... "Wow," she whispered, squeezing him hard before she released him and turned back around. Kyle was watching Andrew with wary dislike, and the rest of her relatives were frankly staring at him. "Sorry. This was kind of unexpected. This is my father-in-law, Andrew Roberts." She almost enjoyed the flinches. "A very welcome surprise."

"I'm sure," Kyle murmured. "For you, at least."

Andrew eyed him steadily for a moment, then looked around at the gathered relatives. "Hi there." His Southern accent dripped out like molasses. "Good t'meet y'all. This here's mah wife, Ceci," he added, as Cecilia joined him.

"Hello." Ceci smiled with charming frigidity at the crowd. "Moments like this make even a rationalist like me seriously doubt Darwin."

"Hi." Kerry was hard pressed to restrain her glee at seeing Ceci, someone who could meet her relatives on equal footing and boot them in the rear with exquisite courtesy. It was seriously like having the cavalry riding over the hill. "When did you guys get here? Did you see... Ah." She felt Dar's presence at her elbow, and a warm hand touched her back. "Hey."

"Hey," Dar said. "Now the puppy-sitting makes sense."

"Hm." Kerry regained her balance. With Dar and Andrew bracketing her like a pair of sturdy bookends, life had gotten much better with startling rapidity. It wasn't that she didn't have confidence in Dar alone, but Kyle's specialty had always been intimidation, and Andy simply was who he was, his scarred, yet potent strength making her old adversary seem almost childlike in comparison.

Maybe Kyle felt it. Certainly, he backed up a few steps, pretending to take more interest in obtaining a glass of wine from one of the servants. Then he looked up as a cluster of people approached and grimly smiled.

Kerry turned, only to be face to face with her mother and another pod of relatives. "Ah...uh..."

"Kerrison...Oh." Cynthia Stuart stopped a little short, blinking at her unexpected guests. "Why, Commander, it's good to see you. And Mrs. Roberts, how nice it is to have you here."

Ceci's eyebrows lifted almost imperceptibly. It wasn't quite the reception she'd expected, given their last meeting. However, one took what one could get, and if she got caviar instead of fish turds, all the better. She dusted off her annoying company manners and presented them, knowing she'd get no help whatsoever from her beloved spouse. "Thank you so much for welcoming us in such a distressing time. We always do seem to be meeting under the worst of circumstances, don't we?"

Cynthia pursed her lips. "You know, that's very true. Perhaps we could invite you to a Christmas party or something in the future?"

"Well, I'm a pagan. Solstice, perhaps?" Ceci smiled charmingly and watched the comment fly over Cynthia's head and splat against the white walls.

"Of course. Lovely," Cynthia answered vaguely. "Ah..."

Dar was having an absolute ball watching the expressions on the faces of Kerry's family. Their reactions ran the gamut from puzzlement to outrage. Dar made sure she smiled at each of them. Out of the corner of her eye, she saw Kyle slip away as a curious cameraman approached, drawn most likely by Andrew's tall, uniform clad form.

Having had enough fun for the moment, Ceci took Cynthia's proffered hands. "We knew it was a rough time for everyone. Glad we could be here to give you our sympathies in person. You have a beautiful home."

A camera flashed.

"Why, thank you," Cynthia replied warmly. "Oh, do come and let me introduce you to my brother Anthony. I believe he collects your work."

"When he finds out who I am, hopefully he'll continue to do so." Ceci smiled politely and held a hand out to Andrew. "We'd love to meet him."

"One less thing for you to have to worry about," Kerry murmured, turning her head so that only Dar could hear her. "What a gorgeous surprise, and what perfect timing."

"Mm," Dar grunted, giving the press a polite smile. "I could use a drink of water, how about you?"

Amazing how dry that suddenly made her throat. "You bet." Kerry edged out of the view of the press, who seemed intrigued by their new target. "Dad looks great."

"Yeah," Dar whispered back. "I've never seen all those decorations before. I can't believe Mom got him to wear them." She eyed them and gave her father a pointed look before she gently steered Kerry through a nearby doorway and into a small alcove just off the reception room. Here there was a linen draped table with glasses and a pitcher of water. She poured two glasses and handed one to her lover.

For a moment, they sipped their drinks and regarded each other. Then Kerry sighed. "Night of surprises."

Dar nodded. "Some not so good."

Kerry stared into the depths of her glass and swirled its contents. "Yeah. Damn. I forgot how much I hated him." She was surprised to see her hands shaking, then realized the rest of her also shook. "Wow."

Dar took the glass out of her hand and put it down. She took Kerry's cold hands in her own and warmed them. "It's a little chilly in here."

"Yeah, it is." Kerry felt lightheaded. She took some deep breaths and the shakiness subsided as her racing pulse slowed and steadied.

Dar noted the pale tinge to Kerry's normally golden complexion. "You all right?"

"Yeah." Kerry nodded, relaxing a bit. "It was so good to see Mom and Dad." She smiled at Dar. "When we heard they'd left Miami, I should have guessed they'd be coming here." She turned her head and spotted a nearby bench. "Sit for a minute?"

Dar took a seat next to her, and they let out simultaneous sighs. "Here." Dar handed Kerry back her water and watched her take a swallow. "Tough crowd."

Kerry rolled her eyes.

"They make my family look like the Waltons," Dar continued. "On Thanksgiving."

Kerry snickered, almost spitting out some of her water.

"If one more of them had made one more snippy comment about your weight, I was getting ready to spill a glass of that disgusting dry champagne down their backs," Dar went on. "Especially since the last time most of them saw a gym was high school." Another snicker from Kerry encouraged Dar to add, "And even then, they probably just danced in it."

Kerry cleared her throat. "Very true. They're not much into the physical fitness scene; that was one subject that never really came up. It was fine and accepted to starve yourself into rapier thinness, but to actually consider...ugh...sweating, forget it."

"I think you're very cute when you sweat." Dar crossed her ankles and swallowed some water.

"Let's not go overboard," Kerry replied, giving Dar a wry look. Then she sighed. "Okay, I've had my Dar break, I'd better get back out there. I think my other cousins just got here." She stood up and twitched her dress straight. "Want to come meet them?"

Dar put her glass down and joined Kerry near the doorway. They paused and looked over the gathering, spotting Andy and Ceci near a cluster of older guests. As they were about to step forward, Dar felt Kerry hesitate, and she glanced around to see what the problem was. Kyle was watching them from near the elegant bar, his arms crossed as he spoke in a low voice to two men in dark suits. "I don't like the looks of that."

"Me either. C'mon." Kerry deliberately turned and walked in the other direction, towards two younger women looking self conscious and trying to be casual in black lace dresses neither did any justice to.

THE STUDY WAS very quiet, almost somber. Kyle ignored the ghosts watching from the corners and strode across the rich carpet, swung behind the desk, and sat in the leather chair with stolid arrogance.

For a moment, he hesitated and laid his hands on the surface, then he shook his head and opened the center drawer. There were a few papers on top, and these he pulled out, impatiently flicked his eyes over them, and then tossed them on the desk, one after the other. "Nothing there."

He put the papers back into the drawer and closed it, then went to the first file drawer on the right hand side. Inside, a series of hanging files were lined up in a typically neat row, labeled with the senator's projects.

Most were empty. Kyle frowned, thumbing through them. "I know these weren't finished. Don't tell me someone's come in to get them already. I'll have them skinned."

He shoved the files towards the back, then hesitated as he felt resistance. Pulling the folders forward, he craned his neck to see what was blocking them in the back of the drawer. "Maybe they fell down in there...Eh, what's this?"

He tugged out a manila envelope, its edges frayed and partially split. It was fairly thick, and he put it down on the desk, opened it, and looked inside.

The scent of paper and laser ink hit him. Curious, he removed the first few pages and tilted them towards the light on the desk to see better. "Ah hah," he whispered and chuckled softly under his breath. "Now here's something I can use."

He read further, a look of consternation appearing on his face. "Where in the hell did he get this?" he wondered aloud, then his eyes narrowed. "And why didn't he tell me about it?"

He drummed his fingers on the desk, then picked up the envelope and tucked it under his arm as he got up to leave. "Maybe that's why he put a stop to my plan of stripping those contracts." He chuckled as he headed for the door. "Now I can kill two jackasses with one grenade."

MUCH LATER IN the evening, Dar found a moment to pause and lean against the wall, hoping the ordeal was almost over. It had been a very long night, with a lot of stress, and her shoulder had gotten so painful, it was hard for her to move her arm without screaming.

But now, people were leaving. That was good.

Good riddance. Dar felt very little empathy for the wool suited, hostile eyed people who surrounded her beloved partner with appraising stares and veiled comments. Family, yes, but almost all of them either resented Kerry for what she'd done to her late father, or for her current lifestyle. Or for her choice of life partners.

Fuck them. Dar mentally enunciated the words with grim sat-isfaction. She then looked up as she felt someone approaching. *Ah.* "Hi, Dad."

Andrew Roberts found a spot on the wall next to her and claimed it. "Hey there, Dardar," he rumbled softly. "You don't look so hot."

Dar sighed inwardly. She'd never had much luck in fooling her father about when she wasn't feeling well. "No, you're right. I'm tired and grumpy, and my shoulder's killing me." She saw Kerry walking across the room towards her with a forceful and determined stride. "Uh oh."

Andrew chuckled. "Hey, Dar?" He eased closer and motioned with his jaw to the reception room doorway where Kyle was standing, just watching Kerry. "Who is that feller?"

"An asshole who deserves to be run over by a Mack truck," Dar replied without thinking. "A total bastard who made Ker's life a living hell for a long time."

"Yeah?" Andrew's voice was gentle.

"Yeah," Dar answered, before she greeted Kerry. "Hi. Bet you have a headache."

Kerry had opened her mouth to speak, and this statement derailed her a little. "Um...yes, I do, as a matter of fact. How did you know?"

"Same way you know it's time for me to go get more drugs," Dar replied with a faint smile. "Unless you're ready to retire for the evening."

With her back turned to the room, Kerry looked up at Dar, and for a moment her determinedly cordial mask slipped, reveal-ing a rawly anguished expression. Her voice, however, remained quiet. "I think I've had about enough for the night, yeah. If I have to hear one more person come up with one more euphemism for you and me being lovers, I may have to kill someone."

There was an awkward silence. Kerry glanced up to see Andrew scratching his jaw. "Sorry, Dad. I figured you already knew." She peeked at Dar, almost smiling at the faint blush. "I mean, you are a sailor and a man of the world and all of that stuff."

Andrew chuckled. "I surely did know, kumquat. I just usu-ally call you two sweethearts, is all."

That coaxed a smile from Kerry. "Did my mother invite you two to stay over?"

"Yes." Ceci appeared on Kerry's other side. "Now that I've spent the evening bludgeoning your relatives with highbrow art talk. Good goddess, Kerry—you have a more annoying family than I do, and Andy will tell you that's quite the radical statement."

Kerry sighed. "Thanks." She looked around. "I hope you insulted the hell out of them. They deserve it."

"Yes, they do," Ceci said. "Tell you what. Let's plan on getting your people together with my people some time, and we'll bus them off to the Dade County Fair. I'll take pictures."

Andrew snorted and chuckled under his breath.

"They don't deserve the funnel cakes," Kerry said dryly. "C'mon, let's get out of here, Dar."

Angie stuck her head around the corner of the doorway. "Kerry, they want to get one more set of pictures, then we're done."

Aggrieved, Kerry sighed again. "For what? This is supposed to be a solemn occasion, Angie. I feel like we're performing s..." she glanced at Andrew and half smiled, "...bears."

"The local paper." Angie gave her an apologetic look. "They're doing an entire special section on him."

Kerry closed her eyes. "Great." She opened them and looked at Dar. "Why don't you go on upstairs; I'll meet you there in a few minutes. I need to have a word with my mother, anyway."

Dar considered for a moment, then nodded. "All right." She pushed away from the wall, and gave Kerry a gentle rub on the arm before she circled around her and headed for the door.

After a moment, Andrew caught up to her. Dar started to say something, then just decided to conserve energy and remained silent, ignoring the curious looks as they left the reception room and headed for the wide, open staircase. Cameras popped in the foyer as they crossed it, and Dar winced at the bright light. "What the hell's that for?" she muttered.

Her father merely looked at her and snorted, shaking his head.

"Ms...ah...Roberts." One of the reporters stepped into her path. "Can we get a moment to talk with you?"

Several choice replies came to mind, but then Dar recognized the lapel badge as one of the major business papers and decided Alastair didn't deserve all the grief. "Sure." She put a hand on the stair banister and waited. "What can I do for you?"

The man and his companion closed the distance between them as he took out a pad. Dar was mildly relieved no cameras were involved and decided to be patient and wait for him to get his act together. "Did he really rate the Wall Street Journal?"

The man looked up and gave her a half grin. "He was involved in a lot of behind the scenes issues."

"Ah."

"For instance, we know he's been promoting an investigation

that calls into question the government contracts ILS has been given this past year. Did you know that?"

Dar took a moment to absorb the unexpectedly public information. "I did. But I try to stay clear of political entanglements—our legal department handles that."

"Your company would have been badly hurt if it'd been successful," the man said. "So I guess that makes this an opportune event for you, huh?"

Dar remained quiet for a few breaths, balancing her inner feelings with her responsibilities. "People dying is never an opportune event, mister. No matter what he was up to, and no matter how he felt about ILS, he was still my partner's father."

"Even after those hearings? Pretty nasty," the man said. "No one'd blame you for holding a grudge."

"I don't waste my time on grudges," Dar lied in a sincere voice. "I don't think he did, either. But it makes good press, doesn't it?" She redirected the attack with a smile.

The man's eyebrows quirked. "Someone else could pick up the ball there, y'know. Those contracts are worth a lot of money."

Dar shrugged. "All our contracts are worth a lot of money, and that's why we pay the legal department. I suggest you talk to them if you need any more details." She lifted her hand off the banister and took a step back. "Excuse me."

"Thanks for chatting, Ms. Roberts. Have a good night," the reporter replied courteously. "Sir." He gave Andrew a nod, before he turned and rejoined the milling crowd.

"Pansy ass," Andrew grunted.

"Shh." Dar muffled a short laugh. "C'mon." She turned and walked up the stairs, shaking her head.

Dar was glad to get away from the noise and the crowd. She didn't like them to begin with, and the pain was shortening her already ragged temper. "Damn, I wish I was home." She sighed as she reached the door to the green room.

"Ah bet." Andrew opened it for her. "Let me take a look at that there arm of yours."

Dar's brow edged up.

"Don't you give me that look." Her father scowled at her. "Git."

"Yes, sir." Dar entered the room with Andy and closed the door. The room was dark, as they'd left only one lamp on, and she let out a silent sigh as she absorbed the quiet, dim peace. She kicked her shoes off first, then pulled her jacket off and froze in mid motion, clenching her jaw against a gasp.

"Easy there, Dardar." Her father caught up to her and gently eased the jacket off her shoulders. "Lemme see that…Good Lord."

Dar glanced at her arm. "Looks worse than it feels," she lied.

Andrew turned her into the light and touched the bruised skin with gentle fingers. "Looks a sight worse than it did back down south. Thought you been taking it easy." He lifted his eyes and studied her face. "That does not look good to me, young lady."

Dar managed a rakish grin. "Yeah, well, it's your fault."

Andrew blinked at her in astonishment and pointed a finger at his own, medal bedecked chest. "Mah fault?"

"Yep." Dar walked to her bag and dug out her bottle of pills, then opened it and spilled one out onto her palm. "I did something yesterday I shouldn't have."

Her father snorted. "Are you telling me ah taught you to be a dumbass?"

Dar swallowed the pill and washed it down with a little of the bottled water she kept in her overnight bag. "Nope." She put the bottle down and faced him. "You taught me chivalry. Kerry was sick as a dog and couldn't stand up, so I picked her up and carried her to the bed."

Andrew covered his eyes. "Lord."

"Yeah, well." Dar trudged back to him and turned. "Mind unzipping me?" She felt a light touch, then the fabric around her shoulders relaxed. "Thanks." She glanced back at him. "And you would have done the same damn thing, so there."

"Huh."

Dar picked up her nightshirt and ducked into the bathroom. She peered at her reflection and grimaced at the spreading extent of her injury. *No wonder they freaked. Damn, that looks almost as bad as it feels.* With a sigh, she slid her dress off and carefully got into her nightshirt, trying not to lift her arm more than she had to. "I'll be damn glad when this is over," she called out.

"You and me both, Dardar," Andrew answered.

Dar went back into the room and sat on the bed. Andrew sat in the chair facing her. They regarded each other in silence for a moment, then Dar exhaled. "I hate what this is doing to Kerry." She hesitated. "And I hate that it's because of us, because of our relationship that it's so bad for her."

Andrew mulled that over for a bit. "Yeap," he finally exhaled. "It was like that for your ma and me too. Her folks, my folks...Hurts like hell sometimes."

They both thought about that in companionable quiet.

"Dar?" Andrew finally looked up at her, the dim light glinting off his pale eyes. "What'd that feller do to Kerry?"

Dar studied his face. "Kyle?"

"Hm."

"Just a lot of things. Why?"

Andy shifted. "'Cause that young lady ain't afraid of much, and she's scared of him; and I want to know why that is. And 'cause he makes mah eyeballs itch."

How should I answer that? Dar wondered. So much Kerry had told her was so very private, and she knew her lover had kept it that way for a reason. Would she want anyone else to know? Would she want anyone else to hear the things she'd finally told Dar, getting past that one last barrier before she committed herself to their relationship?

Maybe not.

There had been shame in Kerry's eyes when she'd told her. It was a secret she'd held inside for a long time, and something she'd offered up to Dar in a trembling voice, as though somehow it might have made her feel differently about Kerry. Instead, it had just made her angry she hadn't been there to stop it.

As she considered, Dar peered down at her hands, clenched together and tensed. Her mind went over Kyle's vaguely threatening manner. Would he try to hurt Kerry further? Her brow creased, then she nodded a tiny bit. He'd try to make her as miserable as he could, wouldn't he?

She lifted her eyes and found her father patiently watching her. "I think...I think the worst thing he did to her..." She paused, trying to find the right way to phrase her thoughts. "I think the worst thing he did was he forced Kerry to see just how little she counted as a person with her own parents."

"Mm." Andrew considered that. Then he glanced sharply at her. "How?"

Her father sensed something, Dar realized suddenly. "He...did something to her, and when she told her parents, they didn't believe her." She hesitated. "They believed him and made her apologize to him, and he laughed at her."

Andrew got up and sat on the bed next to Dar. He looked into her eyes with a serious expression. "Paladar, did that man hit her?"

"No." Dar felt suddenly back in adolescence, facing the one person she had never lied to, and had always trusted more completely than anything or anyone else in her life. "He raped her, Daddy."

Andrew went very, very still, not even breathing for a long, long moment.

Dar blinked and was surprised to feel the warmth of tears rolling down her cheeks. She wiped them away with an irritated swipe of the back of her hand. "How could they not believe her? Damn! I could never understand that."

Andrew remained very quiet for a moment, then he exhaled and took Dar's hand, carefully folding his fingers around hers. "I thank the good Lord that you cannot understand that." His voice was low and a touch hoarse.

Dar studied the scarred hands holding hers. "Dad?"

Andrew looked up at her. "Hm?"

"Sorry I gave you such a hard time when I was a kid," Dar said. "I didn't realize how lucky I was."

Andrew shifted, then circled her with one long arm and gently hugged her and brushed his lips over her hair as she tucked her head against his shoulder.

"KERRISON, A MOMENT, if you please?"

For a long beat, Kerry almost said no. Then she exhaled and walked to her mother. The press had disassembled their equipment, and the hall was almost empty, and she wanted nothing more than to escape and find Dar and just get a hug. "Yes?"

Cynthia glanced around, then looked at her. "I know this evening was terribly upsetting for you."

Kerry shrugged. "It was more or less what I was expecting. I don't think we'll be staying for the service tomorrow."

Cynthia's lips compressed. "Oh dear." She sighed. "Perhaps if I speak with them—"

"No." Kerry lifted a hand. "Don't bother. I've paid my respects and said my good-byes." She paused, considering her words. "Anything more is just a farce, and we all know it."

"But—"

"Besides," Kerry brushed aside the objection, "I've had about as much of Kyle's slimebag presence as I'm willing to take in this lifetime."

Cynthia remained silent for a moment. "His return was unexpected. Your father did depend on him so. He placed great value on him."

"I know." Kerry looked her right in the eye. "More so than on me. I remember that very clearly."

Cynthia fell silent, visibly biting her lip.

"Excuse me." Kerry stepped around her and walked towards the foyer. She met up with Angela and Michael as they came out of the library, almost as though they'd been lying in wait for her. "Hey."

"What a bitch of a day, huh?" Michael fell in at her side as they walked towards the stairs. "Think tomorrow will be better?"

"I don't give a damn," Kerry replied. "We're out of here in the morning."

"Oh," Michael murmured.

Angie put a hand on Kerry's back as they started up the steps. "If it's any consolation to you, the snarky comments got nicer as the night went on. Even Marsha had to grudgingly admit you take grace under pressure to new heights."

"Fuck them," Kerry said. "They can all collectively kiss my ass."

Her siblings maintained a slightly shocked silence for a few steps. "Well," Michael finally said, "okay. But I bet Dar would start throwing them out the windows if they tried."

"That might be fun to watch," Angie said.

Kerry gave them both pointed looks, then she exhaled, her shoulders dropping and losing some of their tension. "Sorry."

"It's okay, sis." Angie put her arm around Kerry's waist, and Michael did the same from the other side as they walked up the steps together. "Did you know the governor knows Dar's father?"

No, Kerry hadn't known that. "Really? Small world, I guess. Oh, wait. He's ex-Navy, isn't he?"

"Yeah," Mike said. "He said Dar's father is one of the scariest people he's ever known."

"Mm." Kerry shrugged. "I don't think so; not now anyway."

"I like him," Angie said. "And I like Dar's mom. She's so funny."

"Funny?" Michael snickered. "You didn't hear her talking to Uncle Edgar. He had no idea who she was. I mean, he knew she was a famous artist, but he had no clue. I guess he didn't make the connection because she doesn't look anything like Dar. So he's going on and on about how horrible everything is, and man, she took him to pieces." He moved his free arm in a slashing motion. "Whack...whack...whack. Just ripped him to shreds. It was great." He laughed. "She told him having met him only confirmed her theory that you should have a license to enter the gene pool."

Kerry felt a tired laugh emerging and she allowed it. "She's really sharp. I know that's where Dar gets it from, but Dar isn't wicked like that. Ceci goes right for the jugular in small words she's sure are going to be very clearly understood." She smiled briefly. "I'm sorry they decided to go back to the hotel tonight." She glanced at the top of the stairs. "Maybe we should have too."

"Hey," Angie gave her a squeeze, "I know it sucks, Ker, but don't begrudge us the few minutes we've spent with you, okay? We do miss you, regardless of what the rest of these jerks say."

They were at the top of the stairs. Kerry stopped and regarded them both, then she pulled them into a hug. "I miss you guys, too. I've hated losing that part of my life." She swallowed back tears.

They stood blocking the landing in a clump for a long moment, then they all released each other and exchanged glances. Angie pursed her lips and put a hand on Kerry's cheek. "Get some rest, sis."

"Thanks. You too." Kerry managed a smile, then walked away.

THE RINGING OF the cell phone made her jump. Dar turned from where she'd been standing at the window watching the odd snow fall and went to the side table. She picked up the phone, opened it, and checked the caller id before she put it to her ear. "Evening, Alastair."

Alastair released a long breath before he spoke, and that alone put ice cubes in her gut again. "Evening, Dar. How's everything there?"

"Sucks," Dar replied succinctly. "Her family sucks, my shoulder sucks; about the only good thing I can say is that her damn father's dead."

"Saw the news. They sure put a show on there, eh?"

"Jackasses. I had the Wall Street Journal sniffing at me about those damn contracts. I sent them to Ham."

"Good thought. Guess they wanted a sound bite."

"Guess they wanted me to admit I was glad he was dead."

Alastair remained silent briefly. "Ah. Well, then, I'm sorry it has to be me to add more misery to your night, Dar, but this call couldn't wait."

Dar sighed. "Now what?" Her mind ran over the possibilities and she didn't like any of them.

"Just got off the phone with the general," Alastair said. "It's gotten public that Stuart had that information."

Dar's eyes closed. "How did that happen?"

"Someone told someone, who told someone else. You know how it is."

"Shit."

"Mm." Alastair sounded more resigned than upset. "I'd say that describes this entire situation to a T. But regardless, the deal's off if that stuff's still out there, and apparently the general's heard it is."

Dar was silent, her eyes focused on the soft pastel wall opposite her. "Well, it's there somewhere, since I gave it to him and I doubt he burned it. Want my resignation in person or via a letter? I can't change what I did." Her throat caught a little on the words. "I'm not even sure I could say I'd do it any differently, even now."

Alastair absorbed her statement in pensive quiet. "Any

chance you could get those papers back? I mean, you're right there, Dar. I'm sure he kept them close. If those were recovered, the general said he'd be all right, I think."

"He probably made copies."

"Dar, don't make it more complicated than it is," Alastair said. "If he said he'd be satisfied with the damn papers, then let's give them to him, all right?"

She accepted the fact that he hadn't rejected her offer of resignation with a curious sense of personal loss, mixed with a rueful pride that at the very least, she'd done it her way. "I doubt I could find them, Alastair. People are crawling all over this place. I'm sure my rummaging through his office won't be a viable option."

"I see." Alastair sighed. "Well, tell you what, Dar. Why don't you come see me after this whole thing is over, hm? Just let Bea know when you're headed out."

Dar's chest tightened. "Okay." She managed to keep her voice even. "I will."

"Goodnight, Dar. Take care." Alastair's tone gentled. "And give Kerrison my sympathies, too, hm? She looked a bit put upon on the tube."

"Okay. I will. Thanks, Alastair." Dar closed the phone and stared at it, then she simply shook her head and tossed it onto the table. Now what? She'd thought they were okay, and now...

Well, hell. "Screw it. Screw them, screw Gerry, screw it all. This is one damned decision I refuse to regret," she announced to the uncaring green walls. "All of them can kiss my ass."

She walked to the window and watched the damn snow fall as she waited, trying to dismiss the conversation from her mind. Kerry didn't need to deal with all this now. Neither of them needed to. They'd get out of there, and go home and then...

There'd be plenty of time for them to think about it later.

KERRY TRUDGED DOWN the hallway and reached the door to their room with a sense of definite, finely drawn relief. She turned the knob and poked her head inside, finding pale blue eyes alertly watching her from the bed. "Hey." She entered and closed the door, then leaned against it. Dar was sprawled on one side of the plush, canopied bed, her laptop resting on her thighs and her dark hair in appealing disarray.

"Hey," Dar replied. "I was about to come looking for you."

Kerry had to smile. "Like that?" She indicated her lover's state of undress.

"Mmhm." Dar nodded. "Barefoot and all. I figured I couldn't possibly attract any more attention than I already had today, so what the hell?" She held out a hand. "C'mere."

Kerry shed her shoes on the way to the bed as Dar shifted the laptop, and they somehow ended up in a warm tangle of limbs and bedding in the middle of the comforter.

"Uhrg," Kerry groaned.

Dar pulled her closer and rubbed her back with her fingertips. "Kerry, Kerry, Kerry," she murmured on a breath. "It's over, sweetheart. It's over and done with."

Kerry kept her eyes closed and went almost limp, just absorbing the feel and scent of her lover. "We're leaving in the morning. We're going back to the hotel, getting Mom and Dad, going to the airport, and getting on the first plane larger than a crop duster headed south."

Dar smiled faintly. "You got it."

"And I'm never coming back here again," Kerry whispered. "Ever."

Dar just hugged her closer.

"Ker?"

"Mm?"

"You want to take that dress off?"

"No. Do you?"

Dar studied the figure curled up in her arms, her face buried into Dar's nightshirt. "Well," she smoothed Kerry's hair a bit, "normally I'd jump at the chance, but I'm kinda handicapped on that side."

Kerry slowly lifted her head, her eyebrows scrunching together as she blinked in the dim light. "Oh, damn. I'm sorry." She peered at Dar's chest. "Why didn't you say something? I must have been killing you."

"Nah." Dar shook her head. "It doesn't hurt when you press there." She patted the front of her shoulder. "Only when I lift my arm up."

"Mmph." Kerry raked her hair back out of her eyes, rolled onto her side, and gazed down at her now rumpled clothing with a look of sleepy displeasure. "Yeah, I guess I'd better. Damn thing's uncomfortable as heck anyway." She squirmed off the bed and stood up, then unzipped the back of her dress and pulled it over her head.

Dar merely sat back, enjoying the view. Kerry had a gorgeous back, a cute little V shape that sloped cleanly down from her compact, but smoothly muscular shoulders, then flared lightly through her slim hips and powerful, lean legs. She had a faint golden tan, and the low lamplight caused shadows to form across her skin as the muscles moved visibly under it.

She could see tension there, too, though. "Aspirin's in the

right front pocket of my bag, if you want."

Kerry paused in the act of pulling on her Tweety T-shirt. "Did you take your drugs?"

Dar nodded. "Oh yeah."

Kerry finished pulling down the soft cotton fabric, then fished the bottle of aspirin out of Dar's bag, along with her bottle of water. "Did I ever mention how much I love how prepared you always are?" She swallowed a few tablets and took a sip of the water. "How did everything work out with the lines in Chicago?"

Dar grimaced. "Maybe we should change planes there tomorrow instead of Detroit, so I can go and kick that bastard's ass in person."

Kerry smiled as she trudged back to the bed and climbed back into it. "No, sweetie. You're going back to Miami with me, and right to Dr. Steve's." She laid a finger on Dar's nose. "He's going to spank you."

Pale blue eyes mildly regarded her. "All right, but you're coming with me. While he's taking pictures of my insides, he can run some tests on yours."

Kerry took a breath, obviously caught by surprise. "I don't think I..."

Dar lifted an eyebrow and smirked.

Kerry sighed, dropping her gaze, then she returned the smile. "Okay." She crawled over Dar's body and nudged her to the left. "Move over. I don't want to take chances." She waited for Dar to comply, then snuggled against her lover's right side and put her head on her shoulder.

Dar gently massaged the tight muscles in Kerry's back. A warm puff of air penetrated the fabric on her chest, and she glanced down to see a somber, bleak expression on Kerry's face. "Hey."

Kerry blinked, and a few tears rolled down her cheek to soak Dar's shirt. "I'm so tired," she breathed. "My soul hurts, Dar. Those people trampled all over it."

At a loss for words, Dar relied on touch instead. She pulled Kerry closer and cuddled with her, wincing as she brought her other arm over to stroke Kerry's face with light fingertips, catching the tears that continued to fall and brushing them aside. "Don't let them get to you, Ker," she finally said, very softly. "They're just assholes."

Kerry drew in a shaky breath and sniffled. "I know. I just feel like I spent the day as an archery target." She spread one hand out flat against Dar's stomach and absorbed the warmth of her skin as it moved with Dar's breathing. "I feel as bruised as you look."

"Well," Dar tenderly kissed her on the head, "we're both

gonna head south to heal, then." Kerry relaxed against her as the tension eased from her body. "You know I felt like taking out a fire hose and spraying that room tonight, doncha?"

Kerry remained very quiet for a moment, then she gave up a surprising giggle.

"Yeah," Dar went on, her voice a low drawl, "I would have loved to just blast those suckers right down and watch them slip and slide and crack their asses on that parquet floor."

That image elicited another giggle. Kerry sniffled, rested her chin on Dar's chest, and gazed up at her through tear filled eyes. "Can I tell you something?"

"Sure." Dar gently wiped her face.

"I love you."

Dar hugged her again. "I love you, too."

Kerry exhaled and put her head back down. "You know what the worst thing was?" she asked in a quiet voice.

"Kyle?"

Kerry nodded against her shoulder. "Yeah."

"The rest of them are just ignorant bastards. Him, I'd like to put a rifle bullet through." Dar's temper rose a little, and her nostrils flared.

Kerry slid her hand under Dar's shirt and stroked her thigh. The muscles were tense, and she rubbed her thumb in a tiny circle over them as she considered Dar's words. Seeing Kyle had been a definitely unpleasant shock. It had brought back a lot of bad memories she'd consciously pushed out of her consideration after she'd broken most ties with her family and thrown herself into her new life with Dar.

It had been easier that way. After all, she had in truth left that part of her past behind her, and the reassuring solidity of her relationship with Dar, along with her ever expanding new job, had filled her wants and needs quite nicely, thank you.

It hit her suddenly. Kerry went very still and almost stopped breathing.

He was gone. Her father was gone.

Her world reversed and turned upside down as an unseen weight came off her. She was aware of Dar's snug hold, but she floated in limbo for a long moment as she adjusted to a new reality.

He was gone.

Kerry closed her eyes, and all the tension drained out of her, leaving her limp as a dishrag draped comfortably over Dar's tall frame. Sleep gently overtook her, refusing to erase the smile that now shaped her lips.

Chapter
Ten

THE STUDY WAS full of frazzled looking frustrated men and women. Kyle entered, closed the door, stripped off his coat, and tossed it over the tall back of the chair near the desk. "Anything?" he asked the two men behind the large, square desk.

"No, sir." The younger of the two looked up. "Sir, is there any point to this anymore?"

Kyle gave him a withering look. "Of course there's a point. The governor's going to make his announcement tomorrow, and if we don't find a way to clean up little Mrs. Stuart's family act, we've got a lot of money that's going to pull out like gangbusters." He picked up a folder and studied it. "I've already gotten calls warning me."

"Well, sir, unless you can talk to Mrs. Stuart, I'm not sure we've got anything here." The man sighed and dropped his pencil. "I've checked financial, legal, tax records, DMV, credit...I've never seen people so clean in my life."

"Oh, c'mon." Kyle put the folder down. "You can't tell me a bitch like that doesn't have some skeletons. I don't buy it."

"He's right, sir," said the older man, a gruff, bear-like figure with a thick, grizzled beard and shrewd eyes. "Here's the file recap." He handed it to Kyle. "High school valedictorian, graduated mcl from Miami, worked for ILS for sixteen years, never late on her taxes, no tickets, no police record except for—"

"Except?" Kyle glanced at him. "I knew there was something. What is it?"

The aide shook his head. "An incident several years back involving some fight at a bar. Some kids got attacked."

Kyle looked delighted. "By her?"

"No," the man replied. "She defended them. Put two of the assailants in the hospital, despite the fact they were armed with shotguns. The cops gave her a glowing commendation."

Kyle frowned. "That's not the answer I wanted."

The younger man shrugged. "Never even paid her electric bill late, sir. There's just nothing there." He shuffled some papers. "And forget the parents. The mother's Eastern money we don't want to mess with, and the father's got a military honor sheet longer than my leg."

"Mmm." Kyle's face went still, only his eyes darting back and forth over the documents. "Real hero, huh?"

"Yes, sir." The man nodded. "He was MIA for seven years. Went in after a bunch of guys that had gotten captured and let himself get captured so they could get free." He glanced down. "Medal of Honor for that one, sir."

Kyle snorted. The rest of the staff watched him uneasily. "Well, if they won't oblige us by handing us a scandal, I suppose we'll have to manufacture one."

The door opened. They all looked up to see Cynthia Stuart standing in the doorway, primly erect, her hands folded before her. She took a step inside and looked at all of them.

"Ah, Mrs. Stuart." Kyle put on a charming smile. "We were just discussing transition plans."

Cynthia closed the door and walked forward, scanning all their faces before she reached her late husband's desk and stopped by it. "Please don't waste your time. I've come here to inform you that you are all, as of this moment, fired." She paused and took a pleased breath. "Please leave, or I'll have security escort you out."

For a moment there was nothing but shocked silence. "That would be *now*. At once."

Stunned, they picked themselves up and edged out of the room. They jostled each other at the door and waited to clear it before uttering vicious whispers.

Only Kyle remained, staring at Cynthia with hooded eyes. "I'm sure you don't—"

"Most especially, I certainly do mean you as well, Mr. Evans," Cynthia said sharply. "It's simply a pity that all I can do is fire you."

Even Kyle was caught off guard by the icy tone. "You don't know what you're doing. I've got some information that could be very, very damaging—"

"I most certainly do." She enunciated the words very carefully. "Roger is no longer here to protect you, and you will leave this house immediately, or I'll have security drag you out of it and toss you over the wall." Her voice rose. "You will not stay in my home one more second or visit even one more second's abuse on my children. *Out!*"

Kyle's eyes narrowed as he circled the desk. "Think you can just order me around like that, lady? Better think again."

He was stopped in his tracks, the back of his collar and belt held firmly and yanked, jerking him back several paces. A low, Southern-tinged drawl crawled over his shoulder.

"Ah do believe this lady asked you to leave."

"Let me go." Kyle struggled. He was jerked further back, where he collided with a large body.

"G'head." Andrew lowered his voice. "Fight me, you bastard, 'cause I'm looking for one real small excuse to rip off yer arm and beat you with it." The voice dropped further. "'Cause I can."

Kyle stopped struggling, turned his head, and met Andrew's pale blue eyes.

"And ah will," Andrew rumbled. "Now, you figger my kid kicked yer ass round 'bout a year ago, and she's a damn sight nicer than I am."

For a moment, it could have gone either way, then Kyle glanced away. "If you put it that way, fine. I'll be out of here as soon as I gather my gear. The information I have will certainly screw you over, too, you fucking sailor."

Andrew swung him around and shoved him towards the door, adding a boot to the butt to hurry his progress. Kyle stumbled forward but caught himself on the chair, and, after grabbing his jacket, left the room without a single backward glance.

"Well." Cynthia exhaled. "Thank you, Commander Roberts." She glanced at the door. "I'm afraid he might try to turn this to his advantage, however. He has quite a legal mind."

"And ah have me a smart wife." Andrew ambled across the room and drew back the heavy window curtains. Ceci slipped out, putting the cap on a small, nifty looking video camera. "Who don't like to take chances."

Ceci gave Cynthia a smile. "Well done. Couldn't have done it better myself, though I suspect my daughter could have."

Cynthia Stuart let out a long, relieved sigh. "I have so dreamed of doing that. For such a long time." She collected herself and straightened. "I believe I need a drink after that, however. Will you join me?"

"Absolutely." Ceci curled her arm around Andrew's and smiled. "We should talk."

Andrew looked thoughtfully at the door. "Ya'll go on; I'll catch you up," he said, gently disengaging his arm and heading after Kyle.

IT WAS DARK in the hall, but Dar's night vision was up to the task. She glided down the steps on bare feet without a whisper of sound and crossed the huge foyer with a quick look in either direction.

The big house was quiet, but not silent. Its walls creaked, and there were soft sounds of cutlery clinking somewhere off to one side that indicated not everyone was sleeping. Dar paused in the doorway of the main hall to listen, only moving on when she was sure no one was headed her way.

She wasn't even sure why she was doing this, except that she knew if she told Kerry what was going on, and she hadn't even tried looking, her partner would be upset. It would be like she'd quit, and Dar clearly remembered Kerry's reaction to that the last time she had just given up.

So here she was, slinking like a thief in the night, creeping across the marble floors to the door of Roger Stuart's study. Again she paused to listen, one hand on the knob. Certain that she was alone, she opened the door, slipped inside, and closed the door behind her, thanking anyone who was listening that the hinges were well oiled.

The office was dark. Through one window, a bit of light from outside threw soft gray shadows over the room. A shiver went down her back as she imagined the room's former occupant watching her malevolently from the next dimension, and the stirring of her usually dormant imagination almost sent her right back out of the room. Then her logic centers took hold and she forced herself towards the other end of the study.

Here, shelves of books and handsome oak inlaid cabinets lined the walls. Dar touched a few of the books, but they were mostly never read sets; the cabinets opened readily, displaying cut crystal decanters of whiskey and not much more.

She studied the desk, then turned on the desk lamp and bathed the surface in bright gold. The leather desk pad showed faint impressions, and if she looked at an angle, she could almost make out words, pressed there by a dead man's hand.

One word caught her eye, she leaned closer, and touched the pad as she recognized—even with breaks and gaps—her lover's name. But that was all she could make out, just the "Kerrison," and then part of one word, "bo." For it to be there at all, it had to be recent.

As intriguing as that was, Dar reluctantly tore her attention from it. She pulled out a drawer and hunted through it, finding it mostly empty. The next, and the next were the same, and the fourth contained only a Bible and a folded wool sweater. "Least one of them's useful." But the papers she sought were not there. She straightened, then froze, finding a pair of somber eyes looking back at her. "Ah."

Kerry walked across the room and faced her across the desk.

"What in the dickens are you doing?" She folded her arms.

Rats. Dar leaned a bit on the desk top. "Thought you were asleep. I was just trying to clean up a detail or two."

"Detail?" Kerry looked around and then back at her. "About what? Why are you in here, Dar? What are you looking for?" She kept her voice very low, though not quite a whisper.

Ah well. She had been hoping to put off telling Kerry about Alastair's call until they were on the way home. With the stress of being with her family so high, the last thing Dar felt she needed was to hear more trouble. Now, she had little choice.

"I'm looking for the papers I gave him," Dar replied quietly. "Alastair needs them. Otherwise, the deal is off, and I'm no longer your boss."

Kerry's jaw dropped, literally.

"And they're not here. So," Dar circled the desk, and turned off the light, leaving them in darkness, "let's go back to bed. I can at least say I tried."

"Wait. I thought—"

Dar took her arm. "Word got out that the senator had them." She nudged Kerry towards the door. "C'mon. Don't worry about it, Ker. Whatever happens, happens."

Don't worry about it. Kerry felt numb. She'd woken in darkness to find Dar gone. Instinct had led her to the study, and now... She sighed. Now, she almost wished she'd just stayed in bed. "Okay." It was all just too much. She wrapped her fingers in Dar's nightshirt and let her lead her back upstairs to their room. "Were you serious about—?"

"Yeah," Dar whispered as they nearly tiptoed down the hallway. "But it's okay."

"No, it's not."

Dar closed the door to their room behind them and put her arms around Kerry. "Yes, it is. I don't regret any of it, Ker. Honestly."

Kerry looked up into her eyes and read the truth there. Feeling the tears well up and the ache in her heart shortening her breathing, she put her palm against Dar's cheek. "It's not okay," she managed to get out. "Dar—"

"Shh." Dar kissed her forehead. "I love you. That's what matters to me. You matter to me. ILS can go jump off a bridge, for all I care."

Kerry leaned against Dar and closed her eyes, surrendering to her own mind's exhaustion. It was just a sucky end to a sucky day.

"STUPID BASTARDS...LITTLE whore bitch. Fire me, huh?"

Kyle was furious. He threw his car into drive and headed through the intersection, foot pumping the gas as he just missed a man walking across the street. "Get out of my way, jackass."

It was bitter cold out, and his hands were stiff as he curled them around the steering wheel. Of all the endings he'd expected for the night, this was the last he'd have imagined. From her? The milkmaid? The woman without two brain cells to rub together? "Bitch."

He knew what was behind it. No question. The little dyke whore daughter was behind it. She'd gotten to mommy dearest; probably brought up that old story about what he'd done to her. *Stupid kid.*

It hadn't even been memorable. At least for him. Just another nubile conquest, and he'd even convinced himself she'd enjoyed it. She'd been lusting after him anyway, right? *Yeah.*

"Stupid bitch," he repeated, cursing himself for the nth time for not getting back into the country just a week earlier. The summons from the senator had sounded so important, so urgent. Stuart had wanted him there immediately.

Could it have been for the contracts? Lately, he'd started to get the feeling Stuart was putting him off, avoiding him since he'd been pushing that investigation so hard. But the sudden call had reassured him he was still in good graces, still needed.

Still important.

Well, at least he'd found a nest egg. Kyle patted his briefcase. With what he had in there, he could blackmail himself into retirement, and to hell with it.

The road curved in front of him and he followed it, the snow covered fencing on either side whipping past as he sped up, enjoying the power of the car's engine.

He never looked in the rearview mirror, so he never saw the cold blue eyes that rose up from behind him, or the long arm that reached across his body to grab the steering wheel. He merely felt a huge hand wrap around his mouth, cutting off his scream of alarm as the car swerved and plunged off the road in a moment of icy nightmare.

A huge, dark tree rose up in front of him and he couldn't avoid it, the steering wheel held in an iron grip even as his foot came off the gas and he tried to brake. The front of the car imploded, crushing him from the waist down, in a wave of pain so intense he almost passed out. Almost.

The hand removed itself, and he screamed.

"Ah could jest leave your sorry ass here jest like this," a voice said in his ear.

"Asshole! You bastard! Augh!" Kyle tried to turn to see his

attacker, but he was pinned in place. "You son of a bitch!"

The blue-eyed wraith chuckled. "Yeap. Ah am an asshole, mister. Lotsa better men than you found that out." Andrew clamped a hand on Kyle's jaw and slammed it shut. "But I ain't no bastard, like you are."

"Gprfm." Kyle struggled impotently.

"Ah just wanted you to know, ya'll piece of scum, that what you done way back when to that little girl just come home to bite your ass," Andrew whispered into his ear. "Got anything to say 'bout that?" He released Kyle's jaw.

"I enjoyed every fucking minute of it," Kyle spat.

"Thought so." Andrew took hold of Kyle's jaw and savagely yanked it to one side and slammed the top of Kyle's head with his other hand. A sharp crack sounded in the car over the hissing of the demolished engine.

Then it was quiet.

"May t'Lord God have mercy on ya'll," Andy said, after a moment of silence. "'Cause He's a better man than me." After a slight delay, he slammed his shoulder against the back door, slid out of the car, and cocked his head as he heard sirens in the far, far distance.

A house overlooked the crash site, and there were lights on. He could see silhouettes in the window, and a door slammed nearby, accompanied by the crunch of someone running in the newly fallen snow.

In the other direction, a thick blanket of white formed an unwritten page, and towards the road, headlights approached, their brilliance dancing off the soft surface.

Andrew paused, then looked up and studied the branches for a moment before he crouched and leaped, grabbed a branch, and pulled himself up into the tree. A dusting of snow fell under him, then it all went silent again.

AS SHE WOKE the next morning, Kerry half remembered her dream. It had been something about rabbits. Her eyes drifted open and bemusedly regarded the colorful fabric she was lying on, recalling that every time she dreamed of animals, it was always one of those really weird dreams that made no sense and usually involved her being naked.

She wondered briefly what a psychologist would make of them—especially the one with the talking bears. A smile spread across her face and she turned her head a little, and took in the room with a vague sense of the unreal.

It seems brighter in here today, she thought, eyeing the window which now let in the pale winter light.

Wonder what time it is. Kerry closed her eyes and snuggled closer, reflecting on how much a good night's sleep could do for a person's outlook. She felt much more centered, and she considered that perhaps it was because she'd faced the worst and endured. She'd been tying herself up in knots imagining what her reception would be like, and now...

Well, now she knew. She took in a deep breath, filled with heated air and Dar's scent. It had been as bad, or worse than she'd expected, but knowing, she discovered, was far better than wondering. Knowing, you could deal with, plan for, and defend against. Wondering just kept you unbalanced.

Now she knew the worst, both with her family, and the fallout from Dar's actions with the Navy. Looking at the sun, she realized that life did just go on, despite all its problems. Life would go on now. They would go on together.

"Mmph." Kerry exhaled and wriggled a little in contentment as Dar's arm tightened around her. Dar had been her anchor through it all, she acknowledged quietly. Like a rock she'd stood there, being a windbreak, something to lean against, and a shelter when it all had gotten to be too much. Kerry opened her eyes again and looked up at her lover in deep affection, almost jumping when her eyes met amused blue ones looking back at her.

"Yeah?"

Dar's eyebrows lifted.

"Didn't think you were awake," Kerry said with a sheepish grin. "I was just lying here thinking about how wonderful you are."

The dark brows lifted even further, giving Dar an almost comical look. She laughed softly and stretched in Kerry's embrace, arching her back and tensing her muscles before relaxing back onto the bed's surface.

"Mm...that was like a carnival ride. Can we go again?" Kerry asked.

Dar eyed her with a faint smile. "You're in a good mood. Feeling better today?"

Kerry nodded. "Yeah. How about you?" She carefully touched Dar's shoulder, feeling it move under her fingers as Dar experimentally flexed it.

"Eh. Stiff, but not as bad as yesterday." Dar sounded mildly surprised. "It's not throbbing anymore." Another experimental movement yielded the same results. "Cool."

Kerry smiled and gave her a hug. "Glad to hear that." She regarded the window. "Looks like the weather got better, too. Hey, wanna get dressed and go for a walk? I could show you my favorite sledding hill before we take off."

Dar remembered her last walk in the cold. "All right." She eyed Kerry. "But you better keep me warm. It looks like the arctic tundra out there. And how about we find some breakfast first? I noticed you didn't get much off that table last night."

"I don't like pate," Kerry said. "And neither do you. There're just so many crackers topped with bits of roast beef and horserad-ish I can handle." Her nose crinkled in distaste. "Besides, I wasn't really hungry." A low rumble made her chuckle a little. "I am now."

"So I hear," Dar remarked mildly. "C'mon. I may need some help in the shower."

Kerry grinned. "Now that's an offer I'll never refuse." She paused and laid a hand on Dar's stomach. "Dar, about work—"

"Shhh." Dar ruffled her hair. "Don't think about it. Let's just get through today and get home."

Kerry sighed. Well, there wasn't much she could do about it anyway, was there? Her eyes drifted off a bit. Or was there?

"WHAT DO YOU think?" Kerry spread her arms and indi-cated her body. She watched the expressions on Dar's face cascade from quizzical to thoughtful to outright lecherous. "I meant the clothes, honey." She sighed, blushing at the compliment neverthe-less.

"Oh." Dar laughed. "Hm." She reviewed her lover's choices thoughtfully. Kerry wore a long sleeved flannel shirt tucked into her nicely worn jeans, to which she'd added the cute touch of sus-penders. She also had on her hiking boots. Dar thought she looked adorable. "Are you deliberately going for the non-WASP look?"

"Well, yeah." Kerry put her hands on her hips. "Did it work?"

"I think so," Dar said gravely. "Should I put on my fringed leather vest?"

Kerry's eyebrows jerked up in pleased surprise. "Did you bring that?"

Dar chuckled. "No. I was joking. Would you settle for leather pants?"

Kerry looked at her suspiciously, then went to her bag and rummaged in it. "Oh." She lifted the pants out. "You really have some? I never saw these before, Dar. Where did you get them?" She shook out the soft, burnt caramel colored hide. "Oo...I like."

"Thank you," Dar replied. "And you've never seen them before because I won't wear them at home."

Kerry eyed her. "Too trendy for Miami?"

"No." Dar took the hide trousers from her. "Too hot. I figured

I might get a chance to actually put them on up here, so I brought them along. Give me a hand getting into them?"

Kerry happily obliged, tugging the leather up and over Dar's hips. They fit comfortably, not too snug, and she neatly fastened the buttons and buckled the two criss-crossing leather beltlets that lent a somewhat offbeat touch to them. The leather was broken and butter soft, and she knelt to fasten the straps near Dar's ankles. "Meant for boots, I see."

"Mmhm," Dar said. "I used to have some that went with them." She buttoned the sleeve on a tightly woven wool shirt in a creamy butter color. "Back in my wilder days."

Kerry ran her fingers over the smooth leather, then sniffed it. "I like them. You're a natural for this stuff."

Dar's lips twitched. "I'll take that as a compliment."

"You should." Kerry placed a kiss on the inside of her leg, just above the knee, then she got to her feet and offered Dar a hand. "Breakfast?"

Dar curled her fingers around Kerry's and accompanied her to the door. "Listen, Ker, about last night—"

"Doesn't that sound like a bad romance novel?" Kerry's lips quirked into a smile. "It's not over, Dar." She looked up at her partner. "I'm going to have a look myself. Maybe I have a little insight into where he might have put that stuff. He was my father."

Dar placed a kiss on the top of her head and just smiled.

MICHAEL HID A smile behind an English muffin as they entered the breakfast room, still holding hands. "Morning, sis."

"Hi," Kerry replied, releasing Dar to walk to a seat. "Morning."

"Oh, Kerrison..." Cynthia looked up from her plate and stopped in mid speech, blinking at her eldest daughter. "Goodness." She hesitated. "That's very colorful, dear."

"Thanks." Kerry snapped a suspender at her and sat down.

Dar continued around the table and approached the serving board with pointed determination. She evaded the uniformed server and captured two plates, then proceeded to dump what she considered proper amounts of edible items on them appropriate to both her taste and Kerry's.

"Ma'am," the server murmured at her anxiously, "I'll do that for you. In this household, the family prefers service."

"In my family's household," Dar answered in a normal voice, "they tossed the food down on the floor in bins, and we had to fight for it. Old habits die hard. Excuse me." She ducked around the woman and headed back towards the table.

Kerry covered her face with one hand, her shoulders shaking.

Cynthia rose to the challenge. "Why, Dar, I didn't know you had siblings."

"I don't." Dar set Kerry's plate down, then took the chair next to her. "But we had a dog."

"Ah." Cynthia's brow wrinkled, then she gave a little shake of her head. "At any rate, I'm very glad you chose to join us for breakfast. Did you have additional plans for today, Kerrison?"

"I was going to treat Dar to a walk in the snow." Kerry finished buttering her muffin and took a bite. "And show her around the property. Then we figured we'd head back to the hotel and pick up M...Dar's folks." There was really no sense, she conceded, in stinging her mother with her usual form of address for Andy and Ceci. Not now that things seemed to be improving as far as familial acceptance went, though Kerry admitted that she was probably pushing things a little today. Just to make sure she wasn't backsliding, she picked up a piece of bacon and bit it in half, then offered the other half to Dar.

"Ah, saved the crispy part for me." Dar accepted the treat with a snap of white teeth. She crunched the bacon with a slight wink in Kerry's direction. "Thanks."

Kerry grinned back, then turned her head and met the bemused looks of her family. *Take it or leave it, guys,* she projected at them. *This is who I am.*

"You guys must be fun to watch in restaurants," Mike commented with a snort. "Do you slurp spaghetti together, too?"

"No," Dar said blandly. "It gets too messy. We save that for home."

Angie nearly snorted a piece of melon out of her nose.

"Hey, I bet Richard never did that with you, did he?" Mike asked his younger sister pointedly.

Angie cleared her throat and swallowed. "Definitely not. It took me three dates just to get him to loosen his tie." She took a sip of juice. "He's not a romantic like Dar is."

Round blue eyes pinned her from across the table in outraged shock.

"Yeah, she gets that from her father," Kerry said blithely.

Cynthia had assumed a noble, serene air, apparently content to let the conversation flow over her unimpeded. "Commander Roberts is a terribly nice man. He has quite a lovely sense of humor." She had finished her breakfast and she stood, folded her napkin, and left it neatly in place. "I must attend to some business matters. If you wish, Kerrison, after your plans are completed, perhaps you might stay for lunch."

Kerry considered the somewhat late time of the morning and nodded. "Sure. Our flight's not until three." The funeral service was scheduled for four that afternoon, and the focal point would be at the cemetery, not there at the house. They would be left in peace, at least for a little while.

Her mother nodded, then left the room.

Angie propped her head up on her fist and just looked at Kerry. "You are such a brat."

"Me?" Kerry asked innocently. "Why? I'm not acting out, I'm just acting normal." She crunched another strip of bacon. "I'm not going to sit here dressed in lace and pretend that's how I live. I don't."

"I think you look really cute," Mike said. "Angie's just jealous 'cause she'd never be able to pull off that outfit."

"Neither would you," Angie gave him a withering look, "hippo butt."

"Look who's talking," Mike retorted. "You're the one who gets her clothing at—"

"Michael," Kerry said.

He stuck his tongue out at her.

"Remind me again why I wanted siblings," Dar said to Kerry, with a look of wry amusement. "You know I—" She fell silent by necessity as Kerry stuffed a piece of muffin into her mouth.

"Hush." Kerry put a fingertip on her nose. "You don't have siblings because you're one of a kind." She smiled at Dar's charmed expression. "Now, chew, so we can go explore."

Dar obliged, chewing and swallowing the bit of muffin while she watched her lover and her family trade banter. *At least,* she sighed, *as long as we are here dealing with this disaster, we aren't back home having to deal with the Naval one waiting for me on my desk.*

Dar thoughtfully nibbled another piece of bacon. *My ex-desk.*

Oh well. She'd figure out something. They had savings in the bank, after all.

THEY WALKED THROUGH the grounds surrounding the house, with Kerry pointing out favored spots from her childhood. Then they turned out of the gates and walked along the road, its surface sloping up towards the crest of a nearby hill.

"It's such a different environment," Dar commented, crunching a bit of snow under her boots. "It's like you have two worlds in the North, a winter one and a summer one."

Kerry tucked her gloved hands inside her pockets and watched her breath plume as she exhaled. "That's true. You're more aware of the passage of time up here, I think. I always liked spring and summer better. We were out of school in the summer, and at least for a while, that was fun, because I got to go to summer camp."

"Mm."

"Winter was always full of social stuff," Kerry went on. "Dress ups, and press events, dinners...For a while I tried to get interested in current events so I'd have something intelligent to say when they pointed the camera at me, but after a few instances of that, I got told to just shut up and look good."

Dar looked at her.

Kerry shrugged. "What can I tell you, Dar? They didn't want to hear what I had to say, or maybe they were afraid I'd develop an embarrassing view on something." She chuckled softly. "If they'd only known."

"Did you?" Dar asked. "Develop a view different from your father's?"

Kerry considered the question. "I liked some of his positions on things. I thought his view on keeping families together was good, though now after knowing what was going on with that other woman, the hypocrisy kind of stinks. He knew a lot more about international politics than I did, and I didn't have the maturity to understand the machinations he was going through here locally to control funding and maintain a conservative majority."

Dar grunted thoughtfully.

"I didn't really start disagreeing with him until I was in college," Kerry went on. "When I got exposed to the wider world and the many kinds of people in it."

"Ever talk to him about that?"

"No." Kerry shook her head and leaned forward a little as they started up a steeper part of the hill. "I tried once, but he told me if that's what college was doing to me, he'd put a stop to it."

Dar simply stopped walking. Kerry moved on a few steps, then turned and regarded her. "I want to know something. How in the hell did you become the woman that told me to go to hell in Miami?"

Ah. Good question. Kerry walked back to Dar, took her hand, and led her upward toward the crest of the hill. "It wasn't something that happened overnight. It was something that was building a little at a time, until I got home after I graduated college with my degree, and was told I was being put to work as a spokeswoman/receptionist in one of my father's crony's companies."

They got to the top of the hill and Kerry paused, regarding the view. "I knew I had a choice. Either put my money where my mouth was and get the hell out of here, or stay here and accept the inevitable." She walked to a tall, almost bare tree and patted its bark. "So I came up here that night and spent hours looking up at the stars, and finally made my decision."

Dar joined her. "Not a popular one."

"No." Kerry exhaled. "After I'd accepted Associated's job offer that next morning, I called Brian and told him, then I just packed, told my parents I was taking the job and left." She leaned on the tree. "But they didn't make it easy. He kept after me constantly. They hoped they'd wear me down and I'd just give up and come home."

Dar gazed at her. "And I almost made that happen."

Kerry turned and looked at her. "Almost. But you also were what made me choose my life over their plans for it, and that more than makes up for what might have been, Dar." She decided to lighten up the conversation. "So, here we have my very first decision tree."

Dar studied Kerry's face for a few moments, then relaxed into a smile. "Nice view up here." She indicated the opposite slope. The hill was fairly steep, and featured a long stretch of even whiteness, ending in a clear area at the bottom with only a few trees that might provide a dangerous impediment. "That where you used to slide down?"

"Yep." Kerry sighed. "Wish we had a sled; I'd love to take you for a ride."

"Well," Dar removed her small penknife from her pocket, "first things first."

Kerry walked to Dar and eyed the knife. "Honey, I love you, but you can't cut down the tree with that to make a sleigh for me. I just won't let you," she warned with a serious look. "I'd rather get the car and drive to Wal-Mart."

Dar laughed.

"No, really, sweetie." Kerry took the knife from her fingers.

"Give me that." Dar swiped the tool back. "I wasn't going to cut the damn tree down." She circled the trunk and found a good spot. "Just do a little carving." She set to work with Kerry peering over her shoulder.

"Oh." Kerry smiled. "Okay." She turned away and explored the hilltop, kicking bits of half buried wood around with the toe of her hiking boot. The wind was stiffer up there and it blew her hair back, stinging her eyes with its chill as she gazed down the slope.

"That night seems so long ago," she said to the air. "I was so scared. I didn't know what I was getting myself into, or where I might end up." The branches overhead chuckled together. "But I looked up at those stars, and they told me to follow my heart." She turned and watched Dar. Dar's brow was creased in concentration as she carved careful letters. "And that's what I ended up doing, isn't it?"

"You say something to me?" Dar poked her head around the tree trunk. "Almost done."

Kerry strolled to Dar and kissed her on the nose. "Take your time, Geppetto." She admired the neat heart shaped cut and the curved letters taking form under Dar's skilled hands. "I bet you could carve wood, if you wanted to."

"Isn't that what I'm doing?" Dar finished a K and started on the S. "Or do you mean like sitting on the porch in a rocking chair whittling kind of thing." She flicked a piece of bark out of her way. "I think I'll wait for retirement for that, when I'm too old and creaky to do anything else."

Kerry rested her chin on Dar's shoulder and exhaled. "We can be old and creaky together. Can you imagine what great memories we'll have by then?" She had a touch of wonder in her voice. "What an amazing thought."

Dar finished her work and turned her head. "You like?"

A simple heart, with four initials and a plus sign. Kerry sighed in deep satisfaction. "I love." She kissed Dar on the lips. "Thank you."

Holding hands, they walked back down the hill. Kerry knew they were watched from behind kitchen curtains, knew the whispers, knew the scandalized looks they were garnering, and the only thing that knowledge evoked in her was an intense desire to laugh.

There were cars in the driveway when they got back to the house. One, Kerry realized, was Andy and Ceci's rental car, and she nudged Dar and pointed to it. "Hey!" The other was Richard and Angie's, and she guessed her brother-in-law had come over. The third she didn't recognize.

"Huh. Thought they were going to wait at the hotel for us," Dar commented as they strolled up the walk. "Hope everything's okay."

The front door opened as they approached, and the major domo gave them a brief smile as they entered the house.

It was quiet, but they could hear voices from the solarium, and one of those voices was easily identifiable from its low, drawling tones. Kerry led the way into the garden and waved at the group seated near the end of the glassed-in area. "Hey, folks."

"Goodness!" a clear voice erupted, and a small, silver haired form popped up from the bench like an albino meerkat. "Kerrison! There you are."

Kerry stopped and blinked, then smiled. "Aunt Penny!"

Her aunt hurried around the bench, rushed over to her, and gave her an enthusiastic hug. "Hello, my dear. You look wonderful," Aunt Penny said with enthusiasm. "Hello to you, too, Dar. It's good to see you again."

"Same here," Dar responded cordially, having developed a liking for Kerry's perky elderly relative.

Aunt Penny clasped both of their arms and led them to the benches, where Dar's parents and Cynthia Stuart were seated. "And I've just met your lovely parents, Dar. Wonderful!"

Dar felt her face reacting, saw her father's do likewise, and heard her mother snicker; she realized they both probably wore the same expression. She walked over, took a seat next to her father and exhaled, extended her leather covered legs out a little and regarded her boots as she listened to Kerry and Aunt Penny exchange pleasantries with Cynthia.

"Oh, listen." Kerry broke the flow of conversation. "I have to get something from our room—I'll be right back." She exchanged a glance just slightly too long with Dar as she passed, and touched her partner's shoulder as Dar patted her calf in understanding.

"Right. Ah..." Cynthia frowned. "Well, Penny, tell us what you've been up to? It's been so long."

"Well, dear, since I was banned from your house while your husband was alive, that's not so very surprising, now is it?" Penny rebuked mildly. "But I've been doing some interesting things, so I'm glad you asked."

Cynthia had the grace to look embarrassed. "I'm so sorry, Penny." She sighed, glancing furtively at Ceci and Andrew.

Ceci rallied to the occasion. "Don't worry. Andrew and I are banned from so many households for so many reasons, we don't even bother with Christmas cards anymore."

Andy chuckled. "Ain't that the truth."

Penny patted his knee, giving Cynthia a reassuring look at the same time. "As I was saying, dear..."

DAR SAT BACK to listen, half an ear listening for Kerry moving around the house behind her, and most of her thoughts fastened on what her partner was up to.

"You ready to go home?" Andrew asked in a low voice.

Dar glanced at him. "Does it show?"

Her father patted her knee, then poked it. "Whacha got here, Dardar? Alligator pants?"

"Leather." Dar chuckled, smoothing the hide. "Stuck in the back of my closet."

Andrew studied the garment. "Ah do believe I remember when you got them there pants." He glanced around and lowered his voice again. "D'jya hear what happened last night?"

"No." Dar leaned on the arm of her chair. "What?"

"That there lady fired all them hangers-on," Andrew said. "Just went in and told them to git."

Dar's eyes brightened. "Yeah?" She was pleasantly surprised. "All of them?"

Andrew nodded solemnly. "Yep. Even that feller we all did not like."

Kyle? It had to be. Dar muffled a grin, giving Cynthia mental points she hadn't expected to tender. "Good for her," she whispered. "About damn time. Wait 'til Kerry hears."

Andrew sat back with a satisfied grunt, folding his arms across his chest. He was dressed in his usual jeans, but this time with a heavy sweatshirt against the cold weather and a pair of sturdy military boots. "I do believe she'll be happier for it."

"Sure," Dar said. "She's hated that bastard most of her life. Just wish she'd have been there to see it."

Her father's lips quirked a little. "Wall, just so happens your momma was there with that little camera thing of hers. So we can have us a picture watching session later on."

Dar looked at him in surprise. "You were there?"

"Yeap."

"Huh."

"Didn't think we'd let you kids have all the fun, didja?"

Dar covered her face with one hand and shook her head.

After a moment of watching her, Andrew leaned over again. "Hey, Dardar?"

"Hm?"

"Things work out all right with Gerry?"

Dar stared past the people in the room to the far wall. "Not really. But that was my choice and my fault, so if I pay for it, it's only fair." She kept her eyes forward, even when she felt the warmth of her father's hand on her shoulder. "You taught me that."

The pressure increased as Andy squeezed her arm. "Yeap, I did. But if it's all the same t'you, I think you made the right choice, doing what you done."

Dar managed a smile. "Thanks."

IT WAS A plain wooden door, set in a half forgotten hallway behind the library and the study, the senator's official "working" area. Kerry approached it and rested her hand on the rough, slightly irregular surface for a moment before she turned the knob and pushed the door inward.

Unlike the big study, this room was small, almost intimate. It smelled mostly of books and dust, age and use. Along one wall, under the window, was a desk with an old style wooden desk chair. The other three walls were covered in bookshelves, and they, unlike the outer study, were filled with well-read and tattered books.

Kerry just stood in the middle of the room and looked around. It was, perhaps, the third or fourth time she'd ever been in there, and even though the memories she had were hazy, the room didn't seem to have changed.

This was her father's private office. Here, he worked on the family financial business, or read books that interested him rather than advertised his achievements. Here, on the walls, hung old certificates from his younger years and pictures from his college days.

Kerry knew she only had a few minutes to search, but she had to pause and study the pictures—stern men standing together, her father in the front row near the middle, almost unrecognizable. Almost.

Except that the face in the picture held lines she recognized from the mirror she looked into every day. The truth was there in front of her, a truth she knew she couldn't set aside. She had been a part of this man, no matter what he'd done to her. Kerry touched the edge of the picture frame, staring intently at it. Then she shook her head, went to shelves, and scanned the books on them.

Military histories. He'd loved them, she recalled, and now, thinking that, she remembered his reaction to Dar's father and a little puzzle seemed to click into place. He'd always admired soldiers, heroes. His most prized appointment had been to the Military Appropriations Committee. Surely, he'd taken the time to research Dar's family. Kerry wondered what he'd decided about them. Had he changed his mind? Would he have ever changed his mind about her? About Dar?

With a sigh, she walked to the desk and gingerly sat in the chair, expecting but not getting a protesting squeak from the antique springs. She was reaching for the first drawer when a flash of color to her right caught her eye, and she half turned to look at the desk top.

Pictures were balanced along the back edge of the desk. To her utter surprise, she found herself looking back from one of the frames. Nestled between pictures of Angie and Mike, to one side of a smaller framed shot of her parents together, was not only a shot of her, but a recent one.

Dumbfounded, Kerry brought it closer as if to verify the evidence of her own eyes. She recognized the picture as one she'd had taken of herself for the corporate newsletter on her promotion to vice president, so her expression was appropriately business-like.

It was an original. She could see the softly matted sheen, very different from the print in the glossy catalog. How had he gotten it?

She put it down again, a little shaken. It took all her will-power to turn her eyes from the photo and pull open the drawer to look inside it.

DAR'S CELL PHONE rang. She gave everyone an apologetic look, then stood and stepped outside the room to take the call. "Hello?"

"Well, hello, Dar," Alastair said. "Any luck?"

If there was any consolation to be found, Dar took it from the anxiety she could hear in Alastair's voice. "No. Alastair, those papers could be anywhere. I'm sure he didn't leave them just lying around his house, for God's sake. They're probably in a vault someplace." She hesitated. "Listen, just...We should be home tonight. Have Bea book me on the first flight Tuesday."

Alastair sighed.

"I want a day or so to get things settled," Dar said. "And to give Kerry a few days. She's pretty shaken up right now."

"I'm sure," Alastair murmured. "Take your time, Dar."

Dar leaned against the wall and tried not to feel sick to her stomach. "Hey, Alastair?"

"Hm?"

"I'm sorry."

Alastair was silent for a moment. "Well, you know, Dar, jobs are jobs, but family is the important thing in life." He hesitated. "Right?"

It didn't make either of them feel any better, Dar suspected. "Right." She heard soft footsteps coming down the hall and glanced up to see Kerry approaching. "I'll call you later."

"All right. Bye." Alastair hung up just as Kerry came within earshot. Dar clipped her phone to her leather beltlet and reached out to give Kerry's arm a gentle rub. "No luck, hm?"

Kerry shook her head. "He has...I mean, he had a little private office. I tried there."

"S'okay." Dar produced a smile for her, warm and genuine. "C'mon. I think your aunt was about to tell us funny stories about you and a birthday party."

Kerry rolled her eyes, but allowed herself to be bumped towards the doorway. Just shy of it she stopped and waited for Dar to come up behind her. "He had my picture on his desk, Dar."

Dar's eyebrows shot up in honest surprise.

"I just don't understand." Kerry sighed and continued on into the room, giving her family a smile she didn't really feel.

KERRY WAS GLAD Aunt Penny had stopped by, even though she did tend to tell embarrassing stories about her. *At least one of my relatives,* she reflected, *actually likes me and doesn't mind saying so.* "We just took a walk up to the hill," she said, in answer to her mother's query. "I wanted to show Dar my old sledding spot."

"Goodness, do you still have that Flyer around here, Cyndi?" Aunt Penny asked. "I quite remember young Kerrison here doing battle with a tree on it years ago."

"Ouch." Kerry rubbed her nose in memory. "No, that one's been gone a long time." She spared a sad thought for its passing. "Dar was going to chop down a tree and make one, but I convinced her we didn't have time."

Everyone looked at Dar, who looked back with devastating innocence. "Tell you what. We'll go up to Aspen and I'll make it up to you. You can watch me take out a few trees."

Kerry grinned. "You're on. After your shoulder heals, that is."

"Oh yeah. Get that cleared up just in time fer her to break a laig." Andrew chuckled.

Everyone laughed along with him, even Dar, who folded her arms over her chest. "I wasn't the one who took out six ski instructors and a sled dog. Or that tent."

"Mm...I remember that." Ceci grimaced. "That dog was really mad."

Cynthia leaned forward, placing her hands precisely into her lap. "That sounds very interesting. Do you ski, Commander?"

"Not very well." Ceci ignored the snort from her husband. "Between him and Dar, they cleared the slopes."

Another chuckle made its way around the small circle. "Well, isn't that fun." Aunt Penny patted Kerry on the knee. "Sounds like you have your work cut out for you, dear."

"Yes," Cynthia agreed quickly. "Do stay for lunch, will you, Penny? It's almost served."

They all got up to go into the dining room. Kerry brought up the rear and was surprised when her mother held out a hand, slowing them both down. "What's up?"

"Kerrison, could I speak with you, briefly?" her mother asked. "Alone?"

Ah. Kerry ran over the list of possible subjects and decided it was probably safe, unless her mother was going to give her "that speech," and it was a little too late for that. "Sure." She waved at Dar, who was waiting in the doorway. "G'wan. I'll catch up."

Dar studied her for a moment, then nodded and slipped out of the room, leaving them alone together. "So," Kerry turned and leaned against one of the large planters, "what's on your mind?"

KERRY WAITED FOR the voice to stop, keeping her eyes fastened on the shifting sun outside the glass panes. Then she turned. "I can't believe you're asking me that."

"Kerrison," Cynthia held up a hand, "please, at least consider it. You would be excellent in this role."

"Mother," Kerry took a breath and held her temper, "I'm very happy with the life I have. I'm not changing it."

"I'm not saying you aren't, dear," Cynthia said. "And certainly, I realize you're very attached to your friend Dar, and she would be welcome here, as well."

Kerry regarded her for a moment. "You really don't get it, do you?" She sighed. "No, mother, I won't accept a position here." She paused. "For one thing, you can't afford me. Dar pays me a hell of a lot better than father ever paid anyone."

"But..." Cynthia stopped. "Well, I'm sure..." She stopped again. "It's not just the money, Kerrison. We want you to come back here and be part of your family. Surely you can understand that."

"For another thing," Kerry went on as though she hadn't heard, "I don't like Michigan." She absorbed her mother's slightly shocked look. "I love living in Florida."

"But—"

"Dar and I have a wonderful life together, mother. Why would I want to change that?" Kerry asked in frustration. "Don't you understand yet? This isn't some passing phase I might grow out of."

Cynthia took a seat on a nearby bench and folded her hands. "I do understand that you and Dar are very fond of each other, dear."

Kerry sat next to her. "No, you don't understand. We love each other."

Cynthia was silent.

"I love Dar with all my heart," Kerry said. "She's my life. We're partners in every sense of the word. She's everything I could ever have wished for in someone to share the rest of my life with." She waited for comment and got none. "So, though I'm really glad you fired that bastard Kyle, and the rest of those useless dog poops, I'm not going to come here and take their place."

Cynthia sighed. "Kerrison—"

"I'm going to go home and take my jacket off and play with my dog and soak in the hot tub with Dar under the stars tonight, just because we can," Kerry said. "And, I'll Catch up on my business email and get ready to go back to work."

They were both silent for a few moments. Kerry exhaled and rubbed her temples. "Look, I know that's not what you wanted to hear, and honestly, I do appreciate the welcome you've given both me and Dar."

"Actually," Cynthia murmured, "I quite like Dar. I find her intelligence refreshing."

The way to my heart, Kerry realized with a weak internal laugh, *is through praising my partner. Imagine that.* "It's one of the things I like most about her." She smiled at her mother. "She's smarter than I am."

"Surely not." Cynthia frowned. "You've quite a good brain, Kerrison. You've always had."

"Funny, you and father were always so ready for me to end up as a receptionist." Kerry felt the words slip out. "I never thought my brain ever entered the plans."

"That's not so. He was very proud of your skills, especially when you were in high school," Cynthia said. "He was simply anxious to channel them into something practical."

"I think I found something more practical than reception work to channel them into," Kerry remarked dryly.

Cynthia got up, walked to the frosted windows, and gazed out. "I thought perhaps you would at least think about this, Kerrison." She exhaled. "Yes, I realize you do have your own life and all that, but this is not such a terrible thing I'm asking, is it? We just want you to be a part of our lives, as well."

Kerry searched the ceiling, looking for patience and finding precious little. "Why?"

Cynthia turned. "Pardon?"

"Why?" Kerry repeated. "Why is it so important that I come back here?"

Cynthia frowned. "Is that a serious question? You are my daughter, and a member of our family."

"No, I'm not," Kerry replied quietly. "Have you forgotten? I was thrown out of this family a year ago."

Her mother exhaled. "That wasn't...Your father was very upset at the time, Kerrison. He was simply frustrated and angry. As were you."

Kerry looked at her. "I'm sorry. You all stood there and let him do that. You stood by while they threw me into an insane asylum. Then you let him bully my brother and my sister into shun-

ning me at the hearings." Her voice had gotten louder and louder.
"And now you think I want to come back?" She stood. "Are you
nuts?"

Cynthia stared at her in shock.

"Why in the hell would you think I wanted, or what's more,
needed you?"

"Kerrison!" her mother gasped. "Think of what you're saying.
No one meant any harm to you—"

"Bullshit!" Kerry was really angry now. "You never cared a
rat's ass about me. All that mattered was what I looked like, how
many eligible boys I could bring over to the house for daddy to
wind around his finger, and how soon I could get married to
become a family brood cow."

"Kerrison—"

"Don't call me that," Kerry spat, her breath coming quickly.
"I don't know who the hell you people think you are, or what
gave you the right to bastardize my life for all these years, but—"

The door opened and Dar entered, pale blue eyes flashing,
her hands flexing lightly as she bolted to Kerry's side and glared
at her mother. "What the hell is going on in here?"

Kerry drew in a breath and released it, then touched Dar's
side. She could feel Dar's ribs expanding and contracting, the
muscles under her fingertips taut and almost vibrating with tension. "My mother wants me to give up my job, and my life, and
come home to be her office manager."

Dar looked at her, then at Cynthia, who turned her head in
discomfort. "Nice. I think I can outbid her, though."

Kerry laughed humorlessly.

"What the hell is your problem?" Dar asked Cynthia.

Cynthia looked thoroughly upset. "I'm trying to bring my
family back together. There's no crime in that." She patted her
coiffed hair. "I can see it was a mistake to ask, however."

Kerry closed her eyes and felt sick to her stomach. She leaned
against Dar and felt Dar's arm curl around her in a reassuring
hug. "Why can't you just let me be happy?" she asked in a very
quiet voice. "Is that too much to ask?"

"I..." Cynthia paused, then sighed. "I have no idea what that
is, so perhaps I simply can't understand your viewpoint, Kerrison." She sat down. "I'm just trying to do what I feel is right."

Dar glanced down and caught the reflection of light off the
tears that rolled down Kerry's cheeks. "What's right is for you to
accept Kerry for who and what she is. And stop trying to remake
her into an image that was never her to begin with."

"I have known my daughter far longer than you have," Cynthia said stiffly.

"You never knew her at all," Dar said. "And no, you can't have her back. She was never yours to begin with."

Kerry sniffled and peeked at Dar from under damp lashes. "My, aren't we possessive," she murmured with a wan smile.

Dar looked at her.

"Nice feeling," Kerry whispered. "Thanks."

"Hmph." Dar kissed her gently on the head. "C'mon. Let's go home."

"Wait." Cynthia held a hand up, then walked to them. "Please, let's not leave in anger again." She touched Kerry's arm. "I'm sorry, Kerrison. You're right. I don't understand what it is you want. Please believe that I was only trying to help you."

Kerry sadly looked at her. "I know. I'm sorry I lost my temper. There're just so many things I get so angry about when I think of them."

Her mother glanced down at the marble floor.

"Maybe seeing Kyle brought a lot of that back. He was always the worst."

A soft throat clearing made them glance at the now open solarium door. It was one of the butlers. "Mrs. Stuart? There's a policeman here to see you."

Cynthia blinked in honest astonishment. "To see me? What on earth for?"

"I don't know, ma'am. He mentioned something about an accident," the butler replied. "Shall I show him in here?"

Dar and Kerry exchanged looks, then looked at Cynthia. Cynthia lifted her hands in a tiny gesture of puzzlement, then nodded. "Certainly. Please do so."

THE OFFICER ENTERED, taking off his hat and giving Mrs. Stuart a respectful nod. "Ma'am."

"Come in, Officer," Cynthia said. "This is my daughter Kerrison, and her friend Dar. What can we do for you?"

The policeman gave them both brief nods of acknowledgement, then turned back to Cynthia. "Ma'am, I'm sorry to bother you. I know this is a bad time, but we're investigating an accident that happened near here, and we just need to ask you some questions."

Cynthia looked properly and politely bewildered. "Me? Well, certainly. Please sit down." She took a seat and waited for the officer to join her. Kerry and Dar took advantage of a nearby bench. "I'm sorry, but I haven't been out of the house for quite some time. I'm not sure what I can hope to tell you." She glanced at Dar and Kerry. "My daughter was out for a walk earlier. Perhaps it's she with whom you wish to speak. Kerrison, did you see anything while you were out?"

Kerry shook her head. "No. Nothing except trees, snow, and a couple of buried cars."

"No, ma'am, it's not about something you might have seen." The policeman flipped open a pad and checked his information. "Do you know a man by the name of Kyle Evans?"

It was the last thing any of them expected. "Why, yes," Cynthia replied slowly. "He...well, at least until yesterday, he worked on my...late husband's staff." She fell silent. "Has something happened to him?"

"I'm afraid so, ma'am. He was driving down the highway last night and apparently passed out at the wheel. His car ran off the road and hit a tree." The officer hesitated. "He's dead, ma'am."

Kerry blinked, absorbing the news with a wild mixture of emotions. She took a deep breath and released it slowly, knowing that as a human and a Christian, she should feel some sort of sorrow for the passing of another mortal.

She didn't.

Oh, well. Kerry looked up at Dar, who had an interested, speculative look on her face. "What are you thinking?" she whispered.

"Poetic justice," Dar answered succinctly. "And, gee...now your father will have someone to talk to down there."

Kerry winced.

"Sorry. You asked," Dar murmured. "I'm not going to pretend to be even slightly sorry that bastard's dead. I only hope he didn't ruin the tree."

"My goodness," Cynthia had been saying. "I can't...I hardly know what to say." She shook her head. "What time did the accident occur? He left here just about midnight, I believe."

The officer nodded. "About one a.m., ma'am. Do you have any idea what he'd been doing between the time he left and then? Only takes about a ten minute drive to get where he was."

"I haven't a mortal clue," Cynthia answered, stunned. "He gathered his things and left in quite a hurry. I'm afraid he was quite upset. I had just released him and the rest of my late husband's staff from employ."

"Ah," the officer grunted, writing that down. "Was he a drinker?"

"I have no idea. Certainly in social situations. I never had any reason to believe it was more frequent than that." Cynthia looked at Kerry, a touch helplessly. "Did you think so, Kerrison?"

Kyle, A drunk? "No." Kerry shook her head as the policeman looked at her. "I haven't lived here for over a year, but Kyle was employed by my father for many years prior to that. I never thought he drank, or in fact, did drugs or anything like that." She paused thoughtfully. "In fact, he was a health freak."

The officer nodded again. "That seems right, ma'am. His car had a lot of equipment in it, and gym clothes." He closed his book. "Well, I'm sorry to have to pass that information along to you, Mrs. Stuart. I realize it's lousy timing." He settled his hat back onto his head. "You confirmed when he left here, that's all I really needed. We'll try to backtrack now and see where he went first."

"Officer," Dar said, "it seems like a lot of investigating over a car accident."

The man eyed her shrewdly. "We like to be sure, ma'am, especially when it's a former employee of a government family. We just want to make sure everything's what it seems to be." He touched the hat brim. "Mrs. Stuart, Ms. Stuart, ma'am."

His footsteps sounded loud on the parquet floor, and the door opening and closing echoed softly in the silence that he left behind him.

"Well," Cynthia said, "what a shock."

"Mm," Kerry agreed. "Yeah...Oh my God, I wonder if Brian knows?"

Cynthia gasped softly. "Oh! We should call him at once." She got up and hurried from the room, leaving them behind without so much as another single word.

Kerry sighed and leaned against Dar. "Wow."

"Yeah." Dar's voice was quiet. "You okay now?"

Kerry considered that. "Yeah. I feel better, kinda. I think I was wanting to get that out of my system for a while." She paused. "What I said to my mother, I mean."

"Mm."

"Let's go home."

"You mean it this time?" Dar gave her an affectionate look. "You're not teasing me?"

"Let's go." Kerry stood up and offered Dar her hand. "Let's get Mom and Dad and get the hell out of here. But we have to make one stop before the airport."

Dar followed her out of the room, their hands still clasped. "Where's that?" she asked, as they walked across to the dining room.

"Dairy Queen," Kerry replied firmly.

KERRY TOOK HER hot fudge sundae and sat down at the bench table, her eyes flicking around the interior that called up memories of high school and summer. Most people didn't go for ice cream in winter, though there was a scattering of other people in the store, but that was one of the nice things about living in the tropics, it was almost always summer. Always ice cream season. Kerry dug herself up a spoonful of vanilla ice cream and put it in her mouth. "You know, it's hard to believe."

"What is?" Ceci was maneuvering around a banana split. "That they sell decent ice cream here? I always thought so. We went to Carvel when we could."

"Kyle."

Dar had her arms folded on the table, and she was sucking a thick chocolate milkshake through a somewhat uncooperative straw. She paused in her efforts and looked across the table at Kerry. "Couldn't have happened to a nicer guy."

Kerry twirled a bit of hot fudge on the end of her spoon. "I really want to be horrified that someone died, and you know, I just can't." She glanced furtively at her in-laws. "I can't pretend I'm not glad that happened to him."

"Why should you?" Ceci asked.

"Why should I pretend?" Kerry poked her ice cream. "Because it's polite, and I was raised to be polite. It's not nice to gloat over the fact that someone you hated is dead."

An awkward bit of silence followed. After it had gone on a while, Dar cleared her throat and patted Kerry's hand. "I'm glad he's dead. And I'm glad I wasn't raised politely, because it feels good to be glad he's dead."

Ceci snorted softly.

"No offense," Dar added hastily.

"That feller done wrong by you, kumquat," Andy pronounced, not looking up from his dish of completely vanilla ice cream. "Don't you feel bad about him being dead." He glanced up. "I sure do not."

Kerry glanced up at him, noting the faint smile around the edges of his mouth. "Yeah, I know," she murmured, suddenly unsure. Her eyes shifted to Dar, who blinked and studied her hands, an expression on her face that Kerry had come to know as the one that meant she'd done something she wasn't sure Kerry was going to like.

"Andy's right." Ceci broke the moment. "You've got nothing to feel bad about, Kerry. The man was a jerk, and his jerkiness caught up to him last night. He was probably frothing at the mouth so badly it got in his eyes and made him veer off the road. Poetic justice."

Poetic justice. Kerry pondered that term. As far as she knew, she was the only poet at the table. Finally, all she could do was shrug, and make a mental note to talk to Dar later about that look of hers, though she suspected she knew what was behind it. *Ah.*

Maybe I'll just let it go.

"Mm." She took a spoonful of ice cream and put it in her mouth, then almost choked on the spoon when her name was called from behind her. She turned to see a willowy blond woman obviously heading right for her.

She had about six seconds to figure out who the woman was. Kerry found her early schooling coming in desperately handy as she flipped through names and faces the way her father had taught all of them, searching for this one.

College? No. Church? No. Debating club? No.

"Well, Kerrison! I'm just amazed to see you here." The woman arrived next to the table, her lips twitching into a brief, false smile. "Or maybe not."

"Hello, Corinne." Kerry returned the smile. "How wonderful to see you after all these years." Her eyes slipped past Corinne. "Do you work here?" She spotted a man in what appeared to be a supervisor's uniform behind her.

"Work?" Corinne chuckled. "My husband owns the store. I'm just here picking something up for him. Oh, by the way, I'm sorry about your father."

"Thank you." Kerry replied.

"You're staying in town?" Corinne's eyes darted briefly to Kerry's table companions. "I thought you'd be on your way to the funeral. Or, well, I thought *you* would, at any rate."

Bitch. Kerry leaned one arm on the back of the bench seat, aware of Dar stirring restlessly across from her. "No, we're on our way to the airport. And please forgive my manners. Corinne, this is my partner Dar Roberts, and her parents Andrew and Cecilia." She looked at Dar. "This is Corinne..." She glanced back at the blonde. "What is it now?"

"Henderson." Corinne gave the rest of the table a brief nod and frosty smile. "Well, I'm sure you can't wait to get on your way. It was certainly nice to see you. I'm sure we won't have the pleasure often and everyone," her smile turned sickly sweet, "has been asking about you." She lifted a hand, turned, and went back to her table.

Kerry felt Ceci move, then before her eyes, a brown blob flew through the air and splatted against Corinne's back.

Corinne turned, startled, as Kerry whirled and faced forward, her eyes nearly popping out of her head. "Did you just do what I think you just did?" she hissed at Ceci.

"Sure." Ceci licked her spoon with relish. "Damn good aim, if I say so myself."

Dar wrapped her lips around her straw and put on an innocent look as she met Corinne's staring eyes. Next to her, Andrew merely sniffed and took another bite of his pristine and fudge free ice cream.

Kerry covered her eyes with one hand. "What is it about people around me that encourages food fights? Corinne is going to lose her mind."

"What mind?" Dar asked at the same time as Ceci snorted.

"You know, Kerry, you really should consider giving up Christianity," Ceci said. "All that guilt, all that angst. Go pagan. We just enjoy our mischief and die happy."

Dar grinned as she watched the confused Corinne try to look over her own shoulder at her back, then apparently decide she'd been imagining it all as she slipped into her expensive silk lined leather jacket. She accepted the gloves the manager handed to her, then left, shaking her head, after glancing back at Kerry and finding nothing apparently amiss.

"Old friend?" Dar asked.

Kerry peeked from between her fingers. "Is she gone?"

Dar nodded.

Kerry put her hand down and picked up her spoon. "No, she was never a friend. She was someone I went to high school with who was convinced everything I had, everything I got, was because of my father and not because I earned it."

"Ah."

"Sometimes I believed that," Kerry added softly. "I think everyone did."

"Well, I'm sure everyone doesn't think your father bought Dar for you," Ceci remarked practically. "Way out of his price league, for one thing."

"Hey!" her offspring protested.

Kerry smiled at that and relaxed. "No, I'm sure they don't." She thought back to past times. "I'm sure they don't. I'm sure I don't care what they think, either."

She was sure, wasn't she?

Chapter
Eleven

KERRY HAD NEVER been so glad to get on a damn airplane.
She settled into her seat with a long, relieved sigh and put her
head against the leather headrest, closing her eyes and willing the
plane up and gone. Dar took the seat next to her, and Kerry found
herself mildly resenting the fact that they were in first class,
where there were those stupid console arms between the seats.
She wanted to get rid of hers and curl up in Dar's arms for a nap.
She regarded the lighting controls with a feeling of mild embarrassment at the thought, reminding herself that she was a grown
up who had long ago left the need for a teddy bear and security
blanket behind her. Hadn't she?

Kerry kept her eyes closed as the flight attendant came by and
listened as Dar's low burr ordered them both drinks. Maybe it was
just the whole situation finally getting to be too much. She sighed,
wishing they were already home, wanting the normality of that
back around her.

Even going back to work would be very welcome. Kerry
opened one eye and peered at Dar. "What ever happened with
that UPS?" She hadn't gotten paged again on it, so she figured Dar
had done something or other to clear the issue.

Dar looked up from her Skymall magazine. "I threatened to
cut off the cable feed to the city, and they got the replacement unit
out in six hours. Hey, look, new toys. Want one?" Her long finger
pointed at a page.

Kerry goggled at her. "Could you really do that?"

"Buy you a new toy? Sure," Dar replied, then grinned. "Cut
off their cable? We manage their head end facility, so yeah, if I
wanted to get down and dirty enough, I could." She dug into her
pocket and removed her cell phone. "Now, do you like red or
onyx?"

Kerry peered at the magazine. "Oo." She pulled it closer. "A
Swiss army knife for nerds? Does it have a...Oh, good grief, it

does. How cool." She glanced up at Dar. "We should get these as Christmas gifts for Mark's staff."

Dar considered that. "Mm. Something they can actually use instead of a box of chocolates and a gift certificate to Wal-Mart? Though, those are both useful. Sort of." She waited for the cell phone to be answered, then crisply ordered a case of the knives in each color, sending the order taker into a mini ecstasy of delight. "We should brand them and use them as pitch gimmicks, too. Maybe if José's really good, I'll let him look at mine."

"Why don't you just get him one?" Kerry asked, flipping through the magazine with interest.

"It has sharp implements on it. I don't want to be liable if he cuts his fingers off. Mariana would kill me," Dar muttered as she completed her purchase and closed the phone. "See anything else you like?"

"Mm." Kerry eyes wandered off the page and up to Dar. "Yeah." Then she chuckled, wet one fingertip, and rubbed a spot on Dar's cheek. "Can't take you anywhere, Paladar. Look at you with chocolate all over your face."

"Shh." Dar glanced at the row behind them, where her parents were settled. "Not so loud. You'll get treated to an hour of stories about what I used to do with my food."

"Oh really?" Kerry asked, in a much louder voice.

Blue eyes narrowed. "Kerrison."

Kerry chuckled. "Ah. Why does that sound so different when you say it?" She exhaled and rested her head on the leather again, but half turned to keep Dar in view. "Boy, I'm glad we're going home."

"Yeah?" Dar gazed quietly at her. "Me, too."

Kerry could see the strain around the edges of Dar's eyes. "You look tired."

Dar sighed. "Those damn drugs." She wearily rubbed her eyes. "Between that and what I'm taking them for, I just want to crawl into my damn waterbed and stay there for a day or so."

"I can arrange for that," Kerry said. "In fact, I can arrange for a nice hot water bottle for you to wrap around, too." She was looking forward to seeing their home, and Chino, and settling down on the couch next to Dar with a cup of hot tea, leaving her family and Michigan and all that stood for behind her.

Kerry curled her fingers around Dar's as their arms rested together on the center console. The touch was warm, and it felt good around her chilled hands. Dar gently rubbed her skin with her thumb, and Kerry felt a quiet lethargy steal over her.

Maybe she could doze off until they taxied.

KERRY OPENED HER eyes, blinking them in confusion as she tried to reconcile her memories of the last few moments with what she was seeing. "Uh?"

"We're about to land, hon." Dar smiled, tucking the soft, blue blanket around her.

"Land?" Kerry asked, bewildered. "Did I...?" She glanced outside, seeing the distinctive skyline of Miami through the window. "Son of a... I slept the whole time?"

"Mmhm." Dar stretched her body out then relaxed. She stifled a yawn, glad beyond reason to feel the tightening in her eardrums as the large plane descended. After a few moments, the tires hit, the engines reversed, and they rolled to a halt on the long expanse of runway.

Home.

Dar's entire body relaxed, and she unbuckled her seat belt, quite against the repeated injunctions of the cabin crew. Yes, she realized they were on an active taxiway. Yes, she realized the captain would turn off the seat belt sign when they were safely parked at the gate. Yes, she knew enough to open the overheads carefully because the stuff in them sure enough did tend to shift in flight.

Which was why flying in coach was so scary sometimes. Dar had watched in bemusement on more than one occasion while passengers shoved items no sane person would consider bringing onto an airplane into those aforementioned bins.

She smiled as she remembered a flight where an entire floral arrangement with large blown glass ornaments, being taken to a birthday party, had imploded in flight due to the pressure change. They'd almost had to turn around and land before the rattled flight attendants had identified the sounds. And then the woman had threatened to sue the airline for destroying her centerpiece.

Dar shook her head. People were weird. She glanced out the window as flashing lights caught her attention and saw another plane surrounded by emergency vehicles. "Wonder what that's all about?" She nudged Kerry, who was obediently gathering her personal belongings.

Kerry turned, leaned on the armrest, and peered out of the small window. "Hm. Mostly police, no fire rescue, could be anything. Maybe a hijack attempt?" She watched over her shoulder. "Drugs. See the dogs?"

"Ah, we must be home." Kerry smiled. "This is the only airport I've ever seen that on a regular basis."

"Mm," Dar acknowledged. "Guess we'll read about it in tomorrow's Herald."

"Okay." Kerry settled back as the plane turned to enter its

assigned gate area. "But you have to read me the comics first."

She grinned as Dar gave her a look. They'd developed what was, to Kerry, a charming habit of diving through the morning paper for the cartoons, finding Dilbert first, of course, then sharing the others, and their respective horoscopes. That was after their run and shared shower, while the coffee was brewing for the drive to work.

Work. Kerry gazed pensively at the overhead. Would that schedule be changing? From what Dar said, it probably would. But... She glanced at Dar. They'd figure out something. In the meantime, they'd get a cup of coffee, shed their jackets, and watch the palm trees wave as they drove home.

Kerry sighed happily. She was so looking forward to that. She fairly ached for the normality of it. The plane bumped to a halt, she released her seat belt, and stood up alongside Dar who ducked to clear the overhead. "Sometimes it pays to be short."

"I agree." Ceci chuckled from behind her as they watched Andrew move into the aisle to avoid cracking his head. "And no offense to your home state, Kerry, but I'm glad I'm no longer in it."

Kerry snorted. "Like I wasn't counting the minutes?" She took a deep breath as the cabin door opened and a gust of moderately warm, moderately moist air blew in, tinged with aviation fuel but welcome nonetheless. She shouldered her laptop, edged out in front of Dar, and gave the flight attendant a smile as she exited the plane onto the jetway.

"Ah. Air conditioning in December. I must be home," Dar remarked as they walked up the sloping path. Already, they could hear the clamor of the airport loudspeaker, a combination of English and Spanish that matched the conversations going on around them.

"Oh yeah," Kerry agreed as they walked out of the gate and into the flow of terminal traffic. "I remember my very first experience getting off a plane here. I walked ten feet, put my bag down, stared, and wondered what in the world I'd gotten myself into."

It had been more than culture shock, that was for sure. It had been an exotic, intimidating new world. Now, it was just home, and she welcomed the bustling activity and the riot of color that surrounded them. "You up for a café con leche? It'll take them twenty minutes to bring the car up anyway. You did valet it, right?"

"You bet your..." Dar's eyes wandered. "Yes, I did." She grinned, mindful of her father's inquisitive presence. "You parked or what, Dad?"

"Ah am about to go get me that truck," Andrew said. "Figgered we'd talk to you two later on." He gave Dar a pat on the back and accepted a hug from Kerry, then ambled off with a waving Ceci in tow.

"Bye." Kerry waggled her fingers back. "They're so cute."

Dar arched a brow at her. "I'll go turn in my valet ticket. Did you say something about coffee a minute ago?" She bumped Kerry towards the coffee bar with her hip. "Get me a cheese pastalito, too."

Mm. Kerry obediently trotted over to the coffee bar and leaned against its polished surface as the attendant came over. *"Dos café con leche, dos queso pastilitos, por favor."*

The boy grinned at her. *"Si, Senorita."* He turned towards the espresso machine. Kerry slid onto the stool and idly watched him, enjoying the sharp, distinctive scent of the brewing coffee as she listened to the conversations around her. Football and soccer mostly, with a spattering of stock market, and one very excited discussion about deep sea fishing. She turned around as her coffee and pastries were delivered, paid for them, and received another smile from the server as she left a tip.

She picked up her goodies, shouldered her bag, and headed for the automatic doors leading outside.

Dar was leaning against a support pole, her sunglasses now firmly settled on the bridge of her nose.

"Rats. I forgot." Kerry handed Dar the bag and dug inside her briefcase pocket for her own glasses, a nifty wraparound pair Dar had gotten her not long before. She put her bag between her feet as she straightened and accepted the cup of steaming liquid from Dar. "Thank you, ma'am."

"Ma'am?" Dar laughed and took a sip.

Kerry leaned against her and sucked happily at her drink, enjoying the rich, sweet flavor. The air was cool and equally sweet, and she felt a sense of pure, animal well-being as she watched the confusion of traffic trying to get to the curbside. Soon enough, she spotted Dar's Lexus making its way toward them, and she actually almost felt like hugging it. "Want me to drive? Give your arm a break?"

Dar's face went still for a moment, then she exhaled. "Okay." She accepted her keys from the valet and put her bag in the back seat before Kerry took them from her fingers and circled the car. They settled into the leather seats and Kerry took a moment to adjust the driver's seat forward.

"I should keep a booster seat in here for you," Dar remarked dryly.

"Hah hah." Kerry put the big SUV in gear and edged cautiously into the traffic stream. "How about next time you just put me in your lap?"

"Mm." Dar chuckled softly, sparing a moment to imagine driving with her arms wrapped around Kerry. "Yeah, okay...Hey, pull over."

"Hedonist."

"It was your idea!"

Kerry dodged a speeding Mercedes and settled down to the relatively short drive home. "Hey, Dar?"

Dar had her head tipped back and her eyes closed. "Yeeess?"

Kerry thought a moment of how to phrase her question, then she just shrugged. "Is this really it, at work?"

Dar was quiet, then she shrugged. "Yeah."

"No reprieves? No time off for good behavior?"

A soft chuckle rose from the passenger's seat. "Hon, I've never behaved good in my entire tenure there. Trust me, if I had to come up with a reason to leave, you were the best reason on Earth." She reached carefully behind her with her good arm and tugged her briefcase over and onto her lap. "Want to help me write my resignation letter later?"

Kerry sighed. "Dar, it's not funny."

"I know, I know. I j..." Dar reached inside her briefcase, and her fingers touched a thick sheaf of paper she didn't remember putting inside. She looked into the case. "What the heck is that?"

"What?"

Dar removed the papers and stared at them in utter disbelief. "Dar?"

Dar looked at her. "Did you put this in here?"

Hearing the tension in Dar's voice, Kerry pulled the car over. "Me? Of course not. What is it? The only thing I put in your case this morning was your laptop, because you asked me to."

Dar thumbed the sheaf, the soft rustle of paper sounding loud in the car. "It's the data I gave your father."

"What?" Kerry put the car in park, half turned, and reached for the stack. "How...Wait, are you sure? Maybe it's a copy you put in there, Dar. You had one."

"I'm sure." Dar turned the first sheet over. "I printed this one on recycled; it was my check copy. The other one's on water-mark."

Kerry stared at the words on the back of the page—someone's recipe for pot roast. That seemed so odd and so incongruous, she almost wondered if her father might have scribbled it down for the cooks to try at home. The world seemed strange around her. She braced her elbow on the armrest between them and rested her head on one hand. "I don't get it."

"Me, neither." Dar pulled out her cell and hit a speed dial

button. She waited until it was answered, then cleared her throat. "Hi, Alastair? It's Dar."

"Ah! Oh...uh, Dar, listen, can I call you right back?" Alastair sounded surprised to hear from her. "I'm, ah—"

"I don't care if you're on the john," Dar said bluntly. "I just wanted you to know I have the papers."

There was dead silence, then a splutter. "How did you know where...? Did you get that GPS thing working for cell phones?"

Dar merely waited.

"If you did, why the hell didn't you say so? You know how much money we could make w—" Alastair fell silent. "Holy Jesus, did you say you had the papers?"

"Yes."

Through the phone connection Dar could hear a ball game playing softly somewhere in the far background, but little else. "Alastair?"

His sigh was audible. "Dar, I'm not sure it matters now."

Dar shrugged. "Well, for what it's worth, I have them. Anyway, talk to you later."

More silence preceded his quiet, "I'll call you, Dar." Alastair's voice was now very serious. "Stay close."

Dar closed her phone and looked at Kerry. "Let's go home."

Kerry was staring steadily at her. "It's too late, isn't it?"

"Eh." Dar picked up her hand and kissed the knuckles. "I don't care. C'mon. Let's go. I want you, a soft bed, a warm glass of milk, and a bowl of pitted cherries."

Kerry smiled wistfully at her. "In that order?"

"Any order I can get them in."

Kerry gave in and put the car back into drive, then checked her rearview mirror and pulled into the traffic lane.

After a mile or so of companionable silence, she cleared her throat. "I keep forgetting to ask you, and you did mention it twice, so it's not your fault. What was the deal you set up with the Navy in exchange for that information?"

Dar opened her eyes, and she regarded the fawn header on the Lexus. "Ah. That's right. I guess I never did lay that out for you, did I?"

Kerry glanced at her, then back at the road. "Well, I mean, it doesn't have to be right now, but I was curious—"

"No, now's as good a time as any," Dar remarked. "I should have just told you earlier." Her expression turned pensive. "I agreed to destroy the information and forget what I'd seen, in return for the Navy outsourcing all of their IS to us."

Kerry almost hit the car in front of her. She hurriedly applied her brakes, then turned her head and stared at Dar in utter disbelief. "You what?" A horn honked, and she hastily pulled the Lexus over to the curb again and parked it.

"What?"

Pale blue eyes regarded her warily. "That was my price, if they wanted me to shut up. So they did. Gerry got them to agree to the outsourcing deal." She watched Kerry's face carefully, wondering what she was thinking.

Kerry covered her eyes with one hand. "You blackmailed the US government?"

Did I? Dar rubbed her chin. "Yeah, I guess I did."

Green eyes peeked out from between slim fingers. "Paladar Katherine Roberts, what am I going to do with you?"

Dar smiled wistfully. "I don't know. It was nicer having you think I just chucked it all because I wouldn't leave you," she reflected in a quiet voice. "Just a moment of altruistic heroism I didn't actually have."

Kerry studied Dar for a moment, then cupped her cheek with one hand but didn't say anything. They looked at each other for a moment, then Kerry put the Lexus in gear and resumed driving. Concentrating on the traffic gave her a chance to think about what Dar had told her and how she felt about it.

Was she mad at Dar for not telling her? Kerry nibbled the inside of her lip. *Yeah, a little.* It meant a huge workload for her, and dozens of things would have had to be taken into account. But, on the other hand—given what had been going on at home at the time—had she really wanted to deal with that, too?

No, Kerry admitted. She'd have had no desire whatsoever to add to the stress load she'd been suffering under. So, Dar had probably done her a favor in keeping the arrangement quiet until now. She did wonder, though, about what Dar had said about how she felt.

A quick glance showed her a somber profile. *Dar thinks I'm disappointed*, Kerry realized. *Am I?*

It had been flattering, of course—for her to realize Dar had just chucked everything to be at her side. But...but it had also hurt to know she had caused Dar to relinquish something she knew was so important to her partner: honor, her integrity. Regardless of what ILS had gotten out of the deal, it didn't change the fact that Dar had traded off doing what she knew was the right thing, just to be the rock Kerry had so desperately needed right then.

That was some tradeoff. Kerry felt humbled by it. "Thanks. But the company gaining doesn't matter, because you'd have done it anyway."

Dar's lips curved into a reluctant smile. "So much for my reputation."

Kerry chuckled softly. "I warned you, didn't I?"

"You did." Dar closed her eyes and remembered that moment, there on that airplane coming back from Orlando which she'd almost wished wouldn't land. "Ker?"

"Mm?"

"Thanks."

KERRY STEERED THE big SUV down the slight ramp into their parking area and pulled into the spot with Dar's name on it. She turned off the ignition and rested her arms against the wheel, looking out at the townhouse as Dar started to open the passenger side door.

"Glad we're home." Dar sighed. "Feels like it's been a month."

Home. Kerry took in the lines of the front porch, the Mediterranean stucco of it now warmly familiar to her. She got out of the car and stepped between it and her own, the shiny dark blue reflecting her image as she lightly kicked the parking bumper with her own name stenciled neatly on it.

With a quiet smile, she followed Dar up the steps and stood by as her partner keyed in the lock code and unlocked the door. She remembered the first time she'd stood in just this place, waiting on just that same thing, but this time she tucked her fingers into the back of Dar's waistband and kissed her on the middle of her back as they shuffled inside.

Chino galloped towards them, whining in delight, and Colleen appeared from the kitchen, wiping her hands as she called out a greeting.

Home. Kerry rested her head against Dar's back as Chino jumped up to greet the taller woman. "Hey, Col," she returned, as a wave of exhaustion threatened to swamp her. "We're home."

"And a big welcome to it," Colleen said. "Glad to see you guys. How was the flight?"

"Wasn't awake for a minute of it." Kerry tossed her jacket on the back of the couch. "I'm just glad it's over." She knelt to pet Chino. "Hey, Cheebles. You glad we're back?"

The Labrador licked her face all over and managed to get fur over every square inch of Kerry that she touched. Kerry loved it all and sat on the floor and gathered the delighted dog into her arms.

Home.

"Coffee, Ker?"

"Absolutely." Kerry exhaled happily. "Absolutely."

EYES CLOSED, DAR mentally traced the path her briefcase had taken that day. She'd had it in the green room, taken it with her on the way to the airport, locked it in the car while she was in Dairy Queen. It had gone through x-ray, then been put in the overhead bin for the flight. Taken out again when they landed, it had sat in the back of the car all the way home.

So...when the hell had someone put the papers in it? Dar went over the steps one more time. The only two places that were even remote possibilities were at the Stuart house and in the car while they were getting ice cream, taking into account that someone would have had to get the rental opened and then locked it up again. No one had known they were going for ice cream, so that left the house.

Who had put it there? Cynthia? Kerry's sibs? None of them would have known the importance. *Ah well.* She exhaled. *Probably doesn't matter now anyway.* At least in her own mind, she had them back and some squid wasn't running around with them in Washington.

Dar stifled a yawn and relaxed on the leather sofa in their living room. It was, aside from the low buzz of voices in the kitchen, blessedly quiet in the condo, and Dar dropped her head against the plushy stuffed arm of the sofa, welcoming the rich scent of the leather and the warmth of the long stripe of sunlight that was coming in the front window and painting a golden swath across her body.

She could, she acknowledged dutifully, go into her study and find out what was in her mailbox waiting to pounce on her. She could—Dar wriggled into a more comfortable position and closed her eyes—but she wasn't going to. Tomorrow would come soon enough, and if there was anything of a truly disastrous nature, she'd have been paged before now, right? *Hm.* She pulled her cell phone out and made sure it was on. *Nope; no pages, no calls. Good.*

A cold nose investigated her arm, and she opened her eyes. "Hey, Chino. Did you give up on getting cookies from mommy Kerry?"

Sad brown eyes regarded her, then Chino climbed up onto the wide couch, settled down with a grunt, and licked all of Dar's exposed skin within her reach.

"Aw." Dar stroked the Labrador's soft, thick fur. "I missed you too, baby." She quickly looked around to make sure no one had heard her, then ruffled the dog's ears. "You're such a sweetie, aren't you?"

Chino put her muzzle down on Dar's chest and exhaled happily.

Dar exhaled too. It was over. Damn, she was glad it was over.

Now they could settle down and get on with their life together and concentrate on happier things. Like Christmas, for instance. Dar wiggled her toes in mild glee as she considered the boxes she had hidden in the crawl space. Presents for Kerry, of course, and Chino, but also for her parents, something she hadn't done for many years, and for the assorted friends Kerry had invited over for the Christmas party.

"Christmas party," Dar had firmly insisted. "Christmas, Christmas, Christmas, not birthday."

But Kerry had snickered, which meant she'd at least have to suffer through a cake and a chorus. *Hm.* Dar mentally made a note to ask, in a circumspect way of course, if the cake was to be Kerry's double chocolate mousse, killer cake. That was worth a round of Happy Birthday to You, if nothing else was.

Yeah. Dar grinned and licked her lips at the thought.

"HOLY COW, KERRY," Colleen rubbed her friend's arm sympathetically, "what a nightmare."

"Yeah." Kerry was sprawled on one of the two stools in the kitchen. "You can say that again. Thanks a bunch for staying over here."

"No problem," Colleen said. "I was glad to do it. Chinie's a sweetie, and Dar's folks are great people."

"They sure are." Kerry smiled. "You have no idea how glad I was to see them when they showed up. Oh, my God, Col, I was literally standing in a pit full of vipers, with that bastard Kyle coming right at me when BAM! Talk about the cavalry coming over the hill."

Colleen grinned. "Dar's father is so hooked on you. It's so sweet. You should have heard them when they showed the television report and we spotted you, just before they left. Man, the two of them went off."

Kerry sighed. "That so sucked." She rested her head on her hand and leaned an elbow on the counter. "I don't think I've ever had a lousier couple of days, I can tell you that. After we got back to the hotel, Angie called and told me the staff thought it would be better if I didn't come over to the house, because of Dar."

"To hell with them." Colleen snorted.

"Well, I didn't go," Kerry said. "And it was because of Dar, not for their benefit. She was hurting." She paused. "God knows, I was hurting, too. We needed some space." She thought about that night. "I don't know what I would have done if Dar hadn't been there, Col. I just don't." She could hear a faint tremor in her own voice. "That first night...Jesus. I was so sick. I got a migraine, and

I passed out in the bathroom…"

"Wow." Colleen gave her a concerned look. "What happened?"

"Just too much stress, I guess." Kerry felt irrational tears rising. "But then, Dar happened. She wasn't supposed to come up
until the next day, but she just dropped everything and came that
night. I don't know what I would have done if she hadn't."

Colleen put a hand on her arm and squeezed.

"I think that was the worst I've ever felt," Kerry whispered.
"But Dar held me and made that all go away. It was incredible."
She let out a long, shaky breath. "She saved my sanity."

"Hey." Colleen gently put both arms around her and gave her
a hug. "You poor kid." She patted Kerry's back, then rubbed it.
"I'm glad tall, dark, and daunting was there to make things right,
Ker. I know I didn't start off being a fan of hers, but I'm glad this
time I was so damn, dead wrong."

"Mm." Kerry returned the hug. "Tall, dark, and doofy sometimes. That's how she hurt her arm again. The dork picked me up
and carried me to the bed in the hotel. I was too sick to realize
what she was doing."

Colleen laughed a bit. "Oh, really?"

"Yeah." Kerry got up off her stool, went to the refrigerator,
and took out a pitcher of juice and swirled it. "Want some?"

"Sure."

"Hey, Dar?" Kerry called into the living room. "Want some
juice?"

"Does it have chocolate in it?" the droll answer came back.

"Ew. Orange juice and chocolate?" Kerry made a face. "No,
honey. I'll get you some milk."

"Mmmmmilk," Dar drawled in response as she appeared in
the doorway, looking appealingly tousled in her T-shirt, cutoff
shorts and white socks. Chino came trotting in behind her, yawn-
ing. "Chino wants some milk, too."

Colleen chuckled. "Like owner, like puppy."

Dar paused and put a hand on her hip. She lifted one eyebrow
in mock menace. "You saying I look like that dog?"

"No." Kerry handed her a glass and leaned up to give her a
kiss. "You just act like her—adorably loyal and cute to a fault."
She watched Dar's eyes go round in startlement, then glance at
Colleen and back to her. "Oh, don't go all formal on me now, Dar.
You were the one who was just mooing for milk."

Dar scowled, then her face relaxed into a sheepish grin as she
chuckled and accepted the glass.

Colleen put down her own glass and stood up. "Well, I'll be
getting meself back to the southern reaches of Kendall. You two

take it easy, eh? See you Wednesday?"

"I'll be there, absolutely," Kerry said. "Dar? Well, let's see what the doctor says." She looked at her lover, who merely lifted a brow at her. "Right? You're not going to try teaching us flips until your shoulder gets better, are you?"

"No," Dar replied obediently, referring to the martial arts class they were supposed to resume that week. "I'll just make you all do the work, and I'll watch." She chuckled at their wry faces. "Besides, I can use the pool a little."

"Ah, sure." Colleen shouldered her bag. "She floats while we sweat. Nice." She waved a goodbye. "Later, folks."

Kerry walked her to the door and closed it behind her, then turned and regarded Dar. She crossed the living room and sat down with Dar on the couch, and put her feet up on the coffee table at almost the same time Dar did. Then she rested her head against Dar's shoulder and sighed.

"Nice to be here, huh?" Dar obligingly draped an arm over her shoulders and pulled her closer.

Kerry wrapped her arms around Dar's body and snuggled up as close as she could without actually crawling into Dar's lap. She craved the warmth of her lover's body and the feeling of utter security that her embrace provided. Dar didn't disappoint her. She felt Dar's body shift a little, and she squirmed into a cradle made from long arms and legs that wrapped around her and brought her home in a way that touched her battered soul in just the spot she needed it to.

"Tell you what," Dar murmured as she stroked Kerry's hair, "I vote for a night of shameless hedonism and indulgence. You up for that?"

"Uh huh," Kerry murmured. "But I'd be happy just to have you near me all night."

Dar gave her a worried look. "Well, sure. Where else would I be?" She kissed the top of Kerry's head. "Ker?"

Kerry lifted her head, revealing a tear-streaked face. She wiped the back of her hand across her eyes and sniffled. "Sorry. I don't know what the hell's wrong with me."

Dar didn't know either. It left her at somewhat of a loss to be presented with a problem she had no experience or knowledge to deal with. So she did what she could do, which was wipe the tears from Kerry's face and kiss her gently. "Go ahead and cry if it makes you feel better. Talk to me about it if you want to. But if all you need from me is love, you've got all of that I have, and it's yours for the taking."

Kerry blinked, scattering a few sparkles of moisture, and a tiny, charmed smile appeared on her face.

"What?" Dar smiled back. "Do I have chocolate on my chin again?"

"Milk." Kerry rubbed the residue off Dar's upper lip and gazed at her with a look of utter love. "A night of shameless hedonism, huh?"

"Yeah." Dar found the sea green eyes irresistibly fascinating. "I figured we could start off by ordering something really bad for us from the Italian place, then sort of go from there."

"Will this night of hedonism include hot fudge?"

"Yes."

"Hot tub?"

"Yes."

"Hot...mmfp." Kerry took the kiss as an answer to that question and surrendered willingly to the plan.

IT WAS MUCH later, when Kerry, stifling a yawn with one hand, climbed up the stairs to her office. Her hair was still damp from the Jacuzzi, and she could smell the distinct tang of chlorine on her skin. Mixed with a little fudge. Kerry licked her lips, and couldn't quite repress a grin. *Nothing like a little hedonism to brighten up one's perspective on things, eh?* She spared a moment to think about what her family's reaction would be to their activities of the evening, imagining her mother's face as she described just how skillful Dar was with...

"God, Kerrison, stop it. You'll go blind." She slapped the side of her head a time or two and entered her office.

It felt like it had been a month since she'd been in there. Kerry paused to look around the room, the contents mostly those she'd had on her walls in her apartment back in Kendall: her certificates and awards, her professional credentials, and the first few of her attempts at photography—including a sunset shot of the Miami skyline.

Kerry walked to the photograph and looked at that, then shifted her attention to the eight by ten of Dar, the first picture she'd ever taken of her partner, before they'd become lovers. It had been at the corporate community participation day. Dar had just finished her painting tasks, and she'd been sitting on the edge of a garbage can, dotted with paint spatters and outlined in the sunset's golden light. Kerry had impulsively grabbed Mari's camera and focused it, attracting Dar's attention at the very last second before she closed the shutter button.

Those blue eyes; that suddenly warm grin, aimed straight at her; the connection they'd made even with her behind the camera. After the shot, Kerry had lowered the camera and reluctantly handed it back to Mari, wishing with all her heart she'd thought to bring her own instead.

Kerry touched the framed photo, delivered to her desk in an envelope without any comment a week later. She'd been so excited, and pulled it out and looked at it for minutes at a time when she should have been working.

It had been one of the pictures she'd taken home to show Angie, because there was just something so amazingly sweet about it and even now, looking at it, she couldn't help but smile at the love now obvious to her in Dar's expression. Maybe she'd known all along the promise held in that look.

Kerry leaned forward and gently kissed the picture, and then she turned around, dropped into her desk chair, and rummaged inside the drawer for the packet of receipts she'd gone upstairs to retrieve. A square of glossy paper blocked her search, and she pulled it out impatiently, turned it over, and put it on the desk out of the way. The lettering was now uppermost and she sat there quietly and reread the invitation to her high school reunion. Slowly, a smile crossed her face. She picked up the invitation, left the receipts behind, and trotted out the door and down the steps with her still damp hair bouncing along. "Hey, Dar?"

"Yeeeeeess?" Dar's low purr answered from where she was sprawled on the couch. "Something else I can do for you, beautiful?"

Kerry's hormones almost made it down the stairs before she did. She scooted across the tile floor, slid to a halt next to the couch, and bumped her knees right next to Dar's arm. "I have a favor to ask."

A lazy blue eye regarded her. "Anything."

Kerry knelt down and offered her the card. "I didn't realize this was on the back of that letter I got the other week."

Dar examined the card, then looked at Kerry in some surprise. "You want to go to this? Really?"

"No." Kerry smiled. "I want *us* to go to it." She leaned on the couch edge. "There're a lot of prissy gits I want to show up."

"Whatever you want, Ker." Dar clasped her fingers around Kerry's. "Do we have to wear leather?"

Kerry's eyes twinkled appreciatively. "Maybe we do."

Dar edged over on the couch and pulled gently. Kerry took a seat on the edge of the cushion, then laid her body diagonally over Dar's. They gazed quietly at each other for a minute in silence, only the air conditioning humming along in the background.

Kerry lifted her hand off Dar's shoulder and traced the planes of her face with careful fingers. Blue eyes followed her motion, then lifted and seemed to reach out to capture her, drawing her inward and downward until her body was pressed against Dar's and she replaced her fingers with her lips.

"Mm." Dar closed her eyes as she smiled, her hands coming to rest on Kerry's sides and teasingly tickled up and down them. She felt Kerry's ribs expand outward under her cotton shirt as she took a deeper breath and continued her motion, enjoying the familiar contours under her touch.

She knew every inch of Kerry's body—all its planes, all its quirky irregularities. She loved the softness of her skin, and the slowly building strength she had felt grow under it to cover the sturdy bones that had seemed so very close to the surface when they'd first met.

"You know what I was voted most likely to?" Kerry whispered. "In high school?"

Dar almost lost the question when Kerry's lips descended on hers and their bodies pressed tighter against one another. "Bet it wasn't that," she rumbled softly, as they paused to breathe. "Run for president?" She took in a breath filled with Kerry's scent and reveled in it.

Kerry chuckled, shaking her head slightly as she deferred answering for another kiss. She felt Dar's hand slip under her shirt, warm against her skin as fingers traced slow circles across her ribcage. "Nothing."

"Eh?" Dar eased Kerry's shirt up and gently cupped her breast.

"Nothing," Kerry repeated and inhaled sharply as her body reacted to Dar's touch. "Said I'd never leave home." She kissed Dar. "Never go anywhere." Her voice broke slightly on the last word. "Never—"

"Never experience this?" Dar ducked her head and nibbled Kerry's nipple, then cupped her hand around Kerry's neck and passionately returned the kiss.

A soft groan trickled through Kerry's throat, dusting her own lips with warm breath. "Mm...yeah." Kerry lifted her head, her eyes half closed, nose-to-nose with Dar. She looked into the passion-darkened blue orbs beneath her. "*I* never thought I would either."

"Feel this?" Dar teasingly slid her hand down Kerry's body.

Kerry's expression unexpectedly gentled. She kissed the spot right above Dar's heart. "No, this. To be loved for myself." She kissed the spot again, then shifted back up as Dar lifted her hand and laid it on Kerry's cheek.

"Neither did I." Dar raised her head and they kissed again. Kerry's arms relaxed as she eased forward and slipped one bare thigh between Dar's. "I think we both lucked out."

Kerry hugged her, sparing a moment of passion for one of joy.

Dar hugged her back, finding peace in her choices and accepting them. Then Kerry slipped her hand down and under the waistband of Dar's cotton shorts, and all nobler thoughts evaporated. She grabbed the front of Kerry's shirt between her teeth and yanked, letting out a growl as Kerry ducked out of the fabric and got under Dar's half shirt, finding a tastier target beneath it.

"Hell with leather." Dar gasped. "Let's just go in our god damned socks."

"Hehehe."

IT WAS DARK and not quite dawn when Dar woke up. The condo was quiet, and she could hear the soft patter of rain against the window not far over her head.

It was Monday. Now that the weekend was over, she had to face the reality of the week, and the private knowledge that today might, in fact, be her last one at ILS. She'd already decided not to tell anyone; in fact, she hadn't even talked about it with Kerry. She would just go up to Houston on Tuesday, and then the announcement would come out and that would be that.

So today she would spend cleaning up loose ends, taking solace from the knowledge that at least she was leaving the company in a good position, though losing the Navy contract would be a definite blow. It would work out, though, she was sure. The company could take the hit.

Dar's thoughts drifted a bit, coming around to her still sleeping partner. She could see dark circles under Kerry's eyes and that led to her one real worry about the whole deal. She could leave, and it would hurt her, but she was afraid it would hurt Kerry worse, to have to take over everything now, after what she'd just been through.

Or maybe...Dar exhaled. Maybe Kerry would just chuck it all too. Maybe she should, rather than risk a health Dar was beginning to suspect was more at risk than she was willing to admit.

Troubled, she stared at the ceiling, in the rare position of being out of control of her own destiny and not liking the feeling at all. Instead of being soothing, now the incessant patter of the rain made her edgy, half of her wanting the day to start and half of her dreading it.

Her entire body started when the cell went off near her head. She jerked to one side and reached for it, hissing at the sharp pain in her shoulder. "Shit."

Kerry woke, her head moving and her eyes blinking dazedly.

"Huh?"

"Phone." Dar grabbed it and opened it, rattled and off-balance. "What?" Her heart was thundering, adrenaline pumping through her from the ominously early call. Trouble?

"Uh...Dar?"

Alastair. Dar's throat went dry. "Oh. Sorry." She glanced at the clock. "Good morning."

"Ah, yes, well, thanks." Alastair cleared his throat. "Listen, sorry to call you so early."

Dar felt her heart settle into her guts. "It's earlier where you are." She was aware of Kerry's eyes on her in the dimness, and of the light touch now on her belly, wordless comfort as Kerry seemed to sense her distress. "What's up?"

"Well, I guess you military types are all early risers. I just heard from Washington," Alastair said.

Dar didn't say anything, but she felt her heart rate speed up even more.

"Fact of the matter is, Dar, I didn't think the general was going to buy into us."

"Yeah, well..." Dar heard the husky note in her voice.

"But he did," Alastair said. "I thought he'd ask for ten acres of corroboration, but you know what, Dar? He said your word was good enough."

Dar was a little surprised to feel the sting of tears in her eyes. "Did he really?"

"Yes, lady, he did," Alastair replied. "Never heard a man sound so relieved, I'll tell you that. Anyway, I just wanted to let you know. And, by the way, he wants to make the announcement to the press at the base down there. You'll be available?"

It was all too sudden. "Uh...yeah. I guess. When?"

"Friday."

It was still too much. "You'll be there?"

"Sure, I can be. Dar, are you all right?"

Dar felt more confused than all right. Everything had unexpectedly turned over again, and she needed time to sort it all out. "Want to come to my birthday party? It's this weekend."

The long period of silence at least gave her time to right her mental balance, while her boss was thoroughly knocked off his. She glanced down at Kerry, who had nestled back down with her head on Dar's shoulder and was merely waiting, her fingers tracing an absent pattern on Dar's belly. The important fact surfaced. At least Kerry would be all right now.

"Uh, sure, Dar. I'd love to," Alastair finally said, in a direly bewildered, but reasonably appreciative tone. "Should I bring flowers?"

"Nah. A bathing suit."

"B...Hey, how about I call you back later, huh? After breakfast?"

"Talk to you later, Alastair. And thanks." Dar closed the phone and put it down, then put her arm around Kerry and hugged her.

"Everything okay?" Kerry asked.

No. Yes. Who the hell knew? "I love you. Everything's perfect."

Kerry made a happy sounding grunt and gave her a hug.

The rain eased back into a friendly rumble, and the soft gray light of dawn now became a welcome sight. *Life,* Dar acknowledged, *is a damn, damn funny thing sometimes.*

It really was.

Chapter
Twelve

"HEY, KERRY."

Kerry turned, hearing a somewhat familiar voice. She spotted Lena approaching her, looking painfully uncomfortable in her linen skirt suit and pumps. "Hey." She went back to stirring the two cups of coffee she'd been preparing. "How's it going?"

"It's okay," Lena said. "I think I'm sort of getting the hang of working here. They haven't thrown me out yet."

Kerry stifled a smile. "I'm sure you're doing fine." She turned again and leaned on the counter. "How did things work out at home? Any changes?"

Lena was briefly silent. "You mean, did the bitch let me come home? No. She dropped the charges, though. Thanks for having those lawyer people talk to her."

"At least that's something." Kerry gave her a sympathetic look. "And it was no problem for us to do that. I'm glad she took the advice."

Lena nodded. "Hey, I saw you on television the other night. Sorry to hear about your father and all that stuff." She seemed a little uncomfortable. "But I'd be glad as hell if my parents croaked."

Kerry took her cups, sat down, and patted the table next to her. She waited for Lena to take a seat. "You say that, but it's not true."

"Sure it is," Lena said. "I mean, you ain't had happen to you what I have."

Kerry rested her chin on her fist. "Lena, they're still your family, no matter what they did. There are things my family did to me that I didn't like or appreciate either, but they're still my family."

Lena shrugged. "Mine sucks."

"Mine does too, sometimes," Kerry said. "When my father found out I was gay, do you know what he did?"

"Freaked?"

"Threw me in a psycho ward."

Lena's eyes nearly popped out. "Yeah?"

"Yeah," Kerry said with a sad sigh. "He hated my being gay. None of my family likes it. Well, maybe my brother and sister don't really mind, but..."

"Wow." Lena pondered. "So you must be glad he's outta here, then, yeah?"

Kerry took a breath to answer, the facile lie forming inside her mouth. Then she hesitated. Was she glad? "It's not that simple. He was my father."

Lena shrugged again. "Yeah, well, my old man's an asshole, and if he jumped in front of a truck, I'd clap." She got up. "Anyway, thanks for the help. It's been pretty cool bringing home a like, real paycheck."

Kerry managed a smile and also stood. "Well, glad things are going all right."

"You going to be at the group thing next week?" Lena asked with a slight hesitation. "They were, like, asking me."

"I'll be there." Kerry picked up the two cups. "I'm sure we'll have a lot to talk about this week."

"For sure." Lena half grinned, then she disappeared, leaving Kerry to cross the hallway back to her office in silence.

DAR SAT QUIETLY in her office, just taking the time to look around and study the space as if it were new to her. Then she exhaled and focused on her visitor, who had just seated himself across from her desk. "So."

"So." Alastair nodded. "All's well that ends to our advantage, eh?"

Dar lifted a hand and let it drop on the desk. "Something like that. Listen, I'm sorry about what happened with Senator Stuart. I should have talked to you before I did that."

Alastair soberly nodded again. "Yes, lady, you should have. I'm the last person who's dinging you for getting a life, Dar, but y'know, you're not the only one who'd have had their tail roasted because of that."

Dar got up, walked to the window, and gazed out at the water. Her shoulder was back in its sling, and she leaned against the warm glass with her good hand, having no real response for what Alastair was saying.

"Now, I'm not saying anything about you taking off for parts north, hear?" Alastair joined her at the window. "Totally understood that, Dar. Totally."

"Yeah." Dar exhaled. "But when did I turn into Dudley Do-

Right, is that what you're asking?"

"Er..."

Dar turned and leaned her back against the glass, feeling the sun as it soaked through her shirt. "Kerry was right."

"Eh?" Alastair backed up, and hitched up his trousers to perch on the corner of her desk. "Right about what?"

"I was too close to the Navy contract." Dar met his eyes. "I should have assigned someone else to do it. It was personal."

Alastair rubbed his jaw. "Ah."

"It was too personal." Dar exhaled. "Getting those bastards meant more to me than protecting the company, and I can't pretend that didn't happen."

Alastair folded his arms over his chest. "So, what am I supposed to do with you? If you recall, we got those contracts in the first place because it was personal to you, lady."

"I know."

"We've gotten more than one set of those in the recent past," Alastair continued. "Including the couple that, if my noggin's working right, let you finagle keeping on some staff from an obscure little software house we picked up a while back."

"Hmph." Dar tilted her head. "Yeah, that's true. I should have talked to someone about this, though. Not just handed that crap over to someone who hates our guts like the senator did."

Alastair sighed. "Well," he lifted both hands and let them drop to his knees, "I don't know, Dar. From what Ham tells me, Stuart went hush on the whole investigation of us right after you tossed him those papers."

Dar's eyebrows lifted.

"So, who knows?" Alastair said. "Maybe you did us a favor after all."'

"You don't really believe that."

Alastair shrugged. "Lady, I'm ready to believe anything at this point. That man's going to hand me the keys to a couple of billion dollars tomorrow, and, in the long run, that's what counts with the folks who write our paychecks."

"Eh." Dar made a face.

"How's the arm?"

"Killing me," Dar admitted, glad of the change of subject. "It's been a long damn week." She paused, then looked up at him. "I'm taking some time off over the holidays. We're going out on the boat."

"Good!" Alastair nodded firmly. "I think you need it, y'know? Get some space around you, and all that."

"Get my head together," Dar said with a wry smile. "Thanks, Alastair."

Alastair got up and waved a hand at her. "I sure didn't do a thing, Dar. Glad it all worked out." He checked his watch. "You and Ms. Stuart free for lunch? I'd love to try some of that Cuban food you're always telling me about."

"Sure." Dar sat down and exhaled, feeling a sense of belated relief. At least for now, things were all right.

At least, for now.

KERRY TOOK A slow sip of her coffee as she leaned on the railing and absorbed the early morning sun with a feeling of complete and total pleasure. It was just after dawn, and she was already dressed in her swimsuit, with a pair of cotton shorts and a tank top thrown over it, her bare toes curling against the stone balcony as she sniffed the clean, salt air.

"What a gorgeous day," she said softly, then looked to her right as she heard the whine and hiss of the condo's golf cart approaching. "Hey."

Dar got out of the cart and headed for the garden gate. "Hey, yourself, cute stuff." She opened the door and disappeared, to reappear moments later as she entered the kitchen and padded out onto the balcony next to Kerry. "All loaded up and ready to go."

"Cool." Kerry offered her a sip of coffee. "I made some breakfast. Want to bring it out here and share?" She waited while Dar obligingly ducked inside and returned with a small tray of eggs, toast, and fresh fruit. They sat down together at the metal and glass table and traded forkfuls as the sunlight poured across the space.

"You know," Dar leaned back and propped her feet up against the railing, "I'm really looking forward to today."

Kerry looked at her. "I can tell. You've been smiling all morning. I am too."

Dar returned her gaze. "Was that a map of the Caribbean I saw in the study?"

Kerry grinned, her nose wrinkling up appealingly.

Dar chuckled, clasped Kerry's hand over the table, and rubbed her thumb against the knuckles. "My little pirate. I can't wait to sail the high seas with you."

Kerry's green eyes were fairly ablaze with an intense joy.

"If I'd known you'd react like this, I'd have suggested a cruise a lot sooner," Dar remarked mildly.

"It's not just the trip," Kerry said with a tiny, wry smile. "It's being out alone with you for a whole week. You have no idea how much I want that right now. It could have been a cruise, or a remote cabin in the woods, or a hike in the wilderness; I wouldn't have cared."

"I would," Dar said kindly. "Mosquitoes and leaves for TP do not put me in a romantic mood nearly as much as salt air and you in that green swimsuit."

Kerry blushed. "You must think I'm weirding out. It's just that so much has happened in the last little while, I really want some time to just..." Her jaw shook a little, and Dar squeezed her hand in concern. "Live."

"You got it," Dar whispered, intently watching Kerry's profile. The green eyes turned to hers with a look of almost painful vulnerability. "I think we've earned that."

"Me, too." Kerry nodded as she got up and walked to Dar, put her arms around her and gave her a hug. "Dar, will you do me a very big favor?"

"Sure. Name it." Dar enjoyed her hug, almost getting lost in the faint coconut and butter scent of the lotion Kerry was wearing. A hand touched her cheek, and she looked up into Kerry's face, surprised to see utter seriousness there.

"Please," Kerry murmured, "please be careful and take care of yourself, Dar. If I ever lose you, I'll die."

Dar's jaw dropped in alarm, and she half turned and took hold of Kerry's body with both hands. "Kerry..."

Kerry's forehead dropped to touch hers. "I had this nightmare the other night. The one you woke me up from?"

"Yeah?" Dar nodded anxiously.

Kerry fell silent for a moment. Then she sighed. "I was...in that hospital again. In the CCU. Only..."

Dar could feel her shaking. "Easy."

"Only it was you in that bed, and I couldn't...I couldn't stop...you...I..."

Kerry's knees buckled and she would have fallen, but Dar caught her, pulled her down on her lap, and held on for dear life. "Easy, sweetheart. It was just a dream." She could feel the jerks as Kerry sobbed. "It's okay."

Chino poked her nose under Kerry's arm, snuffled worriedly, and licked the skin within her reach.

"Ohh." Kerry finally took a deep breath and sniffled. "God, I'm sorry."

"It's okay." Dar gently stroked her back. "Take it easy, honey. I'm here, and I'm not going anywhere. I won't ever leave you, Kerry. Never."

Kerry sniffled again. "I...don't know where that all came from. I was just...sitting here thinking about what a great day it was and..." She sighed. "Jesus. What the hell's wrong with me?"

She impatiently wiped the tears off her face.

Dar hugged her tighter. "I...um..." She paused to collect her thoughts. "I think you're just stressed out, Ker. It's been a bitch of a week, and you're on overload."

Kerry remained silent for a bit, stroking Dar's hair with an almost hypnotic regularity. "Yeah. I think you're right." She exhaled. "Boss, can I take next week off? I need to decompress before I go on a wild vacation with someone I love more than life itself."

"Sure." Dar smiled. She felt a distinct sense of relief at not having to order Kerry to do exactly what she'd just requested. "I'll see what I can do about scaring you up some company."

Kerry exhaled. "Only if the company is tall, dark, and daunting and has blue eyes."

Dar waited a moment before asking, "You want to hang out with my dad?"

It worked. Kerry snickered through her remaining tears, her body shaking with laughter.

"I could arrange for that, I guess," Dar went on with a sigh. "I was hoping you'd rather spend time with me, but—"

She was stopped by a gentle kiss on the lips. Then Kerry rubbed her cheek against Dar's and smiled. "Thanks. I needed a laugh."

"Mm." Dar tilted her head and stole another kiss. "I needed *that.*"

They snuggled for a moment longer, then Kerry regretfully got up and ruffled Dar's hair. "Okay. My head's on straight now; let's get ready to party." She held a hand out to Dar and led her into the condo, with Chino frisking at their heels and occasionally between their legs.

DAR STRETCHED OUT her legs in the warm sand and wriggled her toes contentedly as she watched the crowd milling around the island. It was late afternoon and the party was in full swing, with buckets of assorted seafood on one side of the neatly made campfire, and a standing bar with plenty of ice, beer, wine coolers, and champagne for the guests on the other.

She herself had downed four or five Bacardi Breezers and was in a pretty darn good mood, sitting there in the shade with a plate of lobster, shrimp and rice balanced neatly on one thigh. Kerry was on the other side of the fire, talking with Maria, Duks, and Ceci, and another knot of guests was clustered around where Alastair and her father were trading tall tales.

Nice.

Dar bit into a spicy shrimp and chewed it contentedly. The island looked great, nothing like she, in her childhood, had ever imagined it could become. There were comfortable beanbag chairs scattered around, and neatly dug in Lucite tables for drinks and dinner, and to one side the most incongruous looking Christmas tree she'd ever seen.

It was purple, for one thing, and had bright pink flamingo and bright green palm tree lights. And it was surrounded by piles and piles of presents. Some were theirs, some were their guests— all of whom seemed to be having a great time.

Dar rocked her head a little from side to side and hummed along with the music emerging from the strategically placed speakers. It was one of Kerry's favorite songs and Kerry danced a little to it.

Oo. Dar grinned. *That is so cute.* She took a swig from her bottle and leaned against the tree, glad of the cool breeze and the gorgeous day, and another successful party.

"Hey there, Dardar." Andrew appeared suddenly and plopped down beside her. "Penny fer your thoughts."

Dar glanced at Kerry, then glanced back at him and blushed.

"Heh," her father chuckled. "You having a good birthday?"

"Yeah." Dar nodded. "It's great. The best part is having you and Mom here, though." She gave him a quiet, serious look. "Means a lot."

"Mmph," Andy grunted. "Well, it means a lot to us too, honey." He folded his hands and propped them against an upraised knee. "Sometimes ah just have to slap the side of mah head 'cause I can't believe Ah'm having all this back, after going and losing it."

Dar thoughtfully reflected on this very long speech. "Does it ever feel like a dream to you?"

"Yeap." Andy nodded. "It does."

"For me, too." Dar adopted the same pose, resting her hands on her knee. "I look back to where I was a year ago, and it's like remembering a whole other lifetime." She gazed off across the ocean, its surface lightly ruffled with the odd wave. "It's so hard to believe, sometimes I just have to think it's a dream." She paused. "A dream I just hope I never wake up from."

They watched the revelers in silence for a while.

"Well," Andrew eventually commented, "better a dream than a nightmare, that's for sure."

"Mm," Dar agreed.

Andy drew in a breath. "Dardar, when you were a kid, you wanted something real bad." Dar looked at him. "Was a time you made a choice, but the Navy didn't like that choice much. So they told you no."

"Yeah," Dar said. "That they did."

A small silence ensued. Andy seemed to be deep in thought. "Wasn't the Navy that said no to that, Paladar. Ah made that choice for you." He looked at her. "Ah told them to tell you no."

Dar met his eyes with only the faintest of smiles. "I know. I've always known."

Andrew just stared at her, a stunned look on his face.

"It...um..." another half smile, "was in the computer files." Dar looked out at the horizon. "For a while, I thought maybe you figured I'd embarrass you by not measuring up, and that was just your way of making sure I didn't have to go through all that."

"Ah did not think that," Andrew muttered huskily.

Dar just nodded. "Then I figured maybe you knew me well enough to know I'd never have fit in with the Navy." She exhaled. "Then I finally just settled on knowing you made decisions the same way I did: you trusted your guts and let the chips fall where they fell."

Andrew blinked. "You are the damndest thing."

She shrugged. "You made me."

Her father had to chuckle a little. Then he looked at his hands and flexed them. "Paladar, if you'd had your mind set to fit in the Navy, you surely would have, and if you'd set your mind to be a sea dog like me, you'd surely have done that also."

Dar suddenly felt the seriousness of it. "I wanted to. I wanted to do what you did." She looked at him. "And you're right; I could have." Her eyes glinted. "It wouldn't have been easy, but I'd have done it. All the way."

Andy nodded. "Yeap." He looked her in the eye. "And that's why Ah told them not to." He drew a deep breath. "Ah did not want you to do what ah do."

A thousand little tiny puzzles suddenly made sense to Dar. "Oh."

Andrew remained silent, looking out over the waves.

Dar picked at the tiny grains of sand covering her leg. "Sometimes being able to do what you do is a very good thing. Sometimes it needs to be done."

"Yeap," Andrew replied softly. "And some of the times, ah do enjoy it."

Dar looked up at him quickly, but he was still gazing out over the water.

"'Specially when you can help out people you care for." Andrew turned his head to look Dar right in the eye. "Ah do like that."

Dar released her breath and nodded slowly. "You put those

papers in my briefcase."

"Ah did," Andrew said.

"Thanks," Dar replied. "You saved my ass."

Andrew's grizzled brows twitched and he gave Dar a side-long glance. "Ain't that what daddies are for?"

"Only when you're lucky." Dar turned her head towards him and smiled, this time more broadly. "Did you really think I'd be mad at you for getting me turned down?"

Her father blew out a breath. "Lord, Ah had not the first idea what you were going to think about this. Been wanting to tell you for the longest time, and here you just up and trip me. Shoulda figured you knew."

Dar chuckled. "I *was* mad. Then." She looked up and around, and shook her head. "But sitting where I am now, having what I have—it was the right choice, Dad. We both know that." *Time to lighten up a little*, she realized. "Besides, with my usual luck, I'd have ended up in charge of something, and you'd have had to salute me. Then what?"

Andrew thought about that, then he laid a long arm over Dar's shoulders and looked at her. "Ah woulda followed you straight into Hell, that's what. And been proud to do it."

Dar didn't say a word, but her jaw muscles clenched visibly and she swallowed. Andy nodded in understanding and just pulled her a little closer, both of them accepting the moment in all its richness, with a very similar desire for wordless peace.

CECI WANDERED TO where Kerry was sprawled and took a seat on a conveniently placed rock right next to her. "Hi."

One lazy eye opened and regarded her benignly. "Hi." Kerry smiled. "Having fun?"

It was nearing sunset and the fire had been lit, pots of seafood and vegetables sending hints of spices across the island. "Yes, I am," Ceci replied. "You got sunburned."

"Mm. I know." Kerry stretched her tired body and rubbed the bridge of her nose.

They'd managed to string a volleyball net between two half-submerged trees and played several vicious rounds in the water, all the more tough for Kerry because of her relatively short height.

So she was pretty tired out and was glad to retire to her towel spread neatly over the sand and busy herself checking out the inside of her eyelids for leaks. Now she rolled onto her side and propped her head up on her hand. "What a gorgeous day."

Kerry heard Ceci's acknowledgement, but her eyes fell on Dar, and now her thoughts wandered pleasantly off as she gazed at her lover's sunset-lit form.

Mmm. Dar was wearing her black swimsuit and she'd just come out of the water, droplets glistening on her skin as she shook herself dry. Between the golden light, Dar's natural tan, the faintly see-through fabric and the strong body easily visible beneath it...

"Kerry?"

"Hm?"

"Do you go off into these lustful hazes all the time?"

Wide, startled green eyes blinked, then immediately turned Ceci's way. "Uh." Kerry felt a powerful blush warm her skin. "Bu...I...um..."

Ceci snickered unkindly. "Boy, do you ever show your thoughts on your face."

Kerry covered her eyes with her free hand. "Jesus." She sighed. "Sorry about that."

"Why?" Ceci asked. "Despite the Republicans claim to the contrary, there's really nothing wrong with being sexually attracted to the person you're married to."

The comment, as usual, came from around the corner, and unexpectedly struck Kerry's funny bone. She burst into startled laughter, attracting Chino's attention. The Labrador rushed over and kissed her, which only made her laugh all the harder.

"Hey, hey, what's going on here?" Dar's voice floated over. "What's so funny?"

Kerry absolutely could not look up at her. She almost inhaled half the beach as she put her head down and held her stomach, laughing so hard she was finding it difficult to breathe.

Dar took a seat next to her and waited, watching Ceci snicker quietly to herself. "Someone," Dar said, in a low, no-nonsense voice, "is gonna let me in on this joke, right?"

Kerry rolled over and looked up to see Dar's cool blue eyes regarding her over the edge of her sunglasses. She immediately dissolved into giggles again and hid her face. Dar looked at her mother and raised an eyebrow.

Ceci cleared her throat and stood up, having a firm belief in discretion being by far the better part of valor. "Your father's calling me. Gotta go."

Uh huh. Dar slid down onto the sand and stretched out, waiting for Kerry to finish laughing. Eventually, she did, and rolled over onto her back.

"Oh God." Kerry exhaled, rubbing her face. "Your mother."

"My mother," Dar repeated obediently, "was telling knock knock jokes?"

Kerry peeked at her from between her fingers, then smiled

ruefully. "No. It's my own fault. She came over here to talk to me, and I was dozing off I guess, so I woke up and rolled over and...um..." She paused and scratched her nose. "You were in my line of sight."

Dar waited to hear a further explanation, then cocked her head when none was forthcoming. "So *I* am what you were laughing at?" she asked in a tone of mild bemusement. "Didn't think this suit looked that bad." She frowned and plucked at it. "You should have told me that before, Kerry; I mean—"

"Shhh." Kerry covered Dar's mouth with one hand. "No, sweetheart, you look totally awesome." She paused. "That was the problem." She removed her hand. "Apparently my opinion on the subject was um...obvious, and your mother made a joke about *that*."

"Oooohhhh." Dar grinned. "I get it now. She caught you looking."

A tiny smirk tugged at Kerry's lips. "Yeah."

Dar's eyes twinkled. "I'm flattered."

Kerry briefly wondered what would happen if she just pulled Dar's head down for the kiss she really wanted to give her. *Later, Romeo,* she chastised herself with an inward sigh. "Having a nice time?"

Dar uncapped a small bottle of Noxema, took some on her fingers, and spread it over Kerry's skin, getting the nostrils flaring almost at once. Dar bit her lip to keep from smiling and ran her hands across Kerry's shoulders and felt her lean into the touch, the warm skin under her fingers growing perceptibly warmer. "I'm having a great time. What about you?"

"Getting better every second," Kerry replied, her voice husky. She cleared her throat self-consciously and glanced around, then up at Dar, a beseeching look on her face.

Dar chuckled and wiped a bit of the cream across Kerry's pink nose. "I'm going to grab a dry shirt from the boat; you want one?" She handed Kerry the jar and accepted her nod. "Be right back."

Kerry tucked the cream into her bag, sat up, and wrapped her arms around her upraised knees. The crowd was milling around closer now, and she spotted Andrew and Ceci heading her way.

Andy had a large album tucked under one arm and he sat down on the rock next to her and laid it on his knees.

"Hi," Kerry greeted him as Ceci circled around to the other side and sat down. Duks and Mari drifted over, and Mark sat down near her, as well. "Whatcha got there?"

"What ah have here is pitchers." Andrew glanced at the now interested crowd. "Seeing as it's Dardar's birthday, me and Cec figgured you all'd like to see what that kid looked like as a tot."

"Ooohhhh." An eager rumble escaped as Mark scrambled to get a better spot. Everyone crowded around, including Alastair, who put his hands behind his back and peered over Andrew's broad shoulder.

Andrew opened the album to the first page and smoothed down the time-yellowed plastic. "This here's at about five minutes." He pointed. "Yelling already."

Alastair quipped. "Shoulda known."

DAR TOOK A moment to rinse off in the shower before she removed her suit and pulled on a pair of shorts, along with a tank top she tucked into them. Then she regarded her reflection in the mirror. "Hey, beach rat, haven't seen you in a while," she greeted her scruffy mirror image, wind and salt sodden hair and all.

"Aw, you don't look so bad for an ancient, almost thirty-one year old." Dar raked her fingers through her hair to give it some kind of order, then she fished in the small chest of drawers and pulled out a pair of shorts and a soft cotton shirt for Kerry. She wandered through the boat's compact cabin and stopped in the galley to retrieve the quart of chocolate milk she'd tucked into the refrigerator.

It has been a great day, Dar reflected as she walked out onto the stern and uncapped her milk. She took a sip as she watched the crowd out on the island, all gathered together near the fire. She could hear the laughter from where she was standing, and she took a moment to try and understand the wonder she felt at the scene. It was hard to fathom. Here she was, standing on the deck of her boat, looking at her little island, and it was full of her friends, and her family, and her lifelong soulmate and partner.

Mine. Dar took another swallow of milk. *Wow!* Then she smiled and shook her head as she leaned against the pilothouse's support poles. *Life is good. Complex, but good.* She knew she had some tough decisions coming up in the near future, but somehow, those hovered out beyond the holidays, past the golden week she had planned with Kerry.

A whole week, just the two of them out there together. It would give her time to think. It would give Kerry time to heal. They'd both just been through a month of hell together and damn it...

Dar paused and thought about that for a moment. They had been through hell for a month, hadn't they? And the last week had been tough and a bitch. They'd both been off balance and out of temper. And it had only brought them closer together.

Dar put her milk down on the edge of the deck and shivered in the light breeze as the truth of the realization seeped through her. Even with the tension between them, she'd never felt even a hint of fragility in their relationship, no whisper of doubt, no sense of fear that perhaps they were headed down a sad and familiar road to distancing themselves from each other.

It was as though they'd laid down a foundation so strong, that the worst storm could barely dampen the surface.

Dar wrapped that thought around herself as she climbed down the ladder and back across the pontoons, a gentle smile on her face.

CECI INTERCEPTED HER halfway down. "Hi." Her mother had her hands stuck in her pockets.

"Hi," Dar replied, stopping and peering down. "Need something?"

Hm. Ceci considered the question. "No, I've got everything I need right at the moment. But I'd like to give you something, and I'd rather it be in private."

Uh oh. Dar blinked a little. *Now what?* "Um...okay."

A faint grin flashed across her mother's face. "C'mon." She led the way back down the pontoons, past Dar's boat to the one behind it, which belonged to her and Andrew. She was aware of her daughter's intense curiosity as she followed, the long strides making the wooden bridge rock from side to side. "You don't have to worry, it's not anything that would embarrass you in front of your friends."

"I wasn't worried, really," Dar replied. "I just thought we had all the boxes under the tree."

"Mm." Ceci climbed aboard their vessel and felt the boat move as Dar followed her. She entered the cabin but stopped just inside, forcing Dar to stop as well. "One thing." She turned and faced her daughter. "I want you to promise me something."

Dar felt very off balance. She was a little buzzed, and she'd been in the sun all day; her brain wasn't working nearly as well as it usually did. "Huh?"

"Promise me something," Ceci repeated patiently. "It's not that hard, honest."

"Okay. What?"

"Promise me you won't ask me how or where I got this from," Ceci said, feeling more than a bit nervous. "Okay?"

Dar leaned against the doorway, feeling the warm teak wood against the skin of her shoulder. "Okay," she agreed, completely at sea. "I won't. Why would I, anyway? You don't usually ask people where they..."

Ceci had opened a trunk just inside the door as Dar was speaking, and now she lifted something and held it out.

Dar's voice trailed off as she stared at the object, then slowly she reached out and took it. Her eyes absorbed the contrast of slate gray against still vivid color, details meticulously etched by a careful and very patient hand. *Her* careful and very patient hands, which had first built, then painted the model aircraft carrier many years before.

Ceci just watched her. There was so very much about their shared past she could not change, but this one little thing she'd been bound and determined to. It had taken a while, but she'd persisted in gaining back one of the largest bones of contention there had ever been between them. Even Andy had been shocked and angered at her when she'd gotten rid of Dar's models.

Dar finally drew in a deep breath and looked up and away from the ship, her gaze open and wondering. "Wh—"

"Ah ah ah." Ceci shook her head. "You promised." She covered the intense emotion she felt by indicating the chest. "The rest of them are in here. I don't know if you even have room for them, but I..." She heard a slight scraping sound as Dar put the model on the table, then felt the warmth as she approached. "...thought you might..." A hand gripped her shoulder and she felt herself being turned.

Having little choice, she went along with the prodding and found herself facing her daughter, and in the moment their eyes met, Ceci felt like a mother again. But she didn't really get a chance to absorb that before Dar did something very unexpected. She stepped forward and put her arms around Ceci and hugged her.

Good goddess. Ceci managed to respond in kind, wrapping her arms around Dar's strong body and giving her a healthy squeeze. *The last time I did this...*She let out a small breath. *The last time I did this, she was ten years old.* "Dar, I'm sorry. I wish it'd been different for us."

"I don't care." Dar closed her eyes and just hugged harder. "It's different now. That's all that matters."

Ceci was lifted up a little, and she gained a new perspective on why Kerry took such care to remain strong and fit: you could get a little bent otherwise. But it felt good. She hugged her daughter and smiled in relief, thoroughly enjoying the moment.

DAR STUCK HER hands in her pockets and stretched, feeling

a tiny cloud of wonder following her around as she made her way off the bridge. It lasted just long enough for her to get across the sand and realize what everyone was looking at. She could feel the slow burn of embarrassment heat her skin as she heard the laughter and slowed her steps.

Kerry was kneeling beside her father, one arm draped over his shoulders, pointing out something on the page with one finger. As the laughter rose again, she glanced up and their eyes met. In a twinkling instant, the amusement vanished from her face. She stood, gave Andrew a pat on the shoulder and pushed through the crowd towards Dar.

It took all of Dar's considerable self-discipline to not simply turn and leave.

"Hey." Kerry sounded like she was walking on verbal eggshells.

"I didn't realize I was the party entertainment," Dar replied in a clipped tone. Another spurt of laughter and her whole body jerked, stilling when Kerry touched her stomach in a reflex action. It was hard to believe just how angry she was.

"Dar." Kerry frantically sorted through her thoughts for a way to prevent the explosion she could feel about to take place. "Honey, please listen to me, okay? Before you go off the deep end?"

Dar remained completely silent.

"We're your friends and family, and we love you," Kerry whispered. "Your mom and dad are so proud of you, and they want to share their memories of you with your friends. Don't be upset, please?"

Dar stared over her shoulder at the crowd, who hadn't noticed her presence in the twilight shadows. Her face was still and closed, her pale blue eyes remote and very cold. Then, as though a switch had been flipped, she relaxed and sighed.

"I hate those pictures," Dar muttered. "I look like such an idiot."

She shoots, she scores! Kerry wrapped an arm around Dar. "You do not. You were such an adorable baby, Dar. I wanted to just squeeze you." She did so, getting a soft grunt out of Dar. "Especially that one picture with you in the bunny suit."

"Eemph." Dar grimaced. "I'm gonna go wait on the boat."

"No, no, no." Kerry kept hold of her and dug her heels into the sand with a remarkable lack of success in stopping Dar's progress. "C'mon...c'mon, Dar, please?" Her voice broke on the last word, and it actually made Dar stop and turn and put her arms around Kerry.

Oo. Have to remember that. "Come over and look at them,"

Kerry pleaded gently. "Please?"

Dar exhaled unhappily. The very last thing in the world she wanted to do was go look at ugly old baby pictures of herself. On the other hand, it would make Kerry happy. Was she willing to do something she really, really didn't want to do to gain that result? Dar tilted her head and regarded the serious, mist green eyes looking back at her. "I'm not comfortable with people getting this close to me. It's crossing a line I'm not sure I want crossed."

Kerry absorbed that, her lips pursing as she considered the statement. "My life was lived so much in the public view, I didn't even think of that with you. I apologize, Dar. I should have stopped your father." She looked into Dar's eyes. "Forgive me?"

Like I have a choice? A smile pulled at Dar's lips as she surrendered her dignity and simply wrapped her arms around Kerry and started towards the group circling her father. *What the hell.* She endured the sudden glances and grins with wry stoicism. "All right, which one of the seven thousand bad baby shots is he showing you now?"

"Aw, Dar, you were such a sweet baby." Maria smiled at her boss. "So cute."

"Mm," Ceci agreed with a nod, catching up to them as they reached the rock. "I was going to pitch her as a baby model but she bit the photographer."

Everyone looked at Dar, who grinned, then they made room as Kerry and Dar settled at Andy's side. Kerry put an arm around Dar's waist and rested her chin on her shoulder. "What on earth were you doing there?" She pointed at a small, square Polaroid of a perhaps five or six year old Paladar in denim overalls on a very fuzzy, very unhappy looking animal.

"Riding a llama." Dar sighed, remembering the Pirate World Adventure during one of Andy's infrequent leaves. "Neither of us enjoyed the experience, if I recall."

"Ya'll were pulling on his ears, Dardar. What'd ya expect?" Andy drawled.

"Ah, is that where you got the experience to do that?" Alastair asked.

"Yeah." Dar grabbed her boss's ear and gave it a healthy tug as he yelped. "So you better watch it."

The laughter rose again, but Dar felt a bit more comfortable with it this time. She released Alastair's ear, then bent her head to regard the next page.

"HAPPY BIRTHDAY TO you, happy birthday to you...happy birthday, dear Dar..."

Dar listened to the chorus of voices, the cacophony evoking only a relaxed grin from her. They were in a circle around the fire, plates full of food balanced on laps and mugs of alcohol being freely passed around.

Dar was mildly drunk and she knew it. Kerry was even more so, sitting next to Dar with her sturdy legs sprawled out and an arm draped over Dar's thigh. Her head leaned back against Dar's hip as she related a funny story, her warm tones echoing out over the water.

It suddenly seemed oddly familiar. Dar experienced a flash of almost memory as she set her plate aside, put her arm across Kerry's shoulders, and nursed her mug with her other hand. Was it the fire, some sliver of memory from her much younger years, some time spent out camping?

Laughter resounded and Dar smiled as Kerry's voice rose a bit, taking on a subtle, yet deep timbre. The sound echoed slightly, and Dar suddenly felt if she closed her eyes and opened them again...But no, there they still were—at the fire with their friends around them, the Miami night sky twinkling overhead.

Strange.

"Well, I tell you, Kerry, that's a heck of a way to spend a birthday," Alastair said as Kerry finished her tale. "I think I'd have given them up after that."

"Well," Kerry ran her thumb lightly along Dar's inner thigh, "I did...for a long time, until I moved down here." She paused. "And took my life back." Her face settled into a quiet reflection, and the tenor of the crowd changed a little as people took the moment to dig into the excellent stew and munch on crusty garlic bread.

Kerry took a sip of her beer and gazed out over the water, glad of the solid, warm presence she was leaning against. Ceci and Andrew were on the other side of Dar, and Mark was seated next to her, and she found herself very glad to be in this fire lit circle, surrounded by her friends and family.

Her family. Kerry took another swallow of beer, knowing that sitting in the sand covered in salt and suntan lotion wasn't anything her other family would have ever been caught dead doing. Not even Angie or Mike, who loved her, but who loved their privileged lives just as much. "Y'know, Dar?"

"Mm?" Dar selected a bit of carrot sticking out of her stew and offered it to Kerry.

A smile crossed Kerry's face as she accepted the offering— licking Dar's fingers as she munched on the carrot. "I don't think I ever fit in at home."

"No?"

"Nope." Kerry wondered, briefly, what would have become of her if she'd stayed there, had not taken the chance and jumped at the impulsive move to a state as far away from her home as she could get. "Glad I decided to come find you."

Dar chuckled softly. "Me too. Otherwise I'd have had to come to Michigan and terrorize the area until I found you."

"Think you would have?" Kerry imagined coming around the corner in Meijers and finding Dar. "Maybe you'd have," she thought a moment, "found me at some job fair and hired me."

"Nah," Dar mumbled around a mouthful of stew beef. "Something more dramatic. How about...oh...I rescued you from being captured by white slavers and took you away for a life of vagabond excitement and crusading, traveling around the world."

They were both silent for a moment, deep in thought.

Kerry rolled her head back and looked at Dar. "Honey, I love you but you've been watching too much of that late night television again."

"Hey, I could have said we'd go off and become crocodile wrestlers."

Kerry laughed. Dar joined her, pulling her closer and sliding down off the log so they were side by side. Duks started a story of his own and Kerry listened, tilting her head back and regarding the canopy of stars.

Are they twinkling at me? Watching me?

Was her father up there somewhere, finally in a place where lies didn't work and the truth was like a harsh light that could blind if you weren't prepared for it?

Did he know the truth about her now? And if he did, would he ever accept it, or would he go through eternity damning her for being something outside his personal box of understanding?

Kerry found the Big Dipper and traced its outlines. *Goodbye, Daddy.* She let out a small breath. *In spite of everything, I really did love you.*

A soft voice tickled her ear. "Whatcha looking at?" Dar gazed upward with her.

"Just the stars," Kerry replied. "Look at that patch, Dar." She pointed. "You think that looks like a bear?"

Dar pressed her cheek against Kerry's and studied the pattern. "Nah." She shook her head. "A pig."

"A pig?" Kerry lifted an eyebrow. "How about a pig riding a bike?"

Dar didn't answer. She just smiled.

Other Melissa Good books available from
Yellow Rose Books

Eye of the Storm

(2nd edition)

Just when it looks like Dar Roberts and Kerry Stuart are settling into their lives together they discover that life is never simple - especially around them. Surrounded by endless corporate and political intrigue, Dar experiences personal discoveries that force her to deal with issues she had buried long ago and Kerry finally faces the consequences of her own actions. Can their love and support for each other get them through these challenges.

Follow the continuing saga of Dar and Kerry as they face their greatest crises yet.

ISBN 1-932300-13-9

Red Sky At Morning

Continuing from where *Eye of the Storm* leaves off, this fourth chronicle in the Tropical Storm series has Dar Roberts and Kerry Stuart's lives seeming to get more complex rather than moving toward the simpler lifestyle they both dream of.

This story begins with Dar presenting the quarterly earnings for the company. Meanwhile, Kerry encounters plane problems on her way to Chicago to solve a problem, and her flight diverts to New York. Sensing Kerry is in trouble, Dar leaves right in the middle of a stockholder cocktail party leading a colleague to question Dar's commitment to the company.

Dar and Kerry return to Miami to begin a Navy contract and they encounter a cover-up of the worse kind. They end up in Washington to confront the military brass and expose Dar's old friends and in a sense, leave her childhood completely behind.

Originally part of the story posted as *Tropical High*.

ISBN 1-930928-81-5

(To be released in a Second Edition in 2004,
ISBN 1-932300-21-X)